The
Shadow
Prince

Also by Terence Morgan

The Master of Bruges

The
Shadow
Prince

TERENCE MORGAN

MACMILLAN

First published 2012 by Macmillan
an imprint of Pan Macmillan, a division of Macmillan Publishers Limited
Pan Macmillan, 20 New Wharf Road, London N1 9RR
Basingstoke and Oxford
Associated companies throughout the world
www.panmacmillan.com

ISBN 978-0-230-75710-3

1 3 5 7 9 8 6 4 2

A CIP catalogue record for this book is available from
the British Library.

Typeset by CPI Typesetting
Printed and bound by CPI Group (UK) Ltd, Croydon CR0 4YY

for

Paul

and his mother

Les

my love and my inspiration, always

J. T. L.

Prelude

Even the weariest river, they say, winds somewhere safe to the sea. Some rivers grow great as they advance, rushing ever forward in their great surge and plunging headlong into the ocean; others spread and drift lazily onward, turning and looping to find the easiest way to their destination. Lives are like that, too, and I have seen rivers and lives of both types, and others, and have enjoyed their courses and their rapids, their meanders and their still pools, but this river by which now I sit is the last I shall look upon, and this is the last of my many lives. I have that from the highest of authorities.

It was a shadow like the shadow of death that fell over me suddenly as I sat that day, and he who cast the shadow had words with me, and heard my tale, and when I had finished he looked on me and shook his head.

'It is a most preposterous story,' he said. 'You must write it down.'

'Yes. Perhaps I should.'

'You misunderstand me,' he said, and looked at me pointedly from under those heavy brows. 'I mean, you *must* write it down.'

'Oh, I see.'

'And it will be for me to read,' he said, 'but of course no one else must see it.'

'No.'

'You understand, of course?'
'Of course.'

Therefore I take up my quill, as commanded. *Hic incipit liber vitae Richardi Angliae, alias Richardi Greii, quondam dux Iorcis, quondam nauta, quondam princeps, quondam . . .*

But no. This is an English story, about England and an Englishman, and if any story deserves to be Englished, it is mine.

Prey

April 1487

If you want to make yourself conspicuous in a busy scene, stand still.

All around us on the wharf men were giving or obeying orders, loading or unloading boats, fetching or carrying bales – except for two. The people I could see were mostly friends and acquaintances, local river workers, with the usual smattering of boatmen from other ports along the river, but not these two. They were dressed no differently from anyone else, but their inactivity in an atmosphere of bustle and work was enough to single them out.

'Who are they?' I asked my father, indicating the pair. I'd not seen either of them on the riverside before. They were lounging two or three boats along, but seemed to be looking around a great deal.

As I watched they spoke to one of the day labourers and he nodded, looked around and then pointed over in our direction.

Jehan gave them a cursory glance, shrugged and cast off, and then began a strong, steady pull up the river towards a spot he knew near some willows. It was a pleasant spring day, and my only task was to take the rudder and steer a sensible course. Before long we had left the houses of the city behind us and were moving through open meadows that came down to the river on both banks.

My father – Jehan, I mean – enjoyed fishing, a pastime in which I regularly accompanied him, although I was not as keen as he was, and the actual killing of the poor fish after hooking it often made me ill. I was squeamish even then, and could never bring myself to do the deed personally. Nonetheless, I went along on his trips up the river; they were more fun than staying at home, and there was much to be seen as we rowed along. All fishing on the Scheldt was expressly forbidden by town regulations, and in any case the river just below the town was too dirty for good sport. There was a tanning works just above Tournai, where we lived, and in the town itself waste water from fish-gutting and salting was tipped into the river at night when the officials could not see it, or at least were prepared to turn a blind eye. For a good catch it was necessary to go some way upstream, far from the filth and effluent and far too from the prying eyes of the town officials.

This particular Thursday my father had decided that we needed some fresh fish for the following day's meal, and early that morning we had started to load up one of his smaller boats, called a 'bacquet', or bucket, in the local slang.

There was the usual banter from the wharf as we piled our things into the bottom – some lines and a keep net, a pottle with some small beer in it, some bread smeared with butter in the Flemish way – and cast off.

My father took first turn with the oars, and we had been gliding along for about an hour when he grunted and said, 'Odd. There's your two friends again, isn't it?'

I twisted in my seat, and sure enough on the northern bank, but some way behind us, the two men from the wharf were idling along, mounted on two strong-looking horses ambling unhurriedly down the track which followed the river.

'I think it is, yes,' I said, and turned back to concentrate on my steering. Despite what I'd seen of them, idle travellers were still no concern of mine.

Within a short period the two men overtook us and plodded on up the path.

'Take a turn with the oars,' my father said, and we switched positions in the boat. 'Not far now.'

After some time he spoke again. 'Those two are there again. They've slowed down,' he said. 'They were getting a good way ahead of us, but now they're not, and they keep looking back at us.'

Again I twisted to look at the two men. They had gained a great deal on us, but were clearly moving a lot more slowly, almost as if they did not want to outpace us. As I looked, one of them turned in his saddle and looked directly at me. When he saw me looking, he quickly turned his back, but not before a frisson of fear ran down my spine. I suddenly felt that their presence was something to do with me.

I continued rowing, and allowed my father to watch the men for both of us. After all, it could be nothing at all.

Eventually Jehan told me to stop rowing, and we fastened the bacquet to a tree on the north bank of the river. We gave it just enough leeway to swing out with the flow towards the spot where, according to Jehan, the fish clustered, and we set about making ready.

Our two travelling companions had ridden on and were out of sight when we stopped, but by the time we cast our first line they had reappeared, ambling back along the south bank towards us. Jehan looked across, said, 'I'd love to know what those two are up to,' but then lost interest and became engrossed in his hunt. I lay in the bottom of the boat, chewed on a piece of bread and watched the two men as they slowly made their way back towards us. Once again, I could not rid myself of the feeling that their presence was connected with my former life.

'Mynheer Werbecque!'

The call was as loud as it was unexpected, and Jehan and I both sat bolt upright.

The two men had dismounted and were standing on the bank. 'Mynheer Werbecque,' one of them called again, and my father looked over.

'What do you want?'

'You are Jehan de Werbecque of Tournai?'

'I might be. Who wants to know?'

One of the men came down the bank until he was standing on the edge of the shallows. 'If you are Jehan, then this must be your son Pierrechon?'

'I repeat, who wants to know?'

'Come over here. We can't hold a sensible conversation shouting across the river like this.'

'I think this might be danger, father,' I said. 'Don't go over there.'

'I don't intend to,' he said. 'These are not the actions of honest men, following a man and his son all day and then accosting them in the wilderness.' He raised his voice. 'You still have not told me who you are and what your business is.'

'I can't hear you,' the man called. 'Come nearer.'

Jehan used one of the oars to push the boat out so that it floated a little upstream and a little nearer to the south bank, although it was still firmly tied to the tree on the other side.

'Well?'

'We have a business proposition we'd like to put to you.'

'What's wrong with talking to me in town, like honest men?'

'Well, that's it; we don't want sharp ears hearing what we have to say.'

'Illegal, then.'

'More or less, yes.'

My father let this hang in the air for a few moments, and then said, 'Not interested,' and let the flow drift us away from the men and in towards the further bank.

'You haven't heard what we have to say yet. Come over here and discuss it.'

My father grinned at me. 'You know, I don't think we're going to get too much fishing done. I don't know who these men are, but I do know that I don't trust them.'

I nodded agreement, although unlike him I had a shrewd idea of their mission.

They were becoming impatient. 'Are you coming?'

'I think I've got a bite,' he called. 'Just hold on.'

In the reaches above Tournai, the River Scheldt is neither fast-flowing nor deep over most of its length, and the stretch we were in was both slow and fordable. If the men decided to wade or ride to us, we were vulnerable. 'Back the boat up a little and untie the rope,' my father whispered. 'Don't make it obvious.'

I did as I was told while my father made a show, yelling excitedly, 'I think I've got one,' and pointing at some imagined fish a little ahead of us in the stream. He knew that not far away the river deepened, and there we would be safer, as the men would not attempt to come at us across deep water.

All the same, they had chosen their approach carefully. We were isolated in the centre of a narrow river that was also shallow, and although they could not get to us to do whatever they had in mind, by the same token we could not land. Even if we landed on the north bank two men on horses would soon catch a man and a boy on foot once they found a crossing place, and although bridges were not common, there were a number of them spaced out along the river. We were safe where we were, but trapped all the same.

'What do you want?' my father called.

'A word, that's all.' They were giving nothing away.

With the rope untied, the boat spun round in the river and began to drift downstream. The men watched us silently until it became apparent that we were not going to come over to them, and then they remounted and followed us along the bank, clearly in no hurry.

I took the oars, as the stream was doing most of the work, and Jehan steered. 'I think it's about me,' I told him. He looked up sharply; we had not discussed my origins since that first day, two years before, when he had slammed his fist down on the table, and it occurred to me that he had almost forgotten, as indeed I had myself, that he was not my real father. More than that, he knew not who my real father was, or even my country of origin. His lack of curiosity had been my safeguard – and his, had he but known it.

'Why do you think that?'

'Because of who I used to be.'

He adjusted the angle of the tiller slightly and then said quietly, 'And who was that?' It was the first time he had asked me in many months.

'It were still best you do not know,' I said, 'but if they are who I think they are, and have been sent by who I think has sent them, then they have come to kill me. If I tell you who I was, then I place both you and my mother in danger. If you are ignorant of it, then they have no reason to harm you. I wish I could explain all to you, but I cannot. Not yet, anyway.'

'Right,' he said, accepting my word without question. Then he suddenly took charge of the situation. 'We must get ourselves, or at least you, safely off this river. Here in the open we are vulnerable, but as we get closer to town there will be buildings and gardens on the riverbank, and they are bound to lose sight of us, sometimes for quite long periods, while they go round them. That might give us a chance.'

I looked across. The two men were keeping pace with us, their horses moving at a fast walk to match the flow of the river.

The men suddenly speeded up into a Canterbury trot. I looked round to see why.

'Bridge ahead,' Jehan said. 'They'll be there before us. Now we'll see what they're after.'

It was an old stone bridge, its central point highest above the water, and the two men rode onto it and dismounted. 'Pull over, Werbecque!' one of them shouted. 'We mean you no harm.'

My father ignored him, and the speaker promptly gave the lie to his words by drawing a sword from the saddlecloth of his horse and leaning over the bridge. The other moved across to the other bank and came down into the sedge, but the river was too deep for wading at that point, and he came to a halt at the water's edge.

As the bacquet drifted towards the bridge my father said, 'I think you were right; he does mean to kill one or both of us. We need to shoot the bridge. Row as hard as you can, and when I call out, fall flat in the boat until we're through the bridge. I'll take care of our swordsman if necessary.'

The flow took us along, and I heaved heartily on the oars, with my father aiming for the centre of the bridge. 'Harder,' he muttered, 'harder, boy,' and then, 'Flat down! Now!'

As soon as he called I fell backwards, looking up at the underside of the bridge as we passed beneath it. I saw one of the men leaning over, sword in hand, and saw the flash as the blade caught the sunlight as he swung it downwards. Jehan, who had also fallen back over the stern, had in his hand a club that he used to stun fish, and as the swordsman tried to regain his balance Jehan hit his lower arm as hard as he could. I heard the crunch of bone as the arm was driven back against the stone of the bridge, and saw the sword drop. Jehan caught it by the blade just before it hit the water, and then we were out the other side of the bridge and I was looking back at the two men, the one holding his arm and cursing his companion for his slowness, and the other leading the two horses across the bridge towards him.

'Good quality,' Jehan said, eyeing the sword.

I kept on rowing, and watched as the men remounted and

began to trot along the riverbank behind us. 'They're coming again,' I said, and Jehan swivelled to see.

'One more bridge before we get into town,' he said. 'After that they won't be able to follow us so closely. It should be safer there.'

When the river widened we changed places, and he took the oars. His greater strength moved us along that bit faster, but still the two men on the bank kept pace with us, and there was still the problem of the bridge to come.

We made some luck for ourselves, though. Jehan had a townsman's cunning; when I saw ahead of us, on the south bank, a laden cart plodding along towards town and drew his attention to it, he nodded with satisfaction. 'Good, good,' he muttered. 'We can use that.'

He pulled ahead so that we were drifting alongside the cart, close to the bank. 'Whither away, carter?' he called.

The carter looked across, pondered whether it was worth speaking or no, and decided that it cost nothing but the effort. 'Town,' he said.

'Aye, but which part of town?' Jehan asked.

'What business is that of yours?'

'None, carter, except that I know something that may be to your advantage, and save you delay.'

'What might that be?'

'The path on your side there is blocked, a mile or so down. We saw it as we came upstream, not much more than an hour since – a wagon athwart the path, with a horse dead still in the shafts and a wheel broken. They won't have shifted it by now.'

'Neighbourly of you to tell me,' the carter said. 'Thank you. I'll take the path on the other bank, I reckon.'

'Good idea, I'd say,' Jehan said. 'Good day, neighbour.'

'Good day to you,' the carter said, and out of deference to Jehan spat on the land side of the wagon, so as not to give insult.

My father smiled at me and allowed the bacquet to drift into the centre of the stream. We looked across. The two men were still keeping pace with us. Jehan spat on each of his hands and picked up the oars. Suddenly, there was no rhythm in his rowing; the oars were not hitting the water together, and he slumped in his seat instead of sitting upright.

'Are you all right?' I asked.

'Tired is all.' He rested a little and looked at the north bank. The two men were still there. The cart had disappeared from sight around a bend in the river. Jehan idled along, partly drifting and partly sculling with one oar so as avoid coming too close to the far bank. After the bend he leaned over and said to me, 'Can you see the cart?'

'Yes,' I said.

'Tell me when it's nearing the bridge – say twenty or thirty paces from it.'

I let a minute or so go by, as Jehan made desultory passes at the water, and then told him, 'It's there.'

'Right,' he said, and glanced over his shoulder. Then he leaned into the oars, and the boat shot forward. He only gained a moment on the two riders, who were much faster anyway, but that was not his purpose. After a second's hesitation they increased their speed to maintain their position relative to us, but made no attempt to get any distance ahead. Jehan was still pulling hard, and as we neared the bridge his plan became clear even to me, and my dull wits sharpened long enough to appreciate it.

As the cart started across the bridge we were perhaps thirty yards away, and Jehan lengthened his stroke. The feigned tiredness had dropped away completely, and the boat gathered speed. The two horsemen broke into a canter, seeing the bridge ahead. I did not know what plan they had in mind this time, but Jehan's cunning outclassed theirs. By the time we got to the bridge the cart was halfway across, just wide enough to make the crossing without difficulty, but obviously blocking all access to the parapet. We shot unscathed and unhindered under the arch, and the riders, after reining in briefly, stayed on the same side of the river and trotted down the path together.

'Good,' Jehan said. 'They fell for all of it.'

'What do you mean?' I asked.

'I was worried that they might separate onto opposite banks,' he said, 'but they haven't thought that far ahead. We should be safe now.' He eased in his rowing again and allowed the craft to slow down until it was drifting again, controlled only by the rudder.

'They have to stay on the same side of the river now until we get into town,' he said, 'so I'll put you off on the other. It's clear they know my name, so they probably know where we live, so it were best you do not go home yet. When I put you off, go to my sister's house at Ouldenarde; she and her husband will keep you safe until we have sorted this out. Understand?'

'Yes,' I said.

'Be watchful and stay safe,' he said. 'I do not know why these men want you.' He looked up suddenly. 'You have done no wrong, offended no one?'

'No,' I told him. 'None. These men are come from my past, of which I may tell you naught.'

'We'll have you home soon,' he said, 'fear not.'

I was ashamed to have brought such trouble to the door of these good people, but I knew not what more to say to him. 'Give my mother my love,' I said.

'I will,' he said, 'and take ours with you.' He reached into his scrip and put a few coins into my hand. 'This is all I have with me,' he said, 'so it must serve.'

The town was soon upon us, and it was no longer possible for our pursuers to keep us always in sight as buildings interposed themselves. At one point, with the men watching, my father sculled over towards the right bank as if to land. Then, when the men disappeared behind a house, he quickly pulled across to the other side of the river.

'Go, quickly,' he said as soon as we touched the shore. 'Here we are halfway between two bridges, so you have a little time. Hide yourself and then go to Ouldenarde. I'll see you there as soon as I can.'

I leapt to the shore and he pulled away immediately, the boat soon finding the centre of the stream. He arranged his surcoat in a heap and threw a hat on top of it; it didn't look much like a boy asleep, but it might give the pursuers pause for a short time.

I kept to myself the thing that had escaped him, for I did not want to involve him in my problems. I had heard what he had not. When I threw myself flat in the boat, and the would-be assassin's sword had wafted above my head and been taken by my father, I had heard the cries of the men on the bridge, and the words that they had spoken to each other, and I knew who had sent them, for the words, if they had no meaning to Jehan, carried significance for me.

To each other, the men had spoken English.

I watched until he became a speck on the river, and I saw no sign of the horsemen, who must have been behind the houses still. I never saw my father Jehan again.

Prince

August 1473 – August 1485

And what, you might ask, had all this to do with me, Pierrechon Werbecque, a Tournai wharf rat?

The truth is that I was not always as I am now. I began my life honoured by all and clothed in robes of the finest manufacture. It is the robes that I recall best. They were very heavy, and so stiff with brocade that they were sometimes capable of standing up on their own with no support from me. I did not mind that sort so much; if you made yourself very small then the robes no longer weighed on your shoulders, and the burden was eased. You could have a rest, especially in the parts of the ceremony when you were allowed to sit.

Otherwise they weighed you down, fatigued you and made you hot and sleepy, and sometimes I was asleep long before the service or ceremony was ended, and I had to be taken away by Sir Thomas Grey, who was the chamberlain of my household in those days. And there were so many services and ceremonies. I cannot remember all of them or what they were for, but by the age of nine I had experienced a great deal of ceremonial in my short life.

For I was born the second son of King Edward IV of England in August of 1473. I cannot recall the exact date, for my birthday ceased to be celebrated before I was ten. My elder brother, called Edward after our father, shared my own physical resemblance to him. We were all three tall and fair, but the similarity did not extend to health. From when I was first aware of him, my brother was a sickly youth. He had a slight deformity of the lower jaw, so his face looked lopsided, and as time went on his teeth began to fall out and the gaps never seemed to heal. Everyone said, however, that I was a cutting from my father's tree.

I recall few details of that life. My papa was a great man who had wrested the throne of England from those who stood against him. He had been deposed and then returned to win the kingdom a second time, and had won many great victories. In this he was aided by his brother, my uncle Richard of Gloucester, who was later king himself. My mother the queen was the most beautiful woman in England, and there were sisters, three or four at least, and there might have been another one, a baby, although now I cannot recall for certain.

I was honoured and garlanded as a prince always is, and received earldoms and appointments by the score. I was Earl Marshal of England at five and Lord Lieutenant of Ireland before I was six, but I remember nothing of what went on to induct me into these roles.

I do recall the day I became a Knight of the Garter, because it was my seventh birthday, and I was allowed a celebration with my brother and sisters afterwards. I don't remember being made Earl of Nottingham or Duke of Norfolk or Lord of Seagrave or Lord of Gower or any of the other dozen or so titles and honours which attached themselves to my tiny shoulders in those years. In some cases, I do not even remember what the titles were; they are at best the faintest of echoes at the furthest fringes of memory.

I am able to remember my wedding quite well. I was married, a stocky little man of four summers, to a lady called Anne Mowbray. Marriages at such an early age are not uncommon among the nobility, especially where dynastic pretensions are at stake, but I remember that I did not take to the idea even then, and I cried all through the ceremony and the feast that followed. Through the marriage, though, I was able to add another title to my collection – Lord of Mowbray. Of my wife I recall little except her name and the fact that I found her most unfriendly and disagreeable. She would not share her wedding breakfast sweetmeats with me, and scolded me pitifully, practising for later in life, I suppose. She was an older woman, of course – six years old at the time – and the marriage didn't last, as she died of a fever three years later. I was widowed at seven, isolated from the world at nine, and, as far as the world knows, murdered at twelve.

All of these titles were simply a way of ensuring that my father the king got control of the revenues from their estates, offices and benefices. It was not necessary for me to do any work to justify these revenues. There were civil servants to deal with that sort of thing. All I had to do was be, which I did right well, and wear the robes, which duty I performed less well, but almost as often, as it seemed to me.

Sometimes I was scolded for not paying enough attention, but usually I was just put to bed and left there until morning. There were so many ceremonies in those days that a little boy could not be expected to stay awake through every single one of them.

It all came down to the robes in the end; I wore the robes, so I was the marshal, or the lieutenant, or the duke, or the lord, or whatever it was they wanted to call me; but the truth was that I was just a little boy who wanted to go to sleep.

I am now in my seventh life. My first life, a full and happy one, was over not long after my twelfth birthday. My second life, even happier in some ways, lasted some six years, as did my third life. My fourth life was less than a year in length, and my fifth nearly as short – just a year and a half from birth to death. The sixth life – well, you shall hear of that, and the seventh, which will end ere long, as I said, perhaps the happiest of all.

At the Christmas after I was nine years old there came to

my father's court a foreign gentleman who had befriended my father in his worst hour, when he had been almost alone in a foreign land with no money, no place to lay his head and not even a coat to keep out the rain.

This man, Hans Memling, was a painter of faces, and he had been commissioned to paint portraits of my father, mother and uncle. He was polite and kind to me, and encouraged me to try to draw myself, and guided my childish hand. When my father began to spend an hour or so each day sitting for his portrait, I went along to the sittings and sat at the artist's elbow and watched and learned.

Then, being the spoiled princeling that I was, I demanded to be allowed to try myself. I do not think that I had any skill, but it is perhaps not politic to gainsay a prince, even a little one, and Hans gave me paint to mix and then allowed me to apply it to the folds of cloth drawn behind my father's image, to the evident delight of my parents. At this distance in time, I am astonished at his patience, but then I just thought it was my right.

When this simple task palled I was given another role; Hans gave me brushes, paints and a small easel of my own. I realized later that this was no promotion at all, but a way of getting me out of his hair so that he could press on with his work, but he was a cheerful and companionable man with three small sons of his own, and I liked and trusted him. He missed his children, and in a way I became a replacement. Over the few months I knew him, Hans and I grew close.

In due course his portraits were finished, and he went off elsewhere to work, promising one day to return and enjoining me to continue my drawing. I began to miss him immediately.

We in the court prepared to celebrate Easter, but suddenly we were struck by tragedy. My father, though no more than forty years old, became suddenly ill. He took to his bed and in our palace of Windsor people began to move on tiptoe and talk in whispers. My brother was away at his own household in Ludlow with our uncle Anthony, my mother's brother. I was too young to understand what was happening, but the fact was that my father's illness was more serious than I knew, and the country was soon to be thrown once again into turmoil.

'Richard, wake up.'

My mother's voice broke into my sleep, and a rough shaking of my shoulder proved that it was no dream.

'What is it?' I asked. 'What is the matter?'

'Get up. Get up,' she said urgently. She was standing over me, her hair about her ears, and in a state of some distress, looking wildly about her.

'What is it?' I sat up. All around me servants and sisters alike were gathering up clothes, jewellery, headgear and even furniture and transporting it outside.

'We are going to the abbey,' my mother said. 'Now get yourself up and dressed. There is no time to lose.'

'Why are we going to the abbey?' I asked. 'It is not a feast day.'

'I'll brook no argument,' my mother said. 'We go to sanctuary in the cathedral; that's all you need to know.'

'Why?' I asked.

'I have no time to bandy words with you, sirrah,' my mother said, snatching some trinkets from a table. 'Now finish dressing and do as you are told.'

I did as I was bid and made my way outside to where carts awaited, piled high with all manner of goods and chattels. My eldest sister, Bess, pulled me up onto one of them and said, 'Do not move from there, Richard, under pain of stripes. We go at any moment.'

Bess was my favourite among my sisters; sensible and kind, and as beautiful as she was generous. She was already, at sixteen, a lady much admired by many of the young gentlemen about court, many of whom would treat me kindly in the hope of winning a smile from her. I did not care to upset her, so I stayed where I was and watched the preparations, if such frenzied activity can be dignified by the word, go on around me.

Finally the carts were loaded, the servants clambered aboard and Bess settled beside me.

'Why is all this happening?' I asked once the waggon started to move.

'It is my mother's whim,' Bess said. 'She fears for our lives.'

'Why?' I asked, suddenly alert. 'Who could wish to harm us?'

'My mother thinks that it is possible that my uncle of Gloucester, my lord Hastings, my lord the Duke of Buckingham and a host of others might have designs on our lives.'

'Why?' I asked again. 'Those men are all my father's friends. They would not harm us.'

'My mother says 'tis better to be safe than sorry.'

I shook my head. It was beyond belief that any of those named might be anything other than loyal to my father, and I was sure that no one would ever want to harm my mother, my sisters or myself.

It was to the abbey at Westminster we were bound, there to take sanctuary. My mother was no stranger to the place, having given birth to my elder brother there some thirteen years before, and the holy fathers seemed to have had some warning of her arrival, for they had chambers ready, which although not comfortable were at least adequate. It was not intended to be a comfortable existence within those walls, we knew that, but we knew too that it was a safe haven no matter who prevailed in the perennial struggles for England.

Given my mother's fears, however, my thoughts that night were all for my brother's safety. As soon as I felt able I asked her about him.

'Your brother is safe,' she said. 'Be sure of that. Your uncle Anthony is at his side, and no man will harm him while Anthony is there.'

'And will my father go to him, too?'

'Your father, child?'

'Yes.'

There was a pause, and her face changed. 'Oh, my lord,' she said eventually. 'You poor sweet innocent child – do you not know, then?'

I looked blankly at her, and she took me in her arms and whispered into my hair. 'Your father is no more, child. The king is dead, and we are alone in this world.'

'But mother,' I protested, 'I said goodnight to my father but last night before going to my bed, and he . . .'

'And he is gone, Richard,' she said, 'and everything is changed. Your brother is King Edward the Fifth, and you are heir to the throne of England, and we are fenced about by treason, treachery and greed.'

I took in the news, and sensed a little of what concerned my mother. 'And who then will take care of us?' I asked.

'Who indeed?' my mother said, and she stroked my head, and I felt her fear.

Of the politics of what followed I can tell little; that is a matter for the writers of history and Henry Tudor's assiduous re-writers of it. I know now that the news of my father's death had been kept from my uncle Richard of Gloucester, who had been named my brother's and the land's Protector by my father. I know that the Treasury of England had already been looted and its contents spirited away; I know that my mother's brothers and her sons from her earlier marriage, my half-brothers, formed a council to control the country, and I know that they decided to crown Edward king within a matter of a few days. I do not know why they did this, but I know the effect it would have had; according to custom, my uncle Richard's authority as Protector of the Realm would end the moment the crown was placed on my brother's head, and my mother's other family desired this to be done right speedily.

I know too that Richard discovered the news and hastened south, and, meeting my brother and his entourage at a place called Stony Stratford, placed the new king under his protection and escorted him thence to London. Thus did Richard execute the wishes of my father according to his will and in despite of my mother's family. It was, I suppose, the right thing to do.

While these events were taking place, but before the outcome was known, the Chancellor of England, Archbishop Rotherham, presented himself to my mother, carrying with him the Great Seal of England. I remember being amused as he scrambled in through the hole which my mother's servants had knocked in the abbey wall, the better to carry in her goods and chattels which had accompanied us and her share of the realm's treasure that had been taken – by her brothers, I now knew.

'Your Majesty,' he said, falling to his knees before her. 'All England is in tumult. Tongues spread rumours like fire through the land, but I have been given reassurances by my lord Hastings that . . .'

'Talk not to me of Hastings,' she said. 'Hastings is first among those that labour to destroy me and my blood.'

'Not so, mother,' I butted in. 'My lord Hastings . . .'

'This business is not yours, Richard,' she said coldly. 'Now be silent, or be elsewhere.'

'He could be king,' Rotherham gabbled wildly, pointing at me, 'your younger son. He could be crowned tomorrow. If the new king is lost to us, then let us welcome King Richard the Third, who, though but a boy—'

My mother's voice cut in, as sharp and cold as I had ever heard it. 'I am a little deaf on this side, my lord bishop. There are some things which I cannot hear. I cannot hear what you do say . . .'

Not catching her drift, the old fool began to repeat himself.

He got as far as 'Your younger son . . .' when my mother's voice, clear as a bell, forestalled the rest of his speech.

'. . . and, lest I be misunderstood,' she said, 'I cannot hear anything which might be considered treason.'

The old man shut his mouth at last, and silently handed over the Great Seal of England, an act that neither he nor my mother seemed to notice as being as treasonous as his words.

News came that my brother was safe, rescued by one uncle from the clutches of another, and staying at the palace of the Bishop of London, and the new government of England was formed around him. A chastened Bishop of Rotherham returned to retrieve the Great Seal from my mother, my brother's coronation was set for late June, some six weeks away, and he was moved into the royal chambers in the Tower of London. All manner of thing now seemed to be well, but my mother was still disinclined to leave the sanctuary of the abbey. Perhaps she knew something that we children did not.

When the world changed it did so with the speed of a thought, and the status of my brother and myself changed with it. A bishop came forward with the information that neither Edward nor I had rightful claim to the throne, because our father had entered into a marriage with another lady before my mother, and that he was a bigamist, that my mother had never been his lawful wife and that consequently Edward and I and all our sisters were bastards. This meant little to me; I was not expecting to be a king and had never wanted so to be, and there was no difference in my daily behaviour or the way people treated me. I had met my uncle Richard's bastards in Yorkshire, and they seemed happy enough in their status.

A few days later came news that surprised me, although not my mother. My father's friend, Will Hastings, had confessed to treason and had been executed; Bishop Rotherham and several other men were arrested and jailed, and Uncle Richard was to become king – much against his will, or so the story

went. Turmoil, which had never been far from England these
thirty years, had ridden back in triumph over the body of my
father.

My mother fulminated much in private. At first I thought she
was likely to hate my uncle for what had been done to her, as
she was of course queen no longer nor her children royal, but it
was my father she blamed for all that had befallen.

Within a short time it was announced that my lord Protector, which was still my uncle Richard, the Archbishop of
Canterbury and my brother's tutor, that same Flemish painter
Hans Memling, were to request an audience. My mother gave
them an hour at which to attend, and then spent time writing
and rewriting a statement.

When she was satisfied, she called all of us children to her.
'This is hard for me to say,' she began. 'You have heard it
said that your father and I were not married in the eyes of the
church. I fear this is true; it is your father's fault, not mine;
he was trothed to another before he met me. I must now throw
all of us on the mercy of the Lord Protector. I doubt not that
he will act honourably towards us all. This is what I am going
to say to him when he comes.'

She unfurled the paper she had spent so much time on and
read from it. 'I freely confess to you that I entered into a bigam-
ous marriage with the late King Edward. I entered into the
marriage in good faith, but in his last years he confessed to me
of his previous attachment. The evidence produced by Bishop
Stillington is, I believe, correct. I hope that the church will
realize the suffering that I have been through since I learned
these facts, and that both church and state will realize why
I remained silent. In protecting my own name and those of
my children I know that I have sinned grievously, and I beg
both church and state to show mercy unto a woman who had
thought herself to be a wife, widow, mother and queen, but
now realizes that through no fault of her own she may call

herself none of these save one. I have lost all else, but I stand before you still a mother in defence of her children.'

She looked up. Bess, ever solicitous, moved to her side and put her arm around our mother. 'We understand, mother,' she said. 'It is what you must do. Think naught of it.'

My mother received the men in an outer chamber kindly enough, entering the room with all of her children. The men knelt to her, and we underwent the formalities. Then I could wait no longer. 'Hans!' I cried, and threw my arms about the painter's neck.

He was mortified. 'Your Grace,' he began by way of protest, but I was talking so fast that he could say no more. 'Ah, you have come with my uncle Gloucester. Are you going to let me paint some more? Have you seen Edward? What do you think of the fate of my lord Hastings? Did you bring materials for drawing? Have you heard the news? I am a bastard!'

'Richard, that's quite enough,' my mother said. 'Have you no greeting for my lord archbishop and for your uncle?'

Sobered by this admonition, I knelt before the archbishop and received his blessing in silence, and then bowed gravely to Uncle Richard before running forward and butting him in what I thought was his stomach, although I think I aimed a little low. He was a little breathless for a moment, and then I caught my mother's eye, after which I stood quietly. Perhaps my behaviour was a little indecorous for the occasion, but, in my defence, I was still but nine years old.

'Go and make your preparations, Richard,' my mother said, and so I bowed again to all three and went back into the cloister with my three youngest sisters, leaving only Bess and Cecily with her.

She had agreed that it were best if I were lodged with my brother, and when I returned with a manservant carrying my few personal possessions, she handed me over to my uncle, who had promised to care for my brother and me. I returned with the three men to the Tower to settle in with Edward.

I had not seen him for several months. At our last meeting we had been brothers and princes; since then we had lost a father and Edward had become king, ex-king and bastard. We were still loving brothers, of course, but now he was newly an ex-king and I a subject, so I suppose there was bound to be some awkwardness, and at first there was.

In addition, I was unprepared for the change I found in Edward. At first sight I hugged him, but immediately I had to pull back because of the smell.

'What's that?' I asked, making a face.

Edward drew aside his bandage to show me what had happened to him, and my reaction must have shown in my face.

'You too are repelled by me,' Edward said, and turned his face away.

'Ed, I am not,' I told him. 'It was a shock, that's all. I did not know that you were losing more teeth.'

'You had better go,' Edward said. 'Your chamber will be made ready.'

I shook my head. 'Can I not stay here with you?' I asked.

'I don't know,' Edward said.

I looked up at the painter, who had been designated my tutor also for the time being. 'May I, Master Memling?' I asked. 'My place is with my brother, even if he be no longer king.'

Of course he could not deny me, so that night and every night thereafter we slept in the same bedroom. I think it did Edward good.

I settled happily enough into life in the Tower, and I think I had a beneficial effect on my brother. Even in those days I was always eager to be up and about each morning, and was usually, although not always, able to drag my brother outside to play at ball or archery. Other than that the days had little to recommend them; each was the same as the last. Edward refused to go out in public and thus we were confined to within the walls of the Tower. Then Master Memling had the idea of carrying letters from us to our mother, if Edward were unable or unwilling to go himself, and got permission from the Protector. On the first occasion Hans went alone to the abbey, but on the next occasion he asked if I would like to go along. I had had precious few opportunities to wander the streets of London, and furthermore he offered me an intriguing treat.

After we had handed over our letters and visited my mother, Hans led me across to another part of the precinct of Westminster, where a red pole stood outside a shop. 'I want you to meet Master Caxton,' he said.

Master William Caxton was a squat, powerful man with a square white beard and a ready smile. He had spent many years in the Low Countries where he had been friends with Master Memling and, I was delighted to find, was acquainted with my father, whom he had befriended in the days of his exile before I was born. He was a dangerous man to be near, for he was a printer of books, the first in this our realm, and his apron was always liberally besmeared and bespattered with the ink of his trade, and with the slightest touch the said ink would be transferred to the nearest person, which was all too often myself.

He greeted me as if I were an old friend and did not stand on ceremony with me, but encouraged me to join in the work that was going on in the shop. In printing the books he made use of a large machine which he called a press, on which pages were printed one at a time; it looked like the cheese presses I had seen on some of my father's country estates.

There was a layout of metal type which was inked – again a dirty and dangerous process – and then a sheet of paper laid over it. The press came down, the ink was transferred to the paper and then the sheet laid aside until the ink was dry.

On that first day I became taker-off, he whose task it is to remove the paper from the type in one smooth motion so that the page is not smudged. It was a responsible job, but one I took to after some early mishaps. It made for an enjoyable afternoon, and it was easy to get permission from my uncle Richard, from Master Caxton and from Hans to go again, which I did many times, although Edward always refused to join us. He did however get some enjoyment out of my work, for Master Caxton sent him copies of each book to read as soon as it was printed, and I enjoyed carrying the volumes back to my brother – it was good to see the rare look of pleasure on his face.

I began to look forward very much to my printing days, and learned much of the printer's trade thereby. Master Caxton said that it is important work, for it means that all men, and not just the rich with their expensive illuminated manuscripts, will be able to read and enjoy the works of poets, storytellers and philosophers.

Edward and I spent the whole of that summer of our father's death in the Tower. Parliament duly and formally chose my uncle Richard as king, and so he, not I, became Richard the Third in despite of the Archbishop of Rotherham, who had regained his freedom. The following spring the king took us to Yorkshire with him, and we enjoyed an open-air existence as boys should. By the spring after that, though, there were problems. The Duke of Buckingham had risen in rebellion and been executed, and thereafter a man called Henry Tudor had come to the fore, announcing that he would be king and would marry my sister Bess. He was a bastard son of a bastard son, apparently, so had as little right to the throne as any man in England, but such was how things were in those tormented days.

'Why would he want to marry Bess?' I asked the king one evening as we sat, the whole family together, round a blazing fire. 'He does not love her. He doesn't even know her.'

'You are lucky,' King Richard told me. 'The marriages you

know well – mine, your father's – are marriages based on love. Some marriages are based on policy. I fear that such is what Tudor has in mind when he declares his intent toward your sister.'

'But that would do him no good, surely?' I asked. 'His own claim to the throne is poor. If Bess were still a princess then it would make sense, as she would stand third in line to the throne and bolster his claim, but by that law – what is it called?

'Titulus Regulus,' my brother said.

'Yes, that, and by that she is a bastard, and has no claim.'

Edward my brother laughed. 'Titulus Regulus can be repealed,' he said, 'as my uncle here intends one day to do. Then we shall no longer be bastards.'

'But still he has no claim to the throne,' I said. 'My sister's husband will be given an honoured place at court, I am sure, but as you and I begin to breed the crown will ever move further away from his grasp.'

Edward looked at me. 'Do you tell him, Your Majesty, or shall I?'

The king smiled. 'Feel free to display your grasp of the realities of political life,' he said. 'I shall be content to check your accuracy.'

Edward shifted position so that he was facing me. 'The present situation,' he began, 'is that you and I are illegitimate, as are Bess and all our sisters, and Tudor, whether or no he marries our sister, has no claim. However, postulate a further situation' – I think he had been given one too many glasses of wine, for even he was not often so prolix – 'wherein my uncle is deposed as king and Titulus Regulus repealed. You and I then become king and heir, as we were, and Tudor can marry whomsoever he wishes, for it makes no difference. If you and I are both legitimate and alive, then we are the rightful heirs, and Tudor still has no claim.'

He leaned forward, and the king, who could see more clearly than I the line of his argument, nodded silently.

'Postulate then a third possibility,' Edward continued. 'The only way Henry Tudor can claim the throne of England is if the following conditions are fulfilled: my uncle Richard has to be out of the way, Tudor has to be married to Bess and you and I (and thus Bess) have to be legitimate.'

'If we are legitimate then you are king,' I said.

'Unless,' Edward replied, 'I am dead, and you with me.'

He paused to let his words sink in, and as he looked at the king I felt a chill run the length of my backbone. 'Do I have it aright, Your Majesty?' he said.

'I fear you do, Edward,' Richard said. 'Legitimate but dead; that's Tudor's route.'

Things moved fast thereafter, and involved much sadness. King Richard's only son, Edward, died suddenly, aged only ten, and less than a year later the queen too died, although it has to be said that this was not unexpected; she had been pale and coughing up blood for some time. Then Tudor took the opportunity to invade, bringing with him an army of foreign mercenaries and such English lords as did not enjoy the fair and honest way that Richard was ruling. Edward and I were rushed back to the Tower as the safest place, and there we sat and waited for news.

It was not long in coming.

'I think the king has given battle in Leicestershire,' Master Memling told us one morning not long after my twelfth birthday. 'Rumours were rife yesterday. I think it were best we move you to a place of greater safety in case the news is bad.'

'I'm staying here,' Edward said determinedly.

'We can come back if the news is good,' Hans said.

'I'm staying here,' Edward repeated.

'Then I shall go and find what news there is.'

'I'll come with you,' I said.

He considered for a moment and then agreed. 'It can do no harm,' he said, and we walked out into the city to find out what we could.

The news, we heard, was all bad. Rumour gradually hardened into fact as men arrived from the battlefield, and we heard that Richard III was dead and Henry Tudor triumphant. Hans, who had been a good friend of the king's, was aghast. 'All is changed,' he said. 'I must return to the Tower to bring out your brother before it is too late, yet I cannot take you back there.'

'Where should I go?' I asked.

'In that at least I may please you,' he said. 'I think you should spend the rest of this day practising your printing skills.'

Despite the news we had had and the danger that my brother and I were in, I think my smile must almost have split my face, so happy did this proposal make me. How easy it is to be twelve years old.

It is less easy to be cheerful in such circumstances when you are a mature man. Master Caxton and his assistant Wynkyn were doleful and subdued that day. King Richard had been a good friend and patron to them, and they mourned his death as much as any man in England. Hans returned to the Tower, meaning to return with my brother and safeguard us until the waters were less muddied.

I remember that I sang that day as I set about my printing work. It was, I suppose, my last day as an undisputed prince.

Private Citizen

August 1485 – April 1487

By the time Hans came back some hours later, wet and dripping with a doleful story to tell – at least, to Caxton and Wynkyn, as I was not to hear the details until some time later, I was becoming tired. I had spent the afternoon helping Caxton and Wynkyn to print the pages of yet another new book; there seemed then to be no end to them.

I was not to go back to the Tower, it appeared, and Caxton asked no questions but gave us food and shelter, and for a few days more I became an apprentice printer, my apron and face as inky as I liked the livelong day, that being the best of disguises.

No man knew of the whereabouts of my brother. I hoped he had gone into sanctuary with my mother, who had again fled to the abbey with her daughters, but no one could tell me, and, as Hans and Caxton both pointed out, it might be dangerous to ask too often.

Hans meanwhile had been busy locating and sounding out men loyal to the Plantagenets, men who could be relied on. He found several such, but committed our safety to one Sir Edward Brampton, who, despite his name, was a Portuguese Jew who had Christianized and taken English nationality. Faithful to his king, he made arrangements for Hans and me to sail aboard a Flemish boat to Hans's home city of Bruges in Flanders, the territory of Maximilian, an ally of my father's and no friend to Henry Tudor.

I was taken on board under cover of darkness a few days later. Brampton greeted Hans on deck, clapped me on the shoulder, called me 'boy' and led us to his cabin.

'Please forgive my familiar behaviour, Your Grace,' he said, 'but no one must know who you are. You are in great danger.'

'Do you have any word of my brother?' I asked.

'No, sir, I do not.'

'And what of my mother and sisters?'

'I believe they have returned to sanctuary, sir.'

'I would join them,' I told him.

'It would not be safe to do so,' he said. 'Mynheer Memling has your safety at heart, and has acted wisely. We must be vigilant at all times; we know not whence danger might come.'

'May I not even write to my mother to reassure her of my safety?'

'It is not yet time for that,' he said. 'It is sad to say so, but it may be better if she does not know anything about you – that way it is impossible that she give anything away.'

I saw the wisdom of that, accepted the situation temporarily and settled down to enjoy the voyage. As Sir Edward had been so close with the secret, no one knew who I was, and I was passed off as Hans's bastard that he was taking to live with him in Flanders. I had the run of the ship, and found my sea legs quickly; I also suffered the smacks and buffets of the sailors whose work I interfered with, and experienced my first taste of life as a common person.

In Bruges I was kept at Hans's house for some weeks, and made friends with his three sons. There came the day, though, when I went to see Maximilian, who was about to be made King of the Romans, and possibly had other things on his mind at the time. He met Hans and myself in private audience, and was adamant from the first as soon as he had heard what Hans had done.

'We cannot acknowledge him,' he told us. 'The continuation

of the English war would be to no one's benefit, and it appears that this Henry Tudor sits secure for now. It were best we provide for the boy and keep him safe; he can make his own decision when he comes of age.'

I sat while they debated my future.

'You cannot provide for him here, sire, surely?' Hans said. 'He will become a focus of disaffection.'

'Unless we disguise his identity.'

'Surely, sir, your stepmother-in-law would know him.'

'Is that my aunt Margaret?' I asked.

'Yes, Your Highness,' Maximilian said.

'I do not think she would know me,' I said. 'I do not think that she has ever been to England since either Edward or I were born. Is there any news yet of my brother, sir? Do we know if he is safe?'

'We do not, I'm afraid,' Maximilian replied, and he and Hans exchanged a glance that at that time meant nothing to me, but which now I understand only too well. He turned back to Hans. 'Even so,' he went on, 'a young boy running around the palace speaking fluent English might excite some comment. It were best perhaps if the dowager duchess knew nothing of this matter for the moment.'

'I could take him into my home,' Hans said. 'One more boy would not make much difference.'

Maximilian shook his head. 'You are known to have been in England,' he said. 'If they come looking, yours will be the first house they search, and a boy of the right age speaking good English but poor Hollandish will stick out a mile. No, it will have to be somewhere else.' He rubbed his brow. 'I wonder.'

He paused, made a decision, and went on, 'There is one of my officers who might be induced . . .' He stopped again. 'I do espy a kind of hope.'

He drew Hans to one side, where I could not overhear, and

they talked in low tones for some time. Thus was my fate decided.

Hans told me on the way back to his house what was to happen. I would be adopted by a family who had recently lost a child, a boy of about my age, and they would be offered inducements to return to the father's place of birth to allay suspicion.

My new father would take up a post as one of the controllers of the river port of Tournai, and I was to live with him and his wife as their child. No decision regarding my future would otherwise be made until I came into man's estate.

'What do you think, Hans?' I asked. 'Shall I do it?'

'What option do you have?' he asked. 'You are a boy in danger. This way you are safe, and no one need ever know who you are until the time is ripe and you are able to make the decision yourself.'

'And Maximilian? He knows.'

'He is a good man,' Hans said. 'He will keep your secret if you will.'

Thus it was that the following month I travelled with Hans to Tournai. The family lived in a small but clean house a stone's throw from the River Scheldt, where my new father's duties mostly lay. Jehan de Werbecque was a bluff, straightforward man who eyed me with much suspicion at first, but softened when he heard that I was an orphan that needed a home. After we had been shown into the house, Hans left me with him while he went out to buy something to drink, and we sat on opposite sides of the tiny room, each eyeing the other up.

'Who are you?' he asked finally. He was speaking in French, so I had no difficulty in understanding him. 'Who are you?' he repeated.

I remembered again what Maximilian had told me. I was to tell no man who I was; it was a secret between him, Hans and myself. I stood before Jehan as he eyed me across the table, and I felt his fear, but I could not say my name. I opened my mouth to speak, to say anything, but nothing would come out. I did not know what to say. I no longer knew who I was, or how to answer his question.

Werbecque banged the palm of his hand flat on the table and I must have jumped. 'Who are you?' he said again, in Flemish this time, but the words were close enough to English to be understood. It was all too much for me, and I began sobbing.

Werbecque's attitude changed. He reached out and patted me gently on the shoulder. *'Ne sois pas un brayou,'* he said gruffly, a look of compassion in his eyes.

Hans had not told him the truth about me; Maximilian had decided that such knowledge would be too much for the family to carry safely – neither my name nor my nationality were divulged to him. I think that Jehan secretly thought I was the bastard child of a court official, or perhaps of Hans himself.

I had already become used to being a bastard, so to become the son of a household, however humble, was a step up. In any case, as Hans said, what alternative did I have?

Hans returned bearing a bottle, and the three of us sat chatting for an hour or so, the two men speaking Flemish when I was to be excluded and French when I was allowed to hear, until Madame Werbecque returned from the market. Jehan was already regaling me with tales of the river, and had promised me that we would go fishing together, sometimes even out on the open sea, although it turned out later that he had never even seen the open sea.

His wife, Catherine, had been born in Portugal, and had the dark good looks of the people of that country. She and I took to each other at once. Her first action was to fold me in her arms, a sign of affection that I had not experienced for some time now. Then she held me at arms' length and perused me. 'He even looks like my own,' she said. 'What is your name, my boy?'

She too spoke in French, which I understood well enough, but I looked blankly at her. I could not tell even her my real name, but I had none other at hand to use. I looked to Hans for help.

'It were best you do not know it yet,' he told her, 'and you must speak to him only in Flemish or French. Give him a name of your own choosing. He will answer to it, I'm sure.'

'Our boy was called Pierrechon,' she said. 'Would that do?'

'Pierrechon,' he said. 'Yes. It is a most appropriate name.' He did not explain why this was so.

'You surely cannot wish to give him the same name as our lost boy?' Jehan Werbecque said. 'Will it not remind you, always, and me, of what we have lost?'

'Can we ever forget, Jehan?' she asked softly. 'Is it likely we will ever forget our Pierrechon, no matter what name we give this boy? Would we want to forget? Why should he not remind us of what our boy might have been, and be our new boy at the same time?'

Jehan looked at me without speaking for a long moment, and then said gruffly, 'I suppose,' and looked down at the floor.

I felt an arm encircle my shoulders and I was pulled into a warm softness.

'Pierrechon, then,' said Dame Werbecque's voice. 'He is Pierrechon, and Pierrechon is our son. That is enough.'

Jehan was still looking at the floor, but I saw the nod of his head.

So Pierrechon Werbecque I became, or Pierrechon de Werbecque if we were putting on airs, or properly Piers van Weerbecke, *anglice* Perkin Warbeck, a name which sadly clung to me like a wet shirt even when I wished to divest myself of it.

At that time, however, I was glad of the name and of the family.

After Hans had put a bag of coins on the table and said his goodbyes, I was left to settle in. Dame Werbecque pointed at my clothes and made movements suggesting that I should take them off. I shook my head, not wanting to, but she persisted, although she did allow me the privacy of taking off my clothes in another room, and gave me some plain garments to wear. They must have been her son's; they were about the right size for me, anyway.

When I came back into the other room wearing his dead son's clothes, I saw the look of shock on Werbecque's face, and saw that he was on the point of protest. Then I saw the shock disappear, to be replaced by sadness. Then he nodded again and said, 'Yes, he must be Pierrechon; as you say, that is enough – or at least, will have to be enough.' He looked at me. 'You are my son now,' he said, 'no matter who you were before. We will not speak of this again.'

The bag of gold that had come with me lay still on the table. Mynheer Werbecque had not touched it.

In those early days I was not allowed to go outside lest I give myself away by my speech. While Mynheer Werbecque was out at his work his wife gave me instruction in the language of Flanders, speaking to me, telling me the names of objects in the house and putting short sentences together. Our languages must be cousins, for there is enough similarity between them for us to learn to understand each other quickly; I must say I became fluent in a short time, just by listening and joining in when I could.

I remember we had great fun with the simplest of devices; one day she gave me a small piece of bread and a dish, and all that morning was spent placing the bread, on her instruction, *in* the dish or *on* the dish or *near* the dish or *behind* the dish and so on, and my vocabulary grew in leaps and bounds.

Flemish was the language of their family, but the language of the town was French, and in this of course I already had some fluency, having been forced to learn and speak it to my sisters from an early age.

37

After I had been in their family for some weeks, Dame Werbecque conceived the idea of having me go to market with her with my head tied up in a bandage around my jaw, so that no one would call upon me to speak. She gave people to believe that I had an abscess of the gum, and stuffed my cheek with pieces of cloth before we set out, the better to keep up the pretence. Thus I was learning to look and to listen, and my knowledge of the language grew while my intimacy with the Flemish people expanded at the same time.

Thereafter she began to put the word round that the vapours of my abscess had affected my brain, and that I was slow to recover my wits after my illness; thus she bought me a few more weeks during which people asked me no questions, and by the time Christmas arrived I was accepted by all of her circle, by the traders in the market and by the neighbours, and I had developed a trick of going into a spasm if I did not understand a question or was unable to frame an answer, and Dame Werbecque would step in to save me.

In that first winter in the low countries I spake not a word of my native tongue, and learned to converse and even write in Flemish, although I have to admit that their way of spelling is fiendish difficult.

I also learned a few words of Portuguese, the language of my new mother, who was wont to lapse into her native tongue in moments of exasperation, whether with me, with her husband or with the traders in the market. It was easy to understand – easier certainly than Flemish, having similarities with both French and Latin.

I learned to love my new father, who though a gruff and sometimes fierce man, loved his wife and missed his boy, and before long I was truly his son and, as soon as I was fluent, was allowed to accompany him to his work, which was mainly the inspection and taxing of riverboats and their cargoes.

It was interesting, and threw me in with a host of rivermen

and seafarers from all of the nations on earth, so that I picked up words and phrases from many languages and from some of the sailors picked up expressions which I learned not to use in the presence of my new mother.

At times my father went even further away than the quays, right down the river which ran through the city. On occasion he was away many days, going to inspect a ship that might be required to stay in quarantine or that was carrying cargo that was not permitted. Usually the trips we took were no more than a few hours or at most a day or two, but they whetted my appetite to see more of the sea and its ways, and I determined that if I could not be a prince of England then I should be a sea captain, the two occupations being equally desirable in my adolescent mind.

It was good to be an ordinary boy, not bound about by protocol and the formalities of court. Before long I was doing what ordinary boys did – I filched fruit from the market, annoyed traders, swam naked in the river and clambered over walls which were not barriers but challenges. I made friends with the other boys of the wharf, and I dare say that by the time Easter came round my own queenly mother would not have known me – and if she had she would not have cared to admit the fact. Although my new mother took pains to ensure that I was always clean and tidy, when away from her care and watchful eye I was as scruffy a street urchin as Tournai could offer. And I was, in despite of all, happy.

A little after Eastertide I was sitting eating a pilfered apple in the shade of one of the arches of Notre Dame de Tournai. I liked to go there, partly because it was quiet and I was able to think, and partly because sometimes the choir was practising and I was able to sit in the coolness of the church unobserved and listen. I have always enjoyed music, and used to sing for my parents with my sisters.

This day I had listened to the rehearsal and then slipped

outside. I was behind the buttress with my feet sticking out, and naturally the choir's song was still in my head. I began to sing it softly, the words familiar from many a service – '*Tantum ergo, sacramentum, veneremur cernui . . .*' I was still holding the long note of the final 'i' when a shadow appeared beside my feet. I stopped abruptly, but a long, lean face surmounted by a clerical cap looked around the stonework and smiled.

'Sing on, my son,' the man said.

Of course I was now unable to do so, and simply goggled at him.

'Where did you learn to sing like that?' he asked.

'In church,' I told him, truthfully enough.

'And the words?'

'In church, at the services, sir.'

'And have you had lessons in singing?'

I decided that this was not the best time to reveal that I had, and so shook my head.

'You have a pleasing voice,' he said, 'one that should be used to glorify God, and not out here in the churchyard.'

'One may glorify God in any place, surely, sir?' I asked.

'Ah,' he said. 'A philosopher as well as a musician, I see. Well, you are right, of course, but in church is generally seen as a more appropriate place than most. What is your name, child, and who are your parents?'

I told him, and he asked, 'From what parish are they?'

I told him St Jean, by the river, and he asked, 'What would you think to joining the choir, and to singing at the services?'

I told him that I would like it full well, and he arranged to come and see my parents to talk to them about it. 'Tell them that Master Baulde Maquet, the cantor, has spoken to you,' he said. 'We may yet hear you sing in the church.'

If I expected them to be pleased with me, I was sadly mistaken.

'It is not meet that you draw attention to yourself,' Jehan

said. 'We are to take care of you and bring you up, not show you off to the world.'

'You are the son of a boatman now, Pierrechon,' my new mother said, 'and must not have ideas beyond that, whoever you might have been before.' She still had no idea, of course.

She repeated the same sentiments to the cantor when he came to see them, and was given short shrift for her pains. 'But the choir is laden with the sons of fishmongers, boatmen, market traders and the like,' he told her. 'Indeed, is there not a namesake of yours, Gaspar van Weerbecke, a man of lowly birth, originally from Ouldenarde, who composes music for the Sforza family in Italy?'

'My cousin,' Jehan said gruffly. 'Haven't seen him for years.'

'There you are then,' Master Maquet said triumphantly. 'Does that not show that the voice of a common man sings as sweetly in God's ears as the voice of a noble? Why, my own father is an ostler at a wayside inn. It is the talent that attracts the offer, not a boy's birth.'

In due course they allowed themselves to be persuaded, and later that week I went to the cathedral and was given a surplice to wear and placed in the front row of the choir, where Master Maquet could hear my voice more distinctly. I took great care not to know how to read the music that some of the choristers had before them, although truth to tell most had learned the chants by ear and were not accomplished readers of the marks, and I dissimulated too about my knowledge of Latin, and soon got the reputation of being a quick learner. I always felt that the words of Tournai's own special hymn, the 'Salve Regina', spoke directly to me, a sorrowful exile: '*Ad te clamamus exules filii Evae . . . in hac lacrymarum valle . . .*'

I have to say it was a good life. Our days were mostly taken up with singing and playing music, but when we were free the cathedral was surrounded by market stalls selling goods from all over the world, and half the tongues of Europe were spoken in the town's streets. I stayed a year with the choir school, until that day the following spring, when I saw two men standing on a wharf and once again my world was turned upside down and I became again a vagrant and an exile even from my new self.

When Jehan was finally out of sight, I moved away from the river and into the back streets, finding the narrow alleys strangely comforting. I was travelling away from the town centre, which was on the other side of the river, and I knew that the pursuers would not find me in the labyrinth. Ouldenarde was some twenty miles to the north-east, and as I set off there I heard the angelus ring. I should have been in the stalls with the other choirboys, but had I but known it, my boyhood was finished.

I set off cheerfully enough for the house of my aunt, Jehan's sister; she and her husband were kind people and it was a good place to hide. I knew I would not be able to make the journey on foot in what remained of the day, and as I walked along the bank I kept my eye open for boats plying downstream. If someone I knew came past then I might have been able to cadge a ride, although there were obvious dangers in letting anyone else know where I was going. I had with me some of the bread and cheese my father and I had taken with us in the morning, and an apple. This was enough to keep me fed, but ere long I would be in need of water. The Scheldt was filthy, and no man short of the insanely desperate would think of drinking from it. Towards evening, however, I found a tiny stream which flowed into the main river, and I walked along its length for a hundred paces or so. It looked and tasted drinkable, and nearby, at the edge of a wood, I found a tiny hollow that would offer shelter against wind, if not rain. It was a fine evening with no sign of rain clouds, and I decided that this was as good a place as any to spend the night. I sat on the grass, turned my jerkin back to front to keep me warm, ate half of my bread and cheese and took a few draughts of the spring water. Then I settled down and dozed off.

It was the sound of voices that woke me. Sleeping in the forest fills up our senses, so that although asleep we are still alert, and thus never far from the surface. I came awake quickly. The jingle of harness came to me through the night, and the sound of voices too. I thought about asking if I could ride up behind on one of the animals, should they be going my way, even though travellers might not take too kindly to being accosted on the road at the dead of night.

My name saint is Richard of Chichester, whose feast day it happened to have been that day, and who must have been watching over me. He must have been more alert for my safety than I that night, for the travellers stopped to water their horses at the very stream at whose banks I sat. One dismounted and turned to piss into the bushes not five paces from where I was. I was about to stand and reveal myself when from his horse the other called, 'And if he's not in Ouldenarde, what then?'

I froze, terrified.

He was speaking English.

'I know not,' said the other, unlacing his points, 'but now we know what he looks like, and those wharf rats will let us know the moment he arrives back at his home. It may take some time, but we'll have him soon enough.' He stepped back towards his horse and pulled its head from the water. 'Damn this arm,' he said. 'Can't tie knots with it.' He hoisted himself into the saddle and asked, 'Ready?'

For answer the other stepped his horse away from the stream and they ambled away down the road, in no hurry to do their work.

I sat where I was until dawn, unable to sleep. It was clear that it was time for Pierrechon Werbecque to disappear as mysteriously and suddenly into the shadows as he had emerged from them, and at first light I turned my steps north, away from Ouldenarde, away from Tournai and away from the pleasant life of an ordinary boy that I had grown to love.

Pressed Man

April 1487 – September 1487

O ver the next few weeks I wandered aimlessly, filching an apple here or begging a meal in exchange for a day's work there, just another wanderer in a continent of way-walkers. I met students, beggars, itinerant priests, discharged mercenaries and all the flotsam of society. No one asked any questions other than a name to call you by, and no one expected any favours; there was no loyalty, for friendship was a duty that laid demands on a man – all there was was a conversation, and a few miles walk along a road, perhaps a shared hunk of bread and the shadow of a companionship.

At the end of my road lay Middelburg, a small town of no great standing where I found work selling his wares for a maker of purses, needles and pincushions, a man called Jan Strewe, who allowed me to sleep on his floor and eat with his family in exchange for working in the market. I knew enough to be a charming salesman when need be, and my work was effective enough for him to keep me on for the big fair that was to be held in the week before Easter.

On my fifth day with him I had set out the stall as usual in the early morning and was dawdling near it, looking at the wares the other merchants had brought and chatting to the boys on the other stalls. We had a system where whoever was on the next stall would keep an eye on yours while you sauntered about or answered a call of nature, so that nothing was filched, and it was a pleasant way to spend a morning. Mynheer

Strewe's fat son, also Jan, was supposed to be in charge, but he had decided that I was unlikely to make off with the merchandise and had sloped off to talk to the butcher's daughter, more in the hope of cheap meat than anything more amatory.

'Purse stall! Purse stall!'

The peremptory call was clearly from someone who was used to being obeyed, and expected people to jump at her word. I looked around. It was a lady I had seen from time to time wandering about the stalls, usually attended by a maid and a couple of manservants, as she was again today, and I went over in as quick but as dignified a way as I could.

'Madam?' I said.

She was small, below average height. Her call had been in Flemish, but when she spoke to the maid the language she used was English, and my spine began to tingle. 'Choose what you need,' she said. I looked at the manservants; neither one was familiar, and I relaxed a little. No one had any idea who I was anyway; I was just a boy in a market.

The maid selected three purses of medium size and demanded to know if we had any of greater capacity. I was forced to confess that we did not, although if she cared to return when the master was about he might have some more in stock. At this point Jan Strewe the Younger appeared and placed himself at the head of affairs, demonstrating his seniority to me. There were indeed larger purses to be had, and I was detailed to accompany the maid to Mynheer Strewe's house, show her a selection, and, if any were satisfactory, to accompany her to the house where the lady was staying and claim payment.

There was no hardship to this. The maid was comely enough and it was a pleasant day for a stroll through the streets; the errand could, if performed carefully enough, use up several hours of the working day. The lady went off with her male attendants, and the girl and I set off for Strewe's house. Her name was Jane, and she was English, but I had to be careful not to reveal my own nationality. She spoke little French and even less Flemish, so I pretended that I was a Flamande trying to learn English, and we strolled through the town, enjoying each other's company and tripping over a triplet of languages, although truth to tell I understood her full well, as she tried out each phrase in her own language before trying to put it into the others.

We reached Strewe's house and a selection of capacious purses was displayed. A dozen or so were chosen to be taken for the approval of the lady. The master was delighted at such a potentially good sale, and told me to take my time escorting the maidservant home, to make sure to impress her mistress and to return to him, not to the market, with the money and any unsold goods as soon as possible.

When he had told me, out of Jane's earshot, the minimum price he would accept for the merchandise and what discounts I could apply for quantity, Jane and I set off again for the house where her mistress was staying.

'Who is she?' I asked.

'I work – *je travaille* – for her, for the lady – *pour elle, la dame*,' she told me. 'She is a – *elle est – grande dame de la noblesse*.'

'*Ah oui. La noblesse de France, ou de Bourgogne?*'

'No,' she said. 'Neither. *Pas*. Not. *Pas France, pas Bourgogne. La noblesse de Portugal*.'

'Ah. *De Portugal*.'

'*Oui*. And also of – *et aussi d'Angleterre*.'

I stopped dead, sudden fear paralysing me. '*La noblesse d'Angleterre?*' I said, and then, just to be certain, 'England?'

'*Oui*,' she said, unconcerned, and apparently not having noticed my slip. '*Mais demain nous retournons à Portugal*.'

'*La toute famille est ici avec elle?*'

'*Non, seulement le maître*.'

'*Qui est le maître?*' I asked.

Is the master Lancaster or York, I really wanted to know. Is he here in pursuit of me, or is it an innocent trip? Is it someone who might know me, or whom I might know? How much danger am I in?

I looked anxiously at her face, and at the puzzlement on it. What had I said? I looked around desperately in case assassins had suddenly loomed from the shadows.

The frown cleared as I watched. '*Sais pas*,' she said. '*En Français*, I don't know how to say it.'

'*Le nom*,' I said. 'His name?'

She grinned. 'Brampton,' she said. 'Sir Edward Brampton. *Le seigneur Duarte Brampton. Tu le comprends?*'

'*Oui*,' I told her, my mind a turmoil.

'*Tu le sais?*'

'No,' I said, a little too desperately I felt. '*Je ne le sais pas. Je suis intéressé, c'est tout.*'

'*Ici*,' she said suddenly. 'This house.'

She stopped at a doorway, and I waited while she went inside. After a few moments I was called in. It was obvious that preparations were being made for a journey. Servants were moving about, carrying items, and there were boxes and trunks, some packed and closed and others in the process of being filled. Jane appeared with the lady, who looked cursorily at the selection of purses and indicated that Jane could choose which ones to have. Then she disappeared into the recesses of the house.

There followed a period of negotiation, with the maid determined to get the lowest price and I the highest, and in the end, thank the Lord, we were able to agree a price that was less than the most her mistress was prepared to pay but more than the least my master would accept. We agreed that she would tell her mistress that she had paid the maximum, I would tell my master that I had accepted the minimum, and those coins which represented the difference would be split evenly between the two of us. It was a satisfactory outcome for all.

When the matter had been thus resolved I asked, 'Does your mistress require any servants?'

'Why?' she asked, looking at me in an interested way.

'I would serve her and go to Portugal,' I said.

'You must ask the master's butler,' she said, and directed me to a tall, spare gentleman dressed soberly in a dark coat.

I repeated my question to him, and he looked me up and down and laughed, not caring to hide his amusement. 'Do you speak Portuguese?' he asked. 'Can you serve at table? Do you know the ways of court? Do you have any skills other than to cut the purses you also sell? Of course not. And that "Of course not" is also the answer to your question. Good day to you.'

I could of course have answered 'Yes' to each of his questions, but to do so might have excited comment. I decided that I was not to be so easily dismissed. I don't know why, but I had suddenly been taken by the urge to travel to Portugal and to see something of my new mother's native land. I had become used to the itinerant life, I suppose, and of course there was the possibility of adventure and seeing a little of the world. Also in my mind, of course, was that Sir Edward had taken care of me once, and of all men was the most likely to do so again, and also the most unlikely to be party to any Lancastrian plot to destroy me.

'May I speak to Sir Duarte?' I asked.

'You may not,' he said. 'He is busy with arrangements for the voyage. There is no opening for you in this house. Be gone.'

Reluctantly I accepted my fate and stepped through the door. 'Here, lad,' a voice said. 'Want to earn a couple of duits?'

'Yes,' I answered automatically. It was someone I'd seen around the market from time to time – a tallish man, young – not much older than myself – with prominent teeth projecting below a beak of a nose, and thin bony wrists sticking out of the sleeves of his jerkin.

'Then help me carry these cases to the quayside. If you take the three smallest ones I'll manage the biggest, and then we can come back for the rest.'

I happily took the opportunity to go and look at Sir Edward's ship. I had been on plenty of river craft, of course, but never a seagoing vessel, except for the one that had brought me over to the Low Countries, and that had been but a tiny boat.

The quay was no more than a short step away, and it was easy to tell which ship was the one being readied for sea from the atmosphere of bustle and general busyness around it. My companion and I took our burden up onto the deck and a servant, clearly proud of his responsibility, fussily directed us to leave them near a doorway. 'Is Sir Duarte aboard?' I asked.

'Get back on shore,' was his only reply, without even the grace of deigning to look at me.

I opened my mouth to give him a good retort, but my companion plucked at my sleeve and shook his head.

I followed him to the gangplank. 'What do you want the boss for?' he asked.

'Just looking at the possibility of a job,' I said.

'As a seaman?'

'As anything.'

He shook his head. 'Nothing doing,' he said. 'A few of us have tried to get berths on *La Rainha*, but it's got a full complement of crew and passengers. Pity; I fancy a trip to Portugal myself.'

We walked back to Brampton's house and picked up another load of trunks and cases. 'Mind you,' he said, 'there's other ways of getting aboard a ship.'

'Stowing away, you mean?'

He shook his head. 'I wouldn't try that,' he said. 'For one thing, they'll make a good thorough search before they sail, and for a second, if he found you during the voyage Sir Edward would think nothing of tipping you overboard. No, there are other ways – if you're prepared to take a little risk or two.'

'Go on then,' I said. 'I'm listening.'

'It'll cost you those coins I promised you,' he said cautiously.

'I'll buy it,' I said. 'Tell me all.'

'My name's Roos,' he said. 'Can you swim? It only works if you can swim.'

With the tide running from Middelburg down to the south it was not difficult to get the bacquet on the right line, but the north wind was cold and whipping up the white horses on the water, so we had to bail more or less continuously. The craft rocked dangerously, but it was a clear spring day and we could see all around us for many a mile. We were south of Walcheren, heading along the shipping lanes, with the Hollandish coast on our port beam. I was pulling for all I was worth, while Roos lazed in the bow and every now and again sat up to scan the lanes behind.

We had 'borrowed' a bacquet from the quayside at Middelburg in the early hours and set off a couple of hours before the tide turned. It was a hard row at first, but once the water started to flow it moved us along more rapidly and then the north wind got up a little. Though it was chilly the rowing kept us warm and after three hours of rowing turn and turn about we were in what Roos considered the best position.

'You can rest now,' he said. 'You'll need your strength later.'

I shipped the oars and lay back, resting my muscles.

'Better be a little more convincing,' Roos said, more or less to himself, and then began to ladle sea water into the boat, using an old pot he had found. I watched him for a few moments and then turned my gaze to the north, where the sea was clear. 'That'll do,' he said, when there was about a hand's depth of water in the bottom of the boat, and he too lay back. 'Let me know if you see anything,' he said, and closed his eyes.

I sat a little straighter and, taken by the tide, the bacquet continued to drift sluggishly southwards.

This was maintained for an hour or so, and then Roos, who had taken to scanning the horizon behind us with greater frequency, exclaimed, 'Ah! There she is.' He pointed, and sure enough a ship was visible, beating down towards us.

'You certain?' I asked.

'Yes,' he said. 'Only one ship of that type in Middelburg just now. That's the one all right. Let's see what course it's on.'

Even I could see that the ship's sails were full, and that she was sailing on a line that would take her further out to sea than we were. 'We have to get onto her course,' Roos said.

We took an oar each and pulled steadily until we could see that the ship was coming head-on towards us. She was nearing us fast, and I imagined that I could hear the flapping of her sails.

Now Roos was bailing again, throwing sea water into the bottom of our craft. I stood up and waved and called at the approaching ship. By now it was so near that I could see figures on the deck, and then one of them pointed at us and waved. 'They see us,' I said.

Roos promptly reversed the bailing process, now throwing out of the boat the water he'd just thrown in. 'Call them,' he said urgently. 'Call for help.'

I did so, yelling at the top of my voice and windmilling my arms about. There was a slight slackening of one of the sails and a figure hailed me from the bow. 'You in trouble?'

'Sinking,' I shouted. 'Help!'

'Whither bound?'

'Middelburg,' I called. 'Help!'

'Come on!' Roos muttered under his breath, and then he abandoned his bailing and he too stood with his arms aloft and joined his voice to mine. Now the bacquet had set to drifting again, and by this time was almost beneath the ship's bow. I felt as if her shadow were absolutely upon us, when she hailed us again. 'Line coming,' came the call, and first one and then a second length of rope came over the side, snaking out towards us and immediately being pulled back in towards the ship's side by the rush of water. Now the craft was almost upon us, and in a few moments would be gone.

'The rope!' Roos shouted. 'Leap for the rope.'

I waited until the bow of the ship was level with me, and the trailing rope no more than three yards from the bacquet. The line was being dragged in towards the vessel's side and away from us with every foot of headway, and I flung myself across the space, my arms and legs all clutching desperately. Beside me I was aware of Roos's body hurtling over, aiming for the second rope. My right hand caught the line and held for a moment, just long enough for me to bring my left arm over and clutch more firmly. Then my left hand slipped, but I held on with my right as I was being dragged through the sea, bouncing in and out of the waves. I managed to bring my left hand back to the rope and then I was able to wrap one leg and then the other round the rope; the firm grip meant that I could catch my breath. Then, with my stronger purchase I was able to bend my right ankle and hook my foot round the rope for an even firmer grip, and so I had time to spit out the sea water and take stock of the situation.

I looked up at the side of the ship, where, ten feet above me, men were gesticulating and shouting, some of them hauling on the rope so that even without any effort I was being inched slowly out of the water. More men were pointing back into the ship's wake, and I turned my head. Beside me the other rope hung slackly, and I twisted to look along the ship's furrow. In the few seconds I had been clinging to the rope the ship had travelled some forty yards or so, and in the water of the ship's wake I saw Roos's head watching me go. I clung to my lifeline as he grew smaller in the water, but was pleased to see that the little bacquet was close enough for him to clamber aboard before my own hand reached the bulwark of the ship and I was able to haul myself over the side.

I found a group of men standing staring at me. One of them took a bite of the apple he was eating and said, 'Just a tiddler. Throw it back again.' I managed to force a grin.

'Can you get my friend?' I asked.

'Turn back?' he said. 'Never in this world. We would have left you if you hadn't caught that line. Business is more important than drowning boys. Anyway, he'll get to shore; he's safe enough.'

Then I realized what language he had spoken in.

'Is this a Flemish ship?'

'No, Portuguese, but there's a few Flamandes aboard,' one of the men said.

'Get this down you,' a crewman said, and handed me a drink – hot water with some sort of spirit in it, I think. 'How long have you been drifting?'

'Since early morning,' I lied. 'We went out too far, and then the tide caught us and swept us away.'

'Come down to the galley and get dry,' he said. 'We can put some clothes on you and then you'll have to go and see the captain.'

The clothes they found me were a little too big, but they were warm and dry and after a second dash of the water and spirits I was led below to the captain's cabin.

I waited outside while the crewman knocked and announced me as 'That bit of flotsam we picked up, sir.' Then he ushered me into a tiny room with a window at one end and a chest on its side serving as a writing desk. Behind it sat a tall, swarthy man who looked me up and down before saying, 'Well, I hope you realize that you're going to have to work your passage.' It was a strange accent – not Flemish, though he spoke the language well enough – but then I already knew who he was.

'As what, sir?' I asked.

'Couldn't care less,' he said. 'Grummet, ship's boy, ship's cat, galley slave – wherever you fit. You've no experience, I suppose?'

'Not at sea, sir, though I've spent some time on riverboats.'

He grunted. 'Well, that's something, I suppose. So, what name did your parents foist on you?'

For a moment I thought that he had seen through me, but then realized that his irony was unintentional. 'Piris,' I said.

'Right. Well, we'll sign you on for the duration of the voyage . . .'

I knew the answer already, but for form's sake I asked the question. 'Beg pardon, sir, but can you not put me ashore?'

'Where?'

'Here, sir, in Flanders.'

'We're not landing in Flanders,' he said. 'We have a following wind, and I've no intention of losing it. No, you're with us until we arrive.'

'Arrive where, sir?' Again, I knew the answer.

'Lisbon.'

'But, sir,' I said excitedly, 'I can't go to Lisbon, sir. I live here. Surely you can . . .'

'I can have my crew throw you back into the sea whence they fished you,' he said, 'if that will make you happy. Do you think I am in the business of running a ferry service for young boys?'

'No sir.'

'So you see, you must remain on board this ship, under my command, until we arrive in Lisbon. You will be rated as a ship's boy. Are you prepared to work as a ship's boy?'

I did not have any option. 'Of course, sir,' I said. 'I am used to work.'

'Well, then, Piris, you can report to the master, who will assign you your duties.'

'Yes, sir,' I said.

'At sea,' he told me, 'the correct response is "Aye aye, sir".' And thus I became a seafarer.

Although the ship, the *Rainha*, was Portuguese, along with most of its crew, it had men from many different countries aboard. I rubbed shoulders with a couple of Englishmen, two Irishmen, a Scotsman, several Flamandes, a Berber, and most exotic of all, the first black man I had ever seen, a native of Guinea in Africa.

Having no real skills I was put in the charge of the ship's cook and set to work in the galley, helping with the preparation of the meals and serving at the captain's table. From time to time I was required to help out in other areas – hauling on ropes and even climbing the rigging to release sails when the wind was right, although I was asked to do this only twice during the entire voyage. The diet and the exercise did me good; the muscles of my arms and legs hardened, my chest began to expand and the boy began to look more like a man, even over the few short weeks we were at sea.

The ship reeked of spices. Sir Edward traded in them and in peppers from the coast of Africa and sold them in the markets of Europe, and the very wood of the ship was permeated with their essence, making it excessively fragrant and pleasant to sail in.

I enjoyed serving at table the best. The food was of the finest, and there were always rich pickings to eat on the frequent journeys to take the remains of one course away and bring in the next. I made an impression on Lady Brampton, who was on board, returning to Lisbon from Middelburg. She did not make any connection between me and the purse seller of Middelburg, and as Jane had been left in the Low Countries to follow later there was no one to give me away. She seemed to find my manners charming, and was pleased to smile upon me and set me little tasks to do. One night she suddenly had a desire to hear someone sing, and as I had been heard singing while going about my business I was the one picked on. She took evident delight in my music, and as a result over the remaining three weeks of the voyage I became virtually her own servant, paging for her and serving her at table.

When the coast of Portugal became visible off the port bow and the experienced sailors told me that the voyage had but a few days to run, I realized that I had a decision to make. Sir Edward Brampton was the most loyal of Yorkists, a friend to both my father and Uncle Richard, and I had discovered that he was still unwelcome in Tudor's England. If there was a man in whom I could confide, it was he. I determined to sound him out, so one afternoon, when the ship was running swiftly before the wind and my galley work was finished, I scratched on the frame of his cabin door.

He was sitting in a chair that was bolted to the deck, with before him a table that had no legs but swung from hooks in the ceiling, so that it moved gently with the action of the ship.

'Yes,' he said. 'What is it?'

'You are Sir Edward Brampton,' I replied.

'I had not thought you the brightest of sparks,' he said, laying his quill on the table, 'having gone to sea in a leaky bucket, but to come and tell me what my name is after four weeks of serving me at table and confinement together in the same ship suggests that at the very least you have been drinking sea water.' He looked at me. 'Did you wish merely to establish my identity, or is there a purpose to this visit?'

'You know me, sir, and I know you. We have met before.'

'I repeat,' he said. 'You have been serving me at table these four weeks. Now for God's sake get out of my cabin.'

'You misunderstand me, sir. I mean that we have had previous acquaintance, before you rescued me.'

'I don't recall,' he said. 'What ship was it?'

'I cannot remember its name, sir. I was much younger then, and I was not then what I now seem to be.'

'Not an idiot, then?'

'Do you recall, sir, ferrying a passenger secretly across the narrow seas 'twixt England and the Netherlands in the days after the battle of Bosworth?'

He looked warily at me. 'There were many passengers who took ship secretly in those days,' he said. 'Why should I remember one young boy in particular?'

'Because of who that boy was,' I said. 'Do you not recall one passenger in particular? One, no doubt, whose safety was paramount?'

He leaned back in the chair, looking keenly at me, and spoke slowly and carefully. 'Every man fleeing a disaster sees his own safety as paramount. I repeat, why should I remember one young boy in particular?'

It was clear now that we were fencing with each other, and that nothing would be settled unless one of us broke cover, and it was equally clear that it had to be me who did so; Brampton was too cautious and guarded to say what he was thinking. I might be a spy, although in truth a spy that he could dispose of easily enough overboard if he chose to do so.

'I think you know why, sir,' I said, 'but just to set your mind at rest and prove that your suspicions are correct, I am that small boy. I am Richard, once Duke of York, once a prince of England, but bastardized by Act of Parliament.'

He stared at me in silence for a long moment, and then leaned back in his chair. 'Miraculous,' he said, and then asked, 'Do you know what today is?'

I shook my head, uncertain. 'Sunday, is it not, sir? We had prayers this morning.'

'Sunday indeed,' he said, 'and not just any Sunday, for today is Easter Day. I had no hopes of seeing a miracle this day, but I have observed one all the same. Today is the day of the Lord's Resurrection and, it appears, of that of Richard of York too. The Lord be praised.'

I detected the irony in his voice, and then he stood up and reached out to me, grasping my arm and dragging me towards him. I thought he wished to embrace me, but he pulled me over to the window where he could get a better look at me. 'Mmm,' he said after a long scrutiny. 'You could be him, I suppose. There's a certain similarity. But why did you tell me you were a Flemish boy named Piris?'

'I did not recognize you, sir,' I lied. 'I could not give away my secret to just any man. But you know it now, sir; you know who I am, and I know too that you are a good and faithful friend to my family.'

He stared at me, and then shook his head slowly from side to side. 'I don't know who you are,' he said. 'I know who you say you are, but that is by no means the same thing.'

'But you saw me, on that boat crossing the channel two years ago. You recognize me from then, do you not?'

He shook his head again, saying, 'Piris, Piris, Piris. First, I cannot identify you as the same boy I saw two years ago. You look like him, it is true, but I could not swear that you and he are the same person – I simply do not know either of you that well, and all small boys look alike, and all small boys change as they grow. Second, even if I could identify you as that boy, I don't know who he was. An acquaintance of mine, the face painter from Bruges, told me who he thought the boy was, and I had no reason to disbelieve him. On balance, it is more likely than not that he was telling the truth, but I didn't want to know too much lest I incriminate myself. I had only his word for your identity, so I could not swear to who you are, only to who you say you are.'

'I see.'

'So you see, all you are while on board this ship, and no matter who else you claim to be, is a ship's boy.'

I tried not to let my disappointment show. 'I see, sir,' I said, 'only . . .'

'No "onlys",' he said. 'Ship's boy. You can return to your duties.'

'Yes, sir.'

'Aye aye,' he murmured, correcting me.

The matter was not mentioned again, although on several occasions I caught Sir Edward's eye on me, and wondered if he might have some plan in mind. On the day we reached Lisbon I was going about my duties below decks when word was passed for me to go to the captain's cabin. I tapped on the door and entered, but there was no sign of Sir Edward. Only Lady Brampton was in the room.

'The captain sent for me, madam,' I said.

'No,' she replied. 'The captain has gone ashore with various duties to perform while we are waiting in the Lisbon lanes. It is I that sent for you.'

She pointed to a footstool and motioned for me to sit. Then she asked, 'What do you do now?'

'Madam?'

'Where do you go?'

'I do not know,' I said, truthfully enough. 'I suppose I shall try to find another ship to take me back to Flanders. Sir Edward might be able to put in a good word for me, or I could wait until one of his own ships was returning, if he would allow me passage.'

'I wonder if you would consider another possibility,' she said. 'Sir Edward and I have a large house on the Serro dos Almirantes, and I am much in need of a pageboy. You do not speak much Portuguese, I know, but I am sure you could learn it quickly, especially as you already know three of the languages of seafarers. Your duties would be to attend on me, wait at table and run errands when required. It would not be seemly for you to carry out these tasks were you any older, and in any case you would not be able to do so for more than, say, two years, but if you were to perform your duties well then other possibilities for employment would open up before you. So, what say you?'

I was not sure that a position as a page was a step up from a cathedral chorister, but it was better than selling purses, and at worst it was a job that offered a roof over my head and regular food, at least for the time being, so I said, 'Thank you, madam. You are most gracious. I should be delighted to accept.'

Once again, my manners impressed her. 'Go then, and prepare yourself. We go ashore this afternoon, when my husband returns, and you shall accompany me.'

I rose, bowed and exited, and went to find the one spare shirt and one pair of hose that were my own.

Later that day, my shipboard duties being over, I was given a few small coins as wages by the master and clambered onto the deck, ready for my new life in Serro dos Almirantes.

In due course the captain's boat pulled alongside and Lady Brampton came on deck. She looked around for me and beckoned, and then she clambered over the side with all the aplomb of a seasoned seafarer and descended into the boat. I dropped my small bundle into the scuppers and threw a leg over the taffrail.

'And just where do you think you're going?' a voice bellowed beneath me.

I looked down. Sir Edward was standing in the boat, staring up at me.

'Sir, I am . . .' I began, but Lady Brampton's raised hand stopped my tongue.

'He comes at my command, Sir Edward,' she told him. 'I have taken him on as a page for the time being.'

'Indeed?' Sir Edward said. He stood silent, contemplating me, and from my perch I was able to see a number of conflicting emotions working within him. When he spoke, however, he was calm and controlled. 'I see,' he said, politeness personified. 'Pray come down then, Master Piris, and find yourself a place to sit.'

The politeness continued throughout the boat trip and the cart ride as far as the house on Serro dos Almirantes, where I was shown to a small attic room, which was to be my quarters. I had barely thrown my bundle onto the small bed when a servant's head appeared through the trapdoor. 'You Piris?' he asked. When I told him I was he went on in French that was almost recognizable as such, 'Master wants you. In his room. Now.' His head disappeared, and when I got to the trap, his body had too, so I was left to find my own way to where Sir Edward did his work when he was at home.

'Come in,' he said when I scratched on the door frame, and pointed to a stool. 'Sit.' He was writing or doing some calculations, and I waited silently. Then he raised his head. 'You're not staying,' he said.

'Sir?'

'I don't contradict my wife in public, so it was impossible to say anything before, but don't get comfortable in that attic. You're not going to be a page – at least, not in this house.'

'But, sir,' I began. He held up a flat, square hand, palm towards me, between his face and mine.

'I've no complaint with your work,' he said. 'In any other circumstances I would let my wife have her way, but with you claiming to be who you do, I can't afford it. I don't want you in this house or associated with me in any way. I'll not see you destitute, so there's a little money for you.' He placed a small purse on the desk. 'There'll also be some new clothes so that you're presentable, and I'll give you a recommendation to any captain or merchant that you like, or arrange for your passage back to the Low Countries, but you won't stay with me, you'll leave my house within the hour, you won't speak to my wife and I don't know you. I repeat, I don't know you, and I've never known you and, above all, I don't know anything about who you claim to be. Is that understood?'

'Is this because I told you of my past?' I asked.

'It is, and thank God you did, for how could I have explained to anyone your presence in my house if this had come out later? I am already in danger every time I go near English waters, and harbouring a fugitive who claims to be a Yorkist prince, whether he is telling the truth or no, would condemn me to death. No, you go, and I don't know anything about you.'

'I am no one to know,' I said. 'I am just a bastard – a king's bastard, I grant you, but of no value to anyone.'

'There is something that you clearly do not know,' he said. 'I hesitate to tell you, but the knowledge will make matters clear. The Act of Parliament that turned you – I mean, of course, Richard of York – into a bastard was repealed by Henry VII before the end of the year in which he took the throne, so that he could marry Edward IV's daughter, the Yorkist heir. Richard of York is presumed dead, like his brother . . .'

'So it is confirmed,' I said sadly. 'Edward is dead?'

'I fear so,' Brampton replied, 'and 'tis cried abroad that dead King Richard had him killed . . .'

'He did not,' I said hotly. 'Edward was alive the day after Bosworth.'

'I dare say,' Brampton went on, 'but knowing that, you must also know that if you are in truth who you claim to be, your appearance – a resurrection, as I told you – would stir up a hornets' nest in England which would not be calmed for twenty years. You see why, don't you?'

I nodded. I had not thought of this before now.

'I knew he'd married Bess,' I said, 'but I didn't know about the repeal.' I remember pausing as realization flooded into me, and then I looked up into his face. 'This means that I am King of England by right of birth.'

'It is precisely the pronunciation of words such as those which make it certain that you do not stay here,' he replied. 'I did not hear you speak treason in my house. I will not have you speak treason in my house. I am an Englishman as well as Portuguese, and listening to the sentences you have spoken could lead me to the gallows. You must go.'

'I understand,' I said. 'I shall do as you say.' Then I added, in an undertone, only just getting to grips with the enormity of it. 'I am the rightful King of England.'

'You do not mean to pursue this claim, surely?' he asked.

'I had not thought about such a thing happening to me,' I answered. 'It is too much to take in all at once. I would need support. I would need to declare myself, and raise an army . . .'

'With respect, Piris, it would not be easy for a boy of what, fourteen, to do such a thing. Even if your claim were recognized by anyone, you would be throwing England back into a nightmare from which it has only recently awoken – civil war, political uncertainty, and at the end of all that all you can offer is the prospect of a monarch who is still a minor. The people would not stand for it.'

'But they would help, wouldn't they, when they saw that my cause was a good one?'

'I would say that it was unlikely, at best.'

'And you – you know the justice of my claim. Will you support me?'

He did not take too long a time to think before he proffered an answer. 'No,' he said. 'I will not – and I'll tell you why. I am a prosperous businessman, importing spices and pepper and selling them all over Europe. I am a member of the Grand Council of King João of Portugal and am in favour at most of the courts of Europe. I can move freely and safely, except in English waters, and I have a settled life. One day, I might even make my peace with Tudor. There will come a time when even he will need spices, and business always takes precedence over all other considerations. No – as I said, I am prosperous, and I would never do anything – anything – which would jeopardize all that. Your right to reign, if you have a right, is as naught placed beside my right to live peacefully. I am a merchant, and the price for young Yorkist princes is low this year; that for settled monarchs like Henry Tudor is high and rising. I dare say you may well find remnant Yorkists, disaffected Englishmen and assorted hotheads who are prepared to help you, but in the main people simply want a quiet life. I do not think I am unusual in my desires, and I do not think I shall be the only one who turns his back on you.'

'Then where should I go?'

'Truthfully?'

'Yes.'

'Home. Go home to your mother and father in Flanders. Use your musical talents, or learn a skill – take over your father's trade, if you have to, but give up any idea of overthrowing Henry Tudor. It is simply not going to happen.'

'If I came to you and asked where I should go to find the best support for my cause, where would you advise me to go?'

'Home,' he repeated. 'It's still your best option. But to return to reality, what's to be done with you now – a return passage to Flanders, service with another master, what?'

'I have enjoyed the work on the ship,' I told him, 'and would not be averse to a little more adventure. I will go home in due course, I think, but I would like to see a little of the world first. Could you get me a place on a ship?'

'As Piris,' he said, 'I might be able to, but not as Richard. You want adventure, do you?' He pointed to the little bag of money, and I leaned over and picked it up. 'I am sending you to an inn for a couple of nights,' he said. 'Your bill shall be paid. You are not to approach this house or any member of its household. If I find you a position I shall communicate with you directly at the inn. You can read and write, I presume?'

'In English, French and Flemish,' I said. 'Oh, and Latin.'

'Good,' he said, 'although to tell you the truth I wouldn't

mention the Latin; it raises awkward questions.' He raised his voice to call. 'Francisco?'

A servant came through the door, and Sir Edward pointed at me. 'This is the boy I told you about,' he said. 'You know where to take him.'

The inn was comfortable enough, and although I found their Portuguese food a little spicy, it was palatable, and I enjoyed being on dry land for the first time in weeks.

I had time to think, too. The idea of being King of England had never occurred to me before, but now I knew the throne was mine by right. I began to consider the possibility, and thence to ponder a course of action. No one would take a homeless fourteen-year-old boy seriously, I supposed, but assuming I were older and more mature, where could I best garner support? The answer was not long in coming – the south of Ireland, where my father had had many friends, and which had been staunchly Yorkist during our struggles with the Lancastrians. There had been an earl – Desmond, was it? And so I drifted into sleep.

No word came from Sir Edward for a couple of days, and then on the third day a message came; it bore no signature or seal, but it was delivered by one of his men, and in any case there was no one else in Portugal to communicate with me.

I was to report to a certain house in the city, and there to present myself to its master for a possible position as his page. He was aware of my interest in going to sea, and had been informed by 'a certain knight' that I was an efficient worker in all areas to do with a ship, but lacked experience. He was a man of the sea, and opportunities for travel were bound to arise.

When I arrived at the house I began to suspect that Sir Edward was having a joke at my expense. The man I reported to was a Portuguese knight, Pero Vaz da Cunha, known behind his back as 'Bisagudo', which I discovered meant Hatchetface. One of his eyes had been put out in a sea battle, but he seemed to see as much with the remaining eye as other men did with two. His ferocity was legendary, and he was not the man I would have chosen as my master.

On the other hand he was close to the king and, like Sir Edward, had access to the Grand Council of the realm, so if there was a path to success which had to be trodden, he was one who could put a young man's feet firmly on it.

Privateer

September 1487 – September 1489

Da Cunha took me on without a private interview: without, indeed, speaking a single word to me. I was dressed in the appropriate livery and then given instruction in my duties by the other servants, mainly in French as I spoke but little Portuguese at that time, and I learned to do them well – holding his stirrup when he mounted and his horse when he dismounted, carrying his gloves or his handkerchief, offering him water or wine at table and attending his retiring at night. My silence was apparently seen as impressive; further, because I could not understand what was said to me, I learned to read the language of my master's body, to anticipate his needs – sometimes, even, to be aware of what he desired before he knew himself that he desired it. It is a trait much treasured in a servant, and I felt myself valued. It is also a trait which is highly valuable to the servant himself, especially to a servant to one such as Bisagudo, who communicated in blows and buffets when his desires were not met immediately. My lack of Portuguese led to a number of these blows from time to time, but my quickness in other ways meant that the stripes were few.

The court of King João II was a peripatetic one, drifting from the hills of Lisbon to Santarém or to the coast at Setúbal, and my master drifted with it in the wake of the king, and I, still flotsam, drifted behind him, and so we all floated for a year.

One evening towards the end of that time my master entertained to dinner a man whose conversation aroused my former interest in sea voyages. By this time I had learned enough Portuguese to follow the conversation, and was aided by the strange fact that the two men were speaking different languages to each other; my master Portuguese and the visitor Italian, although the languages are so close to each other that a man with a smattering of one and some knowledge of French or Latin could follow easily enough what was being said, as seemed to be the case between the two.

The wine was beginning to flow when my master came to the point. 'So, senhor, in what way do you need my help?'

'Just to speak to the king,' the visitor said. 'He will listen to you as to no other. You are a seaman. You know the possibilities. If I am to put my theories to the test I need to go further out to sea, and for that I need ships. Portugal can provide those ships.'

'And everything else,' da Cunha said. 'It is Portugal's expertise which allows you to dream in this way. We build the ships, we train the pilots and we navigate in a way no other nation can. We make maps, and we know the winds and the seas better than anyone. Why should we share all this with anyone else?'

'What you say is true, senhor,' the visitor said, 'but this expertise is of little use if it is not used to seek new lands, to boldly go . . .'

My master held up his hand. 'You have rehearsed all this many times before, Senhor Colom. I am a businessman. If you wish me to use my influence with the king to fit out an expedition to Cipango and Cathay then there must be a little something in it for me.'

'Think of the trade possibilities. The first man to find a route to the Indies will line his pockets . . .'

My master smiled. 'I think not,' he said. 'The first man comes home covered in glory; it is the second who makes the money.'

'Then be the second, if you wish – but help me blaze the path.'

'I sail in three weeks,' da Cunha said.

I pricked up my ears; this was news to me.

'I lead an expedition. You are welcome to accompany me to demonstrate your ideas and methods. The king would be more likely to pay attention to a practical demonstration rather than a theory. It won't get you a ship, but it might get you a sympathetic audience.'

The Italian leaned back in his chair. 'Thank you, senhor,' he said. 'I should be delighted to go to sea again under your command.'

It turned out that my master had been handed the command only that day, although some of the preparations had already been done before an admiral had been appointed. Few were privy to the purpose of the expedition, and even my sharp ears could not find out the answer. All the same, I was one of those chosen from the household to go along on the expedition and wait upon the captain and his Italian guest, and right glad I was of it.

The expedition was huge; twenty caravels were being fitted out, and there were soldiers aboard each one – a military expedition then, as well as a trading one. A fleet as large as that could not contain a secret for long, and soon rumours began to fly.

When I discovered the truth I could not believe what I had been told, and my heart leapt within me.

I heard it from the lips of my master himself, one day when I accompanied him to the court. 'Now I may reveal all,' he said, 'and you may tell the servants what you know. We are to sail to a foreign country to take it, by force if necessary, and to restore a dispossessed prince to his rightful crown.'

I stared at him. 'My lord,' I breathed, scarcely daring to hope.

'King João will not stand for usurpation,' da Cunha went on. 'The blood royal must be defended, no matter what the realm. If God's anointed are to be cast down, we descend to chaos and anarchy.'

'Thank you, my lord,' I said.

He looked at me curiously. 'I don't know what you want to thank me for,' he said.

'Is this the work of Sir Duarte Brampton, sir?' I asked. 'Did he have a hand in it?'

'I don't think so,' he replied. 'He has an interest, obviously, given his business, but he's no more involved than anyone else. Why do you ask?'

I looked surreptitiously from side to side, to make sure that we were not overheard. 'Do you know the identity of this prince, sir?' I asked.

'Of course I do, boy. What is wrong with you today?'

'And did Sir Duarte reveal it to you?'

'No, I had it from the mouth of the king himself.'

'So the king knows of me?' The slip was past my tongue before I could stop it.

'You?' da Cunha said. 'What have you to do with this?'

I could feel my heart sinking within me. 'Nothing, sir,' I said quickly. 'What country do we sail for, sir?' I asked.

'Çanaga,' he said. 'I thought you knew that.'

'Çanaga? Not England?'

'England?' My master stopped dead in the street and turned to look at me. 'Invade England with twenty ships and two hundred men?' he said. 'Who would be so foolish – and what quarrel does Portugal have with England? Where do you pick up your tittle-tattle, boy? England? I've never heard an idea so preposterous.'

He stalked off down the street, leaving me floundering in his wake. 'England!' I heard him snort once more, but thereafter he was silent on the subject.

The unlanded prince was not me at all, then, but a man called Bemoy, King of the Jaloofs in the land of Çanaga. He had arrived at the court of King João some weeks before and had been received with all honour, and he was to sail with us.

To great excitement the flagship's company was augmented by the group of Africans who had been the guests of the king. I had become used to seeing black men in the streets and markets of Lisbon and Setúbal. Their skin was darkened by the burning sun in their own country, they spoke a language unknown to Europe, and it was said that the colour of their skin reflected the blackness of their souls, for they were heathen who had never heard the word of God. I found them no better or worse than any other man, I have to say, for all their lack of faith.

The group was led by this Bemoy, as I said a prince in his own land, but who had been driven away by a usurper. Bemoy had appealed to King João for help, and in return for promises of trade and the ritual of baptism, the king had given him the twenty caravels, which were waiting in Lisbon roads, an enormous force, and the services of my master as captain-major. As expected, our mission to Çanaga was not solely one of trade.

On the day the group came aboard, da Cunha took me aside where none could hear. 'You are to serve this man,' he said.

'The black prince?'

'The same.'

'But sir,' I protested, 'I do not speak his language . . .'

'No matter. He speaks some of ours, and I have little doubt that with your ear for languages you will begin to pick up some of his ere long. I want to know his words, his plans, his very thoughts. I want to know about his own land – I particularly want to know if his people dig gold from the ground.'

'He will have his own serving men, sir, surely?'

'So ingratiate yourself. He will be honoured to be sharing a servant with the Captain-major and his other guest. Remember now, his very thoughts. You are my eyes and my ears.'

I was a tall youth, but I came only up to the armpit of Bemoy.

He was a man of about forty years old, with short, crinkled hair and, unusually for men of his race, a bushy black beard. He was dressed not in his native garb, but in Portuguese dress appropriate to the depth of winter, although it was a fair spring day. Apparently the men of Africa feel the cold more acutely than Europeans do, although by way of recompense they can bear the searing heat much better. He and his men had been on a Portuguese ship before, but they did not always remember to duck their heads, and there was frequent contact between the beams of the ship and the pates of the Africans; within a short time, therefore, I was following my master's instruction and learning some of their language, although not, perhaps, words which I might be able to drop into a normal conversation.

Da Cunha did not give up his cabin to the Africans, as he normally would for an honoured guest, but they were given a large area 'tween decks where they slept, rolled in blankets on the deck. They did not eat our meals, but for a couple of hours a day the galley was given over to them, and Bemoy's cooks made merry with rice, spices and chickens.

Senhor Colom, the Italian adventurer, was as interested in the group as the Captain-major was, but for a different reason. By virtue of his travel on the seas he could speak a few words of their Çanaga tongue, and he was anxious to learn more about the tides in their river, the direction of the winds at various seasons and other matters to do with exploration and his un-discovered route to the Indies. He questioned them constantly, with me standing by to serve food and drink if necessary, and to listen and learn if not.

I soon learned to like Bemoy. He was intelligent and interested, answering and asking questions and debating the answers with Colom. He also told me his story; he did not know mine, of course, but he sensed a sympathetic ear. He had been cast out of his own land by a rival who had invaded from the east, and was anxious to recapture it. He and I practised our Portuguese on each other, and bit by bit I learned to speak and understand his language a little.

In the days before we were to sail Senhor Colom filled the cabin with charts, quadrants, astrolabes and, above all, stories. As well as being a sailor, he produced and sold marine charts with his brother Bartholomew. He had sailed extensively in the Ocean Sea, which is where he had learned open-ocean navigation.

'Two years ago,' he told me, 'I presented my plans to King João. I proposed that the king equip three ships and grant me a year in which to sail out into the Ocean Sea, search for a western route to the Orient and return.'

At this point my master came into the cabin. I fell respectfully silent and looked away from Senhor Colom, but da Cunha was in a good mood. 'He turned you down,' he said.

'He did,' Colom admitted. 'I don't see why. It was a reasonable request.'

'That may have been,' my master said, 'but nothing else was. Tell us what else you asked for. Listen to this, Piris.'

Normally he called me 'Boy', but when it became 'Piris' it meant he was in a rare good mood, so I relaxed and did as he said.

'It wasn't all that much,' Colom said defensively. 'I just asked to be given the title of "Great Admiral of the Ocean", that I be appointed governor of any lands I discovered . . .'

' "All lands" is what I heard,' da Cunha put in.

'It's a distinction without a difference,' Colom said, 'and I asked for one-tenth of all revenue from those lands. The king thought about it, but his council of experts rejected it. They said I had underestimated the distance to be travelled.'

'And had you?'

'Naturally. If I'd told them the true distance I would have had even less chance of getting what I wanted.'

Da Cunha laughed, found what he had come to the cabin

for, and left us, me to unpack and stow his gear, Cristoforra Colom to his measurements and calculations.

I enjoyed Colom's company. He was an adventurer, a teller of tales, and a man who lived life to the full and was larger than it was. He was the sort of man I aspired to be.

He told me that he had sailed to England and Ireland with Portuguese vessels, and even that he had travelled well beyond Ultima Thule into the Ocean Sea, and had landed on a cold land in those waters. His stories may not all have been true, but they livened up the evenings on the voyage.

He had in previous times undertaken long passages to Portuguese Guinea, south of where we were now bound, and to the new Castilian colonies in Las Canarias. He had knowledge of the Cape Verdes and the fortress of Elmina on the Gold Coast. On all these he had observed the winds and the tides. 'If you want to cross the Ocean Sea, young Piris,' he said, 'you must let the winds guide you. They blow in circles. To go west, go first south and the winds will turn and take you away to the west. To return, you must climb further to the north and let the west winds bring you home.'

We sailed from Lisbon in the spring, south-south-west for two hundred leagues as far as Las Canarias. My duties were light, and the main one of these was to see to the comfort of the prince. He was, it has to be said, not a demanding master. Once we came into warmer climes he would spend his days lolling on the afterdeck, eating delicacies brought to him by his body servant and practising his Portuguese on me. We spoke of many things – Portugal, the Low Countries, of which I was still officially a native, of wine, which was unknown in his country although his people made and enjoyed beer, and of the customs of his own tribe – the various mutilations that were performed on boys and girls alike as part of growing up, their diet and their system of government.

'We have a king,' he told me, 'who stole the throne. He is

a bad man, an evil usurper. But good things may come from bad; he has given me the chance to see a little of the world and to observe how other nations behave. All in all, I think I prefer Portugal to Jaloof.'

'Why then do you wish to return?' I asked him.

He looked at me, his eyes wide. 'Because it is what I must do,' he said. 'It is my duty. What kind of a prince would I be if I abandoned my people to live under a cruel tyrant? I would be no better than he if I deserted them to live an easy life in Portugal. It is not fitting. Can you understand this?'

'Of course,' I told him, but my next thought – 'Better than you can know' – I kept to myself.

'But what if you lose?' I asked. 'It is possible that the tyrant might kill you.'

'Then my country will be no worse off than before,' he said, 'but I will have my honour.'

From Las Canarias we sailed due south, heading past treeless desert dotted with tiny landmarks known only to the navigators – a rock shaped like a sailing ship, a white hill, a fortress where Arabs sold negroes, and a long stretch of desert. The coast is covered with sandy dunes, like that of the Low Countries, and is edged with a very white sandy beach, on which the sea breaks violently. Behind the dunes the land is wooded.

Finally, after many days, we sighted the thick tuft of trees standing close together that our pilot said indicated the mouth of the Çanaga. At this point, by the action of the river on the landward side and the ocean on the seaward, the coast is reduced to a peninsula, and is so narrow that we could see over it into the estuary beyond.

To gain this estuary was not easy, though, and we anchored half a mile or so offshore while the matter was discussed.

Da Cunha did not wish to land on the ocean beach, which would leave the ships vulnerable to the waves that for the most part rolled violently from the northward and would do much damage by this perpetual agitation to the ships' cables as well as their masts and rigging.

We moved therefore further south and into the opening of the estuary, but here there was difficulty in keeping the ships on their moorings, as they rolled so prodigiously starboard and larboard, with the gunwales almost to the sea, that it was all but impossible for a man to stand fast on the deck. This was because the flow from the river estuary was almost as strong as the flow of the ocean itself, and the ships were buffeted hither and thither.

I found myself one afternoon on the deck with Colom. 'Why do we not simply go into the river mouth?' I asked him. 'The peninsula will protect us from the ocean swells, even if we still have to cope with the river's outflow.'

'I'll show you something,' he said. He sent one of the men for an empty wine bottle and a length of thin rope, and then dropped the bottle into the sea, waited until it filled and then drew it out again.

He handed it to me. I looked at him, puzzled. 'What's this for?'

'Taste it.'

I decided I might as well humour him, and raised the bottle of sea water to my lips. He smiled when he saw the look on my face. 'Observations?' he asked.

'It's fresh!' I said.

'It is,' he agreed. 'Now tell me why.'

I looked landward. 'The force of the river?' I said tentatively. 'Is it so strong that it brushes aside the sea water?'

'It is,' Colom said. 'Even out here, more than a league from the shore, the water is still fresh. What does this tell you about the river?'

'That it's fast-flowing,' I said, 'and with tremendous force, as we have seen.'

'Yes. What else?'

I had to confess that I did not know.

'It tells us that it's long,' he said. 'The rapidity is due to the distance it travels between its source and its mouth. It also means that the channel is narrow for at least some of its length. Flows like that could catch an unwary captain unawares.'

There were other dangers, too. The men who lived in the jungle on the south bank were known to eat men of other tribes, or so Bemoy had warned us, and thus we remained anchored while da Cunha and his distinguished guest worked out what to do next.

Colom and some of the pilots went out in a small boat to inspect the estuary, and returned with further bad news.

'The entry to the river is made difficult enough by the speed of flow,' he reported, 'but that's not all. The current brings down sand and sludge, and when that meets the ocean it gets pushed back towards the land where it heaps up. Effectively there's a bar across the river.'

'But there's a channel through?' asked da Cunha.

'Yes, but it's not always in the same place. It shifts further out or further in, depending on the ocean currents, the force of the river and the winds.'

'Can we get in?'

'Personally, I wouldn't take the whole fleet in, and any ships that went through would need to be warped through. The bar totally prevents large vessels entering the river. Some of the smaller ones could do it; if I were Captain-major I wouldn't take the risk with the bigger ships.'

Da Cunha grunted. 'I shall not,' he said, 'but we must at least explore. Those are my orders.'

'Has Bemoy spoken to you of gold?' da Cunha asked me when I was clearing away the remains of his supper that night. 'Is there gold to be had in his land?'

'He says not,' I told him. 'Gold is mined in Guinea and traded by the Arabs, but he says his country does not have any.'

'I suppose he would say that,' da Cunha muttered. 'All right; go and bring him in, and pass the word for Colom.'

By this time I was becoming more proficient in the language of Jaloof, as Bemoy's country was called, and thus I found myself called in to translate and interpret; oft-times, as now, only da Cunha, Bemoy, Colom and myself were present.

'Tomorrow we will begin to explore the river,' da Cunha announced. 'I shall take a small party and cross the bar. We will set off at first light. Tell Bemoy he may come with me or not as he wishes, but that I need two of his best men as interpreters and maybe as guides. Colom, you will stay here. Piris, you will come with me to ensure that the black men speak no treachery to their fellows.'

Bemoy immediately agreed to come, and at first light three small boats were readied to carry the Captain-major and his party, soldiers for our defence and sailors to row. One other boat set out before us, to find the gap in the bar and stay to mark it while we passed through.

It was, in the end, an uneventful day. Beyond the bar was a small low-lying island of sand. The north bank was largely desert and scrub, while the south was given over to luxuriant jungle. Some of the soldiers were landed on the island, but there was nothing there, and the jungle gave no sign of being inhabited. The Captain-major stayed all day, prowling about, and eventually announced that a fort would be built on the north bank. Even to my untutored eye, this was the best site. With no cover to the north, any enemies approaching could be seen for some distance. To the south both channels and the far bank were clearly visible even from the height of a man, and more so if ramparts were to be constructed, and the site was so positioned that it commanded not only the far bank but also the mouth of the river.

'Where's he going to get the stone?' I muttered.

'Holds are full of it,' one of the sailors grunted. 'That's why we lie so low in the water.'

He turned out to be right. I was astonished to discover that wood and stone had been dressed in Lisbon and transported out in our caravels. This stone proved an insurmountable problem, as with it aboard there was no place in the bar where a caravel could get through without running aground, and it was necessary for each ship to unload its cargo into the ships' boats for transportation. This took an inordinate amount of time, and stretched the patience of sailors and Captain-major alike to breaking point.

Once the first caravel was unloaded and its stone taken over the bar, the ship itself was warped through to protect the fort site, and by the end of the next day the second ship too had been lightened enough to be floated through, the sailors straining at the oars as they pulled against the rapid flow of the river. Bemoy and his men had transferred to this ship, and before the day was out he and a few of his followers were rowed ashore with a guard of ten soldiers, and chickens were sacrificed and their entrails read in an attempt to propitiate the spirits of the riverbank. That this had not been achieved was evident on their faces when the ceremony was finished, and as a result Bemoy was uneasy about the construction, and asked to speak to da Cunha about it. He was so adamant and agitated that I returned with him to the ship, accompanying him to my master's cabin.

As soon as we entered he began to pour out words, too fast for me to keep up. 'The Captain-major must be aware of the dangers at hand,' he said. 'This place where he wishes to build his fort is not of my territory, which is further up the stream. I know not if the land be sacred to the spirits of this land, or indeed if it be cursed, but I cannot guarantee the safety of any building placed here.'

'It is the wish of King João,' da Cunha replied, 'and if the king requires it, then it must be so. The site commands the approaches to the river, which it must do if we are to explore further. Militarily there is no place better – and we can go nowhere else until I have secured the position.'

I put this to the exiled prince, and he turned to me and said urgently, 'It is a bad place. The spirits are unhappy. You must tell the Captain-major that it is an evil place and that it is wrong to build here. Tell him, please.'

Da Cunha listened while I spoke, and then said, 'Does he have a single, sensible reason or rational argument? No. He was supposed to have accepted Christ. He was even baptized and took the name of João after our king, and now he tells me about spirits! Tell the heathen bastard that the Captain-major of the Portuguese expeditionary force is not obliged to listen to anyone except the King of Portugal or his accredited representative, and further tell him that if I hear another word on this matter I shall put his head on the battlements of the fort for decoration.' He paused, and then said, 'On reflection, perhaps you need not add that final part.'

All were required to work. On days when my translating skills were not needed I was mustered with one of the working parties and sent ashore to help with the construction of the fort. My task was to help make bricks with the mud which the river provided in unlimited quantities and straw that was gathered on the south bank and dried. It was hard work, but satisfying when the bricks were baked hard in the sun, for then I was set to carrying them across to the fort and finally to laying them, a skill which was taught me by an old sailor who deployed a plumb line and a foul tongue to set his walls straight. He took much pride in his work, and taught me his skill, which I have put to good use many times in the years since. I became adept at the work, and pleased the old man so much that he begged me off the making and baking and deployed me solely on the laying with him. Seeing a building taking shape under my hands gave me more satisfaction than any other task I have ever done.

The exception to all this was Bemoy, who pointed out to da Cunha that he was a prince, and did not undertake manual work. My master rolled his eyes, but allowed the prince his privilege as long as his attendants worked. All this time, however, Bemoy's fears had not been allayed, and once again he asked to speak to the Captain-major about it.

Da Cunha reluctantly agreed, and I was called back to the ship to interpret. Before we could turn to Bemoy's worries, however, the Captain-major revealed that he had other thoughts on his mind. Bemoy had told King João that far to the east of his country there lived men who were neither Arab nor negro. His description of their religion had excited the king, who decided that they must be the subjects of the famed and much-sought Christian emperor Prester John, and this excitement had transmitted itself to my master, who had become obsessed with finding this legendary land.

As soon as I came over the side of the ship my master began again to rehearse the questions which he knew full well Bemoy had answered before the king.

'Ask him the name of the king of this eastern land,' da Cunha told me. 'I think 'tis Prester John.'

Bemoy did not know the king's name. No one from his nation had been to this far land; they had only the word of travellers who had met other travellers who had met yet more travellers who had been there. It was many months' journey, through terrain that was impassable; thus said Bemoy.

'Ask him if there is a sea of gravel 'twixt here and there,' my master told me.

'A sea of what?' I asked.

'Gravel. In Prester John's land it is said that there is a sea that men call the Gravelly Sea, that is all gravel and sand, without any drop of water, and yet it ebbs and flows in great waves as other seas do and it is never still, never in peace, no matter what the season. Ask him if he knows of such a sea.'

I did so, and da Cunha did not need the services of an inter-preter to understand the look on Bemoy's face as my question progressed. When it was asked, he looked at me, looked across at the Captain-major, grinned broadly and shook his head. 'Tell the captain that I have never heard of such a thing,' he said finally.

'And what of the great river?' da Cunha asked.

'The Çanaga?' I asked.

'No, no – the river that runs out of Paradise, full of precious stones without any drop of water, and the small trees that grow till midday, but in the afternoon enter into the ground again, so that at sunset they have totally disappeared. Has he heard of such things?'

Again I put the question to Bemoy, and again he shook his head.

'What about the men?' da Cunha asked. 'Has he heard of them? In the desert there are wild men, that be hideous to look on. They are horned, and they speak nought, but grunt, as pigs, and have but three toes upon a foot. Has he heard of such men?'

Again I asked Bemoy, and again he shook his head.

'Speak to our captain,' he told me, 'and tell him not to concern himself with these fairy tales, but to be aware of the dangers at hand. The spirits of this place are angry, and his fort will not stand. Tell him again that it is a bad place and that he must not build here.'

Da Cunha ignored him, and I ushered the prince out before the Captain-major's mounting temper got the better of him.

There was something wrong, all the same. At the mouth of the river was where the Berbers traded, but they made no at-tempt to navigate the river itself. That they left to fools like us, the Portuguese, for upstream from the mouth of the Çanaga there were black men in canoes who came down the river to attack. They tried to swarm over the side of the caravels, and spread death wherever they went, for their spears and arrows alike were tipped with a deadly poison for which there was no cure, and from which men died, threshing and flailing about, their blue lips covered in froth, in a matter of hours.

Our ships' guns kept these natives at bay during daylight hours, for we demonstrated our power by blowing one of their canoes out of the water when first they essayed to attack us, but we were not safe in the hours of darkness. During our second week in the river one of the watch fell asleep and that ship was attacked and burned before our eyes, with the ululations of the victorious natives echoing through the night. No man slept on watch thereafter, for if the natives did not kill him, da Cunha would.

The African sun beat down fiercely, and the discomfort was even worse for those who were, like me, fair-skinned, for we burned more easily than the swarthy Portuguese. Colom showed me how to make a sun hat; I was much mocked for it by the rest of the crew, but it kept me cool. The heat was bearable, but soon men began to die from a strange fever. Bemoy had warned against drinking the river water, and for once my master listened to him, although Colom also had to put a word in. Men went ashore in water parties each day, seeking clean streams to the south, but regardless of how far they went and how clean the water seemed, men began to die of the flux.

Work on the fort continued, but now Bemoy and his men became restless. They wanted to go home, and right soon, but da Cunha was not prepared to brave the torrents of the Çanaga until the mouth of the river was secure. He asked Bemoy to go ashore and seek the local natives, to communicate with them and offer them friendship and trade, but Bemoy refused, saying that he was a king and not someone to be sent into danger like an envoy. He did agree, however, to sending some of his men into the forest to seek them out and negotiate.

The expedition was not a success. His people did not speak

the same language as the local natives, and arrows were shot from the cover of the forest. One of Bemoy's men and two of the Portuguese were hit by the poisoned weapons and died before they could be got back to the ship. One of them, a priest who had been sent from Portugal to effect the conversion of the river people, was dismembered, roasted and eaten before our eyes the same night, the natives gathering round a big fire on the south shore and taunting us with their shouts and the noise of their drumming.

Bemoy was angry at the loss of his follower, and dragged me again into the Captain-major's cabin. 'I insist that we continue upriver,' he said. 'Tell his worship that his function is to deliver me and my men to our nation and restore me to my throne. That is why these soldiers are here.'

'Let him believe that if he wishes,' da Cunha said, 'but we go nowhere until my fort is finished.'

When I had translated, Bemoy laughed. 'His fort will never be finished,' he said. 'The spirits of the river will see to that.'

I translated, and da Cunha looked at the floor for a long time. Then he said, 'Tell this man that I tire of him and his demands. Tell him that I and I alone decide when we move upriver, if we ever do. Tell him that if he is unhappy with my decision then I will gladly put him and his men ashore, and he has feet to carry him whither he might go. Tell him I will hear no more on this subject.'

He indicated that I should open the door and be gone, and I translated for Bemoy, who stood stock-still and stared at him. 'He does not treat me like a king,' Bemoy said. 'He is a man without a semblance of respect.'

Still staring at the papers which lay on the table in front of him, da Cunha said softly, 'Piris, unless you get that man out of my cabin before I count to five, I will have to hold you responsible for what happens to him.'

Somehow I got Bemoy through the door, but he was

quivering with anger, and once away from the Captain-major he began to shout and demand that I return to the captain and make representation to him again. 'He has no respect,' he said. 'No respect for me as a king, and no respect for me as a man. It is not to be borne.'

His agitation spread to his men, and there were some raised voices in the 'tweendecks. Bemoy explained to them what had happened, and the atmosphere became angry and, I felt, a little dangerous. Before long there was a clattering and then a group of crossbowmen appeared on the steps leading to the upper deck. The black men fell silent, and da Cunha appeared behind them. 'What's afoot?' he asked me.

'Nothing, master,' I said. 'Lord Bemoy feels that you do not pay enough attention to his wishes, as he told you before.'

'And why the jabbering from these others?' he asked.

'They feel keenly for their lord's honour,' I said. 'He is a man of great station in his own land.'

'Do they talk mutiny?' he asked.

'No, sir,' I said. 'Most assuredly not. Lord Bemoy is irritated merely.'

'Do you take yourself off to your bed, Piris,' he said. 'There will be no more interpreting this night.'

'Do you not think, sir, that it might be better if I stayed – lest there be any misunderstanding?'

'So it is you that talks mutiny?'

'No sir,' I said swiftly, bowed to Bemoy, explained, 'My master bids me return to my duties,' and went up the steps.

The rest of the night was quiet, although I heard later that my master had doubled the guard and the whole of the fleet was alerted in case there should be any attempt at insurrection.

There was not, of course, but trouble erupted again at first light. I went ashore with the building party to continue the construction of the fort, but we found that the level of the river was rising and that the foundations were being undermined.

Da Cunha decided to come himself and have a look at them, and Colom clambered into the boat with him. The foreman of our building party pointed out the problem.

'The level has been rising for a couple of hours now,' he said. 'We'll have to wait for it to subside before we can do any more work, and even then there's no guarantee that it's not going to happen again.'

Da Cunha grunted and splashed around a little, but it was evident that the waters were still rising. 'Leave it for now,' he said. 'We'll come and look later.'

We rowed back to the ship and discovered that Bemoy and his men had gathered on deck, anxious to know what was going on. At my master's direction I told him what had happened, and asked if he knew anything about this flooding.

'It floods this way in my own country,' he told me, 'further upstream.'

'Why did you not tell me?' da Cunha demanded.

'I did not know the extent to which it happens. In my country the river level rises, but the river does not break its banks the way it does here. Our river gorge is narrower, and the water rises up the side and the flow becomes faster, but I have not seen this before.'

'How often does it happen?'

'Every year at about this time.'

'And how long does the flooding last?'

'That I do not know. In my country it sometimes continues for two or three months before it subsides.'

'You should have told me about this,' da Cunha said, angry now. 'My men's time, my time, the time and supplies of the expedition and of the kingdom of Portugal – all have been wasted because you said nothing.'

I got barely halfway through translating this when Bemoy gave back as good as he got.

'I did tell you,' he said. 'I told you what the spirits said; I told you that it was a bad place to build, I told you that the fort would never be built and I told you that the water was not good. I did not know why this would be, because I do not know the spirits of this region, but I told you all that I could.'

Again, my translation was hardly begun when da Cunha too began to shout. 'You told me what was convenient,' he said, 'never the whole truth. I know not what you sought to hide, but your interest was never in what we were to do here, but in what we could do to restore your throne. That and that alone was your concern. Now, what else have you omitted to tell me?'

Bemoy's men, not understanding the words but knowing full well what the tone of voice meant, began to advance towards da Cunha.

'Master,' I said urgently, 'speak not so angrily. You do excite Lord Bemoy's men, and they understand you not. I beg you, sir, do not alarm them.'

For answer he swung the back of his hand at me and knocked me clear to the deck. From there I watched what events now unfolded as warm blood cascaded in a stream down my cheek.

'You are an ignorant, arrogant man,' Bemoy said. 'That boy is the only way you and I can communicate effectively, and you knock him to the floor. Such is how you have treated my words. I will speak to you no more.' He turned his back on my master, who promptly reached out to pull him round again.

One of the Africans must have thought it was an attack, for he stepped forward and placed himself between his prince and da Cunha, in the process barging into my master. Da Cunha lashed out, knocking the man down, and suddenly the Africans, seeing an apparent assault on their leader, leapt forward, and a free-for-all began on the afterdeck. Da Cunha needed no further stimulus; he had been spoiling for a fight all morning, and this gave him all the leeway he needed. His sword appeared in his hand, and he swung it to knock aside the next man who stepped between him and Bemoy. The prince turned, his arms in the air, calling to his men to stop the fight, but although his followers may have understood him, da Cunha and the Portuguese saw only a black man shouting encouragement.

Da Cunha stepped forward and ran his sword into the prince's midriff, twisted it, pulled it out and stabbed a second time, this one to the neck. Before the prince had fallen my master was calling out, 'Treason! Mutiny!' and his men needed no more invitation than that; the black men, mostly unarmed, were killed were they stood. In the length of time it takes to count to a score the deck was covered with a silent carpet of black bodies, and the Portuguese stood covered in their blood.

I rose to my feet and looked at the slaughter. A stillness had fallen over the ship.

'Get rid of this filth,' da Cunha said. 'Throw it overboard. Swab party, I want these decks clean by the beginning of the next watch or I'll know the reason why.' He turned to me. 'You told me they were not plotting treachery,' he said.

'No more they were, sir,' I told him. 'They showed no signs of—'

'Is this not a sign?' he shouted. 'Attacked on my own deck, by God, and you kept silent about it?'

'Sir, I knew nothing . . .'

'Out of my sight,' he said, sending me reeling again with a push. 'Make yourself useful with the swabbers. I'll decide what to do with you later.'

It was Colom who calmed him down, pointing out that he spoke as much Çanaga as I did, and had seen no evidence of plans to mutiny. My master fell silent and asked me for no further explanation, but I had already decided that my days as his page were over.

My left eye was damaged in some way. Da Cunha's ring had torn the skin and muscle beneath it, and I could see but faintly, and much fluid leaked out. One of the other men bound it for me, and after a few days the wound healed and most of the power of sight returned, but I was never able to see perfectly out of it again.

Our party stayed only a few more days at the mouth of the Çanaga. The floodwaters continued to rise, the fort was swamped, and it was clear that it was never to be completed. The men continued to die of the flux, and da Cunha had no intention of taking any part of his flotilla upriver into the un-known; the men who might have been his guides were all dead, and so was the opportunity to seek out Prester John. On the fourth day after the death of Bemoy we warped the two ships out of the river and nosed our way out into the open sea, and the flotilla, lighter now by a great deal of stone and some forty men, turned north for Lisbon and home. Lighter though the ships themselves were, the mood was not; evil had been done, and I was not the only one to feel a heaviness of spirit.

We came into the harbour at Lisbon towards the end of the year, and here too the atmosphere was palpable. Something had happened, it was clear, but we could not learn what it was until the Captain-major had gone ashore and dealt with all of the formalities. In the meantime we sat in the roads.

We soon learned what it was, and it was the death knell for the hopes and dreams of Colom. I was packing his charts and equipment in the cabin when da Cunha returned.

'Dias is back,' he said the moment he came in.

Colom looked up. 'And?'

'He did it. He rounded the southern tip of Africa and sailed north. He found the Indies, and has returned with dozens of different spices and animals.'

'Oh.'

Colom seemed to shrink, and slumped onto a stool. 'That's that, then.'

Da Cunha nodded. 'Sorry,' he said, and placed a number of documents on his sea chest.

Colom saw my face and explained. 'With an eastern sea

route to the Indies now under its control, Portugal will no longer have any need to search for a western route over the Ocean Sea. I'm finished here.'

'What will you do?' I asked.

'I do espy a kind of hope. If the route is Portugal's, then there is one power which might still need a western route.'

'Spain?' I hazarded.

'The very thame,' Colom said. 'I mutht once more learn to lithp my wordth and thpeak Cathtilian.'

He smiled ruefully, and I continued to pack his goods. He left our ship that day to try his luck with Ferdinand and Isabella, and I never saw him again.

I too left the ship, and with it the service of my master. I felt few regrets. I had enjoyed the freedom of the Ocean Sea and the chance to see Africa, and in the early part of the voyage the company of Bemoy and Colom had been entertaining and interesting, but the turn that events had taken had disturbed me profoundly, and I had no wish to continue in the service of such a man as da Cunha. In addition, during my time at sea I had turned sixteen years old, and entered man's estate.

My destiny beckoned, and now at least I had some inkling of what it must be, as well as a sobering premonition of what could happen to a king who had failed to win back his throne.

Pêcheur

September 1489 – January 1491

I had no difficulty at all in finding a captain willing to take me back north. I was now a veteran seaman of two long voyages, had seen strange parts of the world and could tell tall tavern tales to top the stories of any man in Christendom, so I was an asset to any crew.

I worked my way slowly north, crewing mainly on coasters carrying cargoes from Lisbon to the cape of Finisterre and from there to Brittany. Later I went as far as the entrance to the Baltic Sea and back. I kept this up for a little under a year and then one day I wandered into a tavern in Caen. I had just been paid off from a Flemish caravel carrying livestock along the Norman coast, and when I ordered a flagon of cider I turned to find a man sitting beside me on the bench. 'I've seen you before,' he said.

'Is that right?'

'It is. You were on a ship in Calais harbour. I gave you a hand hauling some tackle aboard.'

'I was never in Calais,' I told him. 'It must have been two other people.'

He had the grace to grin. 'Lisbon, then – or any place where one shipmate might want to lend another a hand.'

'Like a drink?' I asked, and his eyes lit up.

'I thought you'd remember eventually,' he said, and I turned and motioned to the tavern-keeper to supply another measure.

'Pierre, isn't it?'

It was my turn to smile at his guess. 'Might be,' I said, and sat down.

'Looking for a berth?'

'Might be. You offering one?'

'Might be,' he said, and raised his flagon. 'Your health, Pierre.'

'And yours . . .' I replied, and raised an expectant eyebrow.

'Pierre,' he said. 'We're all Pierres here.'

He did well out of my pay that night. He managed to get another two flagons out of me, and they, in addition to those he had already winkled out of some other supposed ex-shipmate, meant that by the time the tavern-keeper decided to close his doors he was much the worse for wear. 'Put me back on my horse, Pierre,' he said when I had helped him through the door. 'Strap me into the saddle.'

'Where is it?' I asked him.

'Where's what?'

'Your horse.'

'I don't have a horse,' he said. 'I do not ride mere animals. I am a man of the sea. My saddle is my ship, and my steed is the widespread sea itself. Take me back to my ship.'

'Where is it?' I asked.

'Ah,' he said, and tapped the side of his nose. 'Wouldn't you like to know, eh? How do you know I'm not going to rob me? Hang on, how do I know you're not going to rob me?'

'Because you have no money,' I said.

He tried to stand straight, felt about his person and came to the conclusion that I was right. 'Perfectly correct,' he said, albeit with some difficulty. 'In that case, you may escort me to my ship.'

'Where is it?' I repeated.

'In the sea,' he said. 'Where else would you keep a ship? Home, Pierre, take me home.'

Home, when we eventually found it, was indeed a ship, with

just two crew aboard, one an old man and the other a boy. I got Pierre up the gangplank and into his bunk and then sat exhausted on his deck under the stars. I had intended simply to rest for a few minutes, but I must have closed my eyes and the next thing I knew I was being shaken awake.

'Do I know you?' he asked, staring at me.

'I brought you home last night, Pierre,' I told him, once I had got my bearings. 'We shared a number of flagons.'

He grunted. 'Your story does have a certain plausibility,' he said. 'Why are you still here? Looking for a berth?'

'Might be,' I said again. 'Offering one?'

'Might be,' he replied, and then a grin crossed his face. 'I remember you now, Pierre,' he said. 'Good night, wasn't it?'

I signed up for the voyage and went back to the inn I was staying in for my gear. Truth to tell, there was little enough of that. A change of work clothes, a couple of good shirts and breeches that da Cunha had been going to throw out, a couple of books and a fine set of silk clothes I had been given for a pageant I once performed in in Lisbon; that was all I had to my name, and I took them back to the ship. Pierre had a cargo of raw wool destined for one of the Flemish ports and was hoping to pick up something there to bring back. He was a wheeler and dealer, a chancer, the owner of the little ship and a trader in anything that he might happen to have about his person when he met a potential buyer. He was the owner of a glib tongue and a sparkling eye, and never was there a man who enjoyed life as much as he.

The ship was called *Buoc'h*, which is Breton for 'cow', so called, according to Pierre, because it was ungainly but steady. At first it was the chance to get back to the Low Countries that attracted me as much as Pierre himself – or rather, Pierre Jean, to distinguish him from me, who was plain Pierre. The other two crewmembers from the previous night, needless to say, were Old Pierre and Young Pierre, and there were another eight or ten seaman, all routinely called some variant on Pierre by their master – Pierre Cochon, Gros Pierre, Grand Pierre and so on. I never received an epithet, and remained plain Pierre throughout.

I had hoped to learn some seamanship; a small crew meant a lot of different jobs to be done, but my main occupation turned out to be clacking the wool to make it presentable for reselling. It was a dirty, smelly, tedious job, scraping the lumps of mud and dung from the greasy fleeces and flinging them over the side; naturally it fell to the rest of the crew to deal with it while Pierre Jean stood at the helm and directed the ship on its course. I learned precious little about sailing, but more than I could ever want to know about sheep dung.

In due course, however, Pierre Jean saw that I was interested, and so he taught me to use an astrolabe and a cross-staff by both night and day, and they were certainly skills that came in useful later. I got to know Pierre Jean pretty well during our time at sea. 'Can you read, Pierre?' he asked me one night.

'Well enough,' I said.

'And write?'

'Yes.'

'Me too. Not much good with figuring, though. How are you with figures?'

'I cope,' I said. 'I don't get short-changed when I buy a drink, anyway.'

'Come with me to see the agent when we get to Antwerp,' he said. 'See what you think.'

By the time we got to Antwerp I had had enough of clacking and was ready to sign off, but I went along with him as he asked to see his agent, an elderly Spaniard called Gomez. 'Brought my lad with me to do the heavy lifting, if there is any,' Pierre Jean said as we came into the warehouse. 'A new lad – a bit dim, but his muscles work.'

'What have you got this time?' Gomez asked.

'Wool, cleaned and clacked. Twenty-four bales, twenty-eight pounds each.'

Gomez sucked his teeth. 'Wool isn't making what it did,' he said. 'There's a glut of inferior stuff on the market.'

'That's what you told me last time,' Pierre Jean said. 'Still, no matter. Can't be helped. How much?'

'Let's see,' Gomez scribbled on a piece of scrap sheepskin with a piece of charcoal. 'Twenty-four bales at twenty-four pounds . . .'

'Twenty-eight,' Pierre Jean corrected him.

'Just so, twenty-eight,' he said. 'That's six hundred and thirty-two pounds, at nine duits the pound, that's 5264, less commission at ten per cent; that's 4196 duits. At 160 duits to the guilder – that's twenty gulden. Let's say twenty-two, shall we, and stay friends?'

'Sounds about right,' Pierre Jean said, and spat on his hand.

'Just a moment,' I said. 'Is that some new form of Spanish counting, Señor Gomez? Your arithmetic seems a little inac-curate.'

'No, no, I assure you,' he began, but I held up a finger.

'Don't say too much,' I told him. 'Just check again. I think you may have made a little accounting error.' To emphasize my point I drew my seaman's knife from my belt and began to pare my fingernails.

'I'll check, then,' Gomez said.

Pierre Jean was standing, his hand open and ready to clasp Gomez's to seal the transaction, but I held a hand up. His lips mouthed 'What?' and I winked.

'You know, you're quite right,' Gomez said after some more frenzied scribbling on the sheepskin. 'That's not twenty gulden at all, it's tw . . .' As his lips began to form the number I raised my eyebrows, and he hastily adjusted, '. . . thirty.' He paused, saw my face, and said, 'Four. Thirty-four. My apologies, Mynheer Meno.' He produced a small bag and began to count out coins.

'You have used Señor Gomez's services before, have you, Pierre Jean?' I asked.

'Twice, yes.'

'And how much wool did you bring last time?'

'About the same.'

'And the time before?'

'About the same.'

'And how much did Señor Gomez pay you on each occasion?'

'About the same,' Pierre Jean said. 'I mean, about twenty gulden . . .' He suddenly got my drift.

'Strange, isn't it,' I said conversationally, 'that although the price of wool has been going down all this time, you received the same amount of money for your cargo as was offered this time – and yet Señor Gomez has discovered just how much he has miscalculated. Perhaps he miscalculated on the other occasions, too.'

'No, I don't think so,' Gomez began, but he knew we had him. 'It's possible,' he said. 'We calculate so fast – mistakes are bound to slip in.'

'It's fortunate, then,' I said, 'that both Mynheer Meno and yourself agree on the amounts of wool and the payments made previously, because that makes it so much easier to calculate how much you have underpaid him.'

Gomez looked at my knife, and decided that he was not going to defend his actions. 'Yes,' he said thoughtfully. 'Perhaps if I added a figure we could both agree on – twenty gulden, say . . .'

'Thirty sounds better,' I said.

'Twenty-five will be fine,' Pierre Jean said, 'but the next time I come, Gomez, we'd better get the best deal you have.'

'We could pose as buyers and ask about the price of wool in the market,' I suggested.

'All right, all right,' Gomez muttered. 'Thirty it is – just keep your mouths shut about this. I have a business to run.'

We stepped from the warehouse onto the wharf. 'Cheating bastard,' I said.

'No more than most,' Pierre Jean said pleasantly. 'It's only business, isn't it? We all do it, more or less. Next time he buys from me, though, I'm leaving the clack on. It weighs nice and heavy. Coming for a beer?'

'Yes,' I told him, 'but then there's something I have to do.'

Later in the evening I managed to get some money out of him, and then the next morning I set off. I made my way first to Ghent, walking now with a seaman's rolling gait. Before long I got work on a riverboat heading upriver to Tournai. I had to put my back into it, getting the worst of the rowing as the newest member of the crew, but looking forward to seeing again the town I had come to think of as home. After more than two years even Tudor's men would have given up and gone home, I reasoned, and so it proved.

I stood on the riverbank and looked up the narrow street towards my father's house. No one paid me any attention; it was a boy that had left and a broad-shouldered man that had returned, and no man knew who I was. I walked up the lane, and there at the door was my mother, standing on the threshold and chatting to two of her neighbours. She was in broad sunlight, squinting against the glare, animated, with a warm smile on her face. I stood across the street, watching, and felt my heart warm with love for her, a woman who had taken in a strange boy, sight unseen, without question, and shown him unconditional love. She looked across, caught sight of me, shaded her eyes against the sun, smiled, and looked away.

She did not know me.

At first I was disappointed, but then realized how much I had changed, and at the same moment I realized the impossibility of revealing myself to her, of starting up again that danger that she was no longer in, of setting her heart racing with joy only to have to tell her that I was going away again, for certain it was that I had to leave. I could no more tell her who I now was than I could tell her who I had once been. I lounged a little longer, hoping that someone might recognize me and so force me to admit who I was, and take the responsibility away from me so that I could see my mother once again and she me, so that we could both enjoy, even for a short time, the pleasures of a prodigal son regained, of a much-loved mother found again, but even as I hoped for it, I knew the impossibility of it. I had to bear my cross alone.

I did not see my father. He was at work, probably. I lingered as long as I dared, hoping to see him one last time trudging up from the river, but perhaps he was working late, or was still out on the stream wending his way back. The first time a neighbour took a second glance at me and allowed his gaze to linger, I rose to my feet and went back down to the Scheldt. There were a number of boats making ready to go downriver, so I begged a ride from one of them in exchange for a day's work, and left Tournai for the last time.

I found my way back to the coast at Antwerp and cast around for work, dragging myself along the dockside from ship to ship and tavern to tavern. I got a couple of days' work coasting, and towards the end of the second day I was paid off in Zeebrugge and decided to reward myself with a drink.

When I turned from the taverner with my pot in my hand there he was, sitting on a bench just as the last time. 'I've seen you before,' he said.

'Is that right?' I replied.

'It is. You were on a ship in Ostend harbour. I gave you a hand freeing a fouled anchor.'

'I was never in Ostend,' I told him. 'It must have been two other people.'

'Let's see, then,' he said. 'It must have been Lisbon.'

'Or any place where one shipmate might want to lend another a hand.' I completed his sentence for him.

'Like a drink?' he asked, and I felt my eyebrows rise.

'Isn't that what I'm supposed to say?' I asked.

'Normally, yes, but I've just got rid of one cargo and fixed up another on the same day, so we sail tomorrow. Pierre, isn't it?'

'Might be,' I said, and sat down.

'Looking for a berth?'

'Might be. You offering one?'

'Might be,' he said, and raised his flagon. 'Your health, Pierre.'

'And yours . . .' I replied. I signed up again. It wasn't a bad life, and I could have done worse.

It was coming on towards Easter, a full three years after I had left Tournai, and Pierre Jean had a new scheme in view to make us rich. 'I know these men,' he said, 'Basques from San Sebastián. I picked them out of the sea a couple of years ago; their ship had been swamped in a storm and gone down. They said if I ever wanted to make good money I should turn up at Finisterre on the Friday after Easter Sunday.'

'Why?'

'They know some good fishing grounds. Secret, see. They've been going to the same place for years – their grandfathers used to go there, but they tell no one. The fishing's too good to share, see. Anyway, they adopted me as their brother, so they said if I wanted to go one year – well, what do you think?'

'Where do they go?'

'Westing, that's all I know.'

'Out into the ocean?'

'Think so, yeah.'

I looked at the ship. 'Well, she's sturdy enough,' I said, 'and seaworthy enough, and we're tough enough. What's the worst that could happen?'

'We could die.'

'Exactly. Let's go.'

We filled our hold with good Breton salt, as Pierre Jean had been told to do by his adoptive brothers, and sailed for Finisterre. We made the rendezvous and asked around the assembled fleet for Pierre Jean's two friends. Sure enough, they were on one of the boats, and a bit of rearranging of the crews meant that one of them was able to come into our ship, and then after a blessing from a priest bobbing on a boat we set sail, west-south-west first until we reached the latitude we wanted, and then due west, sailing directly into the spring sunset. Then, far to the west, there was a southeasterly to run us up to the fishing grounds. I thought of Colom, and what he had told me. Perhaps he was right sometimes after all.

The voyage took nearly six weeks through waters that were stormy but not unmanageable. The flotilla rendezvoused again, and then we were split up into small groups to go to certain areas. These men knew well what they were doing, and each boat had to look out for its neighbour so that all could come home safely. They had a good arrangement – that if a ship was lost the crew's family still got their share of the catch.

And a good catch it was. These fish the Basques call bacalao are big, as long as a man sometimes, and good eating. They swarm in the summer, and are pushed further west by the seals and bigger fish that hunt them through the water. They were heedless of our ships, and the nets were no sooner let down than they were filled and had to be dragged aboard again. For the first couple of weeks we simply dropped the nets overboard and then pulled them in again, but then came the part that surprised me.

There was a large island nearby. Some men had been landed earlier to build what they called a fishing room, which was branches of spruce laid on the ground, and when we landed the catch we landed some of the salt, too, and more of the men were detailed to stay on the flat, rocky foreshore to prepare the fish.

The bacalao were slit down the middle, spatchcocked, spread, salted and left to dry, meat side upwards, in the sun. If it rained they were turned skin side up; otherwise they were simply left. They dried like small planks of wood, and could be stacked or sawn.

After a couple of weeks I took my turn on shore. Once the others had shown me what to do I began preparing the fish in the same way. My first job was as a header, opening the fishes' bellies, taking out the guts and removing the heads.

It was filthy work at first, with the whole of the ground spattered with blood and fish guts, but in due course a wooden stage was erected on which we worked, and the guts and heads fell through this into the sea.

The next job was the splitter, a job which I never really mastered, as it was so specialized. The fish were split and boned, almost in a single movement – in the time it took a man to count evenly to ten the best splitters could bone as many fish.

A job I did master was the next phase, the salting. The amount of salt used had to be precise; too much burned the fish, while too little made it red and unsellable – I fear I ruined not a little in those first days, but soon got the hang of it. Salted and dried fish were easier to transport than fresh, did not rot and had a ready market. They fetched good prices in Bilbao and San Sebastián, and I remembered that I had seen some in Lisbon, although I had never wondered how it got there.

It was not just the fish and the processing that interested me, though. After I had been three or four days ashore I was gutting with a man called Jandro when he suddenly said, 'Don't look yet, or make it obvious. Just move a step closer to me so you can see past that nearest tree.' I reached for another fish and took the step. 'You see it?' he asked.

'What?'

'There, where the fallen tree crosses the next one.'

I flicked my eyes where he was indicating, but I could see nothing. I told him so.

'Straighten up as if you are stretching your back,' he said. 'Look where the fallen tree lies. What do you see?'

'Nothing,' I told him.

'There – flash of red, low down. See it?'

'Yes. What is it?'

'It's a creature of the forest,' he said. 'Some say they're men, but I've never seen a man that colour. Red all over, they are. I think they're apes.'

'Red apes? Are they dangerous?'

'No,' he said. 'They won't bother us. If we leave anything lying around they'll take it in the night, but they never attack us or anything. Never have done so far, anyway. I'll make sure we leave some fish out for them tonight.'

'Leave some out?'

'Mmm,' he grunted. 'Take a few fish and put them on the other side of that stream that runs out of the forest. They take them and sometimes they even leave stuff in exchange.'

'What sort of stuff?'

'Red meat, mostly. Bits of their enemies, maybe.'

I straightened up in surprise. 'And you eat it?'

'Why not? It's not as if they're human. Does it taste all right, that's the only question I'd ask.'

I shook my head and returned to the cleaning. There were occasional flashes of red from the forest as the ape men flitted about for the rest of the day, but they did not show themselves clearly and so I did not get to see one.

We had brought salt with us for salting the fish, but there were hollows in the rocks that the earliest parties ashore had filled with sea water, and soon we were harvesting the salt from these as the water evaporated, and refilling them with buckets, as there seemed to be no tide to speak of. We also prepared extra salt from large pans filled with sea water and heated over wood fires.

The work was back-breaking, and we slept like rocks at the end of the day, but just as Jandro said, the ape men did not bother us, and the day before I was due to go back onto the boat I even got to taste one of them, as a huge hunk of fresh meat was left at the stream. To my mind it was from some animal much bigger than a man or an ape, but Jandro insisted so I said no more, and, besides, it did taste good after five solid weeks of a Friday diet.

We stayed through the summer at the fishing banks, but soon enough there came a change in the air, and the wind too changed, coming more from the north than any other direction. There was a freshness to the breeze that betokened snow, and during my second stint on the rocks as a gutter the boats came in to land their final catch.

'Lot-drawing tonight,' Jandro told me as we set about the fish for the last time. 'Feasting, then home.'

'Lot-drawing for what?' I asked.

'Caretakers,' he said. 'Got to have a caretaker.'

'Taking care of what?'

'The site – the fishing room. A few of us winter here, salting the catch, catching more fish and salting them, looking after the drying racks, that sort of thing. Not every year, of course – just good years, like this one.'

'Doesn't it get cold?'

'Bloody freezing,' he said. 'But it's something that has to be done.'

'Have you done it?'

'Yes,' he said. 'The only way out is to get married; married men don't have to stay. There's a bonus to it, though. You get an extra share if you're drawn; it's only fair.'

That night we all gathered on the foreshore and ate our fill of fresh fish – roasted or boiled mostly, mainly bacalao but with other smaller, oily fish that had got into the net, which were fried in their own oil, and then one of the senior captains stood up and clambered onto a barrel that had been brought ashore from one of the ships. 'Gather round, lads!' he called out. 'Time for the lots.'

Everyone, perhaps five hundred men, stood around him, clustering to catch his words. 'What happens?' I asked.

'Listen,' Pierre Jean said.

The captain said, 'Most of you know what is going to happen.' He reached down and one of the men handed him a large pot with a narrow mouth. 'We need six caretakers,' he called, 'and we're going to choose them now.' He turned the pot upside-down so that we could see it was empty, and then held up his hand. 'Six black pebbles,' he said, and then dropped them one by one into the pot so that we could all hear them clearly.

'Now', he called out, 'for the choosing. Captains are exempt, so all ship's captains be seated.' There was a rustling as the captains sat, including Pierre Jean, leaving the rest of us standing. 'Married men are exempt,' he said, 'so all married men be seated.' More than half the men sat down. Now there were about two hundred of us still on our feet, and I noticed that some of them were shuffling unobtrusively towards where the captain was standing.

'Men who have already been caretakers for a season are exempt,' he called. 'Be seated.' This took out only a few men. 'Old men are exempt,' the captain called. 'Any man over fifty years of age, be seated.' Old Pierre sat, and our ranks thinned slightly, and then he said, 'Boys are exempt; anyone not yet sixteen be seated.' Now it was Young Pierre's turn to sit, and this left yet some hundred and fifty or so of us, and still some of them were almost imperceptibly moving forward.

'Anyone on their first voyage is exempt,' the captain called. 'Such men be seated.'

I was among those who sat, and immediately there were protests from three or four of the men who knew me from the gutting.

'Not you,' Pierre Jean said. 'You've sailed before.'

'Not here,' I said.

'No matter; you've been to sea.' I rose to my feet and held my hands up to the friendly jeers of the rest of the company.

'Any special pleading?' asked the captain.

'My father died last winter,' one young man called out. 'My mother needs me home this time.'

'Fine,' said the captain. 'All agreed?'

There were cries of assent and the young man sat down.

'Any more?'

One man held up a bandaged hand. 'I lost two fingers on a hand line just before we came in,' he said. 'Best I let them heal before I take my turn.'

Again, there was general agreement, and this man and a couple of others who had sustained injuries during the fishing period were allowed to sit.

'Right,' the captain called. 'That's the end of the exemptions. The rest of you come forward and line up here.' He pointed beside him. 'Andraitx, count them.'

There was a sudden rush to get close to him, and I found myself at the back of the throng.

Andraitx passed among us, counting aloud, and then called out, 'A hundred and eight, so a hundred and two whites.'

The captain turned and said, 'A hundred and two,' and white pebbles were produced, counted out and then tipped into the pot. The man holding the pot gave it a good shake, and then the captain turned again to us. 'Right then,' he said. 'Let's start.'

The nearest man stepped forward, pulled his sleeve above his elbow, displayed his bare arm and hand to the crowd and then reached into the earthenware pot and pulled out a pebble. It was a white one. He showed it to the captain and to everyone else, and then dropped it to the ground. To cheers, and waving his arms triumphantly in the air, he went and sat among his shipmates. Now I realized why they had been edging forward – those who drew earliest had less of a chance of drawing a black pebble.

One by one the men stepped forward, bared their arm and then plunged it into the pot. Most men, obviously, drew a white pebble. By the time my turn came, four of the black pebbles had been drawn, with mixed reactions from the recipients. Three had shrugged and accepted their fate, while the fourth, a large black-bearded man, had hurled his pebble angrily to the ground, where it had splintered on the rocks, whipping shards of stone into the ranks of those seated around.

I stepped forward, bared my arm and thrust my hand into the pot. At the bottom lay perhaps a couple of dozen stones. I grasped one of them and withdrew my arm. I opened my hand, and in it lay a black pebble. 'Bad luck,' the captain said, and I joined the small group behind him. When the sixth black pebble was drawn a few moments later the ceremony was over, and the crews began to return to their ships to prepare for the voyage home.

The three Pierres came over to commiserate with me.

'Funny you never mentioned any drawing of lots,' I said.

'Sorry about that,' Pierre Jean told me, 'but I just forgot all about it. You can get out of it if you want – there's always one or two willing to trade places.'

'No,' I said. 'I'll stay. What else have I got to do?'

'It won't be that bad,' Old Pierre put in. 'There's only been a couple of deaths in the last ten years, they say.'

'And look on the bright side,' said Pierre Jean. 'You'll get an extra share, and this has been a good year.'

One or two men did approach me to see if I was prepared to exchange; they offered me half of the extra share if I would, but

I saw no reason to go against fate, and said again I'd stay. One of the chosen men, the black-bearded one, did exchange, and that for just a quarter share, so anxious was he to get home. The man he had exchanged with had wintered before, so he became our de facto leader. The senior captain explained what we had to do, and then we were given supplies for the winter – a couple of small rowing boats, tools such as hand lines, axes and extra knives, all the remaining barrels of salt and a small mountain of warm clothing were unloaded. From different ships came extra tools or supplies that were not needed for the homeward voyage, and then we were left staring out to sea as the boats turned and sailed back east.

Our small party watched them out of sight, and then our leader, whose name was Baleren, turned to face us. 'Best build a shelter, then,' he said. 'Grab yourselves an axe each.'

It had been three years since any caretakers were left, and what shelters had been built then had been destroyed, either by the wind and weather or by the ape men. I had little idea of what to do, but my companions were all hardy Basques who knew their job. As the least talented I was detailed to chop down trees while the others built the shelter. Straight young trees were chosen, and the trunks went to the shelter while the branches were stripped off. A rudimentary hut was put up by the end of the second day, and by the third we were in among the fish again, cutting, salting and drying.

We saw no sign of the red apes. Baleren told me that they went south in the winter, and that we would be unlikely to see anything of them until springtime. The Basques worked biblically, taking every seventh day as a holiday, and the working day got shorter too as sunrise became later and sunset earlier. When the fish were all processed we were formed into three pairs, one for fishing with hand lines, one for gathering fuel and one for watching over the drying fish, processing the previous day's catch, stacking the dried fish, turning them when necessary and preparing food for all, and these duties were rotated, so that no one had time to become bored. As the least experienced, I was paired with Baleren, so once again I was learning.

We were on fuel-gathering duty one day, and I had been left to chop down a tree while Baleren went looking around the area. Suddenly he came back along one of the narrow forest tracks and said, 'Come and look at this.'

I followed him, and after only a few hundred paces we came into a clearing. 'Look,' he said.

At first I saw nothing unusual, but then I began to notice things – small areas where the ground was charred and there were cinders and ash, and larger circles where the grass had not grown and the ground was trampled.

'An encampment?' I asked.

'Yes,' he said. 'Some of the men say that these red creatures are animals, not men, but I think they are men.'

'If they have fires,' I said, 'then they must be.'

He pointed to the larger circles. 'I think these must be where their houses were,' he said. 'See how the ground is churned up more on one side than the other? What does that tell you?'

'They must have round houses,' I said. 'Tents, perhaps, with no floors, and but one entrance. These hollows within the circles, that'll be where they slept, won't it?'

'I think so,' Baleren said. He walked around, counting. 'Five,' he said finally. 'Five houses – maybe forty or fifty people. This camp is the work of men, not animals.'

I could only agree.

When it was our turn to fish I learned to use a hand line rather than the gill net that the boats used. The bacalao is a stupid, greedy fish; it swims with its mouth open and eats anything it sees, even its own young, and will not fight when it has taken a bait. All that is necessary is to drop a hook in the water and wait. When the fish takes the hook you must begin to haul immediately to fix the hook in its mouth. Once this is done it will not resist, and will be drawn to the boat easily. We could catch sixty to a hundred fish each in the hours of daylight and then take them ashore to be salted the next day, and before long our stock of salted and dried bacalao made a discernible hillock on the shore.

'We may freeze to death,' Baleren said, 'but I don't think we'll starve.'

Even freezing was unlikely; there was a vast supply of firewood at our backs and a sturdy shelter to sit in, fresh water at hand and, should we wish it, a change of diet in the shape of the seals and shellfish which clustered round the water's edge.

I learned the whole of this aspect of the fisherman's trade, and my muscles became bigger and stronger as the months went on. It was bitterly cold, and the sea froze over before the year was out, but our wood kept us warm and dry, the fish kept us fed, and by the time spring appeared we had built drying racks, or 'flakes', as the Bretons called them, wharves for the fleet to land the fish, and several large piles of dried and salted fish, finished and ready to be loaded. It had been hard work, but enjoyable, and in good company.

For a time, I had even forgotten to think about Richard of York.

Primitive

January 1491 – September 1491

One day I ventured alone into the forest looking for wood to chop. I had noticed a row of trees that had fallen and, deciding that they would be easier to chop than standing trees I walked on, further along the row. They stretched on for a goodly distance, and before long I realized that their fall had not been natural. They were all of the same age and size, and any gaps had been filled by branches that had been twisted to make an impenetrable barrier.

I stood, hefting my axe, and then I slowly became aware that I was not alone. I saw a man squatting beside one of the fallen trees. His skin was a dark red, and his long black hair was tied in a horse's tail behind his head and pinned with a short length of wood. He wore only a breech-clout. In his hand was a bow, and thrust into the ground in front of him three or four arrows.

When he saw that I had become aware of him, he straightened and stood upright, the bow held loosely in his left hand with an arrow between his fingers. He was taller than me, with a calm and serious mien. At first I thought he was alone, but then behind him I saw other men, and more along the line of fallen trees, all similarly armed and clad.

We looked at each other for a moment, and then he beckoned me towards him. I hesitated, unsure of his intentions, but he made no move to use his bow and beckoned more urgently, looking anxiously away along the line of trees.

I took a step towards him, and his gestures became more

agitated as he saw that I had understood. I realized that if I tried to escape he or one of his companions could bring me down before I had gone five paces. I stepped towards him and stepped through the barrier.

He grinned, motioned me to silence and then turned away, still looking along the line of trees. Then I heard what he was listening for: the sound of someone or something blundering through the undergrowth. Then, faintly at first, but becoming louder, I heard human voices whooping and shouting. For the first time I noticed that there was another line of fallen trees opposite where I was standing, the distance between the two lines narrowing. With a start, I realized that I had wandered into a hunt – the fallen trees I had seen were to stop the hunted beasts from veering away from the killing place. It was just like a boar hunt in England; the voices I could hear were the beaters. I had been directly in the line of the animals' retreat.

We did not have long to wait. The crashing sounds came nearer, and then a group of deer bounded into the space between the two lines of trees. Leading was a large one, obviously a male. He was about the height of a man and had a fine set of branched antlers, while behind him ran four smaller females and three young calves.

He stopped, confused, driven into a triangle of land from which there was no escape, and then turned at bay. The men at the base of the triangle had ready a smaller, slighter barrier similar to a hurdle, and they ran and placed this across his exit, fencing him in completely.

Then the killing began. The red men began to loose their arrows, bringing the calves down first and then turning their attention to the does. Shortly these were all dead or dying, and only the buck remained on his feet. He had a number of arrows in his flanks, but continued to roar his defiance and charge about the triangle.

The red men continued to fire arrows at him, but he seemed

impervious. Some stuck, but many bounced off his hide or antlers, and eventually my friend the beckoner, who seemed to be the men's leader, called out in a loud voice, and the flights of arrows stopped.

He nocked an arrow and stood erect, stepping out beyond the line of trees. Then he called gently, attracting the buck's attention, and the rest of the red men fell silent. The buck turned, hearing the noise, and readied himself to charge. Man and deer faced each other; then the animal charged, lowering its head as it did so. My companion waited until the last possible moment before loosing his shaft. I saw it fly and then glance off the beast's head, and the red man stumbled as he moved backwards and slipped onto the chest-high mass of branches and fallen wood.

I had no time to think. I was directly behind him, in the line of sight and charge of the maddened beast, and I was holding a weapon in my hands. In the animal's final stride I let out a shout and brought my axe down between its antlers. By some luck it did not strike either one, but went directly between them like a butcher's poleaxe and struck the beast on the crown of its head.

The animal did not die immediately, for it continued to charge, with me holding on to the axe shaft, but the axe head was buried in its skull and in no more than three strides it sank to its knees and then collapsed, and I found myself lying nose to snout with it and my hands and face covered in its spouting blood.

I heard a great shout go up from the red men, and then felt myself hauled to my feet and my back and shoulders being pummelled. First among my congratulators was the leader, who clapped me several times on the shoulder and then clasped me to his bosom.

Then he half-pushed, half-pulled me with him along a track that led behind the row of fallen trees. Some of his companions stayed behind, no doubt to prepare and carry the meat, but most came with us, perhaps twenty men, and all singing and shouting a paean to the hunt.

I looked at him, my mouth open and eyes wide, expressing, I hoped, a question.

For answer, he raised his fingers to his mouth, clearly indicating eating. I pointed to the animals, and he made the eating gesture again, beckoned, and turned away along a forest path which was just visible behind him.

I stood, unsure of what to do, but then he turned, beckoned again, and set off along the path. I followed, and his companions crowded along behind me.

The track wound through the trees and led gradually downhill to a clearing where there stood a stockade of woven branches, with a narrow gap giving access to the interior. My guide approached this, and then turned to look back at me. Seeing that I was still following him, he set up a great roar, hallooing and shouting, and answers came from the stockade.

People, the males dressed in a breech-clout and the women only marginally more modestly, appeared in the gap, and I followed my guide through it and into an encampment beyond. There were a number of conical huts – all made apparently of wood, although I discovered later that it was in fact bark – with smoke issuing from the apexes. There were two or three other small fires with a number of naked or nearly naked children tending each one, all looking intently at the stranger in their midst. Every soul there, man, woman and child, was covered in the same red paint that the warriors in the forest were wearing, as was such clothing as they had.

My guide made some announcement, at which there was general elation and the fires were stoked up. I was led to one of the huts, which was also painted red, and given to understand that I should enter.

Inside was smoky but warm. There was a fire in the centre,

the smoke spiralling upwards to a hole, and the uneven floor was covered in the fur of various beasts. My guide sat cross-legged and indicated that I should do the same. When I had complied, several of the other men entered and sat also. One of them, who was somewhat older than my companions, threw some sweet-smelling herb onto the embers, and my guide made a speech which seemed to meet general approval. After this the older man took a tube to which a bowl was attached, put some of the herb into the bowl and lit it, drawing enthusiastically through the tube and puffing the smoke into the air. When the herb was glowing, he reversed the tube and offered it to me.

Not wishing to offend, I took it and held it uncertainly, and with encouraging gestures the man enjoined me to suck upon the tube as he had done. I did so, somewhat too enthu-siastically, I fear, for I promptly fell a-coughing and retching, thinking that my mouth and lungs were afire. This occasioned great entertainment for the men, who laughed heartily, clapped me on the back and took the tube and bowl from me so that each could suck on it. I noted that none of them had similar problems to myself. In due course the tube and bowl, having been passed round the circle of men, reached me again.

More cautious this time, I took only a shallow breath, and found that the sensation was not unpleasant. I held the smoke in my mouth for a few moments, as I had seen some of the others do, before letting it go in a puff of breath. This produced only a mild cough, and again I was congratulated and clapped on the back. This ceremony went on for some time, the tube going round the circle and being refilled whenever the herb burned itself out. I became giddy and wanted only to sleep, and eventually felt myself being laid down and covered. It was an experience I would not have missed, but not one any civilized man would care to repeat, I think.

When I awoke my head was spinning and throbbing, and it was clear that some time had passed, for my companions were still passing the tube around. When they saw me once again awake, however, the ceremony was drawn to a close, and they signalled me to go with them.

Outside some of the animals that had been killed had been quartered and dressed, and haunches were roasting on spits all around the compound. Now the older man was in command, and he led our party towards the largest of the buildings within the stockade, a rectangular one with vertical walls. The interior had long benches along the walls and a dais at the far end.

I was led to a seat. The older man and some of the others withdrew and after some time returned wearing a large, dark robe and a great many feathers of various birds. He made a speech in which he seemed to refer to me, pointing at me and drawing the attention of all to my presence, and there was more cheering and shouting. After this great hunks of meat were brought in and laid before us, and, my appetite being as sharp as that of any of my companions, I set too with a will when invited by looks and gestures to do so.

When the feast was over and all were replete, we were brought small bowls of water to wash our hands and small soft cloths to dry them. Then a large flat stone was brought out by four men and placed in front of the older man, whom I had decided must be the chief, due to his prominence in speech and his position seated at the head of things.

He spoke again, pointing from time to time at me, and there was another great cheer. Then suddenly I found my hands grasped and pulled forward, and as I toppled over more men took hold of my legs, and I was carried into the centre of the hall and laid on the flat stone. It was clear that I was to be a human sacrifice, and I struggled and yelled, but all my limbs were firmly held and I was forced down. Looking up, I saw my guide, the man whose life I had saved, standing above me with a huge club in his hands, his intention to dash out my brains where I lay.

The hall fell silent, and I could hear only my own shouts of terror. Then I too fell silent and awaited my fate. The chief spoke into the silence, and I looked up at the roof of the hall, unable to move. There was a long pause, and then the chief spoke again, and once again there was no response. He spoke a third time, and receiving no answer, he said something in a low voice to my guide, who raised his club, studded with the teeth and claws of different animals, high above his head, ready to bring it down onto me.

I found myself repeating 'Aves' and 'Pater Nosters' and even, to my surprise, brought to mind the 'Salve Regina' from Tournai and began to gabble that. Then, over my own voice, I heard another, higher and sweeter, and then a body fell on top of me, a young girl who spoke urgently and swiftly. She laid herself on top of me and pressed her face on top of mine, and her whole body trembled and shook in the grip of some strong emotion.

And then I recognized the emotion.

She was laughing!

I thought how hard and cruel were the women of this tribe, who could laugh as they watched a man put to death. I lay, shocked into silence as she spoke again, her voice catching on a giggle, and then she laid her head alongside mine and I felt her breath chuckle into my ear.

Looking upwards, I saw the mighty club move, and flinched, but it was being lowered slowly, and then my arms were released and my guide, smiling now, helped me to my feet. The girl rose too, and stood on one side of me with my guide on the other as the chief spoke again to the assembly. My legs would barely hold me up, and I was shaking and taking great gulps of air, unable even to think rationally. I stood there as the chief spoke again.

Then, amid more cheering, a large pot was brought in and two men began to plaster me with the red paint that I had seen on so many of the savages. They spared not my blushes nor any part of my body, for the paint was applied liberally to all parts as the girl and the guide held on to my arms. I was almost fainting with terror, for I knew not what was to happen next. Soon I was completely covered in the paint, and still the shouting and cheering continued unabated.

Then the pot was removed and there was more cheering, and two men bore in a large robe made of the skin of some animal and put it over my head. It stretched to my knees, and with it came a hat and some boots of the same skin. I stood all uncomprehending and the chief turned and sat on the chair that was on the dais, a large thing more like a bedstead than a stool. He drew me down beside him and both he and my guide spoke to me, but I had no more idea of what they said than if a duck had given tongue.

It was the girl that made all plain to me. She pointed to the chief and raised a hand on high; then she pointed to herself and the guide and moved her other hand so that it was lower. They were his children. I confirmed this, miming a babe in arms and indicating first the old man and then the two of them, and enthusiastic nodding showed that I was right. They were brother and sister.

Then she took my hand and placed it between that of her brother and herself, and then raised all three to the old man's heart. Suddenly I understood; what I had thought to be an execution was a ceremony of adoption. My actions in the forest had won their trust, and now I was accepted as a member of the tribe and as their adopted brother.

They must have seen my understanding, for she put her arms about me and her brother, smiling broadly, clasped my hand in his. Though we had no language in common, we were able to exchange names. My guide was Qantoc and his sister Santu, while their father's name was Alacho. I was Wicha, which was as near as they could get to my name. Qantoc gave me my axe, and I presented it to Alacho to further cheering. They had all already spent some time looking at it, and it seemed to me that they were unfamiliar with metal, for I had already noticed that their own axes were made from stone, while their spears were sticks which had been fired until hard. There was more cheering as Alacho accepted the gift, and then the ceremonies were over, and all filed out into the night air leaving me with the chief, the guide and the girl.

By now it was dark, and I was led to one of the bark huts for the night. It was warm and smelled of the herbs they had lit, and the floor was covered in pelts, some of them from the white bears we had occasionally seen. They had been dressed and treated to an extraordinary softness. I lay down gratefully, and was astonished to be joined by Santu, who slid under the pelts beside me and soon made clear her intentions. I was too tired to resist, but acquitted myself well enough, I thought, and the night was passed in good sport before we fell asleep.

On the morrow I was escorted by Qantoc back through the forest to the shore, which I could not have found without a guide. With me went my fur robe and boots, and I remained plastered with the paint, although it has to be said that a fair amount of it had transferred itself to Santu during the night.

With me also went gifts – a stone axe, some pelts and a quantity of the meat of the large deer we had killed. My new friends refused to escort me beyond the stream where we normally left our gifts of food, however, and I bade farewell to Qantoc there and made my way back to our camp.

Baleren and the others had given me up for dead, so my return and the meat I had brought brought great relief to mind and body. In addition, my adventures among the red men entertained them for three long nights as we sat in the hut, listening to the wind without as I told my story and answered their questions. I omitted to tell them of the behaviour of Santu, however; it would not have done to render the men restless with lust.

I maintained my links with the red men, and learned to speak a little of their language. They called themselves 'the people', which in their language is 'Beothuk', and I spent several nights with them and with Santu, usually on our seventh day, on which no work was done.

The growing season in their country was short and as a result the Beothuk did not farm. They fished from bark canoes, speared seals with harpoons and collected shellfish. When I went I usually took some of the salted fish with me, as a gift over and above what we left by the stream. The Beothuk also gathered fruit and berries for food and hunted the large deer I had seen, which they called the 'khalibu'.

Their red colour was not part of their skin, as we had at first thought, but was the result of covering themselves with the same red earth as they had applied to me in the ceremony I had undergone. They used the red earth extensively, covering everything – their bodies, faces, hair, clothing, personal possessions, and tools – with the paint, which they made from the earth, pounded to a powder and mixed with either fish oil or animal grease. I think it must have had some religious meaning, but it also served a practical purpose as protection from insects.

I discovered too that there were other groups in the region, usually related to Alacho's band, and with much the same pattern of living. During the winter, they wore khalibu-skin mantles such as I had been given, with shoes, leggings and mittens of the same material.

Qantoc took me hunting with him, although I was never able to master the bow. He made no comment on my sharing a bed with his sister other than to tell me that Beothuk women were mistresses of their own bodies and thus free to dispose their favours where they would.

'Why do you come here?' he asked one day.

'Because of the fish,' I said. 'There are no fish such as these in my country, and they are a great delicacy.'

He picked up a piece of the stockfish I had brought as a gift, a solid slab of dried, salted fish, and wrinkled his nose. 'This is a delicacy?' he said. 'I fear I must pity your people.'

His father leaned forward and asked, 'Do your people wish to stay here? Will they want land to live one day?'

'No,' I said. 'The fish is enough.'

He nodded. 'There is fish enough in the sea for all,' he said. 'But you and your friends have stayed the whole year round.'

'This happens only when the fishing is good,' I said, 'in case next year there is a shortage. They will not stay every year.'

'I have noticed this. Your men come into the forest to cut wood for fuel?'

'Yes.'

'Is that all they require?'

'When the fish leave, we will leave,' I said. 'The wood is taken only to keep out the cold.'

'The forest has enough wood for all,' he said. 'We shall not begrudge you a few trees from among so many.'

Eventually I managed to get Qantoc to come with me into our camp so I could introduce him to my fellow winterers, but none of the other Beothuk would be convinced, and in the end I stopped asking. All the same, a lively trade was carried on across the boundary stream, the more so when the men discovered that old nails or bits of broken cooking pots could be traded, as the red men were able to beat them out and reuse them as arrow- or spear-heads.

The winter passed cheerfully enough, but as the days continued to lengthen we looked for the return of the fleet. Then, one day, when a fog bank had sprung up, and we were going about our business in that cold silence that fog brings, suddenly there was a noise nearby and two mist-wreathed figures loomed out of the gloom.

'Who goes there?' Baleren asked, and there was an

answering shout of laughter as the newcomers approached close enough to be recognized.

'Pierre,' the laugher cried. 'Looking for a berth?'

I laughed too. 'Might be. You offering one?'

'Might be,' Pierre Jean said, and clapped his arms about me. Pierre Jean and the *Buoc'h* had returned with the spring fleet.

He told me the amount we had each made from our share of the catch, his somewhat larger, as a captain. Old Pierre had taken his money and retired to count his grandchildren, but Young Pierre was back, an experienced hand now and anxious to discover whether it would be sensible to winter in this land, should he be chosen. Most of the rest of last year's crew were back, too.

Last year's money was to help his mother, Young Pierre told me. This year's was for himself.

'And what are you going to do with yours?' Pierre Jean asked me.

'I have plans,' I said cautiously. 'What about you? What are you going to do with yours?'

He looked ruefully at me. 'Pay off my debts,' he said.

'Didn't last year's share do that?'

'Yes and no,' he said. 'I paid them off, but they built up again. Good beer is not cheap, you know.'

'You didn't incorporate my shares into yours, did you?' I asked, a sudden fear clutching at my heart.

'Nay, fear not,' he said. 'I did as you wanted. All the money from your two shares is safe, deposited with that Florentine banker in Bruges, as you asked. You're a man of means now, Pierre, and the share of this summer's catch will turn you into a rich man. You can look at the future with a clearer eye.'

I told the crews what Alacho had said about the fishing, and that as long as we confined ourselves to chopping down trees in the forest then we were unlikely to have any problems with the Beothuk.

When the warm weather came the Beothuk turned their mantles inside out, so that the fur side was outside instead of inside, to hold the warmth, as it had been in the winter, and it was almost time for me to leave and to turn myself the right way out, too. I said my manly farewells to Alacho and Qantoc and more tenderly to Santu, promising to return one day if I could, but in my heart I knew how unlikely that was, especially if my plans came to fruition.

At the end of that second summer in the fishing grounds I was eighteen years old, a man. It was time I was about my father's business.

The Florentine banker Pierre Jean had deposited my money with had keen, deep-set eyes, and they were looking at me most carefully. 'It is very strange,' he said, leaning back in his chair and putting the fingers of his hands together. 'You are, you say, a fisherman, albeit a very rich one. Your investments have done well, and now you bring even more money for me to invest on your behalf. I do not get many fishermen in this office, even rich ones.'

He liked to give the impression of shrewdness, and he may well have been so; more to the point, he had a reputation as an honest man, which is all I wanted.

'You carry out other services, I believe?' I asked.

'Such as?'

'Such as the transportation of correspondence?'

'Oh, that? Of course. You have a package you wish to send?'

'I do,' I said. 'But packages, in the plural.' I placed on his desk a number of envelopes, each securely bound and fastened and sealed with wax. 'Each of these must go directly to its destination,' I said, 'without let or hindrance. I must know when it is received, and I am expecting immediate replies to at least some of them.'

'All that can be arranged,' he said. He looked at the names

of the addressees on the packages and then said, 'You would seem to move in exalted circles for a fisherman.'

'There are precedents,' I said.

'Such as?' he asked.

'Simon called Peter and a few others,' I told him.

He had the grace to smile.

It was but a few weeks later when I received word that replies had been received to some of my missives, and I went to the Italian banker's office to receive them. All held but little in the way of help or encouragement. 'Would you like privacy to read them?' he asked as I broke the seal of the final packet.

'No, thank you,' I said, and scanned the contents, some of which were couched in the most execrable Latin I have ever read and in handwriting that was little better than a scrawl. 'Although I suppose a little help might not go amiss.'

He reached out for the document, but I told him, 'I was joking, sir,' and folded it away.

I found him in Ostend, in a tavern near the harbour. 'I've seen you before,' I said.

'Is that right?' he replied.

'It is. Pierre, isn't it?'

'Might be,' he said, and sat down. 'Looking for a berth?'

'Might be. You offering one?'

'Might be,' he said, and raised his flagon. 'Your health, Pierre.'

'And yours . . .' I replied.

'Have you decided what to do with all that money yet?' he asked.

'I have,' I said, 'and this time, Mynheer Meno, it's going to be different.'

'In what way?'

'I am going to hire your ship to take me on a voyage. You

can trade as well, of course. I don't want your hold space, but I do stand in need of a passage.'

'Where to?'

'Cork,' I told him.

'Where and what the bloody hell is Cork?'

'It's in Ireland,' I told him.

'Ah,' he said. 'Ireland. I see.'

'And,' I told him, 'given your ability to drink and then blab, I'm telling you no more until we're safely at sea.' Then I bought him a few more pots of ale.

It was the next day, moving west along the channel, when he asked me again. 'So, what is it you've decided to do with all the money?' he asked.

'I'm going to use it,' I said, 'to become King of England.'

As his mouth fell open I told him more. In fact, I told him everything.

'I do not care for your choice of clothing, Mynheer Meno,' I said, turning so that the fabric of my clothes wafted outwards. The silks I had worn at the wedding in Portugal were at last being allowed to see the light of day.

'They will be expecting a prince of England, not a Tournai wharf rat or a Breton cod fisherman,' Pierre Jean said. 'You must at least look right. How else will they know you are a prince?'

'But these are clothes designed for a dumb show, an amusement. They are for someone playing at being a prince, not for real.'

'These people are Irish,' he said. 'They've probably never even seen a piece of silk before, let alone worn one.'

'Is it not enough that I much resemble my father?' I asked him.

'Come on, Pierre,' he said. 'Who of these men ever knew your father? And even if one or two of them did, you still need to look the part.'

'Some of the less gaudy items, then,' I said. 'I am an Englishman, not a peacock on parade.'

Thus it was that I stepped ashore in Cork, richly dressed in a white silk shirt and with a dark-blue brocaded doublet and cloak, to find a small procession wending its way along the quay. My letters from Bruges had stirred up the gentry, and I had sent word ahead the moment we tied up, so the populace had come out to see what was going on. The Bishop of Cork with an army of acolytes was preceded by the Host, and behind him came the mayor and aldermen of the city, and behind them my lords the Earls of Desmond and Kildare.

'Who is it?' I heard whispered among the crowd, and the answers were as strange as the language they were spoken in.

'It's the Duke of Warwick himself, the rightful King of England,' said one man.

'Sure, it can't be,' his companion replied. 'Wasn't the man himself here last year, and him looking nothing like this one.'

'No, that one was a fake, and this one is the real thing.'

'No, no,' butted in another. 'This one is the natural son of old King Richard himself, that was killed at that battle.'

By this time the bishop was upon me, and I knelt for his blessing. He murmured the words, placing a gloved hand on my head, and then pulled me up to my feet. 'Is it truth they say?' he asked. 'Are you the prince that was thought murdered? You must tell me truth now, or your soul is damned.'

'I was a prince of England in the time of my father, Your Grace,' I told him, 'but now am no more than a poor traveller upon the face of the earth, an exile from his home and a native of nowhere.'

'God willing, you shall not remain so for long,' he told me, and then stepped aside for Lord Desmond.

'It is you, then,' said the earl. 'I thought I might need convincing, but I see your father in you, and your mother too.'

'I fear others may not be so easy to convince as yourself, my lord,' I told him.

'But let us make a beginning,' he said, and introduced me to the mayor and the other dignitaries as 'Richard, Duke of York and rightful King of England'. No other man had ever called me that before, and I found it strangely moving; for the first time in nearly ten years I was acknowledged by my own name, that which my mother and father had called me, and I was glad, and proud of it.

'I believe you, my son,' the bishop told me, 'but we must make test of you so that all might know the truth. Will you swear an oath upon the Host as to your identity?'

'I will, my lord,' I said immediately, and he signalled the Host-bearer to come forward.

Then he turned to the crowd. 'This man has come among us,' he announced, 'to ask our help in a great venture. So that all may know, he will swear to his identity.' He turned again to me. 'I will suggest to you who you might be,' he said. 'I shall ask you, first in English and then in Erse; do you answer in English so that all may know.' Then he raised his voice again. 'Kneel before God and place your hand on the ciborium wherein resides His body on earth,' he cried in a loud voice, 'and all these people shall witness whether you speak truth or not.' He paused, and the crowd fell into an expectant silence. He pitched his voice higher again, the better to carry across the wharf, and said, 'Do you swear that you are Edward Plantagenet, Duke of Warwick, that was long imprisoned by Henry of Lancaster?'

While my mouth sagged open he spoke words in Erse, presumably the same question, and I shook my head. 'I do not so swear,' I said. 'I am not that unfortunate man.'

A murmur ran through the crowd, and then they fell silent again as he asked his second question. 'Do you swear that you are Richard Plantagenet, son of the body of King Richard III?'

I was about to agree when I realized what he had said. Like the man in the crowd, some must have mistaken which Richard I was, and his intention must have been to clear up that matter. While he intoned again in Erse I was able to gather my wits, and again I denied it.

'Do you swear that you are Richard Plantagenet, Duke of York and surviving son of King Edward IV of England?'

'I do so swear,' I said firmly, and suddenly the crowd of people was cheering and applauding, the Erse words of the question drowned out by the acclamation.

I felt hands lifting me from my knees, and with the Earl of Desmond on one side and the Earl of Kildare on the other I was walked through cheering crowds to a large house in the city centre, where a feast had been prepared. Pierre Jean and Young Pierre tagged on behind, grinning like fools and enjoying the whole proceeding for the adventure it was.

I had taken my first step towards the throne of England.

Pretender

September 1491 – November 1493

If I had expected to find a noble's castle, with food and manners to match Kildare's title (and indeed, I think at the back of my mind I had), I was to be sorely disappointed. The castle was draughty and cold, with only bare stones around the walls instead of tapestries, and a host of evil-smelling dogs that wandered freely about and left their fewmets where they wished – it was not a place for a man to spend too long barefoot. Kildare himself wore rough woollen clothes, leggings tied about with strips of dried animal skin and a long and heavy cloak which lay across his shoulders day and night, waking or sleeping.

His English was comprehensible, but only barely, and not at all if I failed to concentrate fully on his words and use his actions to illuminate the meanings which his words could not. 'We'll get a few men together first,' he said to me. 'Don't you worry about that, your honour; you won't know them at all, but they'll be knowing you, and not a few of them are men who knew your grandfather, God rest his soul, who should have been king by rights before your own father, God rest his soul, and your poor brother, God rest his soul.'

'And then what?'

'And then we'll march on Dublin, and men will flock to your Yorkist banner from the whole of Ireland, and perhaps from beyond the seas too.' He pointed at Pierre Jean: 'Sure, your man here can put the word about and we'll see what turns up. That'll take time, of course.'

'How long?'

He twisted and threw a chicken bone into the corner of the room, where a bundle of dogs began a scuffle that started in a flurry of barking and ended in a whimper as a dispossessed animal had its flank nipped. 'Couple of months,' he said. 'Or more. News'll take time to get around. Springtime, say.' He swivelled again and called, 'Desmond, what you reckon? Springtime before we can raise a force for His Majesty?'

'At least.'

Kildare grunted and turned back to me. 'Until then we'll need to keep you close. Best if you don't stay here.'

'Where should I go?'

Kildare grinned. 'I know the very place,' he said, 'and I'll tell you later.' He looked pointedly round at Pierre Jean: 'When we can be sure that all the ears are on the same side of the head.' He raised his voice slightly. 'And when is it you intend to set sail, sir?' he asked.

'When my lord gives me leave,' Pierre Jean said, and had the effrontery to wink at me. He had elevated me from employee to master as soon as we had set sail. I could not stop myself laughing. He fitted well into Kildare's court, which, if naught else, was relaxed and amusing.

It did not, however, seem to have any sense of urgency about it. I questioned the lord on several occasions about his plans, but he always managed to fob me off – it was no time for a rebellion, it was too cold, it was too close to Christmas, replies to the call to arms had not been received and so on – and one year drifted into the next and winter showed signs of turning into spring and still nothing had happened.

Early in February Pierre Jean, who had been restless for some time, decided to hoist his sail and go. I walked with him down to the wharf, and stood looking longingly around his deck, holding on to a rope. 'Whither away, then?' I asked.

He shook his head. 'La Rochelle, maybe, to start,' he said.

'I've got these fleeces to get rid of, and then I thought I might try my hand at the bacalao again in April, unless something better comes along.'

'What will you do if you're asked about me?'

'Sell you down the river, of course,' he said. 'I have a simple formula – the more money I'm offered, the more I'll find to say. Who do you think will offer the most?'

'Tudor, almost certainly.'

'In that case I'll tell him all I know.'

'The truth?'

'If what you've told me is the truth, then the truth he shall have. If he doesn't like it, of course, I'll tell him what he wants to know, and charge him a little more for it. Or a lot more.'

'Have you any scruples at all?' I asked.

'Of course not,' he said. 'I'm a merchant – everything is a commodity; everything can be sold, especially information. Everything has its price.'

'Or every one?'

'Naturally.'

He accompanied me to the gangplank. 'Do I have to kneel to you now?' he asked.

'No,' I said. 'Not yet. Maybe next time, though, if I'm King of England when next we meet. Let me know how much you get for my story.'

I stepped ashore, and the *Buoc'h* cast off and sailed south. I watched it until I could no longer discern it in the sea mist. Pierre Jean Meno was the most thorough rogue I ever met, but was also the most honest. Like every other man, he was out for what he could get; the difference was that he admitted it freely, both to himself and to others.

I had spent a cold and miserable winter, partly with Kildare in his castle, and partly going about the countryside on a progress round his estates. Springtime came, but there was still no sign of any activity from my Irish allies. The season of Easter was cold and wet, and although a few more men of some quality, such as the Mayor of Cork, John Atwater, came to offer support, they all talked vaguely of some time in the future. Nothing definite was decided. If they thought to make me King of England, they were taking their time about it.

And then suddenly all changed, with the arrival of a ship in the harbour. The packages I had sent out had announced to the monarchs of Europe exactly who I was, that I was ready to assume the mantle of kingship and that I would be grateful for support. Most, of course, simply ignored me; one or two expressed mild interest; only Kildare, as Brampton had suggested, had embraced the idea. Now, however, another player arrived on the scene.

'They've come for you,' Kildare told me in surprise when the captain of the ship presented his credentials. He looked quizzically at me. 'You're not having us on, then?'

'Did you think I was?'

'Well,' he said, 'I have to admit I had my doubts. Anyway, I've given these men permission to land.'

The landing was a sight to see. A troop of crossbowmen filed along the gangplank and then stood on either side of the wharf, forming a guard of honour. A knight clambered from the ship clad entirely in white silk with a heavy white cloak around him and went to the head of the two lines of men. Two other men, each more soberly dressed, joined him, and then the troop executed a sharp turn and advanced in double file and perfect step, their crossbows slung across their shoulders and their gleaming white coats with the red cross of St George across them in stark contrast to the filthy rags of those gathered on the wharf to watch the proceedings. Even more remarkable was that the whole performance took place in silence, the only sound the initial order to march.

The squadron marched through the town, watched by all, ourselves included, who were perched on the battlements until the final barked command to halt. Even Kildare, grizzled old soldier that he was, was impressed and sucked his teeth in appreciation. ''Tis a fine sight,' he muttered, 'but the Lord Himself knows whether or not they fight as good as they march.'

'I wouldn't care to put them to the test, myself,' Desmond said.

We went down to receive them, and the knight advanced with his two companions. 'Have I the honour of addressing his grace the Duke of York, his grace the Earl of Kildare and his grace the Earl of Desmond?' he asked in a powerful voice and also in English.

'You do,' muttered Kildare, and the knight went down on one knee, to the ruination of his breeches, followed by the other two.

'Pray allow me to present myself. I am Chevalier MacDonald of His Majesty's Royal Guard.'

'Which majesty would that be?' Kildare asked. 'Not Tudor, surely? James, is it?'

'I have the honour to be the envoy of His Most Catholic Majesty Charles the Eighth of France,' the chevalier said.

'And you a Scotsman?' Desmond said. 'Does it not break your heart to work for a foreign power?'

The Scotsman ignored the comment and remained on his knees until I raised him up and indicated to the others that they too should rise. 'Permit me, Your Grace,' MacDonald said, 'to present Capitaine Louis de Lucques, one of His Majesty's foremost naval captains, and Monsieur Stephen Frion, whom His Majesty sends to act, should you wish it, as your French Secretary.'

I looked at Frion. He looked somehow familiar. 'Have we met before, Monsieur Frion?' I asked.

'I am honoured that you remember me, sire,' he said, 'for indeed we have. I had the honour to be the French Secretary to your royal father of sacred memory, King Edward IV, and also to his brother, King Richard.'

'But not to Henry Tudor?'

'Indeed I was, sire, for a time, but when my pay was over a year in arrears I was forced to change masters, and gained employment with His Majesty the King of France.'

'Now there's a dog who never changes,' Kildare said. 'Has Tudor ever paid anything with a willing heart?'

'My lord greets you, Your Grace,' MacDonald said, 'and invites you to honour his palace with a visit with a view to discussing further plans for help and assistance against the criminal usurper.'

'Me?' Kildare said.

'The invitation is extended to His Grace the Duke of York, my lord.'

MacDonald cut a strange and exotic figure in those sur-roundings. His uniform was spotless, his manners impeccable and, although he tried to disguise it, his very being revolted against the squalor of Kildare's castle.

'I should be pleased to accept His Majesty's invitation,' I replied, 'but I shall need two or three days to order matters here.'

'Of course,' he said, swallowing hard, no doubt thinking that I would require him to reside in the castle.

I waited for Kildare to invite the three men to stay for a meal or some of the other barbaric refreshments that the place had to offer, but it seemed that such a thought was far from his mind.

After an awkward pause I suggested, 'Perhaps Monsieur Frion and yourself could remain, chevalier, and acquaint me with such information as His Majesty has seen fit to send, while if the good captain needs to ready his ship for sea . . .'

'Of course, Your Grace,' MacDonald said. 'Is there some-where we could confer?'

'Confer, is it?' Kildare said. 'Sure, I never heard it called that before. And what will you be conferring about?'

MacDonald, somewhat bemused, said, 'About His Majesty's plans to aid His Grace, sir.'

'And where am I and Desmond in those plans?' Kildare asked.

'That is a matter for His Majesty and His Grace, sir,' he said. 'Until we have . . . er, conferred, then I do not know.'

Kildare grunted and turned on his heel, leaving us to find our own comfort amid the chaos of his keep.

The next day I thanked Kildare and Desmond for their help, or at least for their intent to help, and boarded the French ship to take me on the beginning of the next stage of my adventure. The ship had to beat well out to the west to avoid the English patrols that Tudor had sent out, having heard of my venture from the reports of the letters I had sent from Ireland as well as from Bruges, and I surprised Captain de Lucques by sighting the pole star, reckoning our latitude and plotting our course for Honfleur.

It was good to have the wind in my hair again after the stuffiness and filth of Kildare's domain, and part of me regretted the course of my life that seemed now to have been plotted. Somewhere to the west Pierre Jean and Young Pierre were heading for the fishing banks, and it was often I turned to look longingly into the sunset, but always I turned my face back. Now the truth of my birth and the duty of kingship were dictating my actions, for once, rather than thoughts of my own safety or of adventure. All the same, I was not sure that I preferred it this way.

On arrival at Honfleur I was pushed into a white suit of armour so that I might be paraded before the populace. I was surprised to discover that I was already being treated as a prince. Greeted by an honour guard of the King's Scots Guards and by yet another chevalier, one Dunbar, I was escorted to a coach in which I was transported in some discomfort to the king's quarters at Molines.

It had been some years since I had been in the presence of royalty, but Charles VIII soon put me at my ease. He was young, younger than me by three or so years, but seemed even younger in his behaviour and enthusiasms. Had he not been a king, one might have thought him simple-minded.

'Are you married, Your Grace?' were the first words he said to me. 'I am.'

'I am not, sir,' I said.

'That's good,' he said, taking my hand. He stood closer than was comfortable, but I relaxed when it dawned on me that this was the result of short-sightedness. 'I have a girl here that you might marry if you like. I wanted her myself, but my sister Anne wouldn't allow it, so I had to marry this other girl. She's Anne, too. I think that's why she chose her really, although she tells me different.'

He pulled me into his apartments. 'You are a prince; you know what it's like,' he said. 'Did you have a big sister?'

'Three of them, Your Majesty,' I said.

He laughed and said, 'Well, you'll know, then.'

His personal chambers were a wilderness. Monkeys and birds chased each other about the draperies, and the bed coverings were much gnawed and befouled by the host of cats and dogs which wandered about.

'So, will you marry her, then?'

'Who, Your Majesty?'

'Marguerite. Someone should marry her so she can stay here. She's lovely – pretty and so much fun. Not like my wife. She's well born. I was going to marry her myself, but my sister Anne . . . Have I told you this?'

'You have, Your Majesty.'

'Well, you can have her if you like. She's the daughter of the King of the Romans.'

'Maximilian?'

'Oh, you know him? Nice man. Says he wants his daughter back, though. If you marry her then she won't have to go. What do you think?'

A sound in the corner attracted my attention. Two dogs were squabbling over what looked like the carcase of a parrot.

'Eh?'

'It is a little early to think of marriage, Your Majesty . . .'

'I am younger than you and I am married,' he objected.

'You misunderstand me, sire. I meant only that I am likely to be preoccupied with the business of regaining my country.'

'Oh, yes – I suppose so. Maybe afterwards, then, when you are king.'

'Perhaps, my lord.'

At this point the door opened and a small group of courtiers entered. I noticed Dunbar and Frion in their midst.

'Your Majesty, His Grace is somewhat tired after his journey, and needs to rest.'

'Quite right,' the king said. 'Good idea. So do I.' He lay down on his bed and then, almost as an afterthought, said, 'You are dismissed. All of you.'

Bowing, and with faces turned towards the royal personage, we left the chambers.

Outside a young girl was wrestling with a courtier. 'Let me pass, damn you,' she said. 'I wish to speak with the mad bastard, and you will not gainsay me.'

'His Majesty has retired for the evening,' one of the courtiers told her.

'Ah, so there's no doubt about who I'm referring to, then,' she said. 'You clearly know who I mean. Just to countenance the phrase is tantamount to treason, is it not?' The courtier blanched, but the girl turned away from him to look at me. 'You're new,' she said. 'Are you a sane man, or as lunatic as the rest of them here?'

'Allow me to present His Grace, the Duke Richard of York,' the courtier said, and then turned to me. 'Sir, may I present the Princess Marguerite of Burgundy.'

She dropped a curtsy. 'I've heard of you,' she said. 'They say you hid away in Flanders in case the King of England tried to kill you.'

'It was Picardy,' I said, 'but otherwise, yes.'

'Is he going to help you to your throne, then,' she asked, 'or are you like me, another exhibit for his menagerie?'

'I hope for help,' I told her. 'His Majesty has graciously brought me from Ireland to that end.'

During the conversation I had time to size her up. She was lively and obviously of great intelligence and I could imagine her being 'much fun' as the king had said, but I could not agree with him that she was 'pretty'; if anything, she was one of the plainest children I had ever seen, her main feature being her grotesquely huge jaw, which jutted some way ahead of her like the prow of a ship. His Majesty was perhaps more short-sighted than I had thought.

'His Majesty is mad,' she said, slipping her arm through mine. 'He is simple-minded, incompetent, easily led and even more easily distracted. The only thing he's any good at is tennis.' I saw the startled looks that the courtiers exchanged, but she merely laughed. 'Look,' she said firmly to them, 'either this lord is as mad as your king is or he is as sane as I am. If the former, then naught I say can make any difference, and if the latter then he'll be agreeing with me by tomorrow.' She turned again to me. 'Of course, what I'm telling you is tech-nically treason,' she said, 'and I really shouldn't make you listen to it, or you would be guilty of it, too, like that fellow there.' She turned and pointed at the courtier she had been speaking to earlier, and a look of fear came over his face. Her desired effect achieved, she turned back to me and grinned broadly. 'So, my lord, I'll leave you. If you have any influence with His mad Majesty, could you ask him to send me home to my father? I'll see you anon. Goodbye.'

So saying, she turned abruptly down a corridor and left me with the courtiers, who all instantly began to murmur excuses and explanations. I maintained a dignified and noble silence and allowed them to lead me to my bedchamber.

And there, in a nutshell, is what my time at the court of the King of France was like. No duties to speak of except attendance on His Majesty (which included the requirement to play tennis against him at any hour of the day or night), inconsequential conversations, mad proposals, wild ideas, parrots, dogs and monkeys, an inadequate king who could see nothing unless he brought it right in front of his eyes, his judgement as clouded as his sight, and a bright, plain girl desperate to be free of it all. It went on thus for five months or so, well into late autumn, and then all changed.

The king and I had spent the afternoon in his tennis court, where he had soundly beaten me, and we retired to relax. His Majesty did me the honour of pouring me a cup of wine, and then, almost as an afterthought, said, 'I knew I had something to tell you. The game put it right out of my mind.'

'Yes, Your Majesty?'

'I have signed a treaty with Henry Tudor.'

I paused, my goblet in my hand, and stared at him.

'What?'

'Not I personally, you understand,' he said, 'but my advisers. Same thing in the end, though. We are allies now, and I have promised not to consort with his enemies.'

'Which of course includes me.'

'I imagine so. Where will you go?'

I was speechless. I knew him to be a creature of whim and fancy, but this was completely unexpected.

'When you have to leave, I mean,' he said. He fondled a dog's ears and added, 'Which I suppose will have to be quite soon.'

'Was I mentioned in this treaty?' I asked.

'Not by name, no – although Henry did want to put you in – but you were implicit.'

'Maximilian won't like it. You're supposed to be allying yourself with him.'

'He can like it or not,' he said. 'He doesn't like me anyway, because I didn't give his daughter back. Hey, perhaps you could go to him – and take her with you. She's pestilence anyway – she's threatened to run away in her nightshift if I don't release her.'

'Why did you keep her anyway?' I asked. 'You can't marry her now, and it wouldn't be right to bed her. What use is she to you?'

'She's a pretty thing,' he said. 'She's fun, and she's nice to have around. I should have married her instead of Anne. I kept her here in case Anne dies, but I don't think she's going to. She's very healthy. Which monkey do you like the best?'

I put down my cup and put my head in my hands. Not for the first time at the court of Charles VIII did I begin to wonder if choosing a head of state by dint of his parentage is really the most efficient way of governing a country.

'Do you have to hand me over to Tudor?' I asked.

''Tis not so expressed,' he said, 'although it might be a nice gesture, as one ally to another. I won't though; I think he might kill you.'

'I think he might,' I agreed.

'I suppose you could take Marguerite with you, if you wanted to go to Maximilian. I like the marmoset the best.'

'I fear, Your Majesty,' I said, 'I might have to travel too fast for the comfort and safety of a young princess. Shall I tell the King of the Romans that his daughter is free to return home if he sends an escort?'

'No, I'll do that,' he said. 'The escort, I mean. You can tell him, yes, if you happen to see him.' He looked up as I rose to my feet. 'Where are you going?'

'Your Majesty has perhaps forgotten that he has promised not to consort with the enemies of Tudor.'

'Of Henry the Seventh, you mean? Yes, I suppose you'd better go. You know the way out?'

I essayed a smile, but he was deadly serious. 'No,' he said, 'I mean the secret way. There's a passage behind that tapestry. I never sleep anywhere that doesn't have an escape route.'

I bowed deeply, said 'Thank you, my lord,' and quitted his life with the minimum of fuss.

Leaving the Princess Marguerite was a little more difficult. She and I had become more friendly as it became less likely that Charles would give me any assistance, and we had been much thrown together when the king went on his progresses through the land. Both completely in his power, I for troops or money and she for her freedom, we had become fast friends.

'You cannot leave me here, Richard,' she said when I told her what had happened.

'I must. If Charles takes it into his head to hand me over to Tudor then I am a dead man. My only hope is to escape. There may be men on their way to arrest me even now.'

'At least, then, promise me that you will go to my father. He will help you and you can tell him of my plight.'

'I must say,' I told her, 'that I have always intended to go to the court of Burgundy. The dowager duchess is my aunt, my father's sister, and I think she will help me.'

'She certainly hates Tudor,' Marguerite said. 'His behaviour after Bosworth was despicable. If you are truly who you say you are then I'm sure she'll help.'

'Her envoys have been taking a good look at me,' I said, 'but I don't know if they're satisfied or not.'

'If I know my honorary grandmother,' Marguerite said, 'she and only she will decide if you are who you say you are.'

I left Paris that very night, booted and spurred and wrapped in an expensive cloak, Charles's last gift to me. He had not changed his mind about helping me, but there was no saying how far Tudor's tentacles reached, and I rode for a night and a day until I arrived in the city of Bruges.

I called first on my former tutor, Hans Memling, and spent a pleasant evening reminiscing about happier times. I told him of my adventures with Brampton, my travels to Portugal and Jaloof and the land of the codfish and of the Princess Marguerite, and the tales paid my bed and board. I stayed that night at Hans's house, and the next morning he arranged an audience with Maximilian.

The King of the Romans was cautiously welcoming, and sent for his stepmother-in-law, my aunt Margaret, the dowager Duchess of Burgundy, who was my father's sister. He was curiously dismissive of my plans. 'Look at it from the people's viewpoint,' he said. 'Henry has been king for eight years; his realm is peaceful, and he is accepted as king. You will find that his people, like all peoples, prefer peace and stability to eternal squabbling. What does it matter to them who sits on the throne? All they want is a quiet life, and time for grandfather to die before father, and father before son. That is the truth – England is Henry's, and it will not be a task easily accomplished to prise it from his grasp.'

I must say I had not expected such a response. 'So what do you advise, sir?' I asked.

'The truth?' Maximilian asked. 'Go home, back to Tournai. Take up your father's post of port controller. Otherwise you risk throwing England, and perhaps Europe too, into another bloody war. We have had a quarter century of instability in England, and at last it is over. Can you take upon your shoulders the responsibility for starting up the war yet again?'

He paused, giving me food for thought. 'And there is another question, too, that is pertinent. If you were to win the war you started, could you rule as well as Henry? He may not be the rightful king, but he is an effective one, and that is what people want. You could crown a dog King of England,

and it would not matter as long as people were able to get on with their lives unimpeded. The truth is that it does not matter who rules a country – it is how he rules the country that is important. In effect, that man, whoever he might be, is the true king.'

My disappointment must have shown in my face. 'I am sorry to speak to you like this,' he said gently, 'and perhaps to dampen your ambitions and dash your hopes, but these are questions that will be asked by every person to whom you go for help – and there is no doubt that you would need help. And therein lies another problem. Those who offer to help you will do so for their own reasons. If France helps you, it will be in order to destabilize England; Scotland and Spain will have their own priorities, as will any other state.'

'But you will recognize my claim?' I asked.

'Recognize it, perhaps,' Maximilian said. 'Act upon it, never. You are welcome to all that my court may provide in terms of food and accommodation. You shall be my honoured guest, should you so desire, as the dispossessed Duke of York, but I will give you no funds or armies. I will help you raise funds and armies, but I make you no false promises. Like every other ruler in Europe, I will keep you safe, but it will be for my ends, not yours.' He shook his head. 'No, if I were you I would return to Tournai and dwell in peace. It is best to stay at home; you are young, and so are perhaps unaware of the inestimable value of a quiet life and a restful night's sleep.'

He paused, and then asked, 'Did you perchance meet my daughter during your stay at the court of King Charles?'

'Forgive me, my lord,' I said. 'I should have told you of her before broaching my own problems. I did see her, and made her acquaintance. She is well, but chafing a little at her enforced stay at His Majesty's court. She . . .'

At this point the servant announced the entrance of my aunt Margaret, who swept into the room in regal fashion. Then her mouth dropped open and her eyes widened as she looked upon me.

'Edward,' she said, and dropped onto a stool.

It has been said that I much resemble my father as he was in his youth, and my aunt Margaret had not seen him since he was in his mid-twenties. She saw me, but in truth she was looking at him.

I spoke to her in English. 'Not Edward, madam, but his son Richard, formerly Duke of York, who now craves your blessing.'

I knelt to her, and she reached out to me and touched my hair. 'You are so like him,' she said. 'For a moment it was him. But you, Richard – they told me you were dead. I sent envoys to Charles, but they did not prepare me for this. You are Edward to the life. But where have you been since Bosworth?'

I explained again what had happened to me. Unlike her son-in-law, she gave me some hope of success; she was enthusiastic about my restoration, and began immediately to press my case. 'Of course, we must help him,' she said. 'We must remove the usurper and restore Richard to his throne.'

'Madam,' Maximilian said. 'Neither Burgundy nor the empire is in a position to antagonize England.'

'Then the French will help.'

'Not after the recent treaty, my lady,' I said. 'I am driven out of France by Charles's friendship with Tudor.'

Maximilian sighed. 'In any case, I have already explained that any help the French might have offered would have been designed to further French interests, not your nephew's,' he said, 'and the same goes for anyone in Europe. If they can see an advantage, they will take it. If not, they'll do nothing. They may recognize you, Richard, of course, and give you a place in court and a title, but there is no one who will help you out of a love for truth, justice and the concept of primogeniture; anyone who helps you will do so only out of political self-interest.'

'And that includes you?' I said.

'Absolutely,' Maximilian told me. 'As I said, I have no intention of helping you – not directly, anyway. I will house and feed you for a few weeks while you visit your aunt and decide what to do next, but if you want a secure future then my advice to you remains the same. Go back to Tournai. Go home.'

'He cannot. It is his destiny,' the Duchess Margaret said. 'He was born to rule.'

'Perhaps,' Maximilian said uncertainly, but he was adamant, and that was where I was forced to leave matters and return to Hans's house, despite my aunt's protestations that I should stay with her. Nonetheless, I remained with Hans but a few days longer, thinking through what to do, until I gave in to her pleading and was received into the household of my aunt Margaret. Maximilian was a little displeased, it seems, but she told him that in her own domains she would act as she pleased, think as she pleased and recognize whomsoever she pleased.

My appearance alone had convinced her that I must be who I said I was, but she and I both knew that that would not be enough to convince others. If I was to sway men to my side then I had to have more than just the look of Edward IV – I had to be a prince in all things.

I found this hard. Over the years, I had become used to treating men on their merits. Whether Pierre Jean or prince, a man was a man; when I had been among the fishermen I had been one of them, and had treated them and been treated by them as one of their fellows. The same had applied when I moved among the earls in Ireland or the courtiers of France; I was at worst their equal, and treated and accepted as such.

Now I had to learn the ways of royalty, ways that I had not learned at the courts of my father and Richard, as I had been too young in the first case and too insignificant in the second. I had to learn to treat all men other than princes as beneath me, where once I had been gregarious and friendly, to maintain a dignified silence where I had been garrulous, to remain still where I had been lively, and to refrain from familiarity where I had been hail-fellow-well-met; in short, to behave as a prince was expected to behave, as failure to do so might of itself be enough to convince men that I was no prince at all. My aunt Margaret fussed around me, determined to ensure that I was comfortable, fed, watered and feted. I lacked for nothing save the freedom to walk where I would and talk with whom I would. She assured me that it was the price of royalty, and advised me to grit my teeth and bear it.

My aunt was careful to school me in all these matters and others of great import – how to walk and how to stand correctly, how to hold my gloves or hat just so, or to look in such a way. It was all flummery, but if I were to convince the important men who held the fates and finances of nations in their hands, I had not only to be a prince but also to be seen as one. The appearance was as important as the reality and, I soon found, it all came down to the clothing.

Kildare and Desmond had not had three shirts between them, which is one of the reasons why my silks had so impressed them, and one of Charles VIII's first actions had been to kit me out with silk hose and shirts, coats and formal gowns, so that I would be able to walk and talk with him without embarrassment to either of us, or indeed to his courtiers, who were if anything more snobbish than the prince himself. The gentry set store by such things, so my aunt decided that I must do so, too.

Truth to tell, it came more easily to me than I first thought it might. My infant mind must have unconsciously registered the ways of my father's court, for I soon developed the manners and ways of speech that she deemed essential, and, although conscious that I was playing a part, I did as she bade me and became aloof and taciturn.

Of course, this cut me off from my fellow men, for there were only my aunt and Maximilian to whom I could talk as equals. My circle would grow slightly when Philip, Maximilian's son, returned to court, but I feared that he had been bred to the purple and might turn out to be an object lesson to me in the aloofness my aunt required. Unlike my normal self, I was on the point of becoming miserable when a ray of sunshine shone over the southern horizon, as Princess Marguerite was returned to her father from the French court.

With her, at least, I could be myself, and there were the shared experiences of the French court to regale the others with in the privacy of the royal chambers. For a time, laughter returned to my life.

When Philip did arrive at court, however, he was not what I expected. Every bit as lively and intelligent as his sister, he had a keen sense of fun. He took my aunt's word as to my identity, and from the first invited me to accompany him as an equal on his progresses through his lands. He was but three years younger than me, and was pleased to listen to my adventures; I think he had heard nothing like them before; although his father was a great teller of tales, they were in the main romances with but a grain of truth.

My presence in the court led to tension, however. Henry Tudor's treaty with France had strained relations between the countries, and Maximilian's decision not to expel me from his court only added to that. Tudor sent envoys to him, but Maximilian pointed out that Philip, not he, was Duke of Burgundy, and sent them on.

Philip met them after consultation with his council, and came into my aunt's chambers afterwards with a serious look on his face. 'I have denied you,' he said to me.

My aunt rose to her feet. 'Philip,' she began, and then, more formally, 'My lord . . .'

Philip's face changed immediately to a mischievous grin. 'I

have told the English envoys that Burgundy officially does not support the claimant – that's you, Richard.'

'Philip!' again from my aunt.

'On the other hand,' he continued, 'I have also told them that the demesnes and estates of my step-grandmother are hers and hers alone, and that I have no powers to control how the Duchess Margaret disburses her own income or what she chooses to do with her own personal resources.'

'I like that,' Margaret said, clearly relieved. 'It is succinct and diplomatic. And artful.'

'And also, as it happens, accurate,' the duke said, and bit into an apple.

'Will Henry accept that?' I asked.

'I doubt it,' he said. 'I imagine that I have enraged him, and the envoys talked of an embargo on English trade with Burgundy.'

Within the month that is exactly what had happened, but by then matters had taken another turn. Maximilian had received word that he had to leave for Vienna, where his father was ill and where there were pressing matters of state to be decided, but before he went there was evidence of the lengths Tudor was prepared to go to convince him that I was not Richard of York.

Henry's envoy, one of the official heralds, Garter King of Arms, was shown into the receiving chamber where we were all gathered. He bowed low to Maximilian, bowed to Margaret and bowed again to Philip, but to me he offered no mark of reverence.

My aunt was furious. 'It seems that you do not recognize my nephew Richard,' she said, 'since you do not deign to bow to him.'

'Madam, your nephew Richard is long dead,' the herald replied. 'My master bids me tell you that this is no Prince of York, and that he can show you the tomb of the prince, should you wish to see it.'

'A tomb is but a sepulchre, and may contain the bones of any thing,' I said, 'just as a crown may encircle the head of any man; but only a true king may wear it rightly. I marvel and am astonished that you think me dead. When I am enthroned in my kingdom, which I hope will be right soon, I shall not forget those words, while you, sirrah, will have cause to regret them.'

'It is well known, sir, that you are no prince, but a base-born native of Tournai, one Perkin Warbeck, the son of a bourgeois of the town, and whatever celebration Your Graces may make of him, you will find yourselves to be deceived in the end.'

'The name is Pierrechon Werbecque, to be precise,' I corrected him, 'and my aunt is already aware of the time I spent masquerading as that boy, so Tudor's lies can have no effect here.'

'You stand in my house, sirrah,' my aunt said to him, quivering with rage, 'and yet treat me, a princess of England, and my nephew, a prince born, with scorn and contumely. You will bear yourself with more decorum else, herald or no, I shall have you committed to prison to consider your behaviour.'

At this point Maximilian murmured something which I did not catch.

'No sir,' she replied, still furious, and turned back to the herald. 'I give you no credence, sir, but am aware that it is your master who has made you learn these words and say them in this way. Nonetheless, you must learn your manners in the presence of a princess.' She looked at the captain of the guard and indicated the herald. 'Throw him into the cells,' she said.

'Madam, you may not . . .' Philip began, but too late, for the guard was already escorting the herald out. As he was led away, his eyes were fixed on Maximilian. Not for a moment did they flicker towards me.

'Do not presume to tell me what I may and may not do in my own domains,' Margaret said.

'See, just what I told the English envoys,' observed Philip to his father, and both men burst into laughter.

For a moment Margaret stood with consternation on her face, and then she too laughed and said, 'All right, then, I shall observe the protocol. I shall let him cool his heels awhile, but I shall send to have him released within the hour. Diplomatic immunity, it has to be said, is a most inconvenient concept.'

Despite Tudor's wiles, however, by this time those in England who had retained their Yorkist sympathies were beginning to hear the rumours that I had returned, and some began to make their way over to my aunt's court at Malines, bringing money and promises of support from others still at home. Even from within the very court of Tudor himself they came, while their ranks were also swelled by exiled supporters of York and disaffected men who had not received the looked-for benefits from Tudor. My instructions at first were to stay aloof from them, but they gathered in ever-larger crowds at Malines, and my aunt decided that rumour had gone far enough, and that it was time for them to see me in the flesh and assess the truth of my claim for themselves.

She arranged an audience for some of the greater men among them. I met these lords for the first time that summer, when they entered my presence in Aunt Margaret's reception chamber. I was seated on a throne raised on a dais, and sat in silence as they gazed upon me. I felt most uncomfortable with all their eyes on me, each expecting . . . what? I did not know.

The silence grew, until my aunt said. 'Can you doubt him? Is he not the spit and image of my brother?'

'Your pardon, my lady,' said one of the clerics, 'but your brother Edward the king did not restrain his . . .' He paused, unsure of how to proceed, and I saw grins appearing on the faces of some of the men. There was a danger that the matter was about to become ridiculous.

'You were about to say that my father did not conserve his energies solely for the marriage bed,' I said. 'I know this only by rumour, of course, but I can assure you that I am the son of his marriage to my mother, Elizabeth Woodville. I am the second son and fifth child of King Edward IV of England.'

There was another silence while they assimilated this, and then one of the laymen stepped forward and asked, 'My lord, can you prove that you are who you say you are?'

My aunt said, 'He has satisfied me. I knew him immediately—'

'Nonetheless, madam,' I interrupted, 'it is natural that these lords, not knowing me as you do, will have their doubts. I have no wounds for you to place your fingers in,' I said, 'and know not how to convince you of who I am. I can but try; I can tell you my memories of my father and mother, my brother and sisters, my uncles and the court I lived in. Some of you, perhaps, will remember me as a child, and could question me on matters that you remember – perhaps even better than I do. Perhaps in that manner I can assuage your doubts.'

'Your lordship would do so only if you were able to tell us things that Richard of York – and he alone – could know,' the same man replied.

'And specifically, to be absolutely sure, things that Her Grace his aunt might not know,' added one of the others.

I caught sight of her expression and quickly told him, 'Yes, I see that. The trouble is that I do not know what matters were known only to the family and what were known to all. Perhaps if you were to ask me specific questions . . .'

I paused, and they stared silently at me. The silence grew longer, and still no one spoke.

'How is it that your brother died and not you?' one man asked finally.

'I was not at the Tower in the days after Bosworth,' I said. 'I last saw my brother Edward the morning after the battle, but I went into Westminster and did not return to the Tower. I do not know what happened to him; I never saw him again.'

151

'And how did you escape to Flanders?' They had all heard the story from my aunt.

'I was brought over,' I said, 'but I may not tell you the names of my saviours or their methods; many of them live yet, some in the domains of Tudor, so to speak would put at risk their safety.'

There was a nodding of heads at this; it was a fear that all could understand and most would share.

'Had you been old enough, sire,' put in another lord, 'on which side would you have fought at Bosworth?'

'A strange question,' I said, 'but the answer is clear. I should have fought at King Richard's side.'

'Even though he declared you illegitimate?'

'Not he, but Parliament,' I said, 'having heard the evidence. I did not hear it myself, being too young, but I am told that it was compelling.' I saw some of the older men nodding their heads. 'It was no fault of King Richard's that my birth was tainted, and no fault of my mother's, either. In any case, it would appear that Henry Tudor, in his goodness, has legitimized me again.' I smiled, and it seemed that the crisis had passed, for some smiled with me. I suddenly realized that they were not antagonistic, but men who were inclined towards belief, if only I could convince them of the truth.

'So you too would have been declared a traitor,' the questioner said.

'I fear I would,' I said. 'Truth is a spider's web which has entangled Henry Tudor more than once.'

'Where were you between the summer of King Richard's coronation and Bosworth, when you . . . the princes, I mean, were not seen in London?' another lord asked.

'In Yorkshire,' I said, relieved at finding something I could talk about with some authority. 'Edward and I were taken to Middleham and to Sheriff Hutton, and remained there in peace until Tudor's invasion. It was a happy time, and good country for a little boy. Then we were returned to the Tower, as the safest place.'

Several of the men nodded, and one said, 'Yes, I had heard such talk.'

'If you had heard it then so must others,' a man said gruffly from the rear rank. 'If it were common rumour then this lord might have had it from any source. This proves nothing. None of it proves anything.'

I nodded slowly. I could see that he was right; so could all of my audience.

'Most of what I can tell you is public knowledge,' I said, 'and what little private information I have would mean nothing to you. My aunt has listened to what I have had to say and has asked me questions; I can only say that my answers proved satisfactory to her. I do not know how to tell you more.'

There was another awkward silence. I rose to my feet. 'Perhaps,' I went on, 'if I were not on this dais, displayed like a haberdasher's wares, I might feel easier. Would you mind if I came and just walked around and spoke with some of you? Perhaps that way further questions might spring to your minds, or further memories to mine.'

In answer, there was a general shuffling of feet, which I took for acquiescence, and I stepped from the dais. 'I feel easier like this,' I said, and I sensed that they too preferred this less formal way of communicating. I looked around, anticipating questions, but none came, and I began to move around, looking into faces and trying to find familiarity there.

'Is this in order to seem like your father?' one of the men asked abruptly.

I looked at him. 'I'm sorry', I said, 'but I don't understand.'

'Have you been instructed in this behaviour?' asked another.

I looked blankly at him, and a third lord took pity on my incomprehension. 'It was a habit of His late Majesty's to mingle

153

in a company,' he said. 'He did not like to stand on ceremony –
he preferred face-to-face contact.'

'Thus is information given away,' said a disgusted voice. It
was the man who had first spoken to ask me for my proof, a
tallish lord with broad shoulders. 'He has told us nothing, and
yet you give him freely information about the behaviour of his
father. If he is a poltroon, then you have taught him how to ape
Edward.' His voice was angry, barely controlled.

I turned to protest. 'I truly did not know this about my
father,' I began, and then broke off. Around his neck the lord
was wearing an ornament, a letter 'M' fashioned in gold and
attached to a gold chain. A faint memory stirred at the back of
my brain.

'I know not who you are, sir,' I said, 'but methinks we have
met before.'

Suddenly, the others fell silent. I sensed that I was about to
undergo some form of test. 'Have we indeed?' the man said.
'Under what circumstances, sir?'

I shook my head. I knew there was something. 'May I?' I
asked, and then reached out to finger his chain and its pendant.
It meant something to me, I knew, but knew not what. 'Is this
your own?'

He nodded, and through the chain I felt a tension in him. I
sensed that I was on the verge of revealing something important.

'I have seen one such as this before,' I said uncertainly, and
the sense of expectation in the room became almost palpable.
I looked across at my aunt, but her face bore only a look of
puzzlement. Whatever I had dimly recalled was something she
knew nothing of.

I looked back at the golden letter, and began to grope for
what I needed to bring the memory to the surface. 'I was very
small,' I said, almost to myself, 'and had not long learned my
letters. I remember that I was very proud that I knew that it

was the letter "M". I cannot bring to mind the occasion . . .' I let the golden letter fall back onto his breast and struggled, but the memory was elusively, maddeningly, just beyond my reach. I stared at the 'M', and each man waited.

Then its owner reached up and took the letter in his hand, a hand wearing a golden ring.

And I remembered.

'My wedding,' I blurted out. 'It was my wedding. The "M" stands for Mowbray. It was my wedding day, the day on which I became Lord Mowbray through my marriage, and I did not want to give the shiny letter away, but was forced to do so. The golden "M" was for the knight who won the jousting tourney. It was the prize for the tourney.'

I looked at the man. 'Were you that victor, sir?' I asked.

He stared at me, and then dropped to one knee. 'Your Majesty,' he said. 'My liege, Robert Clifford is yours to command.'

I looked down at him, and then felt, rather than heard, the susurration as robes began to brush the ground. One by one the English lords in the room knelt to me. Across the tops of their heads I could see my aunt, her head nodding and her face split by an enormous smile.

Within a few days, news came that the Emperor Frederick III had died, and that Maximilian had been elected his successor as Holy Roman Emperor. By the same messenger, a summons came requiring me to accompany Burgundy's official ambassador, Duke Albrecht of Saxony, to Vienna for the funeral, and to represent England.

'Now, Richard,' my aunt said, 'recognized by your countrymen and by the emperor, you are a prince indeed.'

Princeling

December 1493 – November 1495

The church, the Stefanskirche in Vienna, was bright, with candles gleaming from every sconce and a silence which cloaked the whole of the building. In its centre a smaller wooden church had been built to house the body of the emperor, and I found it difficult to breathe, the air being thick with the incense and candle smoke which hung heavily over the congregation.

I had ridden to the ceremony with Maximilian as his honoured guest, recognized without question for who I was. Maximilian had arranged an audience only a few days before, in which I presented my case to his court and the assembled representatives of the various nations of the empire and of the rest of Europe. It was an opportunity not to be missed. In order to get the fullest effect and communication, Maximilian had me sit with his Latin secretary, Ludovico Bruno, for two days, preparing the speech (which Bruno delivered, not me) in Latin so that all would understand it.

I did not have as great faith as Maximilian did in the linguistic powers of his peers, but the speech was duly made, and my grievances against Henry Tudor and appeal for help, advice and support were heard by every ear that might be able to do something in my cause. More than that I could not have asked for.

Now I knelt with head bowed, in silence, as the great ceremony went on about me. I was clothed in magnificent robes and in the company of princes and the nobility of Europe, and not a man amongst them challenged my right to be there. I had ceremonial duties to perform as part of the funeral service – offering a banner, helm and shield at the bier, doing reverence and praying for the emperor's soul – doing that which a prince must do on such occasions.

After that I was a regular member of the new emperor's entourage, staying with him even at his wedding several months later. In the spring we set off together to tour the emperor's dominions, with me always riding at the right hand of Maximilian. Finally, after some months clambering through the rocks in the Tyrol, we turned our horses' heads once more towards Flanders.

'I am thinking,' Maximilian told me, 'of offering you Marguerite in marriage. How might you respond to that?'

'It is an honour most unlooked for, Your Majesty,' I said. 'I am delighted and flattered, but I had not thought to marry yet.'

'Well, think upon it now,' he said. 'She is all that you could wish for in a wife, surely?'

'She is indeed, sir,' I told him, not being completely honest. She was vivacious, amusing and intelligent, but I saw her as a friend merely, and was sure that she viewed me in the same light. In addition, she was not at all pretty. I knew how to deflect Maximilian from this course, however.

'I have nothing to offer the princess,' I said. 'I have no estates, nor any income, and no accomplishments save those of a fisherman. I could not in all conscience offer only these to your daughter.'

Maximilian grunted.

'Before I marry, I must win a kingdom,' I said. 'Then and only then can I stand before you, a prince of substance, not shadow, and ask you to give your daughter to me. I am the very essence of a landless knight from a romance, assailed by enemies on every side, my lands taken by a usurper who has taken my sister to wife, and with a world to conquer before I achieve the lady of my dreams.'

'Well said, Richard,' the emperor said, and clapped me on the back. 'A father could not wish for a finer answer. So it shall be, then! First, win your kingdom and then your wife!'

Truth to tell, my words had been calculated to act on him in just such a way. Maximilian was an incurable romantic, a lover of grand gestures and noble ideals. On his way to marry Mary of Burgundy, I had been told, he had concocted a set of stories which he wrote down, telling of all the trials he had had to undergo to win her hand and his adventures on the road to Burgundy – surviving encounters with wild beasts or falls from high mountains, swinging from ropes and evading exploding guns by the skin of his teeth – and each one of them a product of his fevered imagination.

He loved to listen to my own stories – the race down the Scheldt, the leap for Brampton's ship, the death of Bemoy and the endless shoals of cod – and no doubt considered them as fictitious as his own tall tales. He called me an 'umbzotler', which means a wanderer from place to place, and saw himself as cut from the same cloth. In some ways he was most unprincelike, which might be why we got on. He would rather hunt than administer kingdoms, rather walk than ride, rather dine off bread and cheese than a banquet, and habitually dressed like a peasant, to the consternation of the satin- and damask-clad courtiers who surrounded him.

'My grandson will be King of England,' he said. 'A happy thought.'

He had no sooner ridden a dozen paces more when a melancholy thought replaced the happy one. 'Unless you die before you become king,' he said. 'That would be a tragedy.'

'For me, too, sire,' I said, smiling.

He looked up at me. 'I meant for you,' he said, and then returned the smile. 'And for me, of course, also.'

'Unless you were to continue the struggle,' I said. 'That would make it less of a tragedy for all of us.'

'My children too claim their descent from John of Gaunt,' he said, 'but it is not a claim I could pursue . . .'

I reined my horse in. 'If I die on this quest, sire,' I said, 'then it matters not. What matters is what becomes of England. It cannot be left in the hands of a usurper.'

Maximilian looked perplexed. 'I do not see your point,' he said.

'Let me will it to you,' I said.

'Will what?'

'England.'

'What?' His massive jaw dropped open and he stared at me. Behind us the traipsing column juddered to a halt.

'If I make a will, leaving England to you and your descendants,' I said, 'then you have a legitimate claim to the throne if I should die without issue or am unsuccessful in my attempt to wrest England from Tudor.'

'You would do this?' he asked.

'With all my heart, sir. I can think of no man who would better administer the realm.'

'And in return, what do you want from me?'

'Nothing, sire, nothing,' I said. 'Unless you were prepared to lend me some troops and a few ships.' Maximilian had been adamant that he would not help me conquer England, but my suggestion had given him food for thought.

'It is not an impossibility,' he said. 'Let us see how the land lies when we reach Malines.'

When we got there, however, matters did not look at all promising. Robert Clifford, he of the golden 'M', having filled his mind with all the information he could gather from my aunt Margaret, had decamped and returned to the court of Henry Tudor, taking three or four of the others with him. Philip had proclaimed a counter-embargo against England. The

Burgundians were confiscating all the property of English merchants in their country, and the English were doing the same to Burgundian merchants in England and Calais. Maximilian, however, seemed to find it all quite amusing.

'Well, you have set England in a turmoil,' he said, coming into my aunt's chambers where we were all relaxing. He had a sheaf of papers with him, and looked from one to another of us as he spoke. 'And Ireland too. The Earl of Desmond has broken his bond to Henry and raised Munster in your name.'

'What's he doing in Germany?' asked Marguerite. 'What have they to do with Richard?'

'Munster, ignoramus, is a province of Ireland as well as a place in Germany,' Philip told her.

'Correct,' said Maximilian. 'You are proclaimed as Richard IV,' he added. 'I fear Desmond has little support, though; he is as badly organized as he ever was. There will be little comfort there. Meanwhile, Clifford is holding forth in Henry's court. He tells all who will listen that you were once Pierrechon Werbecque of Tournai, but says that you are not entitled to use that name either.'

'So he is telling the truth, then?' I said.

'Sadly, no,' he said. 'He claims that your true identity – forgive me, madam, for I must speak slander here – is that you are the secret love child of my stepmother-in-law and the Bishop of Cambrai.'

'Oh!' gasped Margaret, too shocked to speak, but Philip and Marguerite, after an initial stunned silence, burst into peals of laughter which would not subside.

'Henri de Berghes!' Marguerite cried. 'Surely not! The man is a saint of heaven! A less likely candidate – begging your pardon, madam – would be difficult to conceive.'

'Conceive! Excellent conceit!' Philip cried, and the two of them went off again into uncontrollable laughter.

The duchess snatched the paper from Maximilian's hand.

'He shall pay for this,' she said. 'How dare he spread such rumours!'

Maximilian shook his head. 'Not even your worst enemies would believe it of you and His Grace, mother,' he said. Then, barely suppressing a smile, he added, 'If any bishop were to be suspected, it is more likely his predecessor, given his enviable record in the production of offspring.'

'Oh!' said Margaret again. 'The very idea!'

Seeing my look of puzzlement, Philip explained. 'The last Bishop of Cambrai,' he said, 'was notorious. His illegitimate offspring were sadly under-represented at his funeral – only thirty-six of them were able to attend.'

Marguerite began to giggle, while Maximilian returned to his perusal of the documents. 'Ah,' he said. 'Henry is consolidating his position. You must have him worried, Richard. He has invested his second son, Henry, as Duke of York and King's Lieutenant in Ireland, so he means to stamp his authority. So now there are two Dukes of York. The other is but three years old, mind.'

He read a little further. 'Clifford is officially pardoned,' he said, 'and has named those he says support Richard. Ah! A list! This is his Epiphany gift to you, Richard: some of the more prominent men have been executed.'

'Such as whom?' I asked, and Maximilian passed me the missive with its attached list. Most of the names were unknown to me, but prominent at the top was one I knew well. 'Sir William Stanley!' I exclaimed. 'I would have thought him as loyal as anyone to Tudor.'

'He's married to Tudor's mother, isn't he?' said Maximilian.

'No,' I said, 'that's his brother. All the same, you'd expect some loyalty within the family.'

'No Stanley is loyal except to himself,' Margaret said. 'Thomas Stanley it was who sent his son to my brother Richard before Bosworth as an earnest of his loyalty and then left the lad in the lurch when he turned against the king. Had Richard been a harsher man he would have been within his rights to have Stanley's son killed.'

'And he did not?' asked Maximilian, surprised, his head jerking up from the manuscript he was perusing.

'Such was not my brother's way,' Margaret said.

'Perhaps Stanley knew it and took a gamble,' Philip said.

Marguerite looked across at him. 'God send you never have sons,' she said, 'if you think to gamble with their lives on the mercy of a king.'

'Stanley knew what Richard was like, all the same,' my aunt said. 'Richard should have had him arraigned for treason on the same day Will Hastings was put to death, but he pardoned him instead. He was a great warrior, my brother, but no politician, for all Tudor says.' She paused. 'So Stanley is dead.'

'So it seems,' Maximilian said.

'I cannot find it in my heart to feel sorry for that man, regardless of whether he was a traitor to Tudor or not,' my aunt declared. 'This whole shambles is his family's doing, and was from the outset. Had he and his brother done their duty at Bosworth Richard would have won, and Edward V would still be King of England.'

'I thought Edward and his brother, Richard here, had been declared illegitimate,' Philip said.

'So they were, but 'twas but a subterfuge. They would have been reinstated by now, Edward would be king and Richard – my brother, I mean – would have been back on his estates in the north.'

'And what would I have been?' I asked.

'Probably a relatively unimportant princeling,' my aunt said, with a certain relish, 'looking after your estates and collecting revenue for the king . . .'

'And heir to the throne, don't forget,' Philip put in.

Margaret raised her eyebrows. 'I think not,' she said.

'Edward, if he resembled his father even remotely, would have done his royal duty by now and provided an heir.' She shook her head. 'All this could have been so, if the Stanleys had supported Richard in his charge and put an end to Tudor's nonsense once and for all.' She drew her head up. 'So,' she declared, 'I am glad he is dead, for his treachery to my family, and not for his treachery to Tudor, who has done nothing to deserve loyalty. The wheels of God's justice roll slowly, Richard, but you can be sure your sins will find you out. Even if you're a Stanley.' She took the list from me and perused it, but there were no other names that gave her cause for comment, and she finally laid it aside.

'There is one thing that gives me pause for regret,' I said.

'What's that?' asked Philip.

'That they all seem to be so willing to embrace a lie. Clifford knows the truth of who I am. Surely he has told Tudor that – so why does he not believe? Why this purge of those who would be my supporters? Why not just accept the truth?'

I saw Marguerite shake her head. 'Whoever took you out of the Tower . . .'

'Hans Memling,' Maximilian prompted.

'He, then, did a great favour to your innocence, but has left you sadly lacking in knowledge of the ways of the world,' she said. 'I am but a child, Richard, but I am able to see something that you are not. Tudor knows who you are as well as Clifford does; as well as anyone does who has met you and talked to you. Who you are is not a problem, although Henry will try to tarnish you in the years to come. He simply wants to hold on to power; knowledge of you helps him in that, so although he knows the truth he will never acknowledge it. If you want his throne, Richard, you will have to fight him for it. That's the real truth.'

'Truth is a matter of perspective,' I mused. 'Hans said that to the emperor.'

'He did,' smiled Maximilian.

'You know he's dead, don't you?' Philip said.

'What?'

'Oh, you didn't know? Yes, he died a few weeks ago; it must have been while you were on the progress with my father.'

I looked at the floor, suddenly overwhelmed with a heavy sadness. 'He was a good friend to me,' I said. 'He saved my life, cared for me, and took me to safety, as he thought, with the Werbecques.'

Into the silence Marguerite said, 'I think you should rethink your quest for a throne, Richard.'

'Why so?'

'No king would put truth and the memories of an old friend before a quest for power. Are you really cut out for this?'

The news of the discovery and execution of some of my supporters was grave, and a choice had to be made – either to abandon the enterprise or to go ahead immediately before Tudor discovered the names of other, greater men who would flock to my banner. I plumped for the bolder course.

Thereafter matters moved quickly. I made a will in favour of Maximilian, as I had suggested. It was drafted in the name of Richard, King of England and France, Duke of York, Lord of Ireland and Prince of Wales – Maximilian insisted on the full set, even down to the claim to France, which no one had taken seriously since the days of Henry V, and insisted too that I sign it in the style to which I was laying claim, so for the first time I signed myself with the legal formula as the King of England – *Ricardus Angliae rex, manu propria.*

In return Maximilian found me credit with his bankers, and we were thus able to muster a small fleet of ships at Vlissingen. I sent more letters – to Ferdinand and Isabella of Spain, to the pope, to the kings of France, Portugal, Scotland and Denmark, and to lesser counts and lords throughout Europe, asking for support – and all the time the ships were being loaded with gunpowder and troops. That we were setting off from Vlissingen buoyed me up, for it was from there that my father had set off to reclaim his kingdom some twenty-three years before. He had been King of England six weeks later. Englishmen came to join my cause, but I was disappointed that almost all were common soldiers or adventurers. There were no great lords or earls, no minor nobility, no landowners: just a few knights and assorted tradesmen. There was a minor sprig of the Neville family, George; he was as far as my noble support went.

I have never claimed to be a general. I was fortunate in that I had by my side on this expedition Roderick de Lalaing, one of Maximilian's best captains, who was to be my military adviser, and on only the second day of the expedition he proved himself invaluable.

We sailed from Vlissingen at the start of July, and the next day the fleet arrived off the Kentish coast. There was a pebble shore shelving gently down to the sea, an inviting landing place. We stood off a few hundred yards from the shore and scanned the beach. There was no movement to be seen, and in the end I gave the order to land.

There was general excitement, with men preparing to climb into the boats to take them ashore, when Lalaing appeared in a small rowing boat from his own ship and came aboard mine.

'Sire, we know not what awaits us,' he said. 'I commend caution to Your Excellency. Make not so much haste to be ashore. We must reconnoitre and be sure of what is there.'

Even I could see the sense of that, and it was agreed to send a small landing party to explore the area. 'It would be wise, as far as possible, to send Englishmen,' Lalaing said. 'They know the language, and some may even know the area, and thus we may be able to get a more accurate picture. They are also, perhaps, less likely to be seen as an invading force.'

Again I agreed, and a group of about three hundred

embarked and were rowed to shore. They assembled on the beach, raised their standards and set off inshore.

We watched as the standards disappeared over the line of sand hills, and then we settled down to wait.

It was no more than an hour later that some of them appeared on the beach. We sent a boat in to pick them up, and they told an exhilarating tale.

'We marched a little way inland,' their spokesman said, 'and then a man-at-arms rode up and asked us whose men we were. "The Duke of York's," I replied, and he said, "We ask for no other lord in the world! We will do him all the honour, help and favour we can. Let him disembark, and all his company." Then he said he would bring us some ale, and rode away. I have come to tell you this, sire, so that you might come ashore and be welcomed.'

I was filled with joy by his words, but Lalaing shook his head. 'Let us wait a little longer,' he said. 'If true, it is but a joy postponed; if false, 'twill do no harm to be circumspect.'

We waited almost two hours more, and then at last figures began to appear on the beach, hailing the ships and waving agitatedly. At first there were only two or three of them, and Lalaing sent in some small boats to pick them up. As the boats neared the shore the men began to wade out to them, still shouting and gesticulating, and then more appeared, running over the shingle and hurling themselves into the sea.

The reason for their panic soon became clear. Soldiers, many more than had gone ashore, and some of them on horseback, came down onto the beach and began to lay about them. Soon the beach was littered with bodies. Men threw themselves into the water and were cut down, and the boats dared not go any closer to shore – any man who could not swim out to a boat was killed where he stood. I could only look on in horror.

No more than a score of the men I had sent ashore came back alive to the ship. One of them, a senior man, Richard

Harliston, who had been a naval commander for my father, told us what had happened.

'It is my fault, Your Grace,' he gasped. 'I believed them, and sent men back to ask Your Grace to land. Then, when you did not appear, a troop of cavalry lined up on the sandhills behind the beach. Even then I thought them to be a kind of guard of honour, but suddenly footmen rose up from the hills and rained down on us from all sides. Our men were caught unawares; those that did not die on the beach drowned in the water, and there remain but we few to tell the story. We can have no comfort of this country, sire. These men were armed and accoutred for battle; they were prepared for us.'

'How can that be,' I mused, 'when even we did not know where we were going to land?'

'It suggests, sire,' said Lalaing, 'that the whole of the coast may be warned and ready. We must try further to the north.'

'I am more likely to have adherents in the north,' I told him, 'but if the whole coast is forewarned, with Henry's men standing guard, then we might be better to try elsewhere. He will be expecting us to come from the east. What if we came from out of the west?'

'Where does your best support lie, my lord?' Lalaing asked.

'After recent events,' I said, 'I must confess I do not know.' I looked down at the chart on the cabin table. 'Let us try the West Country,' I said. 'The men of Cornwall bear no love for Tudor, I hear, and I know there are men there who will support my cause.'

'What men, my lord?'

'Great men,' I said. 'There are lords . . .' I tailed away. The truth was that I did not know of any lords who might help me. I was relying on the common people to take me to their hearts and recognize me as king.

There was a long silence, and then Lalaing said, 'To the west, then.'

He returned to his own ship and we set off down the Channel, standing out of sight of the coast so as to avoid any of Tudor's ships that might be looking for us. I enjoyed these days at sea; this was a short hop by my sea-going standards, but a man who has no more to worry about than whether the wind is in the right quarter is a happy man indeed. Such was I as we scudded down the Channel with not a Tudor in sight.

I even revelled in what happened next; a storm blew up, an easterly that gathered strength and then hurled itself down on us and buffeted us down the Channel, throwing us from one side of the ship to the other, tossing and heaving our small ships this way and that, and driving us far to the west.

When finally the squall died down after three days we were out in the ocean, out of sight of any land. Nine of our vessels were in sight, scattered all over the sea, but the other five, including Lalaing's, were nowhere to be seen. A few men had been lost overboard, and not a ship had a full complement. Our own captain was unconscious, having struck his head on a beam at the height of the tempest, and it fell to me to take command, as there was not as experienced a sailor as I among the lot of them. I resumed acquaintanceship with the astrolabe, determined our position and persuaded the crew to set sail for the nearest port – which happened, as luck would have it, to be Cork.

We limped into the port, a sorry sight, the ships battered and bedraggled, jury-rigged and with rags for sails, but I utilized some of the treasure we had brought to buy stores and make repairs, and with the help of the mayor, who remembered me from my stay in the city four years before, in a few days we had found three or four extra crewmen and were ready to go to sea again. For to sea we had to go; Desmond, it appeared, was still in rebellion against Tudor, and was besieging the town of Waterford, further to the north-east on the southern coast of the island. I decided, in the absence of Lalaing, whom I presumed had been blown further away, to sail up the coast and join the siege.

On the voyage, not more than thirty miles from Cork, we had our first bit of luck. We were moving along the coast and had reached a town called, I think, Yochill, when the masthead reported that in the harbour was a ship flying the English colours.

'An English ship is fair game,' I announced to my crew, and told them I was going to take it as a prize. This raised a cheer, and I collected a party of volunteers from among the Englishmen we had left and rowed in small boats into the harbour, while the rest of the fleet remained outside and blockaded the harbour entrance. We landed on the mole and I led the men along the harbour and lined them up alongside the ship.

'What ship are you?' I called into the silent vessel.

Two or three loungers appeared from where they had been lying on the deck, and a figure appeared on the forecastle. 'Who wants to know?' he called.

'I am Richard of England, Duke of York and true heir to the throne, come to claim the crown of England,' I replied. 'I repeat, what ship are you?'

'The *Christopher*, out of Plymouth,' he said. 'What business do you have with us?'

'I commandeer this ship,' I said, 'all who sail in it and any cargo on board in my cause, which is just before heaven.'

'It is not just to take a ship by force, Your Grace,' he said, and came down towards the gangplank. 'To do so is an act of piracy, which must be answered in the courts.'

'I shall give you a receipt for your ship,' I said, 'and return it to you when I have achieved my objective. I shall, in time, pay for all goods I seize. How many crew do you have?'

'But ten,' he said.

'And your cargo?'

'Iron, sixty tons of it, and wine from Spain.'

'Consider your cargo confiscate. I will sell it in the town here. I am sure there will be ready buyers. Is it your own ship?'

'No, sir. I am but the master.'

I stepped onto the gangplank and walked across to him. 'I am sorry to do this to you,' I said, 'but my needs are urgent. I will take all of your men onto my ships, for I have need of experienced hands. You too can command a vessel for me, unless your conscience bids you otherwise.'

He nodded out towards the harbour entrance. 'All those ships are yours?' he asked.

'They are.'

'And if I refuse to hand her over?'

'Blood will be shed unnecessarily,' I said. 'One way or another, I will take her. You cannot get her out of this harbour without a fight.'

He sighed. 'Piracy it is, then. Do what you will, my lord,' he said. 'Give me a paper under your seal that absolves me of blame, assure me that my men will be well treated, and the ship and cargo are yours.'

'A wise decision,' I told him.

It took no more than a few hours to sell the iron and wine to local merchants, although it has to be said that the master blanched at the price we got, and insisted on being given another paper explaining that he had no part in the sale or the prices realized, which had been forced upon him. His crew were rowed out to the fleet, where they were distributed among the ships, and the captain himself joined my flagship as temporary master until my own captain recovered. From this little venture I had gained extra men, an extra ship and some cash and, which was more, had restored some of the faith in me which had been lost along with three hundred men on the pebble beach in Kent. Before nightfall we were on our way, standing out for Waterford.

Desmond was astonished to see me. 'I'd heard you might

be coming,' he said, 'but I thought it was Saxonland you were aiming for.' Like many of his countrymen, he referred to England in that way, and called us 'Saxons'.

I told him what had happened, and he said, 'Sure, never mind. When we take Waterford Tudor'll feel it a hard enough blow. It's solid for him. Now your ships are here we can try a combined attack by land and sea.'

'Not yet,' I said. 'Let us try the soft approach first.' I dictated a demand that the town surrender to me and sent it to be read before all the city gates the following morning. 'It'll be ignored,' Desmond said, and it was, so an attack was decided upon.

'You won't be taking part,' he said, 'and I'm having no argument about that. You'll stay here.' Here was a place called Passage, at the mouth of the river. 'I'm not having you exposed,' he said. 'Now that you're here, you give legitimacy to the cause, and if you should happen to get yourself killed then there'd be nothing worth fighting for.'

I made my protest, but he was adamant, and with the next day's tide my fleet sailed upriver towards the town, leaving me sitting on the headland watching events, like Xerxes at Salamis, and just as useful.

No headway was made on that first day. The walls were stormed in one or two places just to test the town's defences, and the fleet stood out of range while Desmond conducted his observations.

He came back to Passage at nightfall.

'After Waterford, what plans do you have?' I asked him over our evening meal. 'I am newly arrived, and have no knowledge of what you purpose.'

'Waterford is the stronghold of Saxon sympathies in Ireland,' he said. 'After we take it, we march on Dublin. By then the whole of the country will be raised, and will join us in large numbers.'

'I am flattered that so many men of Ireland have rallied to my cause,' I told him. 'It speaks much for their loyalty.'

'Well, now, I'm going to be honest with you,' he said. 'The only one doing any flattering there is yourself. You see, it's not so much loyalty to you, Your Grace. It's more resentment of Waterford and its allegiances. Revenues are taken by England. The wealth of the city is drained away to England; the same applies to Dublin. All over Ireland there are people who resent paying their hard-earned money to a foreign power. What it boils down to is that we want the Saxons out of Ireland, and this is the best way of achieving that, because you give men a focus.'

I stared at him. 'But you're fighting for me,' I said. 'I am an Englishman. If we win I'll be King of England.'

'We'll take Ireland,' he said, 'and then we'll take England. Then we'll give you England, and you will give us Ireland. England will rule itself, and Ireland will rule itself. No more Saxons here, no more Welsh Tudors there. A fair exchange, is it not?'

'I must say, I had never thought to be King of Ireland,' I said. 'It seems to me a fair bargain. But who will rule Ireland?'

'That would be me,' he said. 'Although I doubt whether the title of king would sit easily on these shoulders. I'd have to find another title, I think. It'd amount to the same thing in the end, though.' He stretched and said, 'I'd better get some sleep. We'll take the town tomorrow or the day after, and then you can ride through the gates in triumph.'

'But the main victim will be England?' I asked.

'True,' he said, 'but there are few enough Saxons actually behind the walls. It's a message really.'

He left me to mull this over.

Despite his confidence, however, the town did not fall, and showed no signs of so doing over the next few days. On the contrary, they sallied forth on a number of occasions, and on one of these took a large number of Desmond's men prisoner, and the next morning a row of heads festooned the gateways and battlements.

In the harbour, things were no better. The guns mounted on Waterford's walls were bigger and had a longer range than those on the ships. The detonations were painful even at the distance away I was, and if I went any closer the sound of the cannon was awful, and I was forced to clap my hands over my ears to keep out the horrendous percussions. One of my ships was sunk, hit by enormous stones thrown from the battlements by the town's biggest gun. The defenders even essayed a raid out of the inner harbour, and four of my ships were captured, including the *Christopher*, which had been in my fleet less than a se'en-night.

After a week or so Desmond admitted defeat. 'We can't take this town,' he told me. 'The men's hearts are not in it, and the ships can't get close enough to engage. It's too well defended.'

'What do we do then?' I asked, deferring to him, as always, on military matters.

He shook his head. 'Return to Cork,' he said. 'Return, consolidate, make a new plan.'

Thus the next morning the siege was abandoned and the retreating ships picked me up as they sailed past Passage. The captain of the *Christopher* was livid.

'You promised me, sir, a good price for my ship,' he said.

'I did no such thing,' I told him. 'I gave you a receipt for your ship, and said I would return it to you when I had achieved my objective. That is now impossible, clearly, but, as I told you, I shall, in time, pay for all goods I seize.'

'But when, sire, when?' he wailed.

'When I am King of England,' I said.

He looked at me, shook his head and walked away. Truth to tell, I was beginning to share his disbelief. Unless some noble prince or lord came to my aid, I could not see my venture ending in success.

Before long, success seemed even further away. Tudor sent troops to Ireland, and it soon became clear that Desmond's men were in no fit state to give battle. 'You'll have to disappear,' he told me. 'Go north, away from danger. You've sent your letters off – maybe some other prince will offer succour.' I had written to Maximilian, but felt that I had taken him a step further than he was prepared to go, at least unless there was some success to show. My letters to Charles had not been answered, although my aunt told me that she had received some encouragement from the King of Scotland. If I sailed north, I would at least be nearer to his domains if I had to escape from Tudor's clutches. 'I have friends in the north,' Desmond said. 'They can hide you.'

'And you?'

'I must stay here,' he said. 'The rebellion has to be held to-gether.'

'I should stay, too, then,' I said.

'No.' He shook his head. 'You need to be safe. If I'm fighting in your support it's a legitimate cause; if not, I'm a traitor. If you die, I'm a traitor to Henry. No, I need you safe, at least.'

'But powerless,' I said.

'Now, hasn't that been the case all along?' he said. 'Give us time. We will rise again, don't worry. You'll find that Irishmen have unusually long memories – they remember things that happened generations before they were born. This will not go away, even if you do.'

'Give me England and you'll get Ireland,' I told him. 'I prom-ise it.'

I was smuggled out of Cork into a wet and windy dawn at the beginning of winter. With me went eighty or so of the men who had embarked at Vlissingen: all that was left. By now four men in particular had become my inner circle – George Neville, John Heron, a former mercer, Nicolas Astley, a clerk, and

Edward Skelton, whose family were landowners in Cumbria – loyal and brave men all, but not warriors, not nobility.

We rode north along tracks that could barely be made out as the marsh and bogland encroached upon them, and hid ourselves in hovels made out of turf and filled with filthy smoke. I was entertained by chieftains who covered themselves in grease and wore thick homespun plaid and waged continual and relentless war against their neighbours on every side.

I soon understood what Desmond had meant about Irishmen's memories; at each stop I was regaled with tales of how Mag Aenghus of the Clipped Ear had stolen the cattle of Domhnaill the Awkward and then drowned his kinsman Brian of the Blind Eye who had pursued him to the Pool of Baidhill to avenge the death of his uncle Calbach the Dwarfish and so on ad infinitum, so that the families were still at loggerheads even unto the present day. When I asked how long ago all this happened it turned out to have been before the days of the Conqueror over four hundred years ago.

After a few weeks of wandering through the mire I was delivered into the hands of a chieftain named Conn Ua Domnaill at a castle called Sligech. It was a poor place, filled with cattle and horses, and with the most abominable smell of unwashed bodies. 'I'm not the chieftain,' he told me, 'that's my father, but I welcome you in his name. My father is tied by a blood bond to Desmond, and will see you safe to wherever you wish to go. Where might that be? What is your next destination?'

We were sitting in his smoke-filled hall, with the noise of shouting and screeching all around, feasting on half-raw meat and drinking blood mixed with milk, and my first thought was to respond, 'Anywhere,' but politeness stilled my tongue. Poor it might be, but I was the man's guest. 'I don't know,' I said.

His father arrived the next day, Aedh the Red, son of Niall the Rough. I had but little time to ponder what sort of a man

Niall would have had to have been, to be known as 'the Rough' among people like these, for Aedh had hardly entered the castle before word came that a force was on its way to confront him, and all men were called to arms.

The clan's armour and weapons, like their memories, dated from the time of the Conqueror, but of their ferocity and determination there was no doubt. As a guest of the house, honour dictated that I should fight on the side of my host, which gave me not a little concern. 'What is the quarrel about?' I asked.

'Let me think,' Conn said. 'Yes, Eogan Ua Concobair, the grandfather of these two brothers who march against us today, would not let my great-grandfather water his horses at the stream of the willows . . .'

'Never mind,' I said wearily. 'Where do we fight?'

'Have you ridden a horse in battle?' Conn asked me. He was helping me into a coat of chainmail that he had borrowed from another chieftain. A sword, shield and helmet completed the accoutrement.

'No,' I told him. 'In fact, I've never been in a battle.'

The information stopped him dead, and he stared at me. 'A prince of the Saxons, sure, and never fought for your lord?'

'Never been called on,' I said.

'Not killed your man?'

I shook my head.

'Blooding today then,' he said, 'if we come through it safe. I'd best not put you astride a horse, though. You'd be better on foot.'

I had with me but three score or so of the men I'd left Vlissingen with, but some of them at least were trained warriors, and when I offered them the choice it was clear that they would rather be fighting than sitting in a damp, smoky castle.

'If you're not used to our way of fighting,' Conn said, 'it were best you and your men were in the second line. It is not the place of greatest honour, but if God wills it you will not be needed; my father will destroy the Concobairs.'

We marched out, foot and horse alike, and lined up on the banks of a river a few miles away. 'We have a surprise for them,' Conn told me. 'They didn't think my father was here, and expected to catch us unawares. Now they'll have their eye wiped.' As he had suggested, my men were put in the second line, behind the men of his own clan and perhaps twenty paces from the river itself.

The enemy throng were not long in arriving, and like us they were accoutred in armour and carrying weapons that would not have disgraced a battle of five hundred years ago. They lined up on the opposite side of the river, foot in the centre and cavalry on the flanks, just as our own force was arrayed.

I realized that I was afraid, more afraid than I had ever been before. I hefted the unfamiliar sword in my hand, and gripped my shield more tightly, and then there came a new revelation. The fear I felt was not for myself, but for the safety of those whom I had led into this situation.

'This is not your fight,' I said to Skelton, who was standing beside me.

'I know,' he said. 'No matter. We follow our lord.'

I turned to George Neville on the other side. 'This is not your fight,' I said. 'I have to stay, for I am Conn's guest, but there's no need for anyone else to die in his cause. Take the men and go.' I had appointed him commander; unlike most of the rest of us, he had actually been in a battle – he had earned his knighthood by fighting for Henry Tudor at Stoke.

'We're soldiers, Your Grace,' he said. 'We might as well see it out. There would only be dishonour in leaving now.'

I turned again to Skelton; oddly, he too had fought at Stoke, but on the other side, for the rebels against Tudor. 'He's right, Your Grace,' he said. 'We all knew what might come when we followed you. The path of honour can lead down some strange byways.'

'At least allow the men to go if they wish,' I urged. 'They need not stay.'

Neville spoke again. 'They all know the options,' he said. 'They could have refused yesterday, but they did not. Where you go, we go, even into a ridiculous quarrel like this one.'

I turned to look at the men lined up behind us. The nearest, Heron and Astley, had overheard the conversation, and their cheerful grins suggested that Neville had gauged them rightly. I shrugged. 'So be it,' I said, and turned again to face forward.

For some time the two groups threw at each other nothing more dangerous than insults and epithets, but in the end the invader decided that enough words had been spoken, and part of his cavalry entered the water of the shallow stream away to our right. Some of our own rode down to meet them, and the insult hurling stopped while the two sides tested each other out.

I was unprepared for the ferocity of it. One of the enemy came forward, shouting and roaring, his horse at the gallop, and launched two spears in quick succession at Aedh, Conn's father. The old man ducked under the first and batted the second to one side as he urged his own horse forward. The spearman was ready, his sword drawn, but Aedh rode his horse directly into the other's mount, knocking it over into the fast-flowing water. Then he reined round, and as his opponent rose to his feet, his mail dripping, Aedh swung back-handed and smote his head clean from his shoulders. Head and helmet flew into the centre of the stream, where they eddied a little and then sank, leaving only traces of red in the water. The trunk, meanwhile, sank to its knees and remained upright until the man's own frightened horse righted itself and barged into it, knocking it too into the foaming stream.

A roar went up from both sides, and then the two cavalry detachments met in the centre of the river, hacking and tearing at each other. I saw five, ten, a dozen men go down, blood spouting from their wounds, and friend and foe alike rode over them, intent solely on doing more damage.

For a moment it seemed that the struggle was going against us, as Aedh and his men fell back, regrouping on the near side of the water. Immediately another shout rose up, and the line of infantry on the opposite bank surged forward. A hail of arrows and spears preceded them, and we were hard put to keep our own shields up in the face of it.

Conn was unconcerned. He waited until the worst of the missile shower had passed and then advanced his front line at a run to the bank of the river. We shuffled along in their wake, but our intervention was not needed. Conn kept his own men on the riverbank, thrusting downward at the enemy in the water and denying them access to the bank. Meanwhile Aedh's cavalry had reached the near side of the stream, and there they turned and regrouped before driving back into the water. At the same time the cavalry to our left also began to cross, and it soon became clear that there were not enough enemy cavalry to hold them. On both flanks the enemy troops began to give way, and before long our own horsemen had driven their opponents back so far that even I could see that they had lost touch with their foot.

The fighting continued in front of us, with not a single man of the enemy breaching Conn's line, and then Aedh and some of his men appeared on the opposite bank. Of the enemy cavalry there was no sign.

'Brian, son of Tadhg,' Aedh called out, standing in his stirrups. 'Brian, son of Tadhg.'

The shouting died down, and Conn signalled to his men to stop fighting. A silence fell, broken only by the shrieks and moans of the wounded and dying.

'Brian, son of Tadhg,' Aedh called again.

A man called from near the centre of the river. 'Brian is dead, Aedh Ua Domnaill. There he lies, near the flatstone.'

Aedh spurred his horse forward and looked at the corpse indicated. 'Eogan Blindeye, then,' he called. 'Is he here?'

'He is, but he too is dead,' came the answer.

'Then who commands here?'

'I,' said a youngish man in the centre of the line, his brow streaming blood and his clothes sodden red. 'I, Diarmait Ua Dubhda, command these men.'

'If Brian and Eogan are dead,' Aedh said, 'do we need continue this quarrel? I hold no grudge against you, Diarmait, or any of your blood. Bury your dead and leave with honour, or stay where you are and die with honour. It is all one to me.'

'Do you give us safe passage?'

'As far as your homes, yes,' Aedh called, 'but if I see four men of the Ua Dubhda together carrying arms thereafter, then I claim my right to their heads. I claim your own person as hostage. Agreed?'

'Agreed,' Diarmait called, and there was a general relaxation of tension along the whole of the line. He waved an arm, and his men began to pull back to their own side of the stream, dragging their dead and wounded with them. Conn instructed his own men to do the same, and within the space of a quarter of an hour the river was clear of bodies. There were fourteen dead on our side and, we later learned, more than three score on the other. I was astonished to see that members of the two opposing sides were now mingling and talking like old friends, some laughing and clapping each other on the back. I realized I was never going to understand the way of the warrior.

After supervising the transportation of his dead for burial, Diarmait came across the river to join Conn and Aedh on our journey back to Sligech, and formally put himself into Aedh's hands as a pledge for future peace.

I had fought in my first battle, although 'fought' is the wrong word, for all I had done was stand and wait for the enemy to approach, and had not used my weaponry at all. Still, I had done as much as many others on that day, and I took consolation that the fear I had felt was not for myself, but for others, so I had learned something about my nature.

'Thank you for your help, my lord,' Aedh said to me.

'I did nothing, sir,' I said, 'but stood in line as directed, with my men.'

'Conn should have given you a place in the front line, as having greater honour,' he replied, 'but no matter. You were true to your honour as a guest. Who are you, anyway?'

Conn told him, and he reined in his horse to stare at me. 'So you are the Saxon prince,' he said. 'I have messages for you that could not be delivered to Cork, for you had left.'

I looked at him, waiting, but he said, 'I mean written messages, not words by mouth.'

'Do you know what they say, sir?' I asked.

He shook his head. 'I have not the skill of reading,' he said, 'though it is a wonderful accomplishment, I know. I do know who they are from, however, and some of what they contain. It is the King of Scotland himself who writes to you, and I know that he wishes you to be his guest as you have been mine. You are summoned to Scotland, if you are of a mind to go there.'

Peregrinator

November 1495 – September 1496

Of the thousands of men who had sailed from Vlissingen, there were but four and twenty of us left when we reached the town of Stirling, where I was to be received by the king. I had released all of the men from any bond to me after the fight at the stream. A few had stayed to ply their trade in Ireland, living on blood sausage and milk and fighting their neighbours; some had decided to return to Cork to try to find a passage back to the continent. The rest of us were a tattered remnant of an invasion force, and even I had to admit that we were a sorry spectacle.

The common soldiers were found lodgings in the town, and I and the companions of my inner group were taken up to the castle, where I alone was ushered into the presence of the king for a private audience.

'Your Grace,' he said, rising from his chair and directing me to sit in a similar one opposite his. ''Tis well I know your history,' he said, 'for I do not think that I would recognize you as a prince of England in your present guise.'

He grinned, and I returned it. 'Your Majesty must forgive . . .' I began, but he held up a hand and stopped my flow.

'James,' he said. 'My name is James. You can call me "Your Grace" when we're being formal in public, but in private like this we are just James and Richard. We don't use "Majesty" in Scotland, by the way; we leave that epithet to upstart Tudors.'

He settled back in his chair. 'Apart from what you say and

the word of those who believe in you, I don't suppose you have the slightest evidence that you are a prince of England?'

'None whatsoever, my . . . Your . . .'

'James,' he prompted.

'None whatsoever, James.'

'That's a pity, but no matter,' he said. 'Two men who are strangers can become friends regardless of their stations in life, I think, be they equal or unequal. Whether you are a prince or no, you are a thorn in England's side, and that is all I need to know.'

'That is somewhat cynical, James,' I said.

'I prefer "pragmatic",' he replied.

'Either way, it is the way most of the princes I meet seem to feel.'

'Do you want help or not?'

'I do,' I said. 'I want to drive Tudor out of England.'

'Then we are agreed,' James said. 'What more is needed for the moment? I expect you are tired, and suggest that you retire to your chamber. We can look further into the matter on the morrow.'

I bowed and went off gratefully. Regardless of his thoughts, feelings and possibly even doubts about me, James turned out to be a generous host. He provided me with, which was a blessing in itself, a comfortable bed to lie in.

The next morning his generosity continued. I found sumptuous clothing laid out for me, good food to eat and an invitation to join him in his council chamber at my own convenience. This time we were not alone, but attended by such members of his council as happened to be in Stirling.

'Perhaps you would like to introduce yourself, sir,' the king said to me, 'and tell a little of your history.'

I composed myself, and then began a formal narrative: 'I think you are not unaware, O King, of the misery which befell the issue of Edward, King of England, the fourth of that name.

In case you do not know, I am his son, saved from slaughter by the beneficence of most high and almighty God. For my father Edward, when he was dying, appointed as guardian of his sons his brother Richard, whom he knew to be loyal and who needed not to be loaded with favours to be attached to his sons. But alas, to my misery it happened otherwise than he imagined, for Richard was overthrown, and his successor was not the guardian of our line but almost its extinguisher. Behold, suddenly the cruel tyrant, seized with ambition to be king, ordered that my brother Edward and I should be killed together.'

I paused, and saw that I had their interest, if not their total acceptance or belief, and went on to give an outline of my adventures.

'So, you admit that you are Perkin Warbeck of Tournai, as Tudor claims?' a bearded lord asked when I had finally come to an end.

'I do not know that name, sir,' I told him, 'but I was at Tournai, and lived as Pierrechon Werbecque for some time.'

'Tudor has Englished the name,' James said.

'Your career seems to have lost some momentum,' put in an elderly lord. 'The events at Deal in Kent and at Waterford have undermined your plausibility, I think, and along with them your chances of success.'

I must have bridled a little, for James stepped in to mollify me. 'I think my lord Huntly is referring to your plausibility as a military leader, perhaps, rather than meaning to cast doubt on your identity,' James said.

The lord grunted and nodded his agreement.

'I have never claimed to be a military leader, Your Grace,' I said. 'I have much to learn in that aspect of a king's duties.'

'Clearly,' Huntly said, and shook his head.

'Nonetheless,' James said, 'it will be necessary to counter these reverses if you are to have any credibility at all. People will not follow someone whose career demonstrates a singular

184

lack of success. You have public acclaim, Your Grace, and the support and friendship of powerful princes, but it is success, tangible success in some venture, that will make people look at you in a different light.'

'Might I ask about Deal?' I said. 'The men who went ashore there and were taken – what happened to them? Do you know?'

'Those English who survived were hanged for treason,' said one of the council. 'Of the foreigners taken we know nothing.'

'So Englishmen have died for me,' I said.

'Too many, for what you have achieved,' said Lord Huntly. 'That's what I mean by your plausibility. No man wants to follow a lord whose fortunes are on the wane.'

'We do have the opportunity, I think, to achieve something, though,' James said. 'Tudor faces the threat of domestic re-bellion and foreign invasion, and that insecurity hinders the marriage arrangement which he is anxious to make between his son Arthur and the Spanish princess, Catherine. Both he and I wish to maintain the truce between us for the time being, but of course he is fortifying Berwick and has issued commissions of array in Yorkshire. We hear that he is even paying fees and wages on time, so he must be anxious.'

The table laughed heartily at the king's observation.

'What do you expect from Scotland?' The question came from a lean, bearded lord who sat on the king's immediate right.

'If His Grace feels able to help,' I said, 'I should like to raise an army. If I could march a reasonable distance into England I am sure that there are those who would rally to my cause, as indeed they did in Ireland.'

'And what does Scotland get in return?' asked Huntly.

'The enduring friendship of the new King of England, if nothing else,' I told him, and there was a scornful 'Hah!' to follow my words.

'But I am sure that some arrangements can be made that are satisfactory to both parties,' I offered.

One of the lords muttered, 'Berwick, for a start,' and there was a susurration of agreement.

'You realize, of course,' said Huntly, 'that if you fail in your attempt to take Henry's throne then you are placing Scotland in a situation in which Henry might feel himself to be justified in invading us? You could well bring down the country, if His Grace is foolhardy enough to support you.'

Again there was a murmur round the table, and the king said, 'Our foolhardiness is a constant irritation to my lord Huntly.'

Huntly looked not a whit chastened, and said, 'As long as Your Grace is aware of the dangers, even if this English lord is not.'

'I am, sir,' I said. 'I realize what a risk it is you would be taking.'

There was a silence that stretched uncomfortably until James broke it. 'Thank you for your attendance, Your Grace,' he said. 'We must now debate with our council as to what steps to take. Please consider our castle your own for the remainder of the day until dinner time, when we shall speak again.'

'Your Grace,' I said, bowed and left them to their deliberations.

I went into the town to see that my men were being looked after. Like me, they were revelling in edible food and real beds, and spirits were as high as I had seen them since we quit Waterford.

On my return to the castle I found my chamber filled with clothes, and a tailor anxious to busy himself with them. Skelton, Heron, Neville and Astley had appeared too, with Heron choosing cloth for me, apparently anxious to demonstrate some of his skill in his old trade. 'King James has sent you some of his own garments for now,' the Scottish tailor said, 'which it is my duty to alter for Your Grace. In addition he has ordered me to measure Your Grace's person and make some clothes more appropriate in size and style. I trust that this meets with Your Grace's approval.'

I looked at him. 'I fear,' I said, 'it is a question of funds . . .'

'No matter, sire,' he said. 'His Grace has requested that the bill be sent to him, so Your Grace need have no reservations on that score.'

I happily accepted this aspect of the arrangement, and submitted to being measured for my new suits. The tailor and Heron had barely finished with me when a courtier arrived and asked for my presence in the king's chamber.

'They have agreed to my requests concerning you, Richard,' James said. 'At present, the council will not commit itself to aiding you in an invasion of England, but that, I think, can only be a matter of time. In the meantime you are to have an allowance of one hundred and twelve pounds a month, which should be sufficient for all your needs.'

'Your Grace is most generous,' I said. It was indeed a great deal of money, although it has to be said that a Scottish pound does not have the same value as an English one.

'James, in private,' he reminded me, and then went on: 'Next week we move eastward, first to Perth and then to Edinburgh. You will have to tell your story again, I fear, to the whole council in assembly. If they then approve, matters can be moved on somewhat. There will be a price for Scottish support, of course.'

'I have no doubt of it,' I said. 'But I am sure it will be a price worth paying – for England.'

The council meeting was held in Perth, and I prepared thoroughly for it. 'Emphasize the suffering you have undergone,' Skelton told me, 'and the wanderings far from home. The Scots love to wail about being far away. It will touch their hearts. They enjoy misery. And remember to weep a bit; keep an onion in your kerchief or something. Tug at their heart strings.'

And so my presentation to the council became something of a performance, with exaggeration of the suffering and no mention whatever of the fun I had had; emphasis on the misery of my plight while the joys of honest work were ignored. Maximilian and Philip were painted as fair-weather friends. I did not actually tell them any lies, but I was sailing as close to the wind as I dared. Old Jehan and Pierre Jean would not have recognized my description of the times I was in their company, for in my entire speech there was no mention of laughter. It was, I suppose, justifiable, but I did some good men a great disservice that day.

Huntly in particular listened to my performance unmoved, his face as granite as the city he came from, but other lords were more amenable, and by the end of the session I had had the effect I wanted, for the council voted to support my cause with arms. Their fee was that I should surrender the town of Berwick to James as soon as I was able to do so, and pay him the sum of fifty thousand marks within two years of my coronation. The money was in truth a small price to pay; I did not have it, and would not be expected to pay it if I lost, and if I won then the wealth of England would far outweigh such a sum. On the other hand, I signed away Berwick with a heavy heart, for I remembered the rejoicing at my father's court when my uncle Richard had returned from taking it just before my father's last Christmas on this earth.

James began to work immediately with the idea of crossing the border in spring, although it was fully a year before anything of the sort happened. He arranged wapynschawings, a sort of moot at which the able-bodied put in an appearance to show willing, and I was called in to attend some of these to demonstrate to his subjects exactly what it was they were fighting for. The plan was to cross the border sometime in spring to allow my supporters to rally to me before we advanced south on Tudor. Both James and I wrote letters – to supporters, to

Maximilian and Philip, to my Aunt Margaret, to the pope and to heads of state such as Ferdinand and Isabella – all designed to get international support for my cause.

But in the midst of all this took place the most momentous event of my entire life, on a freezing cold day in Edinburgh just before the beginning of Advent. The rain had come on ferociously in a sudden squall from the north-west as I was dismounting at the main gate, and I had ducked into a stable ready to leave my horse and run across the courtyard and into the castle as soon as a groom had settled him. I remember the rain beating on the roof of the hut, and outside it poured in torrents, making a solid curtain of water between me and the dryness.

I was not the only person in the stable. A group of three ladies stood sheltering, and as I turned around each of them dropped deep curtsies and modestly kept their heads bowed.

'My riding cloak is wide and capacious enough to shelter all three of you ladies,' I said, demonstrating these attributes, 'and I should be delighted to allow you use of it to gain the safety of the doorway.'

'Thank you, Your Grace,' one said, and I wafted the cloak into the air, holding it at the edges so that it formed a canopy over the trio. The two outer girls held up their arms to keep the cloak from the third, who reached above her head to grasp its leading edge.

'I thank you, sir,' she said, and I looked down into her eyes. They were grey with flecks of green and I saw a ready smile with two rows of even teeth. Her hair was a darkish shade of corn-gold, and she was wearing a simple dress trimmed with lace.

'How came you to be here in such weather, my lady?' I asked – anything to ensure that I was able to continue to look into those eyes.

'I came to see to the welfare of my pony, sir,' she said, 'but the suddenness of the storm caught us unawares.'

I nodded. She was startlingly beautiful, and that thought filled my entire mind to the exclusion of all else.

'Perhaps we should make the attempt, my lady,' murmured one of the other women, and I realized with a start that the girl had been as lost in the moment as I was.

They scurried across the gap between stables and entrance way, and I scuttled in their wake. Under the archway they paused, and my cloak was gathered, shaken, folded and returned to me, while I stood gazing.

'I thank you, sir,' she said, when I had the garment in my arms, and turned to leave.

'Madam,' I said hastily, and bowed low. 'Pray allow me to introduce myself. I am Prince Richard of York, guest of His Grace the king in this place.'

'I am aware of who you are, sir,' she murmured, curtsying. 'I thank you for your kindness.'

'I do not know to whom I speak,' I said, anxious to learn, and, truth be told, to keep her there a little longer.

'My name is Katherine Gordon, sir,' she said. 'I pray you excuse me. My ladies and I are required . . .'

'Of course,' I said, bowing once more, and she looked again into my eyes, sending me speechless messages that I could not mistake.

I saw her twice more in the next few days, both times from a distance while I was attending the king. Finally I resolved to find out more.

'Do you know of a lady named Katherine Gordon?' I asked as casually as I could.

He smiled at me. 'Ah, so you have made the acquaintance of our delectable northerner. Delightful, is she not?'

'She is,' I said. 'I have but the slightest knowledge of her, but she is a most attractive lady.'

'In all things she is,' he said. 'She is both beautiful and intelligent, as sharp-witted as any man in Scotland and a match for any in discourse, pure in heart and mind, a paragon of virtue and a monument to beauty.'

'Do you mock me, sir?' I asked gently.

Again the smile. 'Indeed I do not,' he said. 'She is all these things and more. There are but two things that stand between her and perfection.'

'And they are?' I asked, entering into the banter, but none-theless desperate to know more.

'They are her ferocious father and her even more ferocious stubbornness,' the king said. 'She'll not be tamed, and whoever lays siege to her will have to conquer her redoubtable parent to boot.'

'Who might he be?'

'You don't know!' James said incredulously, and threw back his head and laughed aloud. 'She is the offspring of my lord Huntly, with whom you crossed swords in council – Fault-Finder General of this our realm, and she is an apple that has not fallen far from the tree. If you wish to accost the Lady Katherine, I wish you luck, sir, in your endeavours, and pray you survive the encounter.'

Thus forewarned and intrigued, I deliberately sought out the lady, finding her sitting before the fire in the great hall. Her gentlewomen were combining needlework with gossip, but Katherine sat quietly, reading, and looked up at my approach. When she saw me she rose, curtsied, and remained standing.

'Pray be seated, my lady,' I said. 'May I share the warmth of the fire with you?'

'Heat is spread in all directions,' she said, 'so all may enjoy it. Indulge yourself, my lord.'

I smiled and sat opposite her. She waited a few seconds and then resumed her perusal of the book.

'What is't you read, madam?' I asked.

' "Dictes and Sayings of the Philosophers", my lord,' she told me.

'By Anthony Rivers?'

'The same.'

'My uncle,' I told her.

'So I have heard,' she said. 'It contains much wisdom.'

'Indeed,' I said. 'I can just remember him. A pleasant man, but he was executed for treason soon after my brother's accession. I knew the printer who wrought the book, too, William Caxton. I was his assistant from time to time while I was yet a bastard.'

'A chequered life you have had, sir,' she observed. 'And which do you prefer, prince or peasant?'

'The life of a peasant is hard, but has fewer cares,' I told her, 'but it is my destiny to be a prince, and so I must follow where'er the path leads. There are compensations, however; no peasant could ever sit in such enjoyable company as yourself, or look upon such beauty.'

She laid the book aside. 'You interest me strangely, sir,' she said. 'Pray continue.'

I waxed eloquent, telling her that I had never seen such eyes, such teeth, such skin and all the usual twaddle that young men produce at such moments. I knew it was all the sort of cant that I was expected to come out with, but the truth was that I meant it. I had never known what it was to be in love before this; I had pursued girls in both the Portuguese court and the taverns of Flanders, and tumbled them in both places and a few others, but the way I felt about this girl was completely beyond my experience.

She listened to my nonsense with apparent seriousness, nodding sagely and lowering her eyes modestly at the more extreme of my compliments. Then of a sudden she burst out laughing and picked up her book again. 'You bore me, sir,' she said. 'I can look in a glass and see my own reflection whenever I like, and were I so inclined I could reflect on my qualities in the same manner you have done, but is there not more to life than flashing eyes and white teeth?'

'I apologize, madam,' I said. 'I did not think that you would find my recitation of your virtues a source of ennui. Pray, on what topic would you have me discourse, that I might please you?'

'Tell me of your other life,' she said, putting the book down again and leaning forward. 'Tell me what you did when you were not a prince; tell me of your adventures in lands beyond the sea, of hair-breadth 'scapes from a fearsome foe on the field of war.'

'Alas,' I said, 'I cannot. I have been on the field of war, although never engaged in battle. But I can tell you of my voyage to Jaloof and my winter amid the ice-strewn waters of the northern seas.'

'That will suffice,' she said. 'Tell me all.'

And so I did. For the rest of that December afternoon and most of the next day I told her everything, from my days as a printer's apprentice to the freezing fishing banks of the land beyond Thule, and from the first attacks of Tudor's agents to standing in the second line behind Conn's men at Sligech. She listened, rapt, and when I had finished she said, 'What adventures! What would I not give to have shared them.'

'The past is closed to us,' I said, 'but the future lies open, to be shared if you wish it.'

'I am wooed with words,' she said. 'Do you jest with me, my lord?'

'I do not,' I said in all sincerity. 'Never have I seen a woman so beautiful as yourself, so learned, so much in accord with my own . . .'

'If you do not jest,' she interrupted, 'then it is not I but my father to whom you must address yourself.'

I looked at her. 'Now it is my turn to ask,' I said. 'Do you jest with me?'

'I do not,' she said. 'My heart, my hand, my head lay all open to your desires. I could be coy, and deny you, and play the tease, but that is not my nature. As you say yours are for me, so are my feelings for you. I would be yours, my lord, and share the fate that is to come, if you will have me.'

'Gladly,' I said, and meant it, and she kissed me for the first time before the horrified gaze of the other women of the household.

Her father was less amenable. Asked for a private audience, he delayed as long as he could, but finally agreed to meet me in his private chambers. He greeted my proposal with incredulity. 'God knows I'd be glad to be shut of the stubborn wench,' he said, 'but to give her to an adventurer such as yourself is not to be countenanced. No, sir, you shall not have her; she is of royal blood, and shall marry none but her equal.'

'She has no equal, sir, in all the world, which is why I ask for her.'

'And you, sir, are the equal of none, which is why I refuse.'

'It is true that I find myself reduced in circumstances,' I said, 'but I was born a prince . . .'

'So you say, but even if it were true, which you will give me leave to doubt, there is nothing to say that you will become a prince again or remain one if you do.'

'With the help of King James I expect—'

'Expectations are all very well,' he said, 'but it is achievements which will impress me. Come back when you've got something to offer.' Then a thought struck him. 'Why this undue haste, anyway? You can hardly know the girl.' Then he rose from his chair. 'Have you anticipated . . .?'

'No, sir, no, no – nothing like that,' I said, calming him. 'I have observed her, and made her acquaintance merely, and fallen under her spell.'

'And I suppose you're going to tell me she feels the same.'

'I believe she does, sir.'

'Well, you will not be the first I have disabused of such a notion,' he said. 'Many's the man who's been to me and told me what he thinks she feels, only to have his hopes dashed from the mouth of the wench herself. We'll settle this now.'

He strode to the door, flung it open and bawled, 'Fetch me my daughter Katherine.' Returning to his seat, he said, 'Now we'll see.'

The wait was awkward, as we both remained silent. Then there was the sound of approaching footsteps from the corridor, and the door opened to reveal a herald who announced the imminent arrival of the king. James entered with Katherine on his arm, and she curtsied to her father and then to me.

'Your Grace?' Huntly said, clearly taken aback.

'My lords, I heard that my services as an arbitrator might be needed,' the king said, 'and I am thus come to offer myself.' He took his place on Huntly's seat, and looked expectantly at us. 'Pray proceed,' he said, when it was clear that we were both dumbstruck.

I looked across at Huntly, and he said, 'Your Majesty, I sent for my daughter to ascertain—'

'Her wishes regarding His Grace the Duke of York,' the king said. 'Yes, so I understand.'

'This man . . . His Grace has come to me with an offer for her hand,' Huntly began to explain, but again the king interrupted.

'Yes, yes, Huntly, we know all this. What we do not is how you propose to respond.'

'Why, in the negative, of course, my lord. This . . . lord may be who he says he is, and then again he may not—'

'I have fallen in love with the man, not with the title,' came Katherine's voice, cutting in. 'What he is called is neither here nor there, so long as he is always honest with me. Will you be honest with me, Richard?'

'I will,' I said.

'Grant her request, and your daughter may one day be Queen of England,' James said.

'An I do, she may well watch her husband mount the gallows, and she with him,' Huntly replied. 'Have any of you thought of that?'

'We have,' Katherine said, 'and I would prefer the uncertainty of life with Richard than stifling security here at court.'

'And you, my lord of York, what say you to all of this?'

'I have made my Lord Huntly aware of my feelings for his daughter and of what has passed between us,' I said. 'I have asked for his consent.'

'You are aware, I presume,' the king said, 'that for one so close in blood to ourself as the Lady Katherine is, the consent of the king is also required.'

'I am, my lord,' I began, when Katherine interrupted me.

'There will no doubt come a day when the consent of the lady herself is also sought,' she said. 'Perhaps we could start here and now. So far, the only one of those present who has actually asked my views on the matter is Richard himself.'

The king smiled. 'Perhaps, then, my lady, you would be good enough to share them with us.'

'With pleasure, Your Grace.' She paused, taking in a long breath, and then said, 'I realize the suddenness with which all this has happened, but I have fallen in love with Richard of York and he with me, and we would cast our fortunes together and share our destinies, whatsoever they may be. Whether he becomes King of England or no, it is all one to me – prince or peasant, he is the desired object of my heart.'

The king nodded, paused, and then looked at me. 'Richard?'

'It is as Katherine says,' I told him. 'Our hearts and minds are joined, and we wish to marry. Whether I continue in my present state or am reduced again to poverty matters not, so long as we are together.'

'What say you, Lord Huntly?'

The old man looked at the king and shook his head. 'She is a stubborn wench and will not be told,' he said. 'If it is what she wants, and she is aware of all the possible consequences, then so be it, if the king permits. I shall attend her wedding, but not her execution. If she truly loves this man then I know her well enough to admit that she cannot be dissuaded.'

'The king has no objection,' James said, and a broad smile lit up his face. 'Welcome to the family, Richard. So, Kate, when will the wedding be?'

'As soon as possible,' she replied. 'Tomorrow.'

'It's still Advent,' he pointed out.

'As soon as Advent is over, then,' she said, 'so that our shared life and adventures may begin.'

The king shrugged. 'So be it, then,' he said. 'The day after Christmas shall you be joined.'

And so we were. Katherine and I were both attired in virginal white, and the ceremony took place in the chapel of the castle. We made the dowry offering and then Lord Huntly handed his daughter over to me, not a word being spoken by the gruff old man, and I took her by the hand and led her to the altar.

I remember little of the ceremony, save for the shaking and quivering of my hands and voice alike as I took the wedding ring and placed it lightly on each finger of my bride's left hand, whispering the words after the priest – '*In nomine patris*' for the thumb, '. . . *et filii*' for the index finger, '. . . *et spiritus sancti*' for the middle finger and slipping it onto her third finger with the final 'Amen'. I know that I was required to say '*De isto anulo te sponso*,' and then, giving her some gold, '*et de isto auro te honoro*' – with this ring I thee wed, and with this gold I honour thee. During the mass we each prostrated ourselves before God and each other, and while I should have been praying I contemplated this latest turn in my fortunes – from standing mired to the ankles in cow dung on an Irish field to being married to a princess of Scotland in a little under six weeks. It did not compare with my father's reconquest of his realm in the same space of time, but at least it was a start. I turned my head, cold against the stone of the chapel floor, and saw my beautiful bride smiling across at me. I pressed my forehead down for the coolness and thought myself truly a prince for the first time in nigh on ten years.

When I was a boy I remember an old groom telling me a story about a horse he had bred. 'It was one morning,' he told me. 'I was taking your father's stallion to cover a mare when we happened to pass another mare who was being brought to be put to another stallion. Well, your father's horse would not even look at the animal he was supposed to mount, but pushed and barged away from us all and headed for this other mare, who was as desperate to get to him as he to her. We did our best to bring them to their right partners, but neither of them would have any of it. In the end, we gave them their heads, and he mounted her there and then in the public way. They produced a little foal, Jasper it was, the best and brightest horse I ever had; it was love, see. The parents were in love, and that made all the difference.'

The same must have applied to Katherine and myself. We were as besotted with each other as those two horses must have been, and the result was just as inevitable. She fell pregnant almost immediately, and my plans for the impending invasion of England were made alongside our plans for impending parenthood.

We married in winter and loved our way through spring and summer; by autumn, I hoped, with the help of God and King James, I would be a father and a king.

Patriot

September 1496 – September 1497

James reined up and pointed. 'Do you see it?' he asked.

'What?'

'That line – the stones beside the river.'

'Yes.'

'That's the border,' he said. 'Cross it, and you're home.'

'England,' I said.

After all the letters had been sent out, the arguments, the preparations, the wapynschawings and the false starts, I was at last to set foot on English soil again. There had been messages of support from various groups, but apart from Roderick de Lalaing, my old army commander from the Deal expedition, who had arrived from my aunt in Flanders with a troop of German mercenaries and a shipload of equipment, no actual help had been forthcoming. I had assured James that my supporters would meet me at the English border. I had had promises of great reinforcements, and told him that many nobles would come over to me once I entered England and they learned that I had raised my standard. James had raised his eyebrows, but I had persevered in my hopes. All the same, here, as everywhere else, there was just silence and a barren landscape; no supporters had come along the stony roads to greet me.

Katherine was at the home James had loaned us, the royal hunting lodge at Falkland in Fife, at the foot of the Lomond Hills. There she was awaiting the birth of our baby, which was imminent. Naturally I had been loth to leave, but Katherine had insisted.

'Women have had babies ere now with their men from home,' she said. 'If you return with a kingdom what a birthday present that shall be for the wee child. You must go, Richard – destiny ever triumphs over a family's plans.'

So I had left her in early September and travelled with James from Edinburgh to the border, here on the banks of the Tweed.

James had sent cavalry ahead to see if the English were arming in my support, but they seemed more to be in dread of the Scots and Germans, and had retreated into their lords' castles and keeps. The cavalry reported no support for me at all. It was a dreary prospect.

I looked across the river, swollen with the late summer rains. The ground was much the same on either side, but there was a palpable difference. On this side of it I was an honoured guest; cross it, and I became an invader, perhaps a fugitive, one day a traitor and the next, mayhap, a king.

James was reading my thoughts. 'You lead this part of the journey,' he said. 'It must be you who leads the army into England.'

'Yes,' I said again, and turned my horse's head. I spurred down the slope and took up my position at the head of the army. 'The army will advance,' I said, my voice sounding as unsteady as it felt, and we trooped slowly forward at a walk so that the foot soldiers would have no trouble keeping up.

For a mile or so we saw no sign of life, but then we spied some houses on a slope to the east, shepherds' cottages or something of the type. There was no sign of any people except for a slight drift of smoke coming from one of the dwellings, perhaps a cooking fire that had not been extinguished.

Our men marched in silence, but I noted that some of the officers were casting anxious glances toward me. Finally one of them detached himself and trotted over. 'Shall I send some men to reconnoitre, sir?' he asked me.

'Yes,' I said. 'By all means. Yes, do.'

The relief among the others was palpable, and a detachment set off to climb to the houses. I took advantage of the pause to dismount and sit by the side of the track. James's mount came trotting up, and he remained in the saddle as we watched our search party. Their leader came out from searching the last of the small houses and shook his arm from side to side, signifying that there was no one in them, and the party continued up the hill until it reached the crest and then disappeared over it. They were out of sight for some time, and when they came back into view the leader made the same side to side motion before the party began its descent. They had mostly passed by the buildings when I suddenly saw a lick of flame at the thatch of one of the dwellings, and then a crackling sound was borne along on the wind. 'What's that?' I asked. 'It's on fire.'

James looked around. 'So it is,' he said vaguely.

'We've got to put it out,' I said. I ran over to my horse, mounted and cantered up to where the troop was making its way down. 'The houses are on fire!' I called. 'We must put them out.'

The men looked at each other and then at me. 'What's he saying?' one asked. 'What does he want?'

Their officer was bringing up the rear. 'The houses are on fire!' I called to him.

'Yes, sir,' he said.

'Well, do something,' I told him.

He looked at me, genuinely confused. 'What shall I do, sir?'

'Put them out, man. The houses will burn to the ground otherwise.'

I sensed James at my elbow. 'Richard,' he said quietly. 'Richard, be quiet.'

But I was already calling again. 'Put them out!' I called again.

'But sir,' protested the officer, 'we've only just lit them, sir.'

Then I understood. I looked round at James, who shrugged. 'No,' I said, 'no. This is not a punitive expedition, or a raid, or an aggressive invasion. We are here to liberate my people from the oppressor, Tudor, not burn them out of their homes. I am not making war on England or Englishmen.'

James grunted. 'Well, they are,' he said, jerking his head back towards the column of troops, 'and I don't think you'll be able to convince them otherwise. The men have to have their fun, you know, or you won't be able to get them to do anything when you tell them. Give the Germans their women and the Flemish their beer and you have a happy army. Otherwise . . .'

The roof of one of the buildings fell in with a great roar, and a sudden rush of flame shot skywards. 'This is not what is supposed to happen,' I said.

'That,' James said, pulling his horse's head round to pacify it and keep it turned away from the fire, 'is war. I promised you, Richard, that I would go home peacefully when it was clear that the men of Northumberland had come over to you. Have they? Do you see the cheering throng, Richard, welcoming you to your realm?'

He shot out an arm and indicated the bare hillside. 'No, you do not,' he said. 'If we are not friends with the English, then we are their enemies. If they do not side with you, Richard, be assured that they will not side with the company you keep.'

'Stop this, James,' I begged. 'The crown means nothing to me if it is only to be had by spilling the blood of my people and destroying their land with sword and flame.'

'There are no people here for you, Richard, so this is none of your business. It is no longer your triumphal procession, but a border raid. It is my business you meddle in now, sir, and not your own. It's war. Get used to it. You'll be burning a lot more English houses before this expedition is over, I can tell you.'

'No,' I said, 'no, James, I won't. It cannot be this way. These are my people. How can they accept me as their king if I come and cast down their homes and slaughter their livestock?'

'Accept you as king?' James said. 'Good God, man, they don't even accept you as an Englishman. You are a foreign invader, as I am and as those Germans over there are. If you can't be King of England with my support, now, then you never will. Face it and accept it.'

'Then I call it off,' I said. 'I'm not prepared to destroy Englishmen's homes whether they recognize me or not.'

He leaned over. 'This expedition is not yours to call off, sir,' he said. 'I prepared it, I paid for it, and I owe those troops gold because of it, so it goes on, and you and I with it.'

'Not I,' I said. 'Not I, Your Grace. I beg permission to leave the field and return to my wife and family. I will have no part in this.'

He stared at me, and then with a brisk movement of his hand dismissed me.

I made one last attempt. 'James,' I said. 'Think what you do. This is my land you invade.'

'I think not,' he said, and turned his horse away from me.

With a few companions I rode back down the track and back into Scotland, leaving my ambitions in ruins behind me.

Truth to tell, James was not too long delayed in following. Within a couple of days the English advanced with four thousand men and the King of Scotland retreated across his border. I think he regretted his harsh words to me too, as he sent a present of money after me.

I hastened home – how many years had it been since I had been able to use that word? – and arrived just as Katherine gave birth to our son on the 23rd of September. I called him Edward, after my father and brother, and hoped that in spite of all he might yet grow to be King Edward VI of England.

There are advantages to being a royal protégé, especially one who is in high dudgeon, and I discovered some of them over the next few months, as autumn turned to winter and then round through spring to summer again. I was relatively undisturbed at Falkland. James usually remembered to send my monthly pension and occasionally an ambassador or envoy arrived to ask after my welfare, but by and large I was left to myself, and I enjoyed the time with Katherine and Edward and thought not of killing and fighting.

The truth is that I had never been so close to war before, and to the suffering of the people caught up in it. I had seen wanton killing, when da Cunha attacked Bemoy, and had seen fighting in Ireland, but only at second hand. At Waterford I had not seen the results of the battles, being away from the siege at Passage, and though I had seen men die at the ford with Aedh and Conn they had been men who had gone willingly to fight, not peasants whose homes and livestock had been attacked. James's invasion of England had been different, and it was my own people, those I hoped to lead and inspire, who had been suffering, and some of my own men, people I had marched and starved with, who were joining in as enthusiastically as the Scots. If I were to be successful in my venture, it could only be with Englishmen behind me.

James had not given up on me totally, though. Later in that winter of 1496 he refused to surrender me to Tudor, and made another half-hearted attempt to take Berwick at Christmastime. He visited us in April, and told me that there was still strife with Tudor, but that for the moment the border was quiet. He told me too that Maximilian had continued his endeavours on my behalf, offering to negotiate a truce between Tudor and myself and singing my praises to all who would hear. He also told me that he had been offered money by the monarchs of both Spain and France to transfer me to them, and refused both. I knew this already, for one of my visitors had been Pedro de Ayala, an envoy of Their Catholic Majesties, who had offered me a safe passage to Spain and a pension. Katherine had advised against it, and we had turned him down. With James, blessedly, there was no further talk of invasion, and he smiled upon little Edward, embraced Katherine, who was again with child, and left us in peace. George Neville left too, to return to England and face whatever charges Tudor would bring.

James sought peace, too, and found himself on the horns of a dilemma. In spring England began to negotiate a treaty, although the preparations for war continued unabated, and it turned out that part of the price to be paid was me. Tudor demanded that I (or 'Perkin', as he insisted on calling me) should be handed over as part of the agreement, but James was faithful in his commitment to protect me, and no agreement was reached. He did however pay us another visit in late June.

'It were best, Richard, if you were to leave my realm,' he said. 'I will not hand you over to Tudor, as he desires, but equally I cannot put a lasting peace in place while you are still under my protection. He has offered me his little daughter in marriage, and the prospect of peace through that union, and the possibility that one day my own grandchildren might rule over a united kingdom of Scotland and England is too enticing a thought to put aside. The price we have to pay is our friendship – an equal loss to both of us.'

'I am happy here,' I said, knowing how pitiful that sounded. My happiness carried no weight in the negotiations between nations.

'Nonetheless,' James said.

There was a long silence.

'The ship I bought for you is ready,' he said. 'It is in harbour at Ayr, and stands ready to take you where you will under safe conduct.'

'And what of Katherine and Edward?'

'They are welcome to stay here,' James said, 'although in

truth I hope that they will be able to go with you. It would be more . . . convenient that way.'

'Your Grace has been so kind to me,' I said. 'I understand your wishes. I have accepted so many benefits from you, and have never been able to repay them. I have no wish to appear ungrateful, and I understand how the needs of your kingdom must take precedence over all other considerations. I accept your requirements with equanimity, but with regret.'

'Which is also how they are imposed,' he said. 'I am sorry, Richard. The truth is that your political value always lay more in your potential to undermine Henry than any danger which you presented in reality. If I had simply given you official recognition and a place of refuge, I could have negotiated with Henry from a position of strength. Instead, that military fiasco of ours handed the initiative and the propaganda victory to him. Now I am left with no real choice. Your claim to England is as valid as it ever was, but it must be one that now you pursue without my help. I am sorry. I hope you understand.'

'Of course I do, my lord,' I told him, and then added: 'When must I leave?'

'As soon as can be conveniently arranged,' he said. 'Would two weeks be sufficient time to make all arrangements?'

'It would, sire,' I told him.

'You may have lost your kingdom, Richard,' he said, 'but you retain your greatness of soul. You go with honour, and you go as my friend. May God go with you.'

When he had left I went with a heavy heart to tell Katherine the news.

'Where will we go?' she asked.

'We? You are determined to go with me?'

'Did I not promise to share your fate? And what kind of a husband deserts a pregnant wife? And what kind of a father deserts a babe in arms? And what kind of a wife would I be if I even allowed you to contemplate such actions? And what kind of a wife would I be to allow you to face these uncertainties alone?'

'There are no uncertainties,' I said. 'We sail into certain danger, and probable penury, and possible death. Unless of course we go to Flanders and abandon all thoughts of ruling England.'

'That is not a decision I can make for you, Richard,' she said gently, 'but know that I will share and support whatever decision you make.'

I sat that night before my own hearth and looked deep inside me for the answer. I wanted to be king, yes, because it was my birthright and because Tudor was a usurper. If I were king then I would have avenged the death of Richard and the murder of my brother. If I were king then Katherine would be Queen of England and my son would be king after me, and if I were king I would rule kindly and fairly, as my father and Richard had, and leave England a better place than I had found it.

On the other hand there were the struggles that lay ahead. Tudor would not give up his realm without a fight, and he had many lords arrayed on his side, while my own support was dubious at best. I did not know if I could put Katherine through that; nor indeed did I know if I had the stomach for it. I did not like to see men die; the more so when with a word I could have saved them from that sacrifice. I could not understand why a man would wish to die for me. Unless, of course, he saw in me the hope of England.

The temptation to return to Flanders to my aunt and Maximilian was strong, but there was no guarantee that a failed prince would be as welcome there as a confident one had been. I had lost men and armies, and the money they had piled into my support was all gone for ever. I did not know whether their concern for my safety and well-being was as strong from a personal point of view as it was from a political one. Like James, they might be tempted to be rid of an embarrassing failure.

And the last question was the most important. Was it right? Was I making the challenge out of moral duty or out of personal vainglory?

In the end I decided that it was indeed duty, and that all things demanded that I make one last throw of the dice. People had believed in me, and many still did, and I owed it to them to see it out. Tudor, when all was said and done, was still a usurper and a murderer. Justice had still to be served.

I went to bed. Katherine had fallen asleep, and Edward too slept peacefully. Would he want to be a king, I wondered, if I gave him the choice?

We travelled to Ayr where the ship was waiting. I was not amused at its name, the *Cuckoo*, but its captain, one Andrew Barton, assured me that no disrespect was intended, and that she had always borne that name. With that I had to be content, and we sailed south in the early days of July escorted by two other ships whose names I do not recall.

For the first days I kept below, as both Katherine and Edward were seasick, but once they were settled I came on deck and sauntered about. I told Barton I had been at sea a little, and he gave me the run of the ship.

Towards noon I was standing looking towards the east when a voice said, 'Looking for a berth, Pierre?'

I spun around. 'Might be,' I said. 'You offering one?'

We clasped each other.

'I thought you would be King of England by now,' he said.

'It's not as easy as it sounds to conduct an invasion. And you, why are you here and not far to the west?'

'I ran the *Buoc'h* aground,' he said. 'She needs some new planking, so I have to be a common crewman while I have no ship. That or stay at home and drink. Did you not recognize Foucard?'

'Where? Here aboard?'

'Indeed. He's the former master, so they've kept him on

while they get to know her ways.' He shook his head. 'You have some powerful enemies, Pierre. I've met some of them.'

'Who?'

'Don't know their names,' he said. 'Agents of the English king, though, that's for sure. They captured us as we sailed back from Cork that time. Give them their due, though, they paid me well to tell all I know of you.'

'What did you say?'

'What you told me,' he said. 'No reason to hide it, was there? I told them you were the Duke of York but had to pretend to be Pierre Werbecque for a few years and then went to sea with me. They weren't interested in the first bit, but they copied down everything I told them about Tournai and Portugal. The only thing I didn't tell them was where the bacalao are to be found. I'm to let them know if I ever see you again, so after you've landed in England I'll go and tell them, see if I can get some more money.'

'Ireland first,' I told him. 'I want to see if Kildare can offer any more advice.'

'He's the new Lord Lieutenant or some such for King Henry,' he said, 'so he might not want to give you any help this time. The man's like me; he goes where the pay is.' He looked around. 'Perhaps best if I'm not seen talking to you too openly,' he said. 'I have my duties, and no one knows I know you. You want me to tell Foucard who you are?'

'No,' I said. 'If he recognizes me then that's well enough; if not it doesn't matter.'

He nodded, stepped back, knuckled his forehead and said, 'Glad to be of service, sir,' and walked off.

We headed first for Ireland, and landed in Cork, but matters were much changed from before. The mayor welcomed and made much of me, but as Pierre Jean had said, Kildare was now Henry's man and was rooting out Yorkist rebels and handing them over for execution, usually, or trial, rarely, and invariably the second was always followed by the first anyway. In any case the Irish had lost their enthusiasm for rebellion; there was famine in the land, and the problems of England were of no consequence.

While in Cork I was approached again by ambassadors from the court of Spain. Once again they repeated the offer of Their Catholic Majesties, a safe passage to Spain and a pension. This time we gave it further consideration, but I knew that now I had to have one last try at England; anything else would be a betrayal. I spoke with Katherine, once again she advised against the offer. Like me, she realized, as Maximilian had foreseen years before, that Their Catholic Majesties wanted me for their own purposes. The fact that they were also prepared to open negotiations for their own daughter, Caterina de Aragon, to marry Tudor's eldest son, Arthur, told its own story, and in due course we turned their offer down.

One factor in this was the news from Cornwall. Not many months before, the Cornishmen had risen against Tudor and had marched as far as Blackheath, outside London. There they had been beaten in battle by Henry's forces, but word was that the county still seethed with bitterness at their treatment, and merely needed the right leader in order to rise again. If it were to be done, this was the time and Cornwall the place. I might find there the rebel Englishmen who were not to be found in Northumberland, and the great men whose support had been so lacking in the north.

So we sailed for Cornwall, and had been at sea no more than two days when a fleet of warships bore down on us from the east.

'Who are they?' I asked Pierre Jean, whose eyes were better than mine.

'English,' he said. 'I wonder who they're looking for.'

'Well, it was bound to happen,' I said. 'Do you think I'd pass as a Breton sailor?'

'It would be suicide to try,' he said. 'Do you want to jump overboard and try your luck in the sea?'

'I think not,' I said. 'I'll go below and tell my wife all is lost, and then give myself up.'

'Not so fast,' Pierre Jean said. 'There's always something that can be done. See your wife, and then come with me.'

I told Katherine about the fleet, and kissed her and Edward goodbye, lest I never see them again, and then followed Pierre Jean into the bowels of the ship and through into the hold where the provisions were stored.

'What are you planning?' I said.

'Call it the bacalao's revenge,' he told me. He lifted the top from a barrel which had clearly once contained salted fish, and said, 'Get in.'

I looked into the barrel. 'I think I'd rather hand myself over to Tudor,' I said.

'I'm not joking, Pierre. This is the only chance you have left, and even this is by no means certain.'

'I suppose you're right,' I said, and clambered into the salty, itchy darkness.

'I'm putting the lid back on,' he said, 'but I won't be far away.'

'You could live comfortably for the rest of your life if you sold this barrel and its contents to Tudor,' I said.

He grinned. 'I could, couldn't I? You stay there and pray they don't offer too much and tempt me too far.'

I suppose I could not have been in there much above two hours, but it felt like two months. I could hear much of what went on, and heard the scrape as a small boat collided with ours, and the sound of heavy boots on deck as the Englishmen came aboard. Then I could make out the sound of voices, but nothing of what was said.

Pierre Jean told me later what had transpired. The English fleet had stopped our little flotilla and demanded that Barton hand over Perkin Warbeck. The captain was furious.

'Who do you think you are?' he yelled. 'This is a Scottish ship. We're not in English waters and we owe you nothing. This is an act of war. I don't know anyone called Perkin Warbeck. What does he look like?'

Strangely, none of the English had any idea. They had been given the name, but no description and only the barest of details.

Barton told them that he was transporting a Scottish gentlewoman and her family and that she was not to be disturbed. The English accepted this, but insisted on lining up the crew and asking if any of them knew Perkin Warbeck.

The Scots all said, quite truthfully, that they had never heard the name before. The Bretons had no English, and Pierre Jean translated for them as best he could. 'I knew a fisherman called Pierrechon once – he the one?' he told them, but the English ignored him. He had told them the truth, he said, so his conscience was clear.

The English agents wandered about the ship, poking into corners and lifting hatches, but it was clear that what they wanted was baffling to Scots and Bretons alike.

Eventually the Englishmen's leader decided on one last effort, and assembled the crew on deck. 'If any man here can point out to me Perkin Warbeck,' he said, 'then I shall reward him. On my ship I have a chest containing two thousand English nobles in gold. That is the reward for the capture of this Perkin. The man who points him out to me can take that chest away with him today. Each of you look at his companions. The man I seek is a native of Tournai in Picardy. Is there such a man here?'

Pierre Jean translated this announcement into Breton, to no response. 'Listen, lads,' he said. 'We could make some money here. Let's hand over one of our own and say he's this Wobbec; then we can make off with the gold.'

'And what happens to the poor bastard you identify?' asked one of them.

'He'll probably be hanged,' Pierre Jean said, 'so it had better be someone that none of us like. What about you, Foucard?'

Foucard's response took the form that one might have expected, and the laughter of the men convinced the English that no one knew anything about their Warbeck, and they allowed our flotilla to continue.

Pierre Jean came and rescued me from my confinement as soon as it was clear that the English were sailing on.

'Two thousand nobles,' I said. 'How could you bear to turn it down?'

'Oh, it was a hard struggle,' he said, 'but beneath this rough exterior there beats the heart of a true friend. I couldn't sell you for two thousand nobles.'

'Thank you, Pierre Jean,' I said.

'Mind you, if he'd made it three . . .'

I smiled at his jest, but the truth was that the escape had been my narrowest so far. The stolidness of the Scots crew, the language differences of the Bretons, Pierre Jean's wit and the lack of imagination of the English agents had conspired to save me. At no point did any of Tudor's agents mention that they were looking for an Englishman, or I would have been a dead man. At no point did they mention that the man they were seeking had recently been a guest of the King of Scotland, or I would have been a dead man. At no point did they refer to their quarry as the Duke of York or as Richard Plantagenet, or I would have been a dead man. Thus does destiny preserve men for its greater purposes.

I went back to the private cabin and retrieved my farewell kisses from the lips of my wife and child. 'I could not bear it,' Katherine said. 'I did not know where you were hiding. Just as well, I suppose. Are our lives to be always thus?'

'If I don't take England,' I told her, 'I don't imagine that my life at least will have much longer to run. If Tudor takes me that will be the end.' I paused, and then added, 'My love, I must say this, even though it may sound strange. You do believe that I am Richard of York, do you not, and not the Flemish peasant that Tudor thinks I am?'

'Of course I do,' she said. 'You told me of your time in Flanders, whence this story found its beginning.'

'If I fall into the hands of Tudor,' I said, 'he may torture me to make me say that I am not Richard. I am not a brave man, and do not know how long I can hold out before I succumb. It is said that a man under torture will admit to anything simply to stop the pain.'

'So I have heard,' she said, and I saw tears creep into the corners of her eyes.

'This then,' I said. 'I swear to you, on my life, that I am Richard of York and none other, and that aught else that I ever say to you, whether under torture or otherwise, is a lie that has been forced out of me, whether or not you see the instruments of torture. Do you understand?'

'I do,' she said, and one of the tears dropped.

'I would not for my life have caused you this pain,' I said.

'I know,' she whispered, and then became practical again. 'Then there is the matter of this life,' she said, pressing my hand to her swelling belly. 'It is a question of not many days now – perhaps just hours. When will we land?'

'That too is mere hours,' I said. 'Our second son will be born an Englishman. By tomorrow evening at the latest we shall be landed in Cornwall. Then, soon after that, we will know. This is where it begins.' I paused. 'Or ends.'

'Begins, Richard,' she said. 'Begins.'

At first light I went up on deck to watch England come up over the horizon. Pierre Jean was on watch, guiding the rudder with a sure hand. I wished mine were as steady.

'What are you feeling?' he asked me.

I took a moment to think. 'Many things,' I said at last. 'Excitement. Apprehension. A sense of destiny. Fear, above all else.'

'People will come to you,' he said. 'That is for certain, and they will stay with you as long as you show them leadership. But you must give them the direction. A crew with no rudder is no crew at all.'

'I know,' I told him. 'I cannot let others make decisions for me. I found that out in Scotland.'

England was coming to meet us. The ship was still on the water, but England was moving towards us, sliding along our port beam. 'How long now?' I asked.

Pierre Jean looked up. 'At this speed, no more than a couple of hours,' he said. 'See the point over there?'

I followed his finger.

'Once we round that you'll see St Michael's Mount – half in the sea, half on land, as they say round here, built as it was by an archangel. Cornish and Bretons are cousins, you know.'

'Why would an archangel want a fortress in Cornwall?'

'The legend is silent on that point,' he said, and went back to the tiller.

'You want to come with me?' I asked suddenly. I felt that I needed a male friend I could trust implicitly. Heron, Astley and Skelton were still by my side, but Pierre Jean was more to me than they.

I looked over at him, but he shook his head. 'Couldn't make money out of you if I were always beside you,' he said. 'I need some distance. Anyway, land's not my element; water is. I'm going to collect what little pay is coming to me and then go and collect the *Buoc'h*. It should be ready by now.'

I took out the small bag of gold I had brought up from the cabin in case I met him. 'There's not two thousand nobles in there,' I said. 'In fact, I doubt if there's as many as twenty, but take it anyway. It'll get the ship back for you.'

'I don't want your money,' he said.

'I know,' I told him. 'That's why I'm giving it to you.'

I moved forward. The wind was blowing towards shore, and the ship's sails were trimmed so that we were pushed on a line slightly away and out to sea. I looked ahead, beyond England; there lay Burgundy, and safety; there lay a life of ease with nothing to concern me but the next day's sport. If I were to go there, Tudor would leave me alone, and Katherine and I could live out our lives in quiet obscurity. All I had to do was let England carry on sliding, let it slide away on my left, slide behind me and tell the master to set a course for Bruges.

'What are you feeling?' said the soft voice behind me.

'Fear,' I said. 'No, not fear either; terror. I'm wondering about staying on this course and ignoring England.'

'Going back to Maximilian and Margaret?'

'Yes.'

She was silent for a moment, and then, softly, 'Let's do that, then. What need we a country to rule?'

I shook my head. 'I was wondering about it,' I said, 'not contemplating it. I have to make the attempt.'

'Why?'

'For the sake of the men who follow me, and have put their faith in me. For the sake of my murdered brother and uncle. For the sake of my honour, to do what I have said I will do. For you and our babies. To try my destiny, and above all for the sake of England, to free her from the tyrant. I have cast my die, Katherine, and now I must hazard my life on whatever number it shows.'

I turned to look at her. 'You can go,' I said. 'Pierre Jean will take you to Burgundy, Maximilian will take care of you and Margaret will dote on the babies. You had no hand in casting this die, and need not fear its fall. You and the babies will be safe.'

'Intreat me not to leave thee, or to return from following thee,' she said, and I put my arms around her, and she finished the verses in a small voice which was lost in my chest, 'for whither thou goest, I will go.'

There was a creaking sound, and I felt the wind change on my face. The ship had turned, and was now steering inshore towards the coast of England.

Pragmatist

September 1497

I know not what I expected – for Englishmen to flock to my banner, I suppose, followed by a triumphant march on London through cheering crowds, and Tudor either bowing the knee to me or fleeing once my army hove into sight.

Of course none of these things happened. We landed at Sennen – myself, Katherine and Edward, a couple of servants, the three advisers and three score Irishmen loaned to me by Kildare 'but without any consent from me' as he very deliberately put it. We were watched by a few curious farm labourers and a sprinkling of fishermen, and some of them ventured down to find out what was going on, attracted no doubt by the flowing silk robes that were so like those which had attracted the men in Cork. No man dressed as I was was about to start a fight, there were not enough of us to be an invasion force that offered violence to them, and they were further emboldened by the fact that when they called out one or two of our men were able to answer them in their own Cornish language and say who I was and announce my business.

I bade farewell to Pierre Jean and the crew of the *Cuckoo*. 'If ever you need a berth,' he said, grinning, the only man of them not to bend the knee to me, 'you know where to come,' and I clasped his hand and let him jump back into the ship, which made its way immediately out to sea. Now, truly, there was no way back, and we set out for St Michael's Mount, the castle half in the sea, some ten miles distant.

It soon became clear that Katherine was in no condition to travel. The child was due to come soon, and she would never have made it as far as the castle. Worse, the ascent to the citadel was by means of fourteen sets of steps, each of sixty risers, and in the end we decided to stop at the Monastery of St Buryan, where in addition to a place of rest there was the additional solace that it was a place of sanctuary, somewhere whence she could not be taken against her will.

'I shall stay here, Richard,' she said firmly. 'You must go on. The baby, when it comes, will be born in England, a prince of England. How shall I name him?'

'Richard, then,' I said. 'Richard for a boy, Elizabeth for a girl, and I shall not go. I shall stay with you.'

She shook her head. 'If this land is to be won, it is to be won while your men are new and fresh, at a time when Tudor knows nothing of your whereabouts, and while the men of Cornwall are still smarting from the defeat of last year and ready to try again. Miss this chance, and you might as well not have come to England at all. I shall be safe here – where safer? I am in sanctuary, and behind your lines, and I have my women to see that all manner of thing shall be well. It is peaceful here, and I shall wait for you to return for a first look at our new child. If only it could always be as peaceful as this.' She whispered this last to me, and a part of me was quick to agree – but the greater part was still for the crown.

'After the struggle,' I said to her, 'the peace will be all the sweeter. We will appreciate it more for being hard won.'

'I don't think it is possible for me to appreciate it more than I do now,' she said, 'after that sea voyage, but now do you go and win our realm for us.'

She was not to be gainsaid, and I kissed her and Edward and left the sanctuary of the little church and went outside. It was a dismal setting, a lowering sky on a bleak and treeless plateau, a cheerless place to leave a wife and babes, but I had no choice. Nonetheless a large group had gathered, crowding round to cheer me. Many stayed to march with me, too, but they were landless and in the main weaponless. In addition, they had come foodless and expected to be fed. There were no nobles among them, none of my father's officers and precious few landowners, although admittedly it was yet early days; I expected the gentry to make their way to me when word began to spread.

I realize now though that these poor men came to see rather than to fight, but it was exhilarating all the same, to be cheered and lauded, to be paraded on my horse and to wave and smile and acknowledge their love and loyalty. Now I am a wiser man, but then I was young and green in judgement, with no more experience of the world of politics than a babe in arms.

Mindful of Pierre Jean's admonition, I made sure that I led. Throwing off the silk robes of peace, I donned the white armour that Charles of France had had made for me, selected the best steed of the sorry group that was brought forward for me to choose from, and rode on into the small town of Penzance. In the centre of the tiny marketplace I raised my two banners, the White Rose and the Fleeing Child, and announced myself: 'I am Richard of York, son of Edward of England, and I have come to lift the burden of tyranny from your shoulders,' and I was deafened by the cheers.

The next day we went on to St Michael's Mount, with the crowds growing by the hour. Astley went to announce my arrival to the castle, which was hardly defended and ceded immediately, and I climbed the many steps to the stronghold, thereby, according to the priests, remitting one third of my time in Purgatory.

Two days of rest, and we marched on, through the rocks and the moors, gathering men at every stop – Penryn, Truro, and then on to Bodmin, where I estimated that there must be upwards of three thousand men with us.

I wanted to enter the town in some pomp, and so on the evening that we arrived I decided to wait and enter the next morning in the full light of day. For that night we skirted it to the south and encamped the men at Castle Canyke, an ancient fort to the south-east of the town. We had barely settled them down to rest before there was a commotion outside my tent and one of the Cornishmen demanded to see me and was eventually allowed in with an escort.

'What is it, man?' I asked. 'Can you not see that we all need rest?'

'It is the host of the king, sir,' he said, and pointed back towards the east. 'It comes across Bodmin Moor and will be here by the morning.'

'They are marching now?'

'No, sir, they have stopped for the night, but they will be marching again before first light.'

'You are sure of this?' I asked, and he nodded vigorously.

''Tis the sheriff of the county himself, Your Grace, who leads them.'

'This, then, is our first test,' I said, and turned to Skelton, the only one of us left with military experience, and thus perforce our commander. 'Let the men sleep now, but rouse them an hour before dawn. We will position them on the slopes facing east and let our opponents see our numbers.'

'Better they see our numbers from a distance than come close up and see our lack of weapons,' Astley pointed out.

'Well said,' I told him. 'Station the men alongside their fellows from the same village or town – they will be braver for having friends by their sides to observe them.'

All this was done. I had the men stand in ranks so that the numbers were obvious but the weaponry was not, and an hour after dawn we saw Tudor's men coming along the moor road in a long, snaking file. When they were a long arrow shot away they halted, and we saw their leader, a man identified by some of our side as the sheriff, begin to draw them into battle array.

'I like not this,' I said to Astley. 'Englishman should not fight Englishman. These men are not my enemies, but my subjects. This must not be.'

'There is little you can do about it at this juncture, Your Grace,' he said.

'If there is anything that can be done, then I am the only one who can,' I said.

I spurred my horse forward and began to pick my way down the slope towards the ranks of the sheriff's men.

'Your Grace,' called Astley, and rode up beside me. 'What do you do?'

'I go to seek a peace,' I said. All around me I saw men's heads turning, so I rose in my stirrups and turned my horse's head. 'These are our countrymen,' I called. 'Why should we fight them when they should be joining us? I am no man's enemy, I, save Henry Tudor. If these men will join us, why then, they will march with us, and not against us.' I wheeled the horse, and Astley moved alongside me. 'No,' I told him. 'You stay here. I shall do this alone.'

'My lord,' he protested, but I was not going to be argued with.

'Alone,' I said, and allowed the horse to pick its way down the slope until it found the road. Behind me I saw Skelton and Astley in furious argument. I urged the horse into a trot towards the troops forming up across the road.

'Halt!' a voice called when I got to within twenty yards or so. 'Who goes there?'

'Richard, Duke of York, son of King Edward IV,' I called, 'come to parley with those men sent against me by Henry Tudor the usurper.'

'Archers, prepare your shafts.'

There was an unhurried movement as the front ranks did

as they were told, and I continued to allow my horse to walk forward.

When I was close enough to be heard without shouting, I said, 'I am an Englishman, as are all of you. I have no quarrel with any man of you, and you have none with me. Behind me are the men of Cornwall, your neighbours, and none of them have any quarrel with any man of you, save that it be a private matter. What need then for any man's blood to be spilled here today?'

The man who had been identified as the sheriff rode forward. 'You come against us and against the King's Majesty in arms,' he said. 'Is that not reason enough?'

'I come in arms against no man save Henry Tudor,' I said, 'and even he would I allow to go free were he to hand over this realm to its rightful king and cease his unfair taxation of my people. I loath these taxes, and will repeal them and ensure they are not repeated. Above all, I wish no harm to any man of you.'

'Nor we to you, my lord,' called a voice from the throng, and of a sudden there was a murmuring of agreement.

I advanced the horse a little more, and passed the sheriff, so that I was nearer to his men that he was. 'No man on either side need die this day,' I called. 'I seek only to be allowed to continue on my way to take up my quarrel with Tudor. Howsomany think that my quarrel is a just one are welcome to follow me; howsomany think that it is not may stand aside and let God decide between Tudor and myself. Do I speak fair?'

'Aye,' volleyed forth from a thousand throats around me.

'Let Tudor fight his own battles,' came a voice from my right, and someone else added, 'Aye, he was fast enough to come at us when our cause was just.'

'God save the Duke of York!' came the shout, and the call was passed down the line until there were men shouting who could not possibly have heard a word I had said.

'Give me and my men room to pass, then,' I said, 'and go back to your homes, unless you wish to join me.'

Then an extraordinary thing happened. The sheriff cried, 'Prepare for battle!' and waved his sword in the air, but not a man paid any attention.

'Fight your own fights!' someone shouted, and then again, 'God save the Duke of York!' and those men nearest to me turned and began to walk back down the road.

The sheriff rode his horse ahead of them and called, 'Turn and fight! Face your enemy!'

Suddenly he found a pike inches from his nose, and its owner said, 'I call no Englishman enemy, me, except him that tries to cheat me of what is mine. This duke does not do that, so good luck to him.'

He paused to make sure he was understood, and then trudged off down the road in pursuit of his companions, and the sheriff turned back to stare at me. 'A master stroke,' he said.

'I spake only the truth.'

'No, not that – holding Castle Canyke is what I mean, that place of faeries and hobgoblins. Some of its magic must have rubbed off on you.'

Then there was a roar from behind us as the men on the hillside realized that those who had come to fight them were melting away before them, and the whole force began to move forward down the hill.

'You will pardon me, my lord, if I do not remain,' he said.

'You are welcome to join me,' I said.

'My stewardship is held from King Henry VII, not your father,' he said. 'It would not be meet for me to do so.' He bowed his head, backed his horse a step or two and then turned to canter away behind his army.

Astley was first to my side. 'What happened?' he asked. 'How did you do that?'

I shrugged. 'I told them who I was, and said that I did not expect to have to fight them,' I said, 'so they went home.'

'Such bravery!' he said.

'Bravery! Nonsense! All I did was prevent some deaths by the injection of a little common sense.'

Before he could reply we were surrounded by the men of Cornwall, all cheering and shouting, all acclaiming this first great victory of the campaign, and I accepted the mood of the moment and led them into Bodmin.

I went to hear a mass of thanksgiving in St Petroc's Church, and when I came out, once again in my silken robes, I went into a nearby house that my men had borrowed for my comfort, and there one man after another – clerics, mayor and aldermen, guildsmen and merchants – came forward and greeted me as 'Richard, King of England', and heralds and trumpeters were sent out to proclaim me as king in the streets of the little town.

Just before nightfall, a messenger arrived from St Buryan. Katherine had been delivered of a boy, to be called Richard. My happiness was complete.

We stayed but two days enjoying my little realm, and then moved on, traversing Bodmin Moor and crossing the Tamar, the boundary between Cornwall and Devon, near a town called Launceston. At every stopping place we were joined by more men, but still they were armed with no more than sticks, clubs and farm implements, and there were no gentry or even merchants with them, and not a single titled noble.

A man was brought before me for stealing a chicken, and I punished him with a beating and issued an order that no man should steal from the farms and villages that we passed. Anything that was wanted had to be freely given or be paid for at the going rate. This was morality, but it was also policy; the absence of nobility meant that my force had no arms of any sort beyond simple peasant implements, and if things went badly for us at our next encounter then many of them would have to pass this way again – it was pointless sowing ill will with a harvest looming. It was an admission of uncertain hopes, but it kept options open that might be dangerous if closed.

The Sheriff of Devon was sent to stop our march, and I went forward to his troops and repeated my speech that I bore no ill will to any man.

'And yet you march through Devon,' called their leader. 'That is an act of war, is it not?'

'I go to meet my destiny,' I said. 'If no man stands against me then no man shall be harmed. I am come into my own, and my quarrel is not with you or with any of these men here, but with Henry Tudor, that has usurped the title of king.'

Before he could reply a voice called, 'God save the king!', and I feared that all was lost. Then, as the cry was taken up and repeated, I heard another call, this one saying 'God save King Richard', and I realized that the king they were welcoming was me, and I swept an arm into the air to acknowledge them. Once again, when the cheering died down the army melted away before me with no confrontation, but this time some stayed to lend their support to me. Once again, however, there were no men of mark or quality, and the arms they bore were at best pikes or bows. I needed some Yorkist nobility.

Nonetheless our force, now numbering some eight thousand, continued its march unhindered across the craggy wilderness of Dartmoor, and three days later, on St Lambert's Day, we sighted the walls of Exeter. The gates were shut against us, and we could see armed men lining the walls.

'A stiffer test than the others, I think,' Astley said.

I nodded in agreement. 'I have never been at a siege,' I said, 'much less conducted one. Do we not need siege engines and such things?'

'We do not have them,' Astley said, 'and I misdoubt whether we can get them. Mayhap we should try something that takes a little cunning.'

'Such as what?' I asked.

He spread his hands. 'You are the scholar, Your Grace, not I.'

I sent out a herald to proclaim me at the city gates and demand that they open to me by duty of the allegiance they owed to me, but the reaction here was greatly different from those I had received on the road. My new title of Richard IV was mocked, and the gates remained defiantly shut against me. I should in reality have expected no better, for the town was commanded by the Earl of Devon, who had revolted against my uncle Richard long before Bosworth and had no love for the Yorkist cause. It came down, then, to a siege.

Edward Skelton, it turned out, knew a little, albeit a very little, of siegecraft and took charge of the direction of our forces.

'We have none of the accoutrements which go with a siege,' he told me. 'No engines, no catapults, no guns. We can make ladders and rams, but other than that we have but our bare hands. We can bring fire to our aid, if we can but get close enough to the gate to lay it. I can attempt some of those things, my lord.'

'Please do,' I said. 'If a town is hostile I cannot leave it in my rear.'

'I do not think Exeter is hostile so much as fearful,' Astley said. 'Last year it raised no objection to the Cornishmen marching through it on their way to London, and they are frightened that if they similarly show no resistance this time then there will be reprisals from Tudor. I think the Earl of Devon is there to stiffen their resolve.'

'The town cannot be taken from the west, because of the river,' Skelton said. 'We shall attack the north and east gates.'

The next morning we tried to form the men up in some sort of battle array, but none of them were used to military discipline, and they had no officers of experience who knew what was needed; thus it took the best part of the day just to get them to line up and then stay in the same spot. From the ramparts their cousins of Devon shouted advice and abuse in about equal measure, and watching our efforts clearly made them more confident of driving us away. Skelton sent volunteers in to fire the gate, but the townsmen built a bigger fire on their side, which neutralized our fire, and because they were able to continue feeding the flames, so kept us at bay. He sent men round to the East Gate, and attempted to scale the wall with ladders, but these were cast down, and the fire he laid did not take hold. We retired from the struggle that night with the town unscathed. A few of our men had broken limbs in falls from the wall, and a number had gashed heads from the broken masonry with which the defenders had showered them as they tried to lay the fire, but both sides had managed not to do any major harm to each other.

'We shall have them tomorrow,' Skelton said. 'I shall send your herald again to proclaim you, and, assuming that they ignore us again, make a further attempt at the East Gate.'

In the early hours of the morning he succeeded in getting the fire laid, and before long it was burning merrily. It seemed that the men inside the walls had no fuel for a counter-fire this time, and as the flames began to die down Skelton sent men forward with a ram.

Behind me I heard the hubbub go silent, and I turned in the saddle to see that priests were standing before my followers, crosses raised, and praying. Most of the men fell to their knees. I mumbled my own prayer, and turned to look at the rammers.

At first they seemed to be having no effect, and then suddenly the gates moved, shifted again and then collapsed in a shower of sparks and a sudden flurry of flame.

A great shout rose from our side, and like a great torrent they rushed forward down the hill and towards the open portal. All around me there was shouting as my men encouraged each other onwards. There was no time to think or consider, no time even for fear, for every thought was drowned by the constant noise. I urged my horse forward, but there was nowhere for it to go.

Just inside the gate there was fierce hand-to-hand fighting, and neither the men nor I could make any headway in the press. Then the resistance broke, and our men poured through the gate, shouting and pushing. From the vantage point of my saddle I could see the remaining defenders fleeing up the street in front of them.

'The gate is forced!' Astley shouted. 'Now, sire, now. You must lead your men into the city and claim it. Make haste.'

I urged the horse forward, but it was barely able to advance at a walk. It was no destrier, just some farmer's hack, but it plodded on bravely and placidly into the crush.

'Come, men!' I called, and waved my sword once or twice round my head. 'The White Rose. Follow the White Rose.' I knew I had shouted the words, but I did not hear a syllable of them. I doubted any of the men had either, but then some of the closest to me took up the call, and we surged through the gates and into the narrow lanes of the city. Once again I realized, as I had in Ireland, that I was not afraid; I was no soldier, I knew that, but I was no coward either.

At first there seemed to be no one against us; I went down one lane almost at a canter, outpacing my own troops and desperately looking around, trying to see out of the helm. My field of vision was restricted to a tiny slit ahead of me; I could see the ground, but nothing above my own eye level – the sky could have been filled with Tudor's troops, but I would have been completely unaware of them if it had.

The narrow lane debouched onto a market square, and as I came into this I slowed my horse to a walk, allowing the van of my troops to overtake me. Two men grasped the horse's bridle and for a moment it seemed that we all stood and looked about. I was lost, not knowing which way to lead or even to look, and then I noticed a makeshift barricade on the other side of the square, and behind it the movement of men.

'There!' I shouted, and again, 'there!' and pointed my sword. We began to move again, the leading men outpacing me as before, and I urged the horse forward so that I might charge at the head of my troops.

And then there was an explosion. I instinctively turned my head away, and as I did I felt and heard the impact on my armour. Small things – pebbles, bits of metal, shards of glass – smashed into me, and my horse reared, almost unseating me. It was instantly transformed from a warhorse into the young farm animal that it was in reality, and it took the two men who had taken its head all their strength to calm it down. I looked about, confused, and saw bodies, and around them blood – so much blood – and heard the terrible cries of the wounded.

Then there was a second explosion, and this time the young man at my horse's head took a pace and then fell, a red stain blossoming across his back. He was not dead, but began to writhe and jerk on the ground, his face twisting in agony. My helmet had been struck by something, and my ears were buzzing so that I could hardly hear Astley beside me.

'Gunnery, my lord, they have gunnery behind the barricades!' he shouted, and as he did there was another shattering roar and the horse shied again.

'Back, my lord, back!' Astley shouted again, and obediently I sawed at the reins to get the horse's head round. It was bleeding, I saw, from a wound on its head.

'Retreat!' I called, 'retreat!' remembering just in time that I was still in command. It was an unnecessary order, however, as the men were already crowding out of the square, taking whatever way they could back towards the gate, pushing and running to get away from the superior weaponry.

I allowed the horse to break into a canter, and turned into

one of the narrow lanes that led off the square. Ahead of me was a body of my Cornishmen and then, from my vantage point atop the horse, I saw that there was a barricade here too – old furniture, stones, wood and rubbish blocked this street, and with the realization came the arrows, a volley loosed at point-blank range, and suddenly I was engulfed by a flow of men running away from the new threat.

Back in the square, I saw that men were coming out of other lanes that had seemed safe, and I realized that we had been lured into a trap – the lane before the gate had been left undefended that we might find our way to the square, and all other lanes barricaded and defended.

There was no need to issue an order or a warning, for now every man there was crowding towards the narrow lane we had entered the city by. Now the city's soldiers too tried to crowd into the lane, and slates and stones rained down from the roofs. I looked up, and saw the women and children of the city, the women and children of England, hurling pieces of their homes at me, their faces twisted in hatred.

By now any man who fell was trampled and left for dead, as the men of Cornwall fought to escape. From the side lanes came arrows and crossbow bolts, and my white armour was a natural target for missiles. Step by step, inch by inch, we were driven out of the city, through the burned gate and outside onto the approach road.

The defenders made no attempt to pursue us beyond the walls, and we came to a halt fifty or so yards from the wall. I reined in and looked round; stragglers were still coming from the city, some limping, some dragging shattered legs or holding damaged arms, some carried by their friends. All were weaponless. Even at the ford in Ireland I had not seen such carnage. There the bodies had been far away, and the blood had been washed away by the fast-flowing stream before I had seen them; here they were men I myself had led into danger, bearing wounds that only I had caused to be inflicted, and for many death had been the only reward they had.

'Have we lost many?' I asked.

'Many,' Astley said sombrely. 'A hundred at least, maybe more.'

I was desolate. 'A hundred?' I asked. 'Dead?'

'Yes, my lord.'

I had not expected so much killing. I realized with a start that I had not expected any killing at all. My own men, armed with sticks, stones and billhooks, were not capable of easily inflicting death on other Englishman – I had somehow assumed that those who came against me would be similarly armed, similarly incapable of causing other men to die horribly and messily, with gaping wounds and mangled bodies. I had assumed that their leaders, like me, would be unwilling to have their charges shot down before their eyes. I thought that the other side's leaders, like me, would offer peace before they allowed men to die. I was not ready for this; I could not face what I had done, and I knew too that I could never allow it to happen again. There would be no more men to die in my service.

I turned the horse's head and trotted towards the gate. A row of archers appeared above it, and I called out, 'Who is your leader? I wish to parley with your leader.'

Their arrows were ready to be loosed, but someone, in spite of the noise and confusion, must have got the gist of what I said, for a voice called, 'Stay there, and we will fetch him.'

I sat, my horse quivering nervously and Astley and the others hovering behind as the remnants of the Cornishmen made their way past me, and then a figure stepped into the space where the gate had been and called, 'I am Courtenay. What is your wish?'

'Do you command here?' I asked.

'I do.'

'May I approach?'

He turned, with a gesture moved his archers away from the

wall, and then advanced a few paces beyond the gate. 'Who are you?' he asked, 'and why have you attacked this city?'

'I am Richard IV of England, son of Edward IV. I am the Duke of York, and I attacked your gate because you closed it to me, your rightful king by birth of this realm.'

'And when I translate these words into truth,' he said, 'you are Perkin Warbeck, an upstart boy from Flanders, and you are come into this realm to do mischief unto his Royal Majesty King Henry VII, whom God preserve.' He raised his voice: 'The men of Exeter and of Devon do not consort with traitors, sirrah, as do the men of Cornwall, and you would do well to remember that.'

A roar of approval rose from the garrison at these words, and then there was much cheering.

'I do not expect you to recognize who I am,' I said, 'since you are no doubt a creature who owes his elevation to the usurper, but I wish there to be no more bloodshed this day. Can we reach terms on that?'

'I think so,' Courtenay said. 'Are you surrendering to me?'

I shook my head. 'I am not,' I said. 'However, I do ask for a truce to tend my wounded and enumerate my dead. I wish to retrieve the wounded who cannot walk and the bodies of the dead.'

'I think such can be arranged,' he said, 'so long as those who enter the city do so unarmed and enter streets or buildings only at the direction of my officers, and not under their own volition.'

'Agreed,' I told him.

'Will two hours be sufficient?'

'I hope so.'

'Good. We shall speak at the end of that time, should you wish. Until then, sir, I bid you good day.'

Astley's estimate had been on the low side; almost two hundred lay dead in the narrow streets of Exeter, and all of them men of my own side. The price was too great; although it had taken me some time to accept it, it was at this moment that I knew, in my heart of hearts, that my quest was at an end. I realized at that moment that the desire for the crown had died within me, and that I would never reign in England.

I did not consult Skelton or Astley or any of the others, but kept my counsel, and when the two hours was up I went forward to the gate again, and Courtenay came out to me.

'Well?' he asked.

'I would have your licence to gather my company together,' I told him, 'and that being given, we shall depart and leave your city, and put you to no further trouble unless you pursue and attack us. Give me six hours and you shall hear no more of me.'

'Do you agree not to approach the city again in arms?'

'We do.'

He hesitated briefly, mulling matters over, and then said, 'We give you leave to depart unmolested, a truce which shall last until the sun sets.'

'Thank you,' I said, and turned my horse's head. Behind me I heard the jeers of the men of Exeter, but in my heart I was simply glad that there would be no more killing. I looked at the sky; it was not yet midday, and no matter what anyone else might say, I knew that the adventure was over.

'Send them home,' I told Skelton as soon as we were out of sight of the walls of Exeter. 'Send these men home.'

Some had already made their own decisions and left; others followed them as soon as the order was given, but there were yet thousands who remained and refused to leave. At first we moved along the road directly away from the East Gate I tried again to dismiss the men. They waited, ready to move west towards home, and I realized that they wanted me to make that decision for them.

'Send them home,' I said to Skelton wearily, but they would

not go, and in the end I turned my horse and continued along the road towards Taunton.

'It is not this way, Your Grace,' Astley said. 'This road leads east, into the clutches of King Henry.'

'That I know,' I told him. 'Surely no man could be foolish enough to follow me this way?'

'If you wish to escape Tudor,' he said, 'you must turn here and go west.'

'I do not wish to escape Tudor,' I said. 'I am not running from Tudor; I am running from the senseless slaughter of poor men who believe in me. I run east so that they cannot follow. I run east so that they can go home in safety. If I run west then Tudor will follow me and more of those same men will die. I cannot countenance that. If I go east then they cannot follow, and they will live.'

We continued east, and I was pleased to see that more and more became disheartened and slipped away. By nightfall we were within a few miles of Taunton, and the local lord of the manor took pity on me and gave me a bed for the night.

By morning it was clear that still many men had not grasped that the army of Cornishmen was no more, and still they followed me. We rode into Taunton, and the bishop offered me the use of his house. I confessed my sins to him, and received absolution. For two days we rested, and then I gathered the remnants of the force in a field outside the bishop's house.

'I have told you to go home,' I told them, 'and yet you persist in following me. You need to know that my kingship is at an end; Richard IV is no more. If you stay then the forces of King Henry – I so name him for the first time in the hearing of you all – will attack you and destroy you. We are no match for them, armed and officered as they are. I would pay you, but I have no coin, nothing tangible to show my appreciation. I thank you for your loyalty, but I beg you now to leave me to my fate. I wish you all a safe return to your homes.'

I went up and down the much reduced lines for the last time, greeting those I knew and bidding farewell to all, and then returned to the bishop's house, leaving them there. Most left, and yet there were still those who would not believe and who stayed, hoping no doubt for a miracle, waiting for my return to the field outside Taunton.

After dark Astley came into my chamber. 'Still there are those who will not leave you,' he said.

'If they will not leave me, then perforce I will leave them,' I said. 'I will not stay to see them slaughtered by Tudor.'

I called the few remaining servants and officers together and told them the same thing. 'I hereby release you all from any vows, promises or oaths of loyalty you have made to me,' I said. 'I shall go on from here alone, responsible for no man but myself. The rest of you can escape. If Tudor captures me then he will be content; go, leave me. I shall part hence before morning.'

'To go where, my lord?'

'I know not yet; out of England, for certain. It were best you did not know my plans.'

I slept briefly, and left instructions to be called at midnight. The bishop gave me his blessing, and with all my efforts I could not prevent Astley, Heron and Skelton coming with me, faithful unto the last. I had decided to try for Southampton, a port big enough to have a Breton or Flemish vessel that I could persuade to take us.

We rode to Ilminster and then turned east towards Ilchester and the long straight road that led to and across Salisbury Plain. We turned off that to head across country through Cranborne Chase. The weather was kind to us, and we made good time heading ever eastward, and with no sign of pursuit from the west or Lord Daubeney's men, whom we had been told were approaching from the east. We rode through the night and most of the next day, and then paused for the night at an inn where all the talk was of Perkin, and none of Richard IV. I was now neither of those men, and slept well in the chamber that was made available.

The next morning we moved on, ever south-east towards Southampton. My ploy of moving to the east instead of the more obvious west had worked, for we were untroubled by any of Tudor's men and reached the town easily enough, but there my plan foundered, for the docks were watched, and the wharves and roads had been cleared of all but English ships. There was no way out; I had the choice of running for ever or retiring to a place of greater safety.

Skelton knew of an abbey at Beaulieu that had the privilege of sanctuary, and we turned our horses that way, riding in late that night. We claimed sanctuary and paid the fee, and I exchanged my riding habit for a monk's. We were told to hand in any weapons, but none of us had even one. No one asked our names or enquired as to why we sought or needed to seek sanctuary, and we were shown to stark, bare cells and left to ponder our own sins and mortality.

With the cares of the world no longer on my shoulders, I slept long and peacefully, and the sun was already high in the sky when I awakened. We sanctuarians were free to take part or not in the devotions of the abbey, as long as we attended at least one mass each day and some of the other offices, such as matins or evensong. This was no hardship; I found it a pleasure to sit at the western end of the church and watch the brethren go about their business at the eastern end and listen to their chanting. I felt a great sense of release and peace descend upon me, and on that first day I found myself joining in the chants with an increasing sense of pleasure and joy.

The day after my arrival at the abbey a messenger arrived from Tudor asking if I were indeed there. The abbot refused to give any names, but sent answer that a group of refugees had taken shelter, and a few hours after I was told that a guard had been placed outside the gate.

'Is it permitted to form a guard outside the place of sanctuary in this way?' I asked the abbot.

'It is in a case of treason, my son.'

'I have committed no treason,' I told him, 'and nor have the men who followed me, their lawful lord.'

'I fear the king may not see matters in that light,' he said. 'You must prepare yourself for the full force of the law if you leave this place.'

'I have no wish to leave,' I said. 'My only concern at present is to get a message to my wife.'

'I fear no messages can pass from here,' he told me. 'They would not be allowed beyond the gate.'

'I wish only to tell her that I am safe.'

'You have not seen outside these walls in the time you have been here, I think?'

'No,' I admitted.

'Men and horses are encamped outside the gates. Not a flea on a mouse's tail could pass unmolested. It is you they seek, is it not?'

'It is, father.'

'So I have heard. That is no business of mine; it is a matter between you and God, or between you and the king should you ever leave this place. I must ask if you are prepared to speak to any man who wishes to see you?'

'Not any man, father, but men of authority.'

But when the messengers came, it was not me they asked for, but Heron and Astley. They were offered a safe conduct to the king for one of them in order that they could tell him what they knew and return to acquaint me with his pleasure.

'Accept it,' I said. 'It is the obvious thing to do. Tell the king the truth of what you know and see what he says. If he offers you pardons for yourselves, take them.'

It was agreed that Heron would go, and he set off with an armed escort to make his way into the king's presence.

'He will offer us pardons in return for you,' Astley said. 'Heron, Skelton and I will like as not be pardoned, but it will be dependent on handing you over and saying that you are not who you say you are.'

'Then do it,' I said. 'I have nothing to fear, for truth is an eternal shield, and if Tudor is already convinced that I am not Richard of York then nothing that anyone ever says will change his mind on that. If the chance comes to save your lives, do so by whatever means you can.'

It was as he said. Heron returned with the offer of a full pardon for all three of them, and for me the offer to be pardoned of my life.

'Will you take it, my lord?' he asked.

'Have you spoken false witness against me?'

'No, my lord. The king did speak with me directly, face to face, and I did tell him that I have known you only as Richard, Duke of York, and by no other name, and that these others will say the same thing, and he smiled at me and offered the pardons with no further word.'

'That is because you are of no further use to him,' I said. 'Had you lied and told him that I had confessed to being this upstart boy he thinks I am, you would have had the pardon anyway, but he would have required more of you. But it is of no matter, for he will find men to say what he wishes them to say, and 'tis not impossible I shall be one of them, should he prolong the torture enough.' I recalled what I had told Katherine, and the thought of the rack flashed through my mind, and I found that I was trembling. Astley reached out a hand, but I smiled at him and said, 'It will pass. It is a momentary fit. The fear of death was upon me, but it will pass.'

We passed word to the king's men outside that his offer

was accepted, and that we would hand ourselves over the next morning.

I made my confession that night, to the abbot who listened carefully and gave me full absolution.

'My son,' he asked when he had folded his scapula and kissed it, 'I must ask you a question, if I may?'

'Indeed, father.'

'Your confession included none of the sins for which the king seeks you – there is no admission of deception, or presumption, or falseness of any kind to him or to any other.'

'No, father.'

'Do you not have any wish to confess those sins?'

'If I had committed them, father, I would gladly and freely have confessed them – but I did not.'

He gave me his blessing and I retired for the night.

It was late the next morning, near to midday when the king's messenger called, and along with him the Mayor of Southampton and other officers and dignitaries.

'You are Piers Osbeck?' the king's man asked when I entered the room.

'No.'

He looked puzzled, and consulted a document that he had in his hand. Slowly, he repeated the name. 'Piers Osbeck?'

'No,' I repeated.

'Who, then, sir, are you?'

'I am Richard Plantagenet, Duke of York,' I told him.

His face cleared, and he said, 'Ah! He that claimed to be King of England, but who is in reality Piers Osbeck.'

'Who is this Piers Osbeck?' I asked. 'I have never heard the name in my life before.'

'Beg pardon, Your Grace,' said Heron, 'but it is the name that the king says you were born to.'

'Then the king is mistaken,' I said. 'I repeat, I have never heard the name before this minute.'

'Nonetheless, sir, do you surrender yourself unto the mercy of King Henry?' the man asked. 'Should you be pleased to do so, I have authority to remove you from this place and into a more comfortable lodging in the town. If you do come with me, sir, it must be of your own free will and under no compunction.'

'I do so agree,' I said.

'Then be pleased to make yourself ready, sir. You must not travel in these robes. They are for the holy men alone to wear without these walls.'

'I understand,' I said. 'Do you go and make ready, John, and alert the others.'

'I beg your pardon, sir, but my authority to transfer you extends only to your own person. Your companions must wait here upon the king's mercy.'

'I see.'

'It was so agreed, Your Grace,' Heron said. 'The king was most gracious.'

'You cannot be forced, my son,' the abbot said. 'You must be doing this of your own free will.'

I nodded my head and returned to my cell, where I removed the habit and dressed myself in the robes of the cloth of gold that Maximilian had given me.

My three companions came to say their goodbyes, and then the abbot came into the cell. 'You are aware, sir,' he said, 'that no power save that of God alone can force you from this place? You need not give in to threats or blandishments.'

'No more I do,' I said, 'but to a king who has freely offered pardon at no request from me. I place myself and my life willingly into his hands.'

'Then God be with you,' he replied, and I knelt for his blessing.

There was audible confusion as I came to the entrance to Beaulieu to join my captors. 'Master Osbeck,' protested the mayor, 'you may not wear such clothes as these. Cloth of gold is not for men such as us; it is for princes of the realm and no other.'

'I shall wear my own clothes,' I said. 'I know not of any man named Piers Osbeck, and though I am not he, and not King Richard IV either, I am yet, and shall remain, in spite of all that any man may say, that which God made me, Prince Richard Plantagenet, son of King Edward IV and Duke of York.'

Probationer

October 1497 – June 1498

My hands were not tied, as I had expected them to be, nor was I shackled or constrained in any way. The captain of the horsemen stood inside the inner gate, gazing at me as I approached in my cloth of gold, and then stepped forward. 'My name is Bradshaw, sir,' he said. 'I am to accompany you out of sanctuary, and then place you under guard and escort you first to the abbot's house in Southampton, and thence to His Majesty at Taunton. The king in his mercy has decreed that you are not to be bound or your movement limited in any way unless you should try to escape or refuse to give your parole. Do you understand?'

'I do,' I said, 'and I do give you my parole until such time as you complete your task. Is that sufficient?'

'It is, sir,' he said, and fell in beside me. We walked through the silent cloister, with here and there a monk gazing at me, some hostile, but most with pity. The abbot stepped forward and gave me one last blessing, this time in public, and then I walked out of the abbey, a free prince and a free man for the last, brief time, and into a circle of armed men. They had a horse ready for me, and the captain helped me into the saddle.

He squinted at me, looking into the sun. 'Ready, sir?' he asked.

I nodded, and he clucked to his horse, which set off. My own needed no move from me, for it immediately walked alongside his. I was no longer in control even of a steed.

We rode first, as Bradshaw had said, into Southampton to the abbot's house just inside the West Gate. Technically sanctuary could be extended to this building, but neither the abbot nor I had asked for it to be. My appearance in the town was, I think, simply a sop to the mayor and corporation, the king graciously allowing a small piece of the glory of capturing me being allowed to rub off on them.

We spent the night there, it being too late to dare the rutted paths and trackless moors to Taunton, and again I was not constrained in any way, and I listened intently to the news, which was not all about me. The other item of interest that the soldiers talked about was a new island found for the crown by an Italian adventurer, Giovanni Gabotto.

'He sailed from Bristol in his ship the *Matthew* last year,' Bradshaw told me. 'He sailed first to Ireland and then west, hoping to find Cipango. Instead he encountered an island in the Western Ocean filled with tall trees of the type mariners make masts of and surrounded by seas which were so filled with cod that it was enough to put a stone in a basket to weigh it down, let the basket down into the sea and haul out enough fish to feed the entire crew.'

'Yes,' I said. 'I know this place. I have been to those very fishing grounds.'

'No, sir,' Bradshaw said. 'This is far beyond any island known to man. This Gabotto was the first to travel there. He raised the king's standard and claimed the land for England. He called it the "new found land".'

'That shows supreme logic, if but little imagination,' I said, 'but it is in truth the place of which I speak and to which I have travelled. I have been there with Breton fishermen, and wintered there, and know the natives of the place. Did this Gabotto make any mention of the inhabitants of the land, the red men?'

Bradshaw looked at me, and exchanged a glance with two

of his officers who were dining with us. 'No, sir,' he said, 'although he intends to return next year to explore further.'

'No doubt to seek the "not yet found land", I presume,' I said.

'I suppose so,' Bradshaw said uncertainly, missing the joke, 'although it is said he has already named these yet undiscovered islands after his victualler and sponsor, a Bristol merchant called Richard a Merike, in gratitude for his support.'

I put the new land out of my mind. Such strange coasts and the adventures that went with them were now closed to me, and so, excited as I was by the talk of the new worlds, I closed my eyes and thought not of them.

We arrived at Taunton the next afternoon. The king had taken up residence in the priory, and I thought to have been taken there, but Bradshaw took me first to a house outside the city walls and showed me into a room. 'You must wait here,' he said, 'before we go on to meet the king.'

I sat on one of the chairs and waited, and after some time the door opened to admit a very old man.

'Cloth of gold,' he said as soon as he saw me. 'Presumptuous bastard.'

He had not introduced himself, but he had no need to; his clothing and his attitude told me everything. I was in the presence of Cardinal Archbishop John Morton, Archbishop of Canterbury and Chancellor of England, almost eighty years old, the most powerful man in England after the king and one with an implacable hatred of the House of York. He had baptized me, I believe, although of course I had no memory of the event and he was determined not to have.

'Wrong on both counts, Your Grace,' I told him, kneeling and reaching for his ring.

Morton pulled his hand away. 'You forget yourself, sirrah,' he said. 'You are in the presence of a prince of the church.'

'And you are in the presence of a prince of England,' I replied, and rose to my feet.

There was a slight pursing of his lips, but he gave no other sign. 'That cannot be,' he said eventually. 'You are not Prince Richard, you have never been Prince Richard, and you will never be Prince Richard. You forget, I knew the boy. Perhaps you need to be taught exactly who is who in this realm.'

'I am the third monarch of my family that this king has had in his power, Your Grace,' I told him, 'and I have learned all too well who is who, and what respect he, and you, have for kingship. When do I follow the path of my brother and uncle?'

'I know not of whom you speak,' he said. 'We have nothing on our conscience regarding your brother or uncle, or indeed any member of your family . . .'

I smiled.

'. . . whom I understand still thrive in Tournai. I know about you, boy. I know your history, I know your family, I know your teachers and your fellow choristers, and I know the men who tutored you in your escapade. I knew about you before you knew about yourself; my men were in Tournai within weeks of you, all those years ago, and were there again as soon as you made your false declaration. It is all documented.'

'In Tournai within weeks of me?' I said. 'Within weeks of what? My birth? Did your grace have a premonition of what Pierrechon was to be all those years ago? Or do you simply mean within weeks of my arrival there after the murder of my brother?'

He saw that he had made a slip, and sat heavily on one of the chairs. I said, 'It is not meet that you should be seated in the presence of a prince who remains standing . . .'

'Shut up, Osbeck,' he said irritably. 'I have no time for this nonsense. You are not a prince, and never have been. That is the end of it. I merely wanted to have a look at you before the king did. Now, I need a confession from you,' he went on conversationally. 'I will have it drawn up, although truth to tell it is nearly complete, and you may indeed dictate some parts of it if you wish, as long as they do not differ from the facts – and then you will sign it.'

'And then what will happen?'

He spread his hands. 'I know not, nor do I care,' he said. 'You will be the king's to dispose of. Perhaps he will retire you to a private life – give you employment, mayhap, beside young Lambert, who was so stupid that he aspired to be Warwick. No one who has ever seen Edward Warwick would ever want to be him.' He paused. 'Or he could execute you,' he said. 'After all, you're guilty of treason.'

'I cannot be guilty of treason if I am who you say I am,' I said. 'Your man is not English, I think.'

'A minor detail,' he said. 'As for me, I don't really care what happens to you.'

'We are at one there, then,' I said, and again the pursing of his lips told me that it was not the answer he had expected. 'I have been a king,' I told him, 'with some of the trappings of kingship, and I have been a dead man, and both states are the domain of impostors. I care not what you do with me. Let the king's conscience, if he has one, be his guide.'

He moved to the door. 'Be sure, Perkin, the king's conscience, if he has one, will decide your future, if you have one.'

He twinkled briefly, pleased with his witty line. I found myself strangely pleased that he had discovered a little humour in my plight.

'In the meantime, I shall send you on your way to the king,' he continued. 'In due course I shall send writers to help you prepare your tale.'

Bradshaw returned, and we proceeded to Taunton and into

247

the priory, where I was again shown into a room to await the king; we were to meet alone at first, before he presented me to his council.

Henry Tudor, soberly dressed, entered not long after me. I knelt to him, and he bowed to me before seating himself on a chair that served him in the office of a throne. He motioned Bradshaw to withdraw along with all the other officials and guards who had entered the room with the king. The man hesitated, and Henry turned to him. 'You may leave us, captain.'

'Your Majesty!' The man was clearly on the point of protesting, but Henry waved him away.

'We doubt that this man is capable of lifting a hand to hurt us,' he said. 'You may leave us and wait without.' He reverted to the more personal. 'I shall call if I need you.'

Bradshaw bowed and left.

Henry Tudor did have a silence and dignity about him that was king-like, but his teeth were bad – few in number, widely spaced, and all of them black.

He spent some time simply looking at me, his gaze intense and piercing. 'You may approach us,' he said eventually.

I took three steps forward and then bowed deeply. 'Your Grace,' I said.

'We have decided that the appropriate term of address is "Your Majesty",' he said.

'Your Majesty,' I repeated after him.

'So,' he said. 'You are Piers Osbeck.'

'I am Richard Plantagenet, Duke of York,' I said.

'You are Piers Osbeck,' he said. 'This is our country, and you shall be whom we say you shall be, regardless of who you used to be, or perhaps who you claim you used to be.'

I looked across at him, and he looked back into my eyes. 'Your Majesty is aware of who I am, then?'

'I have always been aware,' he said. 'My spies are not as

incompetent as all that. Admitting to it is a different matter, however. Do you still desire my throne?'

'Your Majesty, I do not.'

He grunted. 'Good. Even so, I cannot admit to being aware of who you are, as you can no doubt understand.'

'I suppose so,' I said.

He indicated a chair. 'Sit,' he said. 'We can talk as equals, Richard, for a time at least. Probably the last time, of course.'

I waited until he had seated himself and then took the chair.

'You will never be recognized by anyone in this country as Richard of York,' he said. 'It is in no one's interests to recognize you, least of all yours. The country is not at peace, but it is not in chaos either, which it would be were you to be allowed the sort of licence you have had hitherto. It is competently run, by the man best equipped to wear the crown. Indeed, there are but two sorts of people who would have England in chaos again, foreigners or fools. The one of these I know you not to be; are you the other?'

I looked at him and then at the ground.

'Think too who would be most harmed by another period of war,' he said. 'I mean she whom you love most.'

'Katherine?' I asked sharply, and started to my feet.

'You misunderstand me,' he said softly. 'No, Katherine is safe and unharmed, and will ever remain so while I breathe. I was referring to England.'

I nodded. He was beginning to make sense.

'I shall make no further assault on your country or your peace, Your Majesty,' I said. 'You have my word on that. Yet I cannot answer to a lie. I am not your Piers Osbeck, and will not admit to it.'

'It is what you will be called,' he said. 'You were him once, were you not?'

'A similar name, and that but briefly,' I admitted. 'I suppose

I need not insist upon the truth, if it is inconvenient to you, but I cannot change who I am, even at the whim of a king. I shall be called whomsoever you wish, as you say, and may in time learn to answer to whatever name it is you desire to call me by, but that is all it is – a name. The office comes with the robes of office. I shall wear your robes, but the title you give me is a description merely, not a definition; what you choose to call me need not accord with what I am.'

'And yet you call us "Your Majesty",' he said. 'On that same basis, is it?'

'The king is entitled to call himself anything he wishes,' I said. 'No man can have any quarrel with that.'

'And you now acknowledge us as king?'

'It is a political reality,' I said. 'Even princes must be realistic sometimes.'

'Well, that admission is not before time,' he said, and stood up. He was taller than I had expected, and milder. The ferocity of his pursuit of me over the years had painted me a mental picture of an ill-tempered individual, but this Henry was calm, even gentle. He walked over to me. 'You must not wear these clothes,' he said. 'Cloth of gold is not fitting.'

'I shall remove them if Your Majesty wishes.'

'Later,' he said. 'Later we will supply you with appropriate attire.'

He resumed the chair. 'I have waited so long for this moment,' he said, 'and now that it has come, I have no idea what to do with it. First, though, I must hold you responsible for many deaths.'

'Yes,' I said. 'I am sorry. I did not seek the deaths of those men at Exeter. I did not expect . . .'

'What? Resistance?'

'I suppose so, yes.'

'I have executed many men for less than you have done. And yet I cannot execute you, for I have pardoned you your life.

Now, however, we must decide on what you are going to tell my council.'

'I shall tell them anything Your Majesty requires,' I replied, 'as long as I do not tell a lie in so doing.'

'Let us see, then. You will admit to claiming to be Richard Plantagenet?'

'I will.'

'You will admit that you once went by the name of Piers Osbeck?'

'No,' I said. 'The name I took when in Picardy was Pierrechon Werbecque. I suppose it is a difficult name to get an English tongue around.'

'So be it. Werbecque, then. You will admit that you came into this realm to wrest the crown from me by force?'

'Yes.'

'And you will submit to me now, and renounce all claim to the throne of England?'

'I will.'

'And renounce all claim to be Richard Plantagenet?'

'Your Majesty knows I cannot do that,' I told him. 'If Your Majesty requires my acquiescence, which I am perfectly willing to give, then you must not ask me that question. All of your questions must be framed most carefully.'

'As must your answers,' he replied. 'I cannot have even the slightest of suggestions in public that you still believe yourself to be Richard Plantagenet. Do you understand that?'

'I do,' I said.

'Good. I can see that we are beginning to understand each other,' he said, 'and are likely to continue to do so. It might even become a pleasure to be merciful. Before I have you brought before the council, I advise that you do not recognize any of them.'

'I shall endeavour not to,' I said, and he nodded, satisfied.

'In that case . . .' He raised his voice. 'Captain, within.'

251

The door opened immediately and Bradshaw poked his head in.

'Take the prisoner to the antechamber. The members of the council are already gathered. Bring him in when the door is opened.' He looked at me. 'We will make a show for them, eh?'

I was led through a maze of corridors and eventually arrived before a large door. The wait was not long. It had been clear to me that the king had been most pleased with his new toy and at the way the toy had behaved. He knew I was going to be little trouble to him.

The door opened and Bradshaw and I stepped inside. The king was seated, while the room was filled with standing men – his council. I cast my eyes about briefly, but immediately dropped my gaze; I did not want to recognize anyone. I stepped forward and bowed to the king. There was a faint murmur – I had not knelt, as protocol demanded, but Henry affected not to notice. He went again through the questions we had already rehearsed, choosing his words delicately.

'You are come here at our will and commandment?' he asked.

'I am.'

'You admit to claiming to be Richard Plantagenet?'

'I do.'

'You admit that you once went by the name of Piers . . .' he hesitated.

'My name in Picardy was Pierrechon Werbecque,' I said.

'You admit that you came into this realm to take the crown from me by force?'

'Yes.'

'And do you submit to me now as the lawful king of this land?'

'I do.'

'And do you renounce all claim to the throne of England?'

'I do.'

I made to kneel before him now, acknowledging that he was king and I was not and would never be, but Henry stopped me with a gesture and said, 'We have heard from you that you call yourself Richard, son of King Edward. In this place are some who were companions of that lord; look and see if you recognize them.'

I glanced briefly round, but then looked at the floor and shook my head. 'None, my lord.'

'I think that will be enough,' the king said. 'Remove him.'

Bradshaw stepped forward and touched my elbow, and I bowed again to Henry. Then, as I turned, a slight movement caught my eye, and I looked up to see a face that was all too familiar. I must have hesitated, for the shock of recognition was great. Among the men standing to my right was Thomas Grey, who had been my chamberlain when I was a child, and was my half-brother, the son of my mother by her first marriage.

I saw the recognition in his eyes, and the pity too, and then we both turned away. I was Pierrechon again now, and must never again claim to be Richard Plantagenet. It was in both our interests that we should not know each other, and as we looked away, faintly, in the distance, I thought I heard a late cock crow.

There remained much to be done. I was under guard, but not held or locked away, and was able to wander at will through the priory. The king sent messengers to St Buryan, first to ask Katherine to leave sanctuary and place herself under his protection, and incidentally to tell her that all was well with me. I waited, anxious to see her and Edward again and to hold little Richard for the first time, but there was no news. The royal household moved on to Exeter, where the king rewarded the defenders and a message finally came that she had been persuaded to come out of sanctuary. In the meantime I had been allocated a guard who stayed with me night and day, and a small room in which to sleep, which was locked at night and had a guard both within and without in case I had thought to escape.

On the afternoon of our arrival in Exeter I was ordered to report to one of the exchequer chambers, there to begin my duties. I was led to the room, told to knock at the door, as was proper for one of my new lowly status, and was called in. There I was greeted by Cardinal Morton, who was accompanied by two young clerks.

'Your duties will begin with your confession,' Morton said. 'You will dictate it to these men, who will write down what you say. Then you will sign it, and the matter will be ended. Is that clear?'

'Yes, my lord. How detailed must it be?'

'The full truth,' he said. 'The full truth, now, no less. There must be no more nonsense from you. Both these clerks are fluent in your language, so there should be no difficulty in making yourself understood.' He looked across at the two clerks, each of whom sat with a writing table on his knee and his eyes on me. 'Are your quills charged?'

'They are, my lord bishop,' replied the elder of them.

Morton pointed at a stool and motioned me to sit. 'Then commence,' he said. He turned and sat himself on one of two comfortable chairs that had been placed either side of the fire.

'I was born . . .' I began.

The two clerks looked surprised and hesitated, and Morton leapt from his chair. 'Enough!' he cried. 'You will make this confession in your native tongue.'

'English is my native tongue,' I said, confused.

Morton brought his face close to mine. 'How long will you continue this charade?' he hissed. 'We know who you are, we know where you are from, we know your parentage, and, above all, we know that your native language is French.'

'No,' I said. 'I speak French, of course, but . . .'

Morton opened his mouth to speak, but a quiet voice forestalled him, saying, 'The confession will be dictated in French.'
It was the king, who had opened the door and slipped in.
Clerks and cleric alike attempted to rise and bow, but he motioned them all back to their places and took a seat. 'You may
begin,' he said, '*en français*.'

The archbishop stepped back so that Tudor could get a clear
look at me.

'*En français*,' the king repeated.

I bowed my head at the royal command, and began again.
'*Je suis né le deuxieme fils du roi Edouard Quatre
d'Angleterre . . .*'

Once again Morton was at my side, his breath hot and
meaty in my nostrils. 'The truth, Warbeck,' he said, 'the whole
truth, and nothing but the truth. The time for pretence has
gone.'

'I agree completely,' I said. His fist, the size of a ham,
slammed into the side of my head, and I fell to the side, off my
stool and down onto one knee. I raised an arm to defend myself
against a second blow, but again the soft voice of authority
intervened. 'Enough, Your Grace,' Tudor said, and Morton,
breathing heavily, stepped back.

The king rose to his feet. 'Do you intend to do as we require?' he asked.

'I cannot be required to say falsehood,' I told him. 'We
agreed that if asked I should tell the truth.'

'As you see it?'

'How many truths are there?' I asked.

He smiled his thin-lipped smile. 'You'd be surprised, my
boy,' he said. 'You'd be surprised.'

He turned his attention to the archbishop. 'I think we need
not detain Master Warbeck any further, Your Grace. If he will
not tell us what we already know to be true, then we can use
the information we already have, and he can sign that.' He

turned to the elder of the clerks. 'Bring the confession,' he said, 'and this man can read and sign it.'

The clerk rose and left the room.

'He can read then, your Perkin?' I asked. Morton took a step forward, and I thought he was going to hit me again, but Tudor restrained him with a gesture.

'Quite well educated, my Perkin,' Morton said instead, and turned to take a parchment from a bundle brought in by the returning clerk. He glanced at it and then handed it to me. 'We have a number of copies,' he said, 'the signing of which will take some considerable time, so you should begin at once. And because we have made so many copies, it should be clear that there is no point in trying to destroy it.'

'It's no Titulus Regulus then?' I said, an unnecessary jibe, and this time Morton did hit me, sending me sprawling and knocking the document out of my hands. The younger of the clerks picked it up. I regained my stool.

The clerk, a youth of perhaps eighteen, stood uncertainly, and Morton said, 'Give it to the prisoner, Thomas. It is the story of his life.'

The boy held it out to me, and I took it and turned the parchment the right way up.

'Give him a pen,' Morton said, and when Thomas held out his quill the archbishop said, 'Sign it.'

'Surely I must first read it,' I said. 'I am sure it is a fascinating document, and I would love to make my acquaintance with your Perkin and his deeds.'

Henry Tudor raised his eyebrows, shrugged and took the seat opposite Morton's. I returned to the stool and read the parchment slowly and carefully from beginning to end.

It was written in French, and detailed in the first part the life of the Pierrechon Werbecque whose life I had taken over. There were errors and inaccuracies, but most of it was true, including his illnesses and details of the neighbours he had encountered, intermingled with some of the men I had known in his guise. There was a long and unnecessary list of relatives and friends which proved only that Tudor's research had been painstaking, if not completely accurate. In the middle it told of my time in Portugal, and became complete fiction only when I set out for Cork. It said, of course, that I was not who I claimed to be, but was the son of Jehan.

'Sign it,' Morton said again when I looked up.

'It contains much truth,' I said, 'but many errors besides, so I cannot sign it. What was it you said, my lord Archbishop? "The whole truth and nothing but the truth?"'

'It is permissible to make amendments,' Tudor said, 'as far as they do not stray too far from the central message.'

'What changes would you like to make?' Morton asked, genuinely interested. He motioned to the two clerks, who charged their pens and waited.

'Well,' I said, 'there is a major error at the beginning, where it says that my father was named Jehan Werbecque.'

'That was his name, surely?' Morton said. 'Or should it be Jan, in the Flemish way?'

'Jehan was my father by adoption,' I said, 'but my true father was Edward Plantagenet . . .'

I got no further, for I found myself knocked once again from my stool, and looked up to see Tudor and Morton leaving the room followed by the elder of the clerks. The younger remained behind to gather up all the tools, and I helped him by rolling up the parchment and finding the quill that I had been holding when I was struck.

'Why do you not just sign it?' the lad whispered. 'They will publish it to the world whether you do or no.'

'Because it is not the truth, Thomas,' I said, 'and there can be no compromise on that.'

'But if you do not sign, they will kill you.'

'Thomas,' I said, 'they will kill me anyway, and one day they

257

must die, and you too must die, so in the end our steps lead us all the same way, and there is no great difference between any of us except that I must die today and you will die tomorrow. I have nothing left in this world except the truth, and I could not face my God if I denied that.'

'Yes, sir,' he said. 'Thank you,' and then he left me alone.

I returned to my small room, and there one of the king's counsellors came to me with further news of Katherine.

'I think you know that she has left sanctuary?' he said.

I nodded. 'She shall be here soon, then?' I asked him. 'It is but a few days' ride, even at a sedate pace.'

'I fear it may be a little longer than that,' he said. 'The king has sent me to tell you that the lady Katherine is in mourning.'

'For whom?' I asked, fear clutching at me.

'It is with heavy heart that I relate this,' he said, 'but your newborn child was too weak. He lived but twelve days; his lungs were not strong. I am sorry to bring this news.'

He left me alone. The loss to myself was but little to bear; it was a son I had never seen, a babe whose face would not come to my sleep in the long hours of the night or be brought to mind in wild imaginings. Katherine, though, having borne him inside her all these months, would feel the pain in every part of her body. I knew I had to go to her, to comfort her, and demanded that he go to find the king.

It took some time to get an audience, and I asked his permission to travel, under guard if necessary, to Cornwall to see her.

'That is impossible,' he said. 'I have had you in my hands but a little time, and to release you again so soon, even under heavy guard, would not look well. There are those already who think I am too lax with you; there are those who call for your death. It must not be.' He looked sympathetic. 'I am sorry for your loss, but I cannot allow you to go. If it is any consolation, she shall be brought to us here as soon as she is well enough to travel.'

And with that I had to be content. Since our first meeting twenty-two months before, I had been from her but twenty days, and in that time our child had died along with my hopes for our future.

It was but a few days after this that she and her escort arrived at Exeter. I immediately asked permission of the king to see her.

He smiled and shook his head. 'I think we have some unfinished business first, do we not?' he said.

This time when I entered the exchequer chamber there was a table, an ink horn and a number of quills, and three separate piles of documents. Morton and his two clerks were there too, and the bishop was almost affable.

'It is a simple matter,' he said. 'We require your signature on each of these documents. When they have all been signed then you will be granted a meeting with Lady Katherine.'

'And if I do not sign?'

He smiled. 'Then no meeting.'

'Ever?'

'Probably ever, but certainly not until you change your mind.'

This time he provided me with a table and a chair, not a stool, and there was even a small fire at my back to keep out the autumn chill. 'I shall leave Thomas here to carry out any minor changes you might wish to make or to translate any English words that are strange to you.'

I looked sharply at him, but he simply smiled blandly. He knows, I thought, and to make my discomfort all the sharper he wants me to know that he knows.

'Take your time,' he said. 'Read them all, ask any questions you will, make any changes as long as they are minor – Thomas knows what is acceptable – and then sign them. Or, if you prefer, just sign them – the signing is all.'

He flowed through the door and I sat in the chair and picked up one of the documents before me. I recognized it immediately. It was the confession, in French, that they had tried to get me to sign before.

'Have any changes been made to this?' I asked.

The boy Thomas shook his head.

'Where does the information come from?'

'The king has been searching for anyone who knows you since you first went to Ireland,' he said. 'It was not difficult information to acquire.'

'No,' I said, musing. 'I made no secret of who I was when I was in Tournai. The more enthusiastically I played Werbecque, the less I would be suspected of being Plantagenet. Ironic, isn't it?'

'I should not be listening to these thoughts, sir. Even to hear them spoken could be construed as treason. I must beg you not to . . .'

'I understand, Thomas,' I told him, 'and shall desist.' I read through the document again, and then turned to the second pile. These were in English, and were a loose translation of the French version, which must have been written first. Much of the list of Pierrechon's relatives and friends had been removed, presumably as being of little interest to people in England, and there were a number of errors; the copyist had been careless, but the mistakes seemed to have gone unnoticed. He had mistaken the first three letters of 'Ouldenarde'; copying them as 'ant' rather than 'oul', and then, in his haste, guessed at the rest, so Ouldenarde had become Antwerp. 'Werbecque' had become 'Osbeck' again, Jehan had been elevated in status, his wife's name was wrong, and, among other errors, I seemed to have acquired an extra grandfather.

'There are many errors,' I told Thomas. 'To correct them will take us a long time.'

'I am at your command, Master Warbeck.'

'Pray do not call me that,' I said. 'It is not, and never has been my name, and as you cannot call me by the name that God gave me, I would lief you called me no name at all.'

'As you wish, sir. But as to the signing?'

'What is this third?' I asked, and took up the other document.

It was as if I had been struck a blow with a fist. 'Mother,' it began baldly, 'as humbly as I may, I commend myself to you,' and went on to say that I had masqueraded as Richard of York and referred to brothers and sisters whom I was supposed to have had, reminisced about our parting and asked for money. And, in the midst of all this, it said that I had heard that my father had died.

'To whom is this addressed?' I asked.

'Why, sir, to your mother; see, there is her name at the foot.'

It was not a name I recognized, certainly not the name of the lady who had briefly acted as my mother, but that was insignificant. 'Is Jehan dead?' I asked. 'Does this say true?'

'I believe so, sir.'

I sat, stunned. I knew, of course, that no man could live for ever, and it had been many years since I had seen him, but I had often thought of Jehan as I had last seen him, rowing one of his bacquets up and down the Scheldt. Suddenly I missed him and his gruffness and strength, and I felt the tears spring to my eyes. In the space of a few days I had lost a son whom I had never seen and a father whom I could never acknowledge. 'I cannot sign this,' I said. 'This is not a letter that a man sends to a newly widowed woman.'

Before Thomas could answer, the door opened and Morton returned. 'I see no earnest scribbling,' he said. 'What is the delay?'

'This letter to Madame Werbecque,' I told him. 'This cannot be sent. She is newly widowed.'

'Do not concern yourself with it,' Morton said. 'Thomas, go outside for a moment.'

The clerk obeyed, and Morton leaned close to me and said, 'Between you and me, the letter will never reach the lady. It is for show only; it is to prove to those who need further proof that you are who we say you are, because the letter acknowledges the fact. Sign it, and I shall guarantee that she will never see it. It is a diplomatic convenience, no more. We cannot afford to have it delivered to her, in any case; she might take it upon herself to deny that she is mother to the child, and we could not have that.' He straightened his back. 'I am informed that my lady Katherine is well rested,' he said. 'She may be anxious to meet you.' He paused. 'Signatures first, though, of course.'

'Would you sign that which you knew not to be true, my lord?' I asked.

'Think what Caiaphas said,' he replied, then turned and left the room, and Thomas re-entered.

'I think I cannot sign,' I told him, 'though I am sorely tempted.'

'Because what you read is not the truth?'

'Yes.'

'Is Piers Osbeck your true name?' he asked.

'No.'

'Then what does it matter if you write it on a few documents? You have said already that they are full of errors. The people who wish to believe them will do so anyway. On the other hand, anyone who studies them with an open mind will see that they do not ring true. If the signature is false too, then they will know that it is all false.'

'I had not looked to meet one so young who is yet so skilled in sophistry,' I said. 'As you said, they will publish it to the world whether I sign it or no. If I do not sign, they will say I did, so if I wish the truth to be known I must sign the documents falsely and leave the world its clues. That is rather a neat paradox, is it not? Are you a philosopher, Thomas?'

'No, sir,' he said, 'although I would like to study it one day.'

'There is the other consideration,' I said.

'Sir?'

'By signing I get to see my lady all the quicker.'

I picked up a quill and grinned across the table at him. 'If I write in a broad clear hand, Thomas, then you might speed matters along by signing a few yourself. Just for handwriting practice, of course.'

I wrote 'per: Piers Osbeck' on about two score copies of each document, but young Thomas refused to essay any for himself, as he was in truth too nervous and in fear of the scaffold.

When the signing was done I went in search of the king's chamberlain and asked to see my wife. Henry agreed to allow us time together, but issued instructions that we were never to be left alone – he did not wish to risk further Yorkist heirs to plague him.

Our first meeting was supervised by the king himself, no doubt curious to see how we would react to each other. He and I were alone when Katherine, still wearing her travel robes, was ushered into the room. She held out her hands to me, and I took her into my arms and we both burst into tears. She assured me that Edward was well, and missing me. Henry allowed us a few moments to hold each other, and then gently but firmly the king pulled me away. Katherine collapsed to the floor in tears, and Henry would not allow me to approach her.

'Most noble lady,' Henry said when her sobs had subsided, 'I grieve as you do, for your child, and it pains me much, second only to the slaughter of so many of my subjects, that you have been deceived by such a sorry fellow as this.'

Katherine looked at me and I smiled, hoping that she would remember our conversation aboard the *Cuckoo*.

Henry went on, emphasizing the lies I had told, the confessions I had signed, my perfidy and wickedness, the way she had been deceived, and the possibility of a new life for one of her worth and station. Only once did she react, when he referred to me as 'this man who was hitherto your husband'.

'He is my husband yet,' she interrupted, 'whatever his present station in life. It was man and woman that God joined together, not prince and princess. No man, not even a king, can put us asunder.' Then, softening, she asked guilelessly, 'Goeth the law not so, my lord?'

'When your husband, then, as you call this man, confessed to his crimes,' the king said, 'I forgave him them and granted him his life. I now order him to confess those same crimes to you, that you might know the extent of his perfidy.'

'My wife already knows all that she needs to know, Your Majesty,' I said. 'She needs no further confession.'

'But I do,' he said. 'Confess all to her, and she and your child shall be treated with honour as long as they both shall live.'

'Your Majesty already knows the full extent of my crimes,' I said.

'Tell her,' he said. 'I would have you confess all to your wife.'

I remained silent.

'Confess,' he said again.

'Perhaps Your Majesty would care to ask me specific questions . . .'

'Not this time, Piers,' he said. 'It must be your own words.'

'My lady,' I said. 'My darling Katherine, you see that I am forced to speak to you thus, which I do out of fear and with shame. I ask for your forgiveness, and beg His Majesty to return you to your father.'

Her eyes widened. 'I shall not leave you,' she said.

'Confess,' Henry said behind me. 'Tell her all. She must hear it from your own lips.'

'Madam,' I said, 'the king bids me tell you that I am not he who you think I am, and that I have misled you into believing so. I am to tell you that I am Piers Osbeck, a native of Tournai, and that my father is . . . was a boatman in that city, and that I came unto your country under false pretences and abducted you and led you into this country in the false belief that I could be king.' I paused. 'Do you understand what I say to you?'

'I do,' she said.

'And so do I,' Henry said behind me. 'Do you now repeat it without all that "the king bids me" and "I am to tell you".'

I did as he said, looking into her eyes, and then said, 'Do you understand why this is necessary?'

'I do.' She held out a hand and touched my face. 'What would you have me do now?'

'I would have you place your trust in this most powerful and merciful prince, who has promised to treat you and Edward with honour and not to desert you.' I held out my hand to raise her to her feet, and as she grasped it she gave my fingers an encouraging squeeze and her eyes caught mine briefly before they were cast down demurely.

She looked at Henry and said, 'I place all my faith, hope and safety in that royal promise.'

'My lady, you will for now be lodged in the household of the queen my wife,' he said. 'You will not for the moment see this man again, until we have decided what is to be done with him.'

'May I not console my wife and mourn our son?' I asked.

He hesitated, but only for a moment. 'No,' he said. 'I am sorry, but matters of state must take precedence over all other considerations. We leave for London immediately. You will travel separately, of course. Once arrived you may meet from time to time, should Lady Katherine desire it, but under supervision, and never alone, as I have said. By the time we arrive your confession will have been distributed to all, and the world will know you for what you are.'

Of Edward, now first beginning to take baby steps in preference to crawling about, naught was said; his existence was ignored by all but his mother and me.

The next morning was All Souls' Day, and I received permission from the king to hear mass in remembrance of the dead who had fought for me at Exeter (and some who had been executed since, hanged and quartered outside the city walls), and especially for Jehan and Richard. I went with the king's party to church, and was recognized by no man. If I had once been a prince, I assuredly was no longer; perhaps more remarkably, I found that I did not care.

Provocateur

November 1497 – June 1498

The king's palace of Sheen is on the Thames. I remembered something of it from time spent there when I was a boy, but nothing in detail. When we arrived there I was taken away to a servant's room in which I was to sleep. I was free to wander throughout the palace and its grounds, but was not allowed to go beyond that, and had to ask permission if I wanted to speak to my wife. I asked on all of the first three days, but was refused. I was now a lowly member of the royal household, and was told that I would soon be allocated duties like any other servant. Katherine, as promised, became a lady-in-waiting to the queen, whom I could no longer call my sister.

I in my turn was placed in the charge of two men, Robert Jones and William Smith, both trusted members of Henry's household. Jones made my position very clear: 'You will wear the king's livery and do all that you are told without question or comment. You will not speak unless spoken to, and you will always refer to the king as "Your Majesty" when speaking to him and "His Majesty" when speaking of him. You will hear nothing, see nothing and speak nothing of anything that you might accidentally observe as you go about your duties. I or Master Smith shall be always within earshot of you; we shall sleep in your chamber. When your duties for the day are completed you may do as you will, except that you may not attempt to speak to Lady Katherine Huntly except in the presence of another person. Is all this clear? Do you wish me to explain further?'

I shook my head. I had been so many things in my short time in Henry VII's power. He had paraded me through the streets on his progress to London – not, as some said, as an object of scorn, although some did laugh at me, but as merely another member of his entourage. I had trailed in his wake from Exeter to London and thence to Sheen. He had displayed me to Parliament, but I had not been required to explain myself, and merely had to sit while members of that house had shouted abuse. I had preceded him down the aisle at church, arm in arm with another courtier; Katherine and I had been displayed at a reception he had held for foreign ambassadors, so that he could show that I really was under his control. Worst of all, he had sent me to act in the office of tipstaff, to escort a former adherent of mine, one of Henry's masters of horse, I believe, though garbed as a friar, through the streets of London to his confinement in the Tower.

I was yet free and unfettered, but it was a freedom that chafed. Outwardly, Henry was treating me with the respect due to a prince, even though he refused to recognize, in public anyway, that I had ever been one, but his clemency was tempered with an element of ridicule, so that his attitude to me seemed to be an elaborate joke to which I was not privy. I developed a way of coping with this, which was to remain silent unless absolutely necessary; not to answer a question is easy – it is simply a matter of turning your head and refusing to acknowledge that it has been asked. Princes learn to do it from an early age, and I had remembered how.

Henry himself I saw little of, but every now and again I would find myself in the same room as him, and he was not averse to engaging me in friendly conversation. One day, passing me in the corridor, he stopped and said, 'You have loyal friends, do you know that?'

'No, Your Majesty.'

'I don't mean Heron and Astley and men of that type,' he

said, 'though they were loyal enough in their way. No, it's James and Maximilian I refer to, people like that.'

I waited, not knowing how to reply, and he went on, 'You are a lively topic in their correspondence. How do you come by such loyalty, I wonder? In any case, you seem to be a most valuable bargaining counter, so I shall not play you until the time is ripe. Lady Katherine is well, as I suppose you know.'

'Yes, Your Majesty. Thank you.'

He nodded, and was about to turn away when I became emboldened by my desperation. 'She tells me that our son has been taken away from her. May I ask why?'

'Because I don't want another Yorkist bastard persecuting my son when I am dead,' he said harshly, and walked off down the corridor.

'What have you done with him?' I shouted, flouting protocol, but more an anxious father than a courtier.

Henry paused, and then turned back. He looked from side to side along the passage, but his officers were well back and diplomatically deaf. His voice was low as he spoke. 'Your boy is safe and well,' he said. 'I give you my word on that. I am a cold man, I am told, and an austere, but I am not the monster that some would have it that I am. Your boy is safe and provided for, although you will never see him again. He will never be King of England, nor aspire to it, for he will never know whose son he is, but he is to be brought up in a family where he is treasured and loved. They know nothing of his birth or history. His mother does not know where he is, and I am not going to tell either her or you, but you need not fear for him. He, at least, is safe from the desperate destiny that has led us both into this pretty pass.'

'It must be difficult for Katherine to bear,' I said. 'She has not spoken of her feelings to me.'

'Nor will she,' he said. 'It is so commanded. I am sorry.'

'An adoptive family can be a loving one,' I said. 'I speak from experience.'

'And to be King of England, rightful or no, is not a task I would willingly place on any shoulders,' he said. 'I desperately wanted it once, as you did, but now I know better. I do not envy my little Arthur.'

'Nor I,' I said.

'You must accept the separation,' he said. 'I am sorry, but it is necessary. Many will think him dead. Let them do so; as long as they think it he is safe.'

He looked me direct in the face, nodded and turned away down the corridor. Edward was never mentioned to me again by any man in that court.

It was a few days after this encounter that I was busy in the king's robing room when the door opened. There was a muted protest, and I turned to see.

She came in. I rose to my feet and stood facing her. She made no move, but waited, and continued waiting, until I recalled what she now was and dropped to one knee. 'Your Majesty,' I said, and she unbent and stretched out a hand for me to kiss.

'You may go,' she said to Smith, who was hovering in the doorway, somewhat agitated.

'Your Majesty, my orders were . . .'

'I care not for your orders,' she said, 'but if you care for your position and, who knows, your head, you will do as I command. You may remain without the door, and I shall call for you when I need you. I do not require that you be within earshot.'

'Madam,' he protested, 'this is a desperate man, and . . .'

She raised a hand. 'If you utter a single word more other than "Yes, Your Majesty", then my husband shall be informed of your behaviour and by nightfall you will be a head shorter.'

She paused, and he mumbled "Yes, Your Majesty" and went

outside. We could hear his keys jingling as he walked off down the corridor and came to rest at the end of it.

'So – you see what I have turned into,' she said quietly, and then she drew me up and put her arms around me, hugging me tightly. I was astonished, and could not speak. After a long time Bess released me, placed her finger on her lips and indicated that I should sit on the bed. Then she sat beside me. 'We must speak quietly, Richard,' she said. 'We cannot be overheard.'

My mouth gaped. 'You called me Richard,' I said. 'You believe me?'

'I knew you from the first second,' she said. 'I knew you from Henry's description and from the way you behaved throughout. It is I that should be kneeling to you and calling you "Your Majesty", if each were to have his true entitlement.'

'And you will tell Henry this?'

She looked at me, pity in her face. 'If only it were that easy,' she said. 'Henry is not as other men. When mercy knocks at his heart it finds the door barred. Henry wants to be king, so Henry will be king, and there is no thing that will stop him, and no thing that he will allow to stand in his way. You must understand this before we speak another word.'

'So I do,' I told her. 'I have always known this.'

'Known, perhaps,' she said, 'but understood, never.'

'I understand single-mindedness,' I said. 'If I understand anything, it is that.'

She shook her head. 'That is the single-mindedness of ordinary men,' she said. 'Henry's is not like that. You went back to Scotland because Englishmen were being hurt in your cause; at Exeter you abandoned the siege because Englishmen were being killed. Mark the contrast; at Bosworth Henry rode over every Englishman in his path, and after he'd won he declared all the survivors traitors. Could you have done that? Could you even imagine yourself doing that?'

I had to admit that I could not.

'Henry has no friends,' she said. 'I have never seen such a lonely man. He is completely self-centred, self-absorbed, self-contained.'

'How could you marry such a man?' I asked.

'I am a woman,' she said. 'I have no choice in the matter. I made what protests I could, but the king would have it so, and so would our mother. If she could not have a Woodville son on the throne, then a Woodville daughter was the next best thing; her grandchildren will rule in this land, and that was enough for her. As she saw it, the blood of her husband and her own blood will still rule England. She died content. In any case,' she said, 'there is no need for me to tell him. He knows, as you know he knows. Morton knows, and Thomas knows, and all those who knew you before know who you are. You must have realized this?'

'I have seen it in their eyes,' I said.

'Knowledge is one thing,' she said, 'but admission is another altogether. If any man of them acknowledges who you are, they know that it will throw England back to the turmoil we have but late escaped from. It is a knife-edge we walk, and we none of us dare slip or fall. That is as true of Henry as of anyone else.' She paused, and I saw softness come into her eyes. 'Henry tells me that you no longer have any desire to be king,' she said. 'Is that true?'

'It is,' I said.

'That is good,' she replied. 'It takes away the greatest danger. Henry will ensure that you are never seen by anyone who knows you and who might let slip the truth. Henry will deny you, and deny you and deny you with his dying breath. No one who knew Prince Richard will come near you. Even I am not here, and I have never been here.'

'But you told Smith you would tell . . .'

'An elaborate bluff,' she said. 'He dare not say anything. Henry has told him not to let me see you, but he dare not dis-

272

obey me, and, having obeyed me, he dare not complain to the king about what I have done. There is nothing to fear there, I assure you.'

She stayed the best part of an hour, chatting of old times, giving me information on what had happened to the rest of the family, and putting me at ease as Bess was always capable of doing. She promised to give my love to Katherine, assured me that my wife's feelings for me had not changed, and kissed and hugged me before she left. 'We may never be able to talk so freely again,' she said, 'but you must know that you are loved.'

She left me happier than I had been for many days.

We spent Christmas at Sheen and settled down for a long, hard winter, with only occasional journeys into London, ten miles distant, to ease the monotony. I began to relax into my part, checking and storing the king's clothes, ensuring that they were free of dust and moths. Matters were relaxed a little, so that Katherine and I were able to walk in the garden, sometimes with no man at all within earshot, and we were able to touch hands and even, on occasion, kiss, although the kisses were stolen and fleeting. It was not the life I would have chosen, but I was no more confined than any man in England, save in the one aspect of relations with Katherine. She was referred to by all now as Lady Katherine Huntly; when I refused to answer to 'Perkin', I had no other name at all. We tried to console each other on the loss of Edward, but we both felt his absence – our family had been complete, and now it was not.

The long winter died, and spring came to Sheen, making it a pleasant place to walk by the river. It is best not to become too complacent.

One day I was sent to find a particular robe that the king wished to wear. I was told that there was no particular hurry, and ambled down to the garde-robe where I slept with my two escorts. As I opened the door there was a sudden scurried movement within. At first I thought it must be one of the cats which were kept in the palace to keep the mice down, but when I ducked forward I saw a small foot sticking out from under a hanging robe. 'What have we here?' I asked.

At first there was no recognition of discovery, but then the foot moved and a small, sturdy boy stepped from behind the garment.

'These are His Majesty's clothes,' I said, mock-sternly, 'and woe betide anyone who interferes with them.'

'Will His Majesty be angry?' he asked.

'Of a surety,' I said, half in jest, but then watched in astonishment as the small boy's eyes filled with tears and his lip began to quiver.

'Do not worry,' I said to him. 'There is no need for the king to know, as long as no harm has been done.'

'You will not tell him?' he said.

'Not I. In any case, I am sure His Majesty would have no real interest in such a matter.'

'And I am sure that he would,' the boy said. Emboldened by my decision not to inform on him, he stepped out of the garde-robe. 'The king knows everything that happens in his palace. Not a sparrow falls but the information is in his grasp within the hour.'

These were not the words of any ordinary boy. I took a harder look at my companion. He was short and stocky, his little rounded belly thrust before him, and his clothes were fine and expensive – too expensive, I decided, to be the clothes of the child of a palace servant I had taken him for.

'Might I ask who you are?' I said.

He looked at me in astonishment. 'Do you tell me that you truly do not know?' he asked.

I was by now ready to hazard a guess, but I had to tell the truth and admit that I did not.

'I am the Duke of York,' he told me. 'My father is the king.'

Just as well then that I had called him 'His Majesty' and

not 'Tudor' as I usually did in private; such things, as the little prince said, had a way of flying back to his ears as fast as thought.

He was almost seven years old that spring, my successor as Duke of York, and second in line to the throne.

'Your Highness,' I said, and made a leg as a good courtier should. 'If I may make so bold, why are you hiding in this garde-robe?'

'I have angered my father,' he said, 'and must needs keep out of his sight until his temper has abated.'

'I see,' I said. 'And what did you do to move your father to anger?'

'I did not do well at my lessons,' he said, 'and my tutor was angry, and did tell the king, and I am like to be beaten.'

I reached into the garde-robe for the garment I needed.

'Music is not an easy subject to learn,' he said plaintively.

'Music can be – nay, is most enjoyable,' I said. 'I have learned music myself, and have derived much pleasure from it.'

'Would that I could.'

'You have only to pay attention to your tutor, surely, and do as he bids. The music, and the pleasure thereof, will come in time.'

'Master Skelton finds little pleasure in it, and he is a master,' he said.

I had seen Master John Skelton around the various royal places. He was remotely related to the family of the Skelton who had supported me, a lean, cadaverous man, well on the way to becoming his name, and irascible and rude to all below him in status. He was proud and ambitious. To their faces he was obsequious to those above him, but scathing and sarcastic when they were not in earshot. I had not had much to do with him, but those who had did not like him much. I did not think him a man likely to have much patience with a young prince who could not learn his lessons.

'Well, perhaps I could help you sometimes,' I said. It was automatic, without thinking, and it changed the course of my life.

'Would you?' he asked eagerly.

'If it does not interfere with my duties, or with your studies with Master Skelton, then I see no reason why not,' I said.

It was an innocent enough answer, with innocent intent.

'What is it you have difficulty with?'

'Singing, and the writing down of songs.'

'Such was my study as a boy,' I said, and we walked together back to the royal chambers, although he made sure not to enter them.

I spoke to his chamberlain, who was amenable to my idea, and thus met the little prince from time to time in the gardens, not clandestinely, but openly for all to see, and enjoyed his company too, for he did not treat me with either suspicion or derision, as most in the court did. I found that he was not lacking in talent, and he soon learned what he had to once he first learned to relax. He was a sturdy little boy, sure of himself and quick equally to anger or laughter. He had been named for his father, but from my point of view he was more like his bluff and hearty grandfather, who was my father too. His elder brother was, like mine, somewhat sickly and no real companion for him, especially as he was often from court in the care of his guardian. I remembered another fun-loving little prince with a sickly, stay-at-home brother and a too-busy father, disregarded because he was not the heir, around whom the whole world revolves, and I pitied him.

He sang in a piping treble, and I was teaching him an old folk tune one day when a shadow fell across us, and a voice asked, 'What do you do, sir?'

It was Skelton, dressed in a robe of green and white and wearing, ludicrously, a laurel wreath around his brow.

'Sir?'

'I asked what you do.'

'I am making music with the young prince, as you see.'

'I see indeed; but it is my sense of hearing that is offended. I marvel that you ennoble the curious sounds that you are making with the nomenclature of music. I see that you are no longer content merely to usurp earthly thrones, but now you must contend with the Muses to usurp the artistic tasks appointed to others. You have mocked majesty, and now you mock the Muses. Having turned history on its head, you must now do the same with music.'

I made the mistake of thinking that he was joking, and smiled at him.

He pointed at the young prince. 'You, sir! Be off with you and about your permitted business! Do not let me catch you again dallying with this coystrowne; in shape, he may resemble a duke, but in shape a horse's turd may resemble a sugar loaf.'

The prince, cowed, slunk away.

I turned to his tormentor. 'Master Skelton, I do but help a little boy,' I said.

'Princes do not need the assistance of Flemish bumpkins,' he replied. 'Do not trespass on my path again; I do meddle nothing with your work.'

'Walk and be naught,' I told him. 'You are no more than a picker of quarrels.' I strode away, but he called after me.

'Unlike you, Rutterkin, I pick quarrels I have a chance of winning.'

It did not end there. When I walked away from him I thought no more of the quarrel, but within a few days I discovered that I had made a most dangerous enemy, and had become a laughing stock into the bargain.

I met Katherine in the garden, as we had been able to do from time to time. We were free to talk and touch, although we were observed at all times, and both of us were closely guarded at night lest we attempt to meet under the blanket of the dark. On this occasion she was, for the first time since our capture, somewhat peevish with me.

'What have you been doing?' she asked in a harsh whisper.

'Nothing,' I said. 'What has happened?'

'I have been mocked, as have you, and naught can be done about it.'

I was used to mockery; the court was full of it as people sought to gain and hold places of influence, and its use was a useful tool in doing down one's neighbour. I had neither hope of preferment nor fear of being cast down, so I was impervious to it. She, on the other hand, was disturbed.

'What has been said?' I asked.

'Have you not heard of the coystrowne poem?'

I shook my head, and she told me all.

Skelton had penned and then recited in the king's court a scurrilous poem with a long title – something like 'Skelton Laureate against a comely coystrowne that curiously chanted, and currishly countered, and madly in his musics mockishly made against the nine Muses of politic poems and poets matriculate'. The coystrowne, the horse's groom, was me.

He had used the image of the horse's turd again, mocked the idea of my being a gentleman, reviled Katherine, whom he called my 'pea-hen', used endless jokes about my apparent Flemish origins and thence drunkenness (all Flemings were renowned as drunkards) and generally made fun of my musical skills, my singing voice and all my pretensions – 'He braggeth of his birth that born was full base' is one line that Katherine could recall. He had even managed to throw my own words back at me, telling the object of his scorn to 'Walk and be naught', and that he was 'a bungler, a brawler, a picker of quarrels'.

'We must not meet until this has died down,' she said. 'I am the object of mockery wherever I go. Courtiers snigger as I pass, and groups burst into mocking laughter when they think

I am far enough away. I complained to the queen, but she is powerless in Henry's court. She told me that Skelton is the court poet, and thus has licence to mock where he will.'

Katherine was young and vulnerable, and completely unused to mockery of any kind. To her it was unbearable, so I agreed to avoid her company for a few days so that people would not see us together and to let the talk die down.

Whether it was the separation from Katherine on top of that from Edward, or the jibes of the exultant Skelton and the laughter of the courtiers, or whether I felt more demeaned than before, or my life as a servant, I know not, but life became unbearable. I was a husband without a wife, and I was neither a prince nor a Perkin. I was a nothing, living only at the whim of an usurper king. I made another decision which changed the course of my life, and decided to leave. I knew I would get no permission to quit court, and was left with no option but to run. Unable to move other than within the king's palace, except for those occasions when we moved to and from London, I was unable to make any plans, and could not share my decision with anyone.

It was early June when I made my move. I was able to beg some spirituous liquor – French brandy, I think – from the pantry, and I made sure that I drank but little of it while my two keepers were happy to swig it until the pottle was finished. It was my good fortune that the ruse worked, and before long they had succumbed and were snoring loudly.

The king's garde-robes were equipped with long ladders for retrieving items from the upper shelves, and I had observed that these ladders were long enough to reach the narrow windows in the upper wall, which gave onto the outside. I slipped from between the two guards and clambered up to the window, levered myself through and dropped to the ground outside.

Now free, I had no idea what to do next. It had been some considerable time since I had had the direction of my own life, and I was unused to freedom. Even a prince is constrained, while a fisherman is governed by the wind. I could not remember the last time I had made a decision – perhaps to desert the remaining Cornishmen at Taunton. I walked down to the river, listened briefly to its sounds, and then turned to follow it to the sea. At the worst I might lose myself in London; at best I would find a ship to take me to Flanders. From there I could negotiate to ransom Katherine and Edward; Tudor would have no use for them except as bargaining counters.

Then I realized that I was playing right into Tudor's hands. He would expect me to head for a port, down the river; he would expect me to try to lose myself in London – and thus he would expect to find me within a short time.

I turned and went the other way, upstream. I had about four hours before dawn started to break; within an hour or so after that my absence would be discovered, and the hue and cry would begin. It was not easy to move fast along the riverbank, and the twisting and turning of the stream meant that at first light I had gone no more than two or three miles. It was a hot, dry summer, and the grass was short – impossible to hide in effectively. I had to find somewhere to hide during the day that was beginning, and eventually found a spinney bordering on the river. I went deep into it and curled up at the base of a tree to sleep; at least no one was likely to be looking for me as close as that to the palace.

It was an interminable day. I slept but fitfully, waking at the slightest sound, and soon realized that I could not go too long without water in that intense heat. The foliage provided some cover, but the sun was relentless. As soon as I dared I crept down to the bank and drank deeply. Then, when I judged it was dark enough to move around unobserved, I set off again along the river, stumbling in the darkness and even falling three or four times, making crashing sounds which felt as if they might be heard for ten miles. When I fell for the last time I lay still, and realized for certain that I was not made for this. I could have coped with walking through the forest by day and sleeping beneath the stars at night, but I dare not do that for fear of being seen, and this threshing about in the dark was leading me nowhere. Unless I stayed by the river I lost my way.

I found a ford not long before first light, and as soon as I felt safe enough I crossed to the other bank and lay in the forest, hidden from sight, I hoped, but no more than a few paces from the river.

By now I was extremely hungry. I had not brought any food with me, and such berries as I found were bitter and unripe. I rolled myself in my cloak and tried to sleep, but I could feel despair creeping over me, and it was still light when I rose and walked on.

It was but a short time later that I stepped out of a copse to see a familiar building ahead of me – the Charterhouse of Sheen. For all my wandering, I was no more than six or seven miles from where I had started out. I was hungry, thirsty and mentally and physically exhausted. I gave in to the inevitable and hammered on the almshouse door.

It opened, I stepped inside and remember saying 'Sanctuary' before my legs gave way and I sank to the floor.

I awoke in a cool cell, bare but for a crucifix on the wall and a stool beside my cot. There was an old monk in a black habit seated on the stool, and as soon as he saw me he smiled and told me to stay down. 'You are weak, my son,' he said, 'but I think a few more hours rest is all that is required.'

Then he left and returned with an older monk, who sat himself beside me.

'You have nothing to fear, my son,' this man said. 'I am the prior here, and none can harm you. Do you wish to tell me anything about yourself, or confess your sins?'

'I was Richard of York,' I said.

He nodded. 'I see. But you have left York now, I see. Are you a pedlar or an itinerant worker?'

'No, father,' I said. 'It is not where I am from; it is who I am. Richard of York. I was of late a servant of the king at the palace in Sheen.'

'Then soon you shall be on your way back there,' he said, 'no doubt to the joy of your friends.'

I was forced to laugh at the unconscious deliciousness of his irony, but in the gloom I think he thought me to be weeping, for he laid his hand on my shoulder and said, 'There, there, you're safe now,' before asking, 'But why did you ask for sanctuary? It is not a privilege granted to this house.'

'The king will be anxious for news of me,' I said.

'The king? Are your connections of such importance, then?'

It was obvious that this unworldly man had never heard of Richard of York, and when the name Piers Osbeck proved unfamiliar to him too, I told him all and asked him to pray for my soul.

'Surely the king cannot mean to kill you?' he asked at the end of my recital. 'He promised you your life.'

'But that was before I ran away,' I said, 'and he might well consider that I broke the parole I gave.'

'And have you?'

'No,' I said. 'The parole was given to the king's officer, and covered only my journey to the king. I did not give Henry Tudor my parole.'

'I think then there is nothing for you to chide yourself with,' he said. 'If the king hears that you are here, he will send men to arrest you, and I cannot prevent that.'

'No,' I said. 'I do not expect you to try, father. And he will hear soon enough, I'm sure.'

'No doubt. Every stone prates in this place.' He levered himself up, his hands on his knees, and said, 'However, I can intercede with him. If nothing else, I may be able to save your life.'

He leaned over and gave me his blessing, and then said, 'Sleep and gain your strength until I return. I am for Sheen.'

I heard later that he rode to Sheen later that day to bargain with the king, refusing to hand me over unless my life was guaranteed. He told me later that Henry had told him that it had never been in danger, and that all he wanted was my safe return. The prior eventually agreed to hand me over under those terms, and after a full day and a night of prayer, retreat and the sacraments I was delivered to the door I had entered by, my clothes clean and soft from the laundry, and handed over to a man I knew only too well.

'Master Bradshaw,' I said, as I stepped back into the sunlight of the world.

Even now, my hands were not tied and no shackles were applied to me.

'I am to ask you, sir, if you will give me your parole as far as the king's presence at Sheen,' Bradshaw said. 'I seek it no further, although the king may require further assurances on your arrival there.'

'You have it, sir,' I said.

'In that case, Master Warbeck, you are not to be bound.'

He had a horse waiting for me, and a small troop of only four men. Clearly my value was falling. He held the stirrup as I mounted, and this time I was allowed to take the reins.

I thanked the prior for his kindness, gave the porter the few small coins I had about my person, and followed Bradshaw along the road back to Sheen; it was a journey we accomplished in less than two hours – such had been my freedom.

The king greeted me as gently as ever, bade me sit and looked closely at me. Once again, only he and I were in the room.

'Your thoughts have turned again to kingship, then?'

'Indeed not, Your Majesty.'

'What then?'

'Escape, that is all. I wanted to be myself – not Richard of York, not Perkin, but me, the essence of me. I wanted to be free of cares; I still want that, and only that.'

'No thoughts of the crown, no plotting with Yorkists, no planning of rebellions?'

'None of those,' I said. 'Just peace.'

'I am compromised again,' he said. 'The prior demanded your life as part of the arrangement. I may not hang you.'

'You could behead me,' I said.

'And thus acknowledge you as noble?' he said. 'I think not – what a host of Yorkist wasps that would bring about my head.' He sat thinking, and then said, 'You must be seen to have been recaptured, and must be seen to have been punished. You shall therefore be displayed, exhibited in London. In the stocks, probably, commoner that you are. Thereafter we shall have to keep a closer eye on you, so you will be moved to the Tower. If you were not happy at Sheen, I cannot see that you will be happy in the Tower.'

'If there be no John Skelton there,' I said, 'I shall be content.' Henry had the grace to smile at that.

As part of my punishment I was displayed to the public gaze for several hours a few mornings later, the day after Corpus Christi. I was fastened about with chains, loaded onto a cart and taken to the Standard, in Cheapside. Miscreants normally had to take with them the objects with which they had offended – his dies for a false moneyer, the short weights for a dishonest tradesman – but I was simply taken as I was. It was my face that had offended, for its resemblance to my father and my use of it as a way of claiming to be Richard, and my face it was which was therefore to be looked upon.

I was not required to do anything other than stand there in silence – the punishment for frauds and deceivers – while the crowd watched me. Some of them threw things at me, but I had now learned to suffer in silence, and in any case there were guards there to ensure that my safety was not endangered.

Afterwards I was returned to Sheen and allowed a final meeting with Katherine before my incarceration. She was to remain in the queen's service, but my escape had reflected on her, and her status had suffered with the unjustified suspicion that she had been aware of it and done nothing. She wept when I left her, and declared her love, as did I mine for her, but it was a love that remained unexpressed. She paused at the door when she left, and I will carry the memory of her lovely tear-stained face to my death, which will not now be long delayed.

On the following Monday I was exhibited on a scaffold of empty barrels, the better to make the point that my promises were plentiful but empty. A list of my offences was read out by a king's officer; I was required only to remain silent, the which I did, and stared out at those who had come to stare at me.

At the end of my ordeal I was paraded through the streets in chains and taken to the Tower, where I was handed over to the keeper, Sir Simon Digby, who formally took receipt of me.

Then the gates of the Tower closed behind me, and the world saw no more of me.

Prisoner

June 1498 – November 1499

I was escorted to the room I was to occupy for the time being. I stepped into it and looked around. It looked more comfortable than I had been expecting, but it was not until I had sat down on the bed that I realized that it was the same room that Edward and I had slept in during our time in the tower fifteen years before – part of the royal apartment. The furniture had changed, of course; it was now more functional and austere with no hint of luxury, but at least it had a modicum of comfort.

I relaxed – perhaps Henry was going to treat me mercifully after all. I waited until my escort removed the chains, and then I lay back on the bed and stared up at the ceiling where Edward and I had seen so many shapes, and I was able to pick out the swan and the rampant lion.

I had been there no more than an hour or so when the door opened and a small, solid man came in, a bunch of keys at his waist and another on his arm. Behind him came the king and Cardinal Morton. I rose to my feet from where I was lying.

The king waved the man away, and we heard him clanking down the corridor. 'Are you chastened?' the king asked.

'Yes, Your Majesty.'

'Anything else to say?' Henry asked sharply.

I shook my head. 'No, Your Majesty. Except that I thank you for giving me such comfortable and, of course, familiar quarters.'

'I wondered if you'd notice that,' he said. 'It's all right. You can relax with His Eminence. Be yourself, as it were.'

I allowed myself a grimace that passed for a smile.

'Your ordeal is nearly over,' the cardinal said.

'I thought as much.'

'You will not be staying here,' Henry said. 'These are royal quarters, and your royalty has been . . .'

He paused, searching for a word, and Morton said, 'Curtailed, Your Majesty?'

'Hmmm. Well, don't get comfortable. As I said, you won't be staying here. It's just to give you a taste, that's all. It would not be fitting for me to see you in one of the less well-appointed rooms. Are you going to give me any trouble?'

I shook my head.

'Good. There are certain preparations that must be made. We shall return soon.'

I was left there a few hours alone. I can only think that Tudor was trying to make a point, although I know not what it was. Then the squat man came back, pushed the door open and poked his head into the room. 'Come on, then,' he said cheerfully, and pointed at the chains. 'Bring them and follow me.'

He waited while I picked up the chains and settled them as comfortably as I could, and then set off at an easy pace along the corridor, pausing from time to time so that I could keep up. We continued along corridors and up and down flights of steps until we reached a heavy door, which he opened using a key and motioned me inside.

'This will be your quarters for the time being,' he said, 'until His Majesty decides what to do with you.'

This room was not so attractive. True, there was a bed, but it was just wooden slats covered by a thin blanket. I could see the handle of a chamber pot underneath it, and in the corner there was a three-legged stool with folded sheets on it. There was no other furniture.

As I looked around the jailer prodded me in the back with one of the keys. 'Strip off,' he said.

'I need my clothes,' I told him.

'Your clothes?' he said. 'They're gentleman's clothes, they are; not for the likes of you. Get 'em off.'

I hesitated, and he said, 'You said you weren't going to be any trouble. I got my orders, son.'

I began to divest myself of my outer garments, and he reached out a hand and took each item from me as I took it off. When I was down to my undergarments I stopped, and he said, 'And the rest; come on.'

'It is not fitting,' I began; but he shook his head and said, 'Orders, my son, orders,' and waited until I was naked.

'Put them on,' he told me, and pointed to what I had taken to be a pile of sheets, but which was in fact two sets of rough doublet and hose, by no means new and not at all clean.

'I can't wear these,' I protested, but he was already going through the door, inserting the key into the lock as he went.

'Please yourself,' he said, 'but it gets very cold in here o'nights. I'd wear 'em, if it was me.'

He closed the door, and I heard the wards turn in the lock. He was right; the cold was already creeping in, and I pulled both sets of clothes on.

I was not ready for what happened next. It appeared that the king had decided against mercy, although a touching little scene preceded this part of my punishment. The door was unlocked, and four men, all unknown to me, came in.

'I beg your lordship's forgiveness,' the foremost of them said, and each of the other men added:

'And I.'

'For what?' I asked, having no inkling.

'For what it is our duty to do,' the leader said.

'Ah,' I replied. 'I am for death, then?'

'No, sir.'

'Then what?'

He paused, and then said, 'Forgive me, sir.'

I opened my mouth to ask again what he was to be forgiven for, and he hit me hard, with clenched fist, on my left cheek-bone. I fell back, my hand reaching up to my cheek, and as I did so he hit me again. Then he grasped me by the shirt and pulled me to my feet. Two of the other men stepped beside me and grabbed an arm each, and the other stepped behind me, knelt, and grasped my legs, holding me immobile. Then the first man beat me about the face, driving his hands again and again onto my chin, my cheeks, my eyes and my nose. I heard the crunch of my nose breaking on the fourth or fifth blow, and the next broke it again. I saw the blood on his fists as they moved in and out, and then my eyes closed, first one and then the other, and I could see no more. I felt the warmth of my blood on my cheeks, and tasted the warmth of blood at the back of my throat. Then I heard, rather than felt, my teeth breaking within my mouth, and felt the pieces drive into my lips as I tried to spit them out. The blows continued, raining down on my face, and only on my face, until I lost conscious-ness in a world of spinning blackness.

I came awake in a firefield of pain, my whole head exploding and throbbing. I found the man standing over me, a look of concern on his face. 'What?' I said, or at least tried to say, but my mouth would not function and a mere grunt came forth. When he heard the noise, though, my assailant's face cleared.

'I am sorry, sir,' he said. 'Can you forgive me?'

I was in too much pain to consider this proposition, and shook my head from side to side. It was the gentlest of move-ments, but the painful sensation it produced was sharp and intense. I had been on the point of rising, but the movement was too much for me, and I fell back onto my pillow.

'Do not move, sir,' he said. 'The pain will go away if you do not move too much.'

I had no intention of moving, and lay still. 'I will put some water between your lips, sir,' he said. 'Swallow if you can; if not, let it moisten your tongue.' I felt the moisture trickle into my mouth, and breathed in sharply as its coldness bit into the cuts and scars on my lips and gums. Before I could swallow I fell unconscious again.

When next I awoke the pain was a little less, although still more than I was ready for. My tongue seemed to have swollen to many times its customary size, but I moved it experimentally around the interior of my mouth and found many sharp spikes, jagged remnants of broken teeth, some with live nerves still attached. I reached up and found my eyes to be greatly swollen too, as was my nose, which did not seem to be the shape I remembered.

My attendant must have noticed the movement, for he rose from a nearby stool and approached me. 'How is the pain?' he asked.

I tried to say 'Better', but the croaking sound that came out was unrecognizable, even to me, as an English word. I felt again, but my eyes were so swollen and tender that I could not reach them. I could see him, but it was like looking through an arrow slit.

He brought some water, and again trickled it into my mouth. I spluttered a little, but most of it went where it was supposed to go. When he turned to replace the bottle, I asked, 'Why?'

The sound must have approximated to the word, for he looked at me and repeated it. 'Why?'

I nodded.

'Why did we beat you?'

I nodded again.

'It was done on the orders of His Majesty,' he said. 'He was very specific. You were to have a thorough beating, but only about the face. No other part of you was to be touched. You will find, sir, that we followed his orders exactly. No other part of your body has any marks or bruises of any sort. And I am very sorry, sir. It was a royal command, after all. We disobey those at our peril.'

'Why?' I asked again.

'I know not, sir.'

Not many days later my assailant, who seemed to be with me night and day, woke me and handed me a clean shift to replace the blood-boltered one I had worn since the beating.

'You are to have a visitor,' he said. 'You have to look your best today. Clothes, I mean,' he amended hastily.

'Who comes?'

'His Majesty the king and my lord Bishop of Cambrai, the envoy of the dowager Duchess of Burgundy.'

'From my aunt?' I asked, excited in spite of myself, and then remembered that I was no longer Richard. My attendant affected not to notice my slip. 'For what purpose?' I asked.

'I know not,' he responded, 'except that you are to have clean clothes and polished chains, so His Majesty must have need to show you off.'

'Mayhap my aunt has prevailed upon Tudor to show mercy,' I mumbled.

'Your aunt?' he said, not pretending to ignore my slip this time. 'And "Tudor"? Mayhap you'd have better chance of mercy if you gave the king his true title and dropped your claims to kinship with his aunt.'

'No matter who intercedes for me, I expect little enough mercy,' I told him, and he shrugged and pulled out a clean pair of hose to accompany the shirt.

'Some ambassadors, too,' he said, almost as an afterthought. 'Spanish, one of them, Señor de Puebla, but I don't know who else.'

My face was still paining, and I was befuddled from the beating, but I walked unaided to the room where the visitors were waiting. I was led in and pushed forward so that I fell to my knees. I remained before the visitors, my head bowed.

'This is my lord Bishop of Cambrai,' Henry said without preamble, 'as you may know from your years of deception. This is Piers Osbeck, that late troubled this our realm with lies and falsehood. He has signed a confession of his crimes in that name, and has stood by without demur while his crimes were proclaimed before him. So that there can be no further misapprehension, we command that you tell his lordship and this other lord why you have practised such great deception on the Archduke Philip and his noble father and grandmother.'

My answer was ready. 'I swear solemnly to God that the Duchess Margaret knows, as well as I do myself, that I am not the son of him who is said to be my father.'

'There,' said Henry. '*Ipsissima verba.*'

The Spanish ambassador stepped forward and reached out, taking my chin and lifting my face toward him. As I looked up I saw the shock in his eyes, and the bishop breathed sharply and stepped back.

'What have they done to you?' the bishop asked.

'*Desfigurado,*' de Puebla muttered, and released me. I allowed my head to drop again.

'You see,' Henry said quickly, 'how his Holiness the Pope and the King of France, the archduke, the King of the Romans and the King of Scotland have all been deceived, as have all the Christian princes with the exception of Their Catholic Majesties.'

I saw de Puebla incline his head in acknowledgement of Henry's recognition of the shrewdness and perceptiveness of his royal masters.

There was silence then, as each man considered what he was seeing. Then the bishop stepped forward. 'I am to tell Her Grace that you are not the son of Edward of England, but of this boatman of Tournai, am I?' he asked. 'That you are not what you once claimed to be?'

I said nothing, but then Tudor said, 'You will answer His Grace.'

I looked at Tudor, holding his gaze, and then at the bishop. Looking him in the eye, I repeated, 'I swear solemnly to God that the Duchess Margaret knows, as well as I do myself, that I am not the son of him who is said to be my father.'

A look of understanding came into the bishop's eye. 'I see the way of it,' he murmured. 'The blessings of God be with you, my son.' Then, glancing at Tudor, he said, 'And may God forgive each of us our sins.'

'Amen,' we all said. The bishop's look turned to one of compassion, and he reached out and traced a cross on my forehead. '*In nomine patris*,' he began, and the other two men joined in the rest of his blessing. Then Henry ushered them out, and I was returned to my cell without a further word being spoken.

There matters were left, and Richard of York disappeared, never to reappear. I suffered no further maltreatment, apart from being put in chains whenever I was removed from my room for any purpose. I was granted some exercise in the gardens of the Tower, and gained some health by allowing the sun to shine upon my face through the tiny window of my room high in the wall. From midday for about four hours that summer the sun's rays heated the floor and one of the walls of my room, and I luxuriated in its warmth. The bruises from my beating faded soon enough, although I lost many teeth and my nose never fully recovered, leaving me sometimes unable to breathe except through my mouth.

In the spring I found myself embroiled against my will in the machinations of the English court. In the room above mine was lodged Edward Neville, Duke of Warwick, the idiot son and heir of my father's brother George of Clarence, who had been a constant trouble to my father and serial rebel against him. I remembered Warwick as a child; he was weak in his wits and completely devoid of understanding. During the reigns of my father and Uncle Richard he had been free to go where he would, moving dreamily from one of his estates to another and no danger to anyone apart from himself. Since Bosworth, however, he had been in the Tower under Henry's control, more because of his potency as a Yorkist rallying point than through any actual danger he represented. After mine and my sisters', his was the best claim to the throne, although both he and his younger sister were attaindered because of their father's treason, and thus legally could not succeed.

I became aware of his presence one day in the spring following my imprisonment, when I had been in the Tower eight or nine months. I was lying on my cot reading one day when I was distracted by a fall of wood shavings that drifted down from the ceiling.

I stood up and looked closely. It was a high ceiling and difficult to make out what was happening, and then I saw an auger boring through the ceiling. A hole appeared and then widened as a knife or similar implement was used to broaden the hole.

I watched, puzzled, and then a pair of fingers emerged from the hole and wiggled about. I put my book down.

'Perkin, be of good cheer and comfort,' a voice said.

I stared upwards. Perkin was not a name that I had ever answered to, and I forbore to do so now.

'Greetings, good cousin,' the voice said.

'Who greets me thus?' I asked, feeling that these words as yet presented less danger.

''Tis I, poor Ned Neville. Who are you?'

'One who has offended His Majesty in some wise,' I said carefully. I could not be sure that it was cracked Ned, and even if it was he would never have known who I was or remember me as I had been when he was a boy.

'How goes it with you?' the voice continued. 'Be of good cheer.'

Then strange things began to happen. One of the wardens

brought in to me a file and a hammer with which, he said, I could cut the bars in my cell and knock the shackles from my legs. I was only shackled when being transported beyond my room, and so had no need of the implements, but he left them anyway. Then I received a sealed sheet of paper, blank except for the words 'for sending news' and containing a length of white thread. Presumably this was for me to dangle letters from my window; I was allowed to send and receive letters freely, and I had always assumed that Henry's agents would intercept and read all of them. In any case, I had nothing secret to communicate with anyone.

I suddenly began to receive visits from a man named Cleymound, who told me he was Warwick's keeper. 'He is kept a poor prisoner, like yourself,' he said, 'and just as unlawfully and immorally detained.'

I pointed out to him that his words were treason, but he took not the hint. He told me that he intended to redress the wrongs done to Warwick and me by seizing the Tower and declaring Warwick as king or, he said, if I were indeed Richard, he would declare me instead. He brought me tokens from what he said were 'friendly parties' – a bent coin, indicating a promise made, a code book to use when I wrote secret letters, a cross painted on parchment. It was so manifestly transparent that he was attempting to provoke me into some treasonous activity that after his third visit I requested an audience with Sir Simon Digby, the Constable of the Tower, and laid all of the facts and tokens before him.

'I do not wish to see this man again,' I told him. 'If there is a plot against His Majesty, I am no part of it, and wish not to be associated with it.'

Within two or three days the hole in my ceiling was blocked up, and there were changes among those guarding me.

It was therefore with not a little fear in my soul that I found myself taken from my room and driven in a closed cart through the streets of London early one March morning. I did not see the building we entered, but I was taken to a well-furnished and comfortable room and left there alone.

About an hour after my arrival the door opened to reveal the king and Cardinal Morton. I rose and bowed, and then knelt.

'Rise,' Henry said laconically, and then seated himself in a comfortable chair. Morton too sat.

'We thank you for your loyal remarks to our constable,' Henry said. 'They were of immediate import in matters affecting us nearly.'

I did not know how to acknowledge this, so I said nothing and kept my head bowed.

'You know, there's one strange thing I've noticed about you,' Henry said.

I looked up at him. He seemed to be not unkindly today.

'Consistency. You've always told exactly the same story. Oh, little details have changed here and there as you remembered things, but effectively you have stuck to the same tale throughout.'

'Because it is true, Your Majesty,' I said. 'I am not given to lying.'

'Yes,' he said. 'I know. At the beginning I hoped I was wrong. I hoped you were a fake and I could just kill you, but you weren't, and I couldn't. Whatever else you were, you were never a feigned boy. Then Bess confirmed it.'

'You told me Bess denied me,' I said.

'She did, and that so vehemently that I knew she was lying. She feared for her brother; she feared that if she acknowledged her brother then it would seal his death warrant, so she lied. She said she'd never seen you before, that you were a pitiful impostor and that I should put you to work in the kitchen like Simnel. She wanted to save your life.'

'She was ever a brave and noble sister,' I said. 'So, in trying to save me she condemned me.'

'I did not intend your brother to die,' he said suddenly. 'I sent those men to the Tower, yes, but their orders were to make safe the Princes – to preserve them, I meant. Unfortunately, those orders were delivered to them by the wrong man, who deliberately and wilfully misinterpreted them. I imagine you can guess who that was.'

I said nothing, and Henry looked at me, noticed something in my face, and said, 'Oh, you may speak freely before Cardinal Morton. He is privy to our innermost thoughts. Who, then, do you think that wilful misinterpreter might have been?'

'Stanley, Your Majesty,' I said.

'You guess aright.'

There was a long pause. Something was different. Something about Henry had changed, and I knew not what. Finally he spoke.

'If you are not given to lying,' he said, 'then we require an explanation of what you told to our captain Bradshaw at Exeter.'

'I do not know to what you refer, Your Majesty,' I said. 'I recall giving him my parole, but little else. We spoke naught of affairs of state.'

'Bradshaw told me that you had told him that Giovanni Gabotto the Venetian was not the first to the new found land, but that you had preceded him there. Does he speak true?'

'Oh, that! Yes, Your Majesty, he does.' I told him how I had gone there with Meno, of the fish and the red men and of my adventures with them.

He nodded. 'It has come to our notice that certain men unknown to you corroborate these statements of yours. Signor Gabotto went on a second voyage more than a year ago, and has not returned; we fear his expedition is lost.'

'I am sorry to hear that, Your Majesty,' I said. 'Those are brave men who venture into those waters.'

'We have sought the advice of our wisest ministers,' the

king said, 'and deliberated long with them. They tell me that a prince may imprison another prince or lord because he fears he will cause insurrection, or that insurrection will come through him, and that is without sin; if he detains him otherwise, he acts through evil intention. So they say.'

I remained silent, not knowing where this was leading.

'You took no part in the Warwick plot,' he said conversationally. 'Why was that?'

'There would have been no point.'

'Because it was bound to fail?'

'Even if it had succeeded, it would have failed,' I said. 'I remember our poor cousin as a child . . .' I faltered. 'I mean poor Warwick,' I said. 'I knew him well; I mean . . . forgive me, Your Majesty, but do I speak now as the man you know me to be, or must I hide . . . ?' I stopped, confused.

'You may speak as Richard of York while we are within these four walls and alone,' the king said. 'You say you remember our cousin as a child?'

'Yes, Your Majesty, and the weakness of his head. I know little of what he is now beyond what I have been told, but I do not think that he would be a suitable king for England.'

'All the more reason then to join in, surely, so that in due course, when he was shown to be what he is, you could take your rightful place on the throne?'

I shook my head. 'Once I might have thought like that,' I said. 'I might have gone along with it, with the plan later to do such a thing as you suggest. But not now. My desire to be King of England evaporated at the gates of Exeter.'

'But do you not see yourself still as the rightful king, in the secret place of your heart?'

'I decided many years ago, Your Majesty, when I first met Charles of France, that a mere accident of birth is not sufficient reason to rule a country, and may be an extremely poor reason. No, let the crown go to him who best knows how to wear it.

Warwick, regardless of his birth, is not the stuff of kings, and nor am I; the right man wears the crown in England, Your Majesty, of that you may be sure. Better that the right man be king in England than that the king be the right man.'

'That is almost a statement of loyalty,' he said, smiling his thin-lipped grimace for perhaps the third time in our acquaintanceship.

'It is more an acceptance of fate and inevitability,' I said, 'but if it pleases Your Majesty then you may take it as one, if you wish, and you will never be disproved by me.'

'And is that why you did not join the plot? Out of loyalty to England?'

'That's the noble reason you can write in your creative history books,' I said, 'but there's a more pragmatic one: I'm tired of trouble – tired of causing it, tired of stirring it up, tired of trying to sort it out. I should have stayed where I was before I got into this – Pierre the fisher of bacalao. Now there I was a happy man.'

'I think we are beginning to understand each other,' Tudor said. 'I wanted to be king because I knew I could do it well. Although I always knew you were Richard, right from the beginning, I knew I would be the better king. And I had fought in the field for England – I was never just going to hand it over to you.'

'Power is an addictive drug,' I said. 'Once tasted it is difficult to relinquish. Maximilian said that of you.'

'Perceptive of him.'

'If, then, Richard of York is set aside,' I said, 'Bess would be next, and if Bess's husband reigns in England and his and her son after him then perhaps we should all be happy.'

'He will, Richard,' the king said. 'He will, and we will.' He paused again, thinking, and then said, 'So. It appears by your actions that you will not cause insurrection, nor will insurrection come through you, so if I detain you, I must be acting through evil intention. I have no evil intent toward you, Richard, and I do not believe that you harbour any towards me.' He paused again. 'Which leaves the problem of what to do with you.'

I waited.

'You know that Their Catholic Majesties are agitating for your death before they will allow their daughter to be betrothed to my son. Had you fallen in with Warwick's plan then I would have had the excuse I needed to execute you. Warwick's actions have condemned him absolutely. He is too much of a fool to be a danger in himself, but only those who know him can know that; any who do not know his limitations will see only the rightful king, and a Yorkist too. For those reasons he has to die – it is a great consolation to me that he is actually guilty.'

He looked at Morton and then back at me.

'Whereas you,' he said, 'are not. Technically, I suppose, you are a traitor, for leading insurrection in Cornwall, but as you were indeed who you said you were it could be construed as a justifiable action. Since those days you have not shown yourself to be disloyal, and I have twice given my word that I shall not execute you. Nonetheless, unless you die there shall be no Spanish marriage. Therefore, we fear we must execute Perkin.'

'Ah.' He had taken a long time to get there, but the news was at least as welcome as it was unwelcome. At last I knew my fate.

The king leaned back and glanced over at Morton again. His eyes seemed to ask a question, and I saw the cardinal's lips purse and an almost imperceptible nod of his head.

'I think I might make you a proposition. You have unwillingly impersonated Perkin these last few years,' Henry went on, 'but we think that now it is time to let the mantle pass from your shoulders. Take some other name and be Perkin no more, and if you accede to my conditions you may walk free.'

I looked up, incredulous, into his face.

'What conditions, my lord?' I breathed.

Henry gestured towards Morton, who unrolled a paper and looked at it.

'To summarize,' the cardinal said, 'you will leave England, which includes Wales and Ireland, never to return during the lifetime of our sovereign lord King Henry VII or of his son the crown prince Arthur. Is this agreed?'

'Yes,' I said.

'Second, that you nevermore claim by word, action or writing to be Richard, Duke of York to any man now alive. Is this agreed?'

'Yes.'

'Third, that you nevermore enter into or remain within any of the lands hereunder specified.' He paused, and looked further down the document. 'They include Spain, Portugal, France, Scotland, the Low Countries, a few more – all those, at least, where Richard of York found support. Is this agreed?'

'Yes,' I said.

'Fourth, that you make no attempt ever to contact the Lady Katherine Huntly, wherever she may be situate. Is this agreed?'

I remained silent. It was an impossible condition. I was about to say so when Henry spoke, very gently.

'To Katherine, as to the world, the man who was Richard of York and Perkin will be dead,' he said. 'She cannot be party to this agreement, nor have any knowledge of it. To her, you must be dead.'

'She may wish to marry again,' I said. 'She may thus be led into sin.'

'She may not marry without the king's permission,' Morton said. 'That permission will be withheld.'

'What of annulment or divorce?' I asked.

'For those, my son, you would have to be alive.'

'I could divorce her before . . . before these events.'

TERENCE MORGAN

'I have spoken to Katherine on this matter, as has the cardinal here,' Henry said. 'She is adamant that she will not divorce you. Even if you were to speak to her yourself, she would assume that pressure had been brought to bear. It must be by his death.'

Morton waited, and then said, 'Is it so agreed?'

Reluctantly, I told him, 'Yes.'

'I will have the papers drawn up,' Morton said, 'and you will sign them. When you have done so we shall commence the next part of your rehabilitation.'

'Excuse me, my lord,' I said, 'but how are the people to believe that I am no more without a trial and an execution?'

'Oh, there will be a trial and an execution,' Morton said. 'We will find some prisoner deserving of death and he will answer to his crimes, but under another name; Perkin will live again, however briefly. Caiaphas need not concern us at all. The proceedings in court will not take long and the prisoner will be too drugged to make sense of what is said to him, so there will be no difficulty.'

'But he will not look like me.'

'He will look more like you do now than you look like yourself as you were before,' he replied. 'Thus is the king's wisdom and mercy displayed in his changing of your face. In any case, our man will of course be wearing the right clothes; it will be enough. The clothes define the office.'

'Only we three in this room will be aware of the personation,' Henry said, 'and the grim but delicious irony that it entails.'

'So,' Morton said, 'Richard is no more, and Perkin is no more. How does it feel to suffer yet another death?'

'The death of the self is also a death, even if the body live on,' I said. 'An interior death is still a death to be fought with all one's strength and wit. The risk of becoming what one hates, committing the one unforgivable act of lying to the self,

302

of speaking the lie that will end all hope of life – these are dangers more terrible than anything to be found on the scaffold, and that is why I can never and will never deny who I am, no matter what you may threaten me with or do to me. You have power over me, true, but it is power only over the body you see before you; it is not power over the self within, and it is most assuredly not power over the truth.'

The two men looked at each other, an amused glance passing between them, and then Morton began to applaud, slowly, his gloved hands beating a rhythm that had no echoes in the stone room.

'Oh, well spoken, sir,' he said. 'A speech worthy of any scaffold, for that is of a surety where it will take you if you repeat it outside this room.' He turned to Tudor. 'But why, Majesty, should we be surprised that such a consummate actor should dissemble so well. Has he not had a whole lifetime of rehearsal?'

'That will do, Your Grace,' Henry said quietly. 'He speaks only what his soul dictates.' He picked up the paper the cardinal had been reading from. 'The contract; is it agreed?'

'Yes,' I said.

'Then you will leave England,' he said. 'I wish you well.'

'If Your Majesty will permit,' Morton said, 'I think we might be able to use . . .' he hesitated '. . . this man in that matter to which I referred?' He let the sentence hang in the air, and eventually the king nodded.

'Very well,' he said. 'His Eminence has a task for you. He will take you to Windsor, where you will meet my chaplain. Then you will leave England.'

'Your Majesty,' I said, bowing, and followed the aged cleric out of the room.

Personator

November 1499 – November 1512

I found him looking over the side of the ship at the harbour side and went up the gangplank.

'I seek to go again to sea, Master Thirkell,' I told him, 'and adventure in the new world.'

He rolled around on his right hip, using the slight movement of the ship to save his energy, and looked into my face. 'And what makes you think that I am hiring?'

'I had heard,' I told him.

He considered this. 'Wharf rat tittle tattle,' he said in the end. 'I'm going nowhere.'

'I would do you good service, sir,' I said. 'I have experience.'

'Experience?'

'Some,' I said. 'I have sailed on Breton and Portuguese vessels, and on Flemish, French and Scottish ones.'

'Over how long?'

'Ten years or so, from when I was a young boy.'

'Speak those languages?'

'Portuguese, Flemish and French, yes. Not the others.'

'Tis no matter,' he said, and turned away to resume his perusal of the harbour. 'I am going nowhere, in any case.'

Of course I knew different, but it is not done to contradict a captain.

'Perhaps, sir, if at some time you were thinking of going again to that new found land, you might give me some consideration.'

'I am going nowhere,' he said again, into the wind.

'Nonetheless, sir, if you were . . .'

There was a long silence, and then he said, 'It is not meet that you speak to me. Master Merrick has the say or nay to who goes on one of his ships. Do you go seek him. If he will have you, then I'll not gainsay him.'

Thirkell, I had found, was not at present in good odour with the crown. He had been with Gabotto, or Cabot as the Bristolians call him, on his first voyage to the new land, but had turned back on the second voyage when his ship's rudder had broken in a storm and he had been forced to put into Cork. He had then returned to Bristol, but not knowing where Cabot had decided to go after landfall he let discretion guide him and had not set out alone. None of the other ships had so far returned, and Henry, predictably, was concerned about his investment – one of the five ships had been funded by him, and he hated to lose money. Thirkell needed to redeem himself.

When I had been taken by Morton to see the king's chaplain, John Esterfeld, who did not known my background or, of course, my secrets, he sat me down and talked me through the events. 'My father,' he told me, 'whose name is also John, is a merchant in Bristol and, like the king, invested money in this venture. He is also Admiral of England for the city and county of Bristol, so it is important that he be seen to be acting in the king's interest. That is why Master Thirkell is to be sent in search of Gabotto.'

'I don't understand,' I said. 'What has this to do with me?'

'Just listen,' Morton growled. 'Your job is not to understand, but to obey.'

Esterfeld looked at him, waited for his nod and then continued. 'His Majesty wishes you to mingle with these merchants and their crew, and find out all you can. In particular, he wishes to know if there are any hints of financial irregularities. You will be given a royal warrant which you may show only to certain trusted people in the event of difficulties. Your contact at the court will be with myself or Cardinal Morton; in Bristol it will be with my father the admiral, or, if necessary, Master Merrick. Is all this clear?'

'Yes.'

'I am told that you have some sea-going experience. That should make it easy to gain access to the ship as a crew member.'

'But when the ship returns to England . . .' I began, and Morton raised a hand.

'Master Esterfeld is not interested in your future movements,' he said. 'By the time the ship returns arrangements will have been made.'

Thirkell had not been on my list of those who could be trusted, but Master Merrick was. He was not difficult to find, but it was a goodly wait to see him. He was not just any merchant, but a king's officer and a customs controller, and had already had part of the new land named for him by Gabotto. Pinned on the wall of his counting room for all to see was a chart drawn by the Genoan, which had the word 'Amerricka' in large letters on the land at the other side of the western seas.

'How far have you sailed?' he asked me.

'I have been to the Azores and Cabo Verde,' I said, 'and once went as far as Jaloof.'

'Under whose command?'

'Usually Portuguese captains; that to Jaloof was under Pero Vaz da Cunha, the one-eyed captain.'

'Yes, I've heard of him. Not a pleasant voyage, I imagine, nor indeed a pleasant man, I hear.'

'It is not my place, sir . . .' I began.

'It's all right,' he smiled. 'But it's immaterial. You've never been in northern waters, have you?'

I was forced to prevaricate. It would not do to say yet that

I had made two journeys to that very land which Gabotto had claimed to have discovered. 'I have not had much experience of them,' I said, 'but I have done some fishing in those waters, some years ago.'

'Then I cannot help you. My complement is full. If matters had been different, and you knew the northern seas well or had sailed with some captains known to me or perhaps had some specialist skills or knowledge, then perhaps I might have been able to help. But, with things as they are . . .' He spread his hands. 'Sorry.'

He waited for me to go, and when I did not he raised his eyebrows. 'I cannot help you,' he repeated.

'Sir, I was told not to put pressure on you except *in extremis . . .*'

His eyebrows shot up in surprise. 'You have a startling vocabulary for an uneducated seaman,' he said. 'How exactly do you propose to put *pressure* on me, *in extremis* or otherwise?'

I reached into my doublet and pulled out the package therein, a waterproof pouch with a single sheet of paper inside. Silently, I handed the pouch over to him. He looked at the seal, looked in astonishment at me, and then looked at the seal again more closely. Then, with a little expression of surprise, he unsealed the bag and withdrew the letter. He turned it over several times, again perusing the seal, and with a final look across at me he broke it and read what Henry Tudor had written. When he had finished he laid the letter down upon a table and looked at me.

'Friends in high places,' he said.

I could find no reply.

'You are to be allowed to sail by direct order of the king,' he went on. 'Who are you? What are you? An agent?'

'Master Merrick,' I said, 'forgive me, but my orders are that my lips must be sealed concerning all that has taken place before I arrived at Bristol, and in no wise can I go against what his . . . what my master has told me. But rest assured that I am not here to observe either yourself or Master Thirkell.'

'You come under a king's warrant and yet you are prepared to work as an ordinary seaman?'

'Yes, sir, although as to specialist skills, well, I can use an astrolabe and cross-staff.'

He shook his head in bemusement and held up the paper. 'And I may not share this information with Master Thirkell or any other save the admiral, and we two must keep it close.' He let out a sigh and said, 'So be it, then. Report to Master Thirkell and follow his orders. You sail for the new found land in five days' time.'

So I returned to the ship victualling in the river near St Brendan's Hill and became a member of its crew, signing on as Richard Wood. After Merrick had come aboard and conferred with him, I found Thirkell looking at me oddly, but he accepted me as a crewmember and then, on the day we sailed, he called me over to him on deck. 'I am told that you can read a router and a chart and have some knowledge of the instruments.'

'A little, sir.'

'Show me.'

I picked up the astrolabe, demonstrated to him how I would use it and then did the same for the cross-staff. He watched, nodded and said, 'I think I may be able to use you. Bring your gear and stow it in my cabin. You can sleep in there.'

The next day we were out of the river and turning our course to the south-west.

'So, how much do you know of whither 'tis we go?' he asked.

'I have some knowledge,' I said. 'We go to the south of Ireland and then westering, is it not?'

'Do you know anything of Cabot's new found land?' he asked. 'Have you heard it spoken of?'

'I know it is ill-named, sir,' I said.

'I think Master Cabot and I may name this land as we wish, for it is new, and we found it.'

'Forgive my plain speaking, Master Thirkell,' I said, 'but we both know that that is not totally true, sir.'

'What? What do you mean?'

'The land is not "new found", at least by you and Gabotto,' I told him.

Thirkell grunted. 'Pay no attention to that charlatan Columbus,' he said. 'What he found . . .'

'I know what he found,' I said, 'because I know Columbus – Colom, we used to call him.'

'You know Columbus?'

'Aye,' I said, 'and sailed with him.' I held up a hand to stifle his astonishment. 'No, not on that voyage – some years ago we were shipmates on a trip to the Çanaga. No, it is your "new found land" that I speak of. Basque fishermen have been going there for years. I have done so myself.'

He leapt to his feet. 'What do you mean?' he cried. 'What nonsense are you talking?'

'For forty years or more,' I said, 'the Basque fishing fleet has been westering to a land far over the western horizon in search of fish. You know this, and so do I, much as they tried to keep it secret. Fifteen years ago, some English ships were there too, long before you arrived. You know this, and so do I, and so does Master Merrick. Was not the matter raised in court?'

He stared at me, thought about blustering on, and then changed his mind. 'That hearing was in closed court,' he said. 'How are you privy to it?'

Esterfeld had told me as part of the briefing, but I did not tell Thirkell that. I saw the change in him, though. 'Don't worry,' I told him. 'I can keep my mouth shut about what I know. I've bigger secrets than yours I need to keep.'

He busied himself with the cross-staff, turning it over and

over in his hands, and then asked, 'How? How do you know these things?'

'Because I was there,' I said. 'I sailed, not on a Basque ship, but on a Breton one as part of their fleet, to the bacalao fishing grounds, maybe eight years ago. Aye, and I wintered there too. A cold time we had of it, but in the spring we filled our hold with salt cod and I came back a rich man.'

'I don't believe you,' he said. 'No one winters there.'

'The Basques do,' I said.

'What manner of man did you see there?' he asked. 'I don't mean your own crew; I mean the people of the country.'

'Strange men,' I told him. 'Forest dwellers, clothed in the hide of a large deer, and painted red all over.'

'And with what weaponry?'

'Bows, spears, clubs,' I said.

He considered my answers. 'You say true,' he said, 'howsoever you learned it. What manner of land is it?'

'Rocky,' I told him, 'with a flat shore and huge forests beyond. I did not venture too far into the forests.'

'No more did I,' he said, 'or any of us. So, then, you are sent to spy on me by the king?'

'Not so, sir. His Majesty has many reasons for wishing to be shut of me, but they none of them are aught to do with you. Is it true, though, that you claimed the land on behalf of the king?'

'We did, yes.'

'Regardless of those men already living there?'

'Our instructions required us to take those lands for the crown which were not Christian lands.'

'Regardless of those men already living there?' I repeated.

'There were no men already living there.'

'There were indeed,' I said, 'for I know them and have lived among them.'

'There were no men already living there,' he said. 'I have

it from the lips of Cardinal Morton himself. After the flood, Noah had but three sons, Ham, Shem and Japheth, and those three men populated the world, spreading their seed through Africa, Asia and Europe. Any creatures in any other land, no matter how seeming men they might be, are no men, and have no more entitlement to the land they live on than do the beasts of the field to the land they occupy.'

'And so says your spiritual leader?' I asked.

'He does.' I will give Thirkell his due; he had the grace to look embarrassed at what he said.

So we set our course once we had found the latitude, and went due west. Some of the men, like Thirkell, were veterans of Cabot's first voyage; some had had friends and relations who had gone with him on the second voyage; all were seamen of some experience, and I found their company convivial and heart-warming. I had often thought of the sea when I had been in the Tower, but never thought that I would sail upon it again. Had Katherine and Edward been with me, I would have been completely happy. Would have been.

It was thirty-two days' sailing to the new found land and I had never enjoyed freedom so much. A prince may be the envy of the world in riches and esteem, but once he has been confined, a fresh wind at his back and the sun shining on his face is something no man would exchange for the cares of state.

We encountered heavy fog towards the end of the voyage, but fortunately none of those floating ice mountains that the Bretons used to tell me about. I have seen one, but only at a distance, which my shipmates assured me was the best and safest way.

Then, as the mist cleared one morning, I saw before me a sight that I had never dreamed I would see again. There was the shore, flat and rocky, and beyond it forest after forest stretched as far as the eye could see. 'The new found land,' Thirkell said, behind me. 'We have found it again. The refound land.' He seemed to consider that he had made a great witticism, and roared with laughter at his jest.

The old hands were already throwing hand lines overboard, weighted and baited with some scraps, and it was no time at all before there were shouts as the first bacalao were hoisted aboard to be grilled for breakfast. If there was ever an easier fish to catch than this one, it must have long since disappeared from the earth.

We went ashore, finding walking on a firm surface strange at first, and Thirkell called the ship's company together to hear what he had to say. 'Our mission here is threefold,' he said. 'First, we are to find John Cabot and his fleet, if possible, and join with them. Second, we are to search for a route to the east, to find Cipango if we can, where all spices and all jewels have their origin. Third, and easiest of all, we are to collect and salt fish, both for our own provisions and also to sell back in Bristol.'

There were cheers at this. Fishing was easier than sailing, and the men were ready for a break in the routine. The ship's company was split into various groups, some to go fishing, some to make do and mend and some to start making the stages for the cod to be split and gutted on. The barrels of salt were hoisted from the hold and brought ashore, and there was a general atmosphere of gaiety.

In the midst of this Thirkell drew me to one side. 'There is one further element of our task,' he said, 'and one for which I think you are best fitted, given the things you have told me.'

He faced inland and nodded towards the forests. 'We need to find out all we can about the red men,' he said, 'if indeed they are men. The king has asked the pope to rule on the matter, but I think we should be safer in treating them as men until we know for sure.'

'Those I met were all men,' I said.

'And that's why it must be you who goes to find them,' he

said. 'I will give you a small party with some weaponry, but I cannot spare very many . . .'

'I'll go alone,' I said. 'Too large a party would frighten them away, and if a weapon were used, even accidentally, it could cause conflict. It were better I go alone and unarmed.'

He considered for a moment and then said, 'So be it. It is a business of which you know more than I. When do you think it would be best to go?'

'Let them see what we are about first,' I said. 'Let them see us fishing and salting, so they know our business is peaceful. We can leave them some fish at the edge of the forest. It would be a good sign if they took it – that would be an acceptance of our presence.'

'Fine,' he said, turning away. 'Three days, then?'

'Three days is fine,' I said.

'And when will you return?'

'Who knows,' I said. 'Perhaps never, which would be a sign that any man can read.'

'Do you have no fear, Richard?' he said suddenly. 'They could kill you, could they not? I have never met anyone so calm in the face of possible death.'

'They might kill me,' I said, 'although they probably won't. In any case, I have been considered dead by so many people for so long that the reality does not concern me. The priests tell us it will be a return home, do they not? Well, so be it; it has been a long time since I had a home.'

Thirkell looked at me, not comprehending a word, and then said, 'So, what do you prefer to do until then – fish, salt or repair?'

'Fish,' I said, and he clapped me on the back.

Then, struck by a sudden thought, he turned and looked back at the forest. 'Do you think they are watching us now?' he asked.

'Almost certainly,' I said, 'although I have seen no sign of them.'

'Nor I,' he said.

We left fish on the fringe of the forest on the first two nights, and in the morning it was gone, although whether taken by the forest dwellers or by animals we could not tell. On the third day I made ready to enter the forest by stripping off all my outer garments, leaving only breeches and a shift.

Thirkell asked me again if I wanted an escort, but I shook my head, waved to all and crossed the ground to where the forest began. I took a last look back and then pushed my way through the undergrowth, looking for a track or some sign that the Beothuk had passed that way, but I could see nothing.

I walked on, further and further into the trees, until I was completely surrounded by them. I noticed some of the black berries I had seen on my last walk in this forest, and I plucked a few and tasted them; they were as plump and sweet as I remembered. I deliberately did not eat too many, for I knew that my belly might protest later if I did.

I was just licking my fingers when I became aware of the presence of someone else. I looked around, and saw a man squatting beside a fallen tree. He was dark, and his long black hair hung freely about his face, and he wore only a breechclout. In his hand was a bow, and thrust into the ground in front of him three or four arrows. When he saw that I had become aware of him, he straightened and stood upright, the bow held loosely in his left hand and an arrow in his right. He was taller than me, with a calm and serious mien. I might have thought that he had bronzed, reddish skin, but in reality he was plastered with the red earth that I remembered so well.

I showed him my hands, both empty, and held them out in front of me, my palms facing him, as I took a step back. He stood for a long moment, looking me up and down, and then he transferred the bow to his left hand and with his right made a sweeping gesture, placing the open hand on his heart and

then outward in a semicircle, ending with his open palm towards me.

I must have looked surprised, for he repeated the gesture,
this time dipping his head slightly.

Looking him in the eye, I too dipped my head and mimicked
his gesture.

Now he pointed at me, made walking movements with two
fingers, and then turned his hand over and raised his eyebrows,
as obvious a way of asking where I had come from as if he had
asked in plain English.

I indicated the forest behind me, and then made a waving
motion with my hand, to indicate water, and three movements
of my hand which I hoped expressed increasing distance.

He nodded, seeming both to understand and to accept this,
and then raised his fingers to his mouth, clearly indicating
eating. I pointed to the fruit, and he made the eating gesture
again, beckoned, and turned away along a forest path which
was just visible behind him.

'Beothuk,' I said, loudly and clearly, in the language I hoped
was his own.

He turned, astonished, and I said, 'I am Beothuk. Are you
Beothuk?'

'You are truly Beothuk?' he asked.

I nodded.

'Who is your father?' he asked, after a pause.

'Alacho,' I answered.

'Alacho is not my father,' he said, 'and I am not of his
family, but I know the sons of Alacho. Can you name them?'

'I can name Qantoc,' I said, 'who is my brother, and Santu,
who is my sister.'

'Alacho has left this life,' he said, 'but Qantoc sits in his
place. If you come to my village I can take you to the place of
Qantoc, if you so please.'

'I should be grateful,' I said, and followed him down the

narrow track. It wound through the trees and led gradually downhill to a clearing where there stood a stockade of woven branches, with a narrow gap giving access to the interior. My heart leapt as I saw this, the very mirror of the village I remembered. My guide approached it and then turned to look back at me. Satisfied that I was following, he looked beyond me, and on turning I saw that I had been shadowed by a number of his fellows, all armed as he was and each with an arrow nocked in readiness. They had, it seemed, been testing my disposition and intent.

I followed my guide through the gap and into an encampment beyond. There were a number of the same conical huts I remembered, and the same small fires with naked or nearly naked children tending each one. Some adults were wandering about, most looking intently at the stranger in their midst. It could almost have been Alacho's village.

True to his word, the red man took me through the forest the next day, and after we had trudged for a few hours I began to recognize things – the shape of a tree, or how the track bent around a particular bush or deviated to ford a stream. I felt a pang of love, and began to feel happy again.

When we reached the stockade my companion called out that he had a brother with him, and I saw movement within. I stepped through the gate and saw Qantoc striding towards me. 'Wicha!' he shouted, and I saw reactions from some of those moving about; perhaps they remembered me from before.

Qantoc took me to his wigwam, where we smoked a pipe together. Alacho had died and Santu was married to a chief's son from another village, with two small children of her own. Otherwise life in the compound was as it had been before, and no doubt as it had been for many years before that.

Qantoc told me that in the years since I had left there had been more and more visitors coming to their land to fish. Ships like my own had come, first in ones and twos, as in previous years, but then in tens and scores, each taking many fish and making little or no attempt to make contact or trade with the Beothuk. He was becoming worried, and some of the elders wanted to move away from the coast permanently, to live in the interior where the khalibu were plentiful and the fishermen did not go.

'Has there been trouble?' I asked.

'Some fighting,' he said. 'Not much. Now that you have returned we will be able to talk to them. But what of yourself? Are you now king of your own country, as you wished?'

I smiled. 'I am not,' I said. I told him of my travails, of the battles and campaigns, of the king's court and of the Tower, but mostly I told him of Katherine and Edward and the lost Richard I had never seen.

'Do you wish me to take the men of the Beothuk to fight for you?' he asked. 'We could sail across the great sea with you, if you will show us the way.'

'I do not,' I said. 'I no longer wish to be king. That part of my life is dead.'

'Then you will stay here,' he told me. 'You are my brother.'

That night there was feasting, and I was given another deer-skin mantle. I was the prodigal son.

I took Qantoc to meet Thirkell.

'He is concerned,' I said.

'He need not be,' Thirkell told me. 'Once we've stocked up we'll be on our way. We'll leave plenty of fish for him.'

'Yet you claimed this land for Henry Tudor,' I said. 'What say you to that now?'

'That's the king's problem,' he said. 'I just did as I was told. You haven't told him that, have you?'

'No.'

'Good. We'll be on our way soon enough. I'm not saying that others won't come along, in due course, but not this voyage; not yet. Perhaps never – that king of ours won't be interested in a land with no gold or precious stones, and the fish is all in the sea. We won't be much bother to him.'

And so it proved. I moved from compound to fish dock freely, but was the only man to do so regularly. Occasionally one or two of the men would come to Qantoc's village with me out of idle curiosity or to have a look at the red women, and one of them in particular found a woman prepared to be as wanton as he would wish, but the Beothuk were suspicious, and I kept the visitations of others to a minimum.

The day came when the ship was stocked up with a plenitude of fish and the water butts were brim full. It was clear that we would be leaving soon to seek the passage to Cipango. I was getting together a selection of unwanted metal to give to Qantoc, when one of the men came over to me.

'The captain wants you,' he said.

'Where away?'

He pointed across the shore, to where Thirkell was supervising the movement of the remaining salt barrels back to the ship, and apart from the stages we had built and two small piles, one of stockfish and the other something I couldn't make out, the rocks were clear. I walked over, and the captain turned to greet me.

'You have wintered here,' Thirkell said. 'What was it like?'

'Cold,' I told him, 'but bearable. I got an extra share for doing so, so I was content.'

'Listen,' Thirkell said. 'I have orders. Secret. Secret even from you. I'm not supposed to tell you, but I won't betray you – not completely, anyway. I am sorry.'

'For what?'

He stared at the ground, then turned away before looking me in the eye. 'My instructions are that you do not return to England.'

'I know that,' I said. 'I have no intention of going back to England. There is an agreement.'

'You don't understand,' Thirkell said. 'You're supposed to die here. I have the orders in writing, from the highest level.'

'From the king?' I asked, incredulous.

'No, not that high, but near enough; from the Cardinal Archbishop.'

'Morton!' I said. 'Well, that makes sense. He it was who suggested I come on this voyage. He has a long-standing quarrel with my . . . family.'

'Who the hell are you?' Thirkell asked.

'I am Richard Wood, seaman,' I said.

He stared at me, and then said, 'He says you are under no circumstances to be allowed to make the return voyage, the which I must ensure by whatsoever means I deem necessary, and that no course of action is closed to me. You realize what that means?'

I stood silently and looked at the forest. 'It means that you kill me,' I said. 'So how are you going to do it? Where?'

'It doesn't mean only that,' he said. 'I can't take you back, that's obvious, but I can leave you here. You get on with the people. There could be worse places to start a new life. And I will have followed my orders. In fact, I could even say that I did kill you.'

'Why don't you just do it?' I asked. 'You'd only be following orders.'

'You're a good shipmate,' he said. 'I'll take my chances with Morton's ire. I misinterpreted his meaning, that's all. It's been done before. Are you happy to stay?'

'I've been all over this world,' I said, 'except for the Orient. Here's as good as anywhere. Will you be back?'

'Who knows,' he said. 'The fishing is good, but here there are none of the riches that make kings happy. They want gold and jewels, not fish and straight-grown wood. A man could be content here, but a king could never be.'

I smiled at his unconscious irony.

'If we find a way to the Indies then there will be no reason to come back here,' he said. 'If we don't find a way, there still won't be any reason. Are we agreed, then, Richard? I leave you here?'

'Leave me some fish to tide me over, and some warm clothing, and I will make shift to live with the red men,' I said. 'I've been threatened with worse fates.'

We parted with a clasp of the hands, and I walked into the forest so as not to see the ship leave without me. I was an exile again, but a free one at least, and I walked back to Qantoc's village in a mood that was lighter than I would have thought it could be.

For the next ten or so years I travelled with them, learning to hunt and track as they did and living their life, accepted by them as one of their own. I met Santu again, but while a Beothuk maiden is mistress of her own body, as Qantoc had said, adultery is frowned upon and punishable by death, so she never again slipped under my bear pelt in the night. We were friends, though, and tied to each other as brother and sister.

Of my time in those lands there is little to tell, except for one incident which is most painful to relate. I had been living with the Beothuk for about two years when it happened. The English and the Basques had continued as they had always done, fishing during the summer months, salting the fish on the shore, doing a small amount of trading with the Beothuk but otherwise keeping to themselves. Others came, however, with different intent.

I was paying a visit to the village of Oubee, the husband of Santu, when word came one day, late in the year when the fishing fleets had all gone home, that a ship had arrived in the bay. He and I went down to have a look. There was indeed a ship there, and I immediately recognized the flag it was flying.

'Portugal,' I said.

'They are men of your nation?' he asked.

'No,' I said, 'but I have lived in their nation, and I know them and their language. I will go and speak to them if you wish.'

'You are not yet wise in the ways of men,' Oubee said. 'If you speak their language, do not let them know it. Then, when they speak one to another, you may learn much.'

'They are great explorers,' I said, 'but more than that, they like to take for themselves the land that they find. If they find nothing of interest to them, then they might move on.'

It soon became evident to the Portuguese that there were no fish to be had. We watched them for two or three days and saw that they managed to catch some small bottom feeders in their net, but it was clear that the effort they expended was more than the sustenance they gained, and they were never going to be able to catch enough to live on. In any case, the water was becoming colder each day, and before long they would not be able to fish for more than a few minutes at a time. The seals too had gone, and so there was no source of fresh meat for the men. They occasionally landed some men as a water party, but did not enter the forest, staying always around the shore.

We left khalibu haunches by the stream where they collected their water, but they did not seem to understand the system, and simply took them without leaving anything in return. Inadvertently, however, we had alerted them to our presence.

The trouble started when one of the boys from Oubee's village was taken. He had gone down to the shore to forage, as they often did, for bits of discarded metal. They always waited until the strangers had gone back to their ship, but this boy was surprised and taken by two mariners who had delayed their return and had been sitting unseen below some rocks. They dragged him off to one of the boats and took him out to the ship.

The boy's companions came back to the compound, terrified,

and Oubee decided to go and trade for his return. He took some pelts and more meat and set off with a half-dozen of us. We left our arms behind.

I was ordered to stay near the chief and let him know what the Portuguese were saying. As we came out of the forest we were spotted, and the Portuguese sent a party to meet us. I noticed that some of them were armed with hand guns. 'Those sticks those men are carrying,' I said, 'make a loud noise and throw a piece of metal at astounding speed. If the metal hits it kills immediately. If the captain gives the order to use them then you must fall to the ground when you see the smoke, and immediately afterward rise and run away before they can do it again.'

He nodded his understanding and then had me repeat it to the other men.

We advanced, our arms out where the Portuguese could see them, and placed the pelts and meat in front of us. Then Oubee spoke, asking them to release the boy in exchange for the gifts. We were too far away for me to hear what they were saying to each other, but several of the explorers gathered and conversed.

Oubee repeated his speech, pointing at the goods and making gestures suggesting the height of the boy.

The leader of the Portuguese took a deep breath and called out, 'In the name of King Manuel of Portugal and of our captain, the honourable Admiral Gaspar Corte-Real, I claim these lands as Portuguese territory and place them under the protection of the Kingdom of Portugal, in the name of the Father, the Son and the Holy Spirit.' Then he crossed himself, held up a hand to us, clearly a sign to wait, and he signalled two of his men forward. They carried a small barrel, which they placed on the ground next to our offerings. One of them stoved the top in with a hammer, and then placed a cup on the ground beside it before the pair of them moved back a couple of paces.

'What do they want to trade?' Oubee asked.

'I think it is wine,' I told him.

'What is wine?'

The Beothuk did not make any form of fermented drink, and thus had never had experience of its powers. 'It is a drink,' I said. 'It is strong, and takes away men's wits and makes them sleepy.'

'I want the boy,' Oubee said. 'Do they not understand this?'

'Perhaps not. Do you want me to speak in their tongue?'

'Not yet,' he said. 'Are you willing to go forward and try this wine?'

'I am.'

I stepped beyond our line and walked to where the barrel had been placed. I gestured, asking if I might try it, and the leader indicated that I should. I knelt and filled the cup half full, and then rose to my feet.

'Go on, lad, get it down you,' one of the two nearest men said in Portuguese. 'Plenty more where that came from.' He grinned at me and nodded encouragingly.

I took a sip. It was wine, but of inferior quality. Still, I had not had a drink of wine for years, so I took a larger mouthful and stood, letting it fill my mouth. I wondered if it might be poisoned, but there would be no point to that, and it tasted like wine right enough.

'Give them all some,' the nearest man said. 'The more the merrier.'

'Enjoy it while you can,' said his companion. 'You'll see no more of it once you get to Lagos, you damned pagan.'

Now this was interesting, and made all clear. I knew of Lagos, a small Portuguese town which had served as a slave market for the last fifty years or so, trading in human misery with African nations who were prepared to sell captured enemies and sometimes even unwanted relatives for a few brass bracelets. I took another sip and then turned and walked back to Oubee. I put the cup in his hand, telling him to taste it, and then said, 'These men mean us ill. They intend to capture some of us and take us back to their land.'

'For what reason?'

'To sell in their market as slaves.'

'Sell? What is sell?'

'To exchange for goods. They mean to keep us as servants, as their property.'

'How can a man own another man?'

'It is their law,' I said. 'Believe me, we should have nothing to do with these men.'

'And the boy?'

'I do not know,' I said. 'I do not know how to get him back.'

Oubee walked forward to the barrel and poured the wine back into it. Then, setting the cup by the side, he repeated that the gifts were in exchange for the boy and only for the boy. The Portuguese stared at him, impassive.

When he had finished he stepped back from the barrel and joined me. 'What will happen now?' he asked.

'I do not know. I have had no experience of negotiations of this sort.'

The Portuguese leader stepped forward again and indicated the barrel. 'We hope you find our gift pleasing,' he said. Then he stepped back and pointed to the ship. 'Bring your relatives and friends aboard, for we shall make them welcome. There is much more wine to be had. Please, come, all of you.' Then he indicated the wine again, pointed to the ship, rubbed his belly and smiled, and opened his arms in a gesture of welcome.

'Does he wish us to go to his ship?' Oubee asked. 'That is what he seems to be saying.'

'It is,' I said, 'but it is not an offer of friendship. I believe that he intends to kidnap any who go on board and take them to his own country to sell.'

'Then we shall not go,' Oubee said. 'Is that what will happen to the boy?'

'Probably.' I thought for a moment, and then said, 'Shall I ask him in his own language for his return? I shall speak haltingly.'

'Try.'

I stepped forward and said in broken Portuguese, 'Give back boy. Chief say, give back boy.'

If the Portagee was surprised to hear a Beothuk speak to him in his own tongue, he gave no sign of it beyond a long thoughtful silence after I had spoken. Then he said, 'Come aboard our ship. You are all welcome. We can drink together.'

'Give back boy,' I said. 'Then we come. No boy, no come, no drink.'

He pondered this, and decided to try to gain an advantage. 'Go and bring out the boy,' he called over his shoulder. 'Let him go. Throw him back; he's just a small one. I've no objection to using him as bait.'

They brought the boy out and sent him across to us, and Oubee raised an arm in acknowledgement.

'Now come,' the leader said.

'Tomorrow,' I told him. 'Talk first.'

'Where did you learn Portuguese?' he called.

'Tomorrow,' I said. 'Tell tomorrow.'

Oubee put an arm around the boy and we turned away. We left the pelts and meat where they were.

'These men are evil,' Oubee said. 'We go inland tonight. I do not want my people stolen by these men.'

'I will return to Qantoc,' I said. 'He too must be warned of this. Will you warn any families you meet?'

'I will,' Oubee said. 'Go now and warn Qantoc.'

It was a journey of about five hours to Qantoc's compound, and it was almost dark when I got there.

Even before I reached the place I knew something was wrong. There was no noise, no fires, no smell of cooking, and I did not see a single family member as I neared the place. I came through the stockade to find only three women, one old man and a child in the clearing.

'What has happened?' I asked. 'Where is Qantoc?'

'We do not know,' the old man said. 'He went with some of the tribe to the ship in the bay, and has not returned.'

'Some of the tribe?' I asked. 'All but you few?'

'Yes. The man on the ship gave a feast, and all were invited. The baby and I were sick, so we did not go, and these my daughters stayed to tend us. All of the rest are there.'

I felt my heart sink. 'When was this feast?' I asked.

'Three days ago.'

I felt my blood run cold. It was as I feared.

I rested until dawn and then walked across the frozen shore. There was a ship moored in the bay, a different one from that at Oubee's village the day before. I called out in Portuguese to one of the men standing guard. 'I wish to speak to Admiral Gaspar Corte-Real on a most urgent matter.'

It took a few moments before he realized what language I was using, and then he asked me to repeat what I had said. I did so, and he went down to the boat and spoke to someone there.

That someone, probably his senior officer, came along the shore and called to me. 'This soldier says you spoke to him in Portuguese and asked to see the captain. Is this true?'

'It is,' I answered him. 'Please arrange it, if you will be so kind.'

'Perhaps you would care to come aboard, senhor.'

'No, I would not,' I told him.

The pair of them stood looking at me for some time, and then the senior one returned to the boat, cast off and was rowed out to the remaining ship. It was no more than an hour later that the boat returned, with three or four more men, one of whom was clearly in authority.

'Are you the one who speaks Portuguese?' he called.

'I am.'

'Please approach.'

'No sir. I do not wish to do so. I wish only to obtain the release of the members of my family, whom you hold against their will.'

'I hold only some aborigines.'

'That is the family of which I speak. They are not slaves, as you intend to treat them, but free men.'

'That is for me to decide.'

'No, sir,' I told him. 'That decision is out of your hands. These lands are the new found lands discovered by Giovanni Cabotto the Venetian, and claimed for his sovereign majesty King Henry VII of England. The people you have kidnapped are citizens of England, and what you have done is an act of war.'

'The pope has decided that all discovered lands should be divided between Spain and Portugal . . .'

'You are well beyond your jurisdiction, sir,' I said. 'I am aware of the papal bull of which you speak, and of the Treaty of Tordesillas of the following year, but they give you no rights over lands this far north. These lands are under English jurisdiction and English law, and I demand, in the name of King Henry VII, that you return his people to their homes.'

'What sort of savage are you, that speaks Portuguese and phrases his sentences like a lawyer?' he asked.

'I am Wicha, a member of the Beothuk tribe that has held these lands since time immemorial. I have sailed the Ocean Sea with Colom and Bisagudo, and I have been to the court of your King João, now deceased, I understand. I know of Cabotto and the others who have sailed these waters. I know of the papal bull which splits the discovered world between your two countries, but I would remind you that your remit extends only to non-Christian lands. These lands are Christian, and thus you must return those whom you have taken to their homes.'

'How can these be Christian lands, when no civilized man has ever set foot here?'

'I repeat, these lands were claimed by Cabotto for England. Your remit has no power here.'

'Nonetheless, my friend,' he said, 'there is nothing that can be done. The aborigines – who, I might add, came aboard our ship of their own free will, have already sailed for their new life in Portugal.'

My heart sank anew. I was too late.

'To Lagos,' I said. 'I know where you have sent them, and why.'

He shrugged. 'They are already three days into their voyage,' he said. 'You know the extent of the Ocean Sea, or so you say, so you will know that they cannot be recalled. Their fate is sealed.'

He stepped a few paces closer. 'You, on the other hand, may stand on the threshold of riches. Do you speak their language?'

'I do.'

'Then why not throw in your lot with me? There are other native villages around here. Help me get their men on board, and I will give you many bracelets.'

'You think I would sell my people for brass bracelets?'

'If you will not, then others will. Or should I offer you gold, then? I take it you know what gold is?'

'I know gold, and I know what gold will do to men. Sail after your caravel and return my family to me, and I will offer you peace and trade. The land here is rich and can supply many of your needs; trade would be beneficial to us both. Refuse to do this and I cannot answer for your safety.'

'You presume to threaten me?' he said. 'Do you know what a gun is? Do you know that I have three on board this ship, as well as the hand guns? You cannot frighten us, and your people are mine to do with what I will, under the terms of the bull and the treaty. Now be gone, and trouble us no more.'

I turned away, but I had already decided that the Portingales should never have a foothold in the new found land, and Corte-Real had just shown me how to ensure that was the case.

The Beothuk have many ways of keeping something dry in water. A bag made from the untorn skin of a rabbit is one such, and halfway through the night I rolled up a couple of flints and my shirt and breeches into as small a ball as possible, put them inside such a skin and tied the top tightly. I held this in my teeth as I let myself slide naked into the water.

It was ice cold, and I was glad that it was but a short swim to where the ship was moored. There are always places where it is easy to clamber up the side of a vessel, especially one lying still in the water, and after some reconnaissance I found handholds and worked my way up to the deck. There were two guards, but they were on the shore side, away from me, and I slipped onto the deck and through a portal before they saw me. Then it was the work of but a few moments to clothe myself in the shirt and hose I had brought.

Moving about the ship was easy. I had spent much time on Portuguese ships, and the lie of them was always the same. Normally the men would have been sleeping on deck, but that was for warmer climes, and they were crowded below. I slipped unchallenged through them down to the lower deck, where the stores were kept, and worked my way along until I found the powder store.

It was as dark as Hades in there, but I knew what I wanted and where to find it. I felt along the bulkhead and found them in a rack there, two or three of the slow matches that the handgunners used to fire their devices. Then I felt around the tops of the barrels until I came to the one that was in use, whose top was looser than the rest, and I took it off.

I knew the next action was the most dangerous of all, and spent some time brushing the deck around where I was so there was no trace of the powder there, and then I knelt and shuffled round in a small circle, pissing the while, to form what I hoped was an impenetrable barrier.

Then I went to the open barrel and forced one of the slow matches down into the powder before taking a small handful of the deadly mixture and returning to my circle of wetness. I placed the powder on the deck, the second slow fuse resting beside it, and took the flints in my hands. I knew that what I was doing could lead to my own sudden death, but I cared not.

I struck the flints against each other and there was a spark, but naught else. I tried again, and this time the spark ignited a few grains of the powder, but they were extinguished before I could make any other move, and I tried again. This time I had it aright, and the spark ignited the powder with a sudden flash, and when it had died down there was a small red glow where it had been. It had set alight the end of the slow match, as I had hoped. I picked up the match, blowing on it to keep it alive, but with my hand cupped around it so as not to blow the spark into the powder. The red glow strengthened and expanded. It was not enough to see by, but I reached out my right hand and felt for the open barrel with the slow match poking from it.

Carefully, and not without a great deal of fear, I clasped the match in my right hand, brought the lit one in my left to it and touched the two together. The second slow match glowed red too, and again I blew gently on it. It needed no further encouragement, and I let go; one end was afire, and the other buried half a foot in the powder. I jammed the end of the second fuse into the barrel to the same depth, and then slipped out of the powder store.

The ship was quiet and still. I waited until my eyes were used to the light and then tried to retrace my steps, but I blundered in the dark and came up the wrong hatchway, so that I found myself in the midst of the sleeping crew instead of skirting them, and had to step round and over slumbering forms as I made my way to where I could get onto the upper deck.

One man roused as I went past him. 'What's up?' he muttered. 'Where you going?'

'Piss,' I said, and he yawned and rolled over.

I waited a moment and then continued, finally finding the right hatchway from the cooler air that was coming through it. I hauled myself up and peeped out onto the deck. There was no one about, and I hauled myself through the opening and stood up.

'And what have we here?' a voice asked behind me.

I turned and looked into the eyes of a guard with an amused look on his face.

'Just want a piss,' I said. I did not want to say too much, for I knew that my Portuguese, while seen as exceptional for a red Beothuk, would not pass muster as a native Portagee.

'Up here?'

'Yes,' I said, and made to step around him. In my mind's eye I could see the fuse burning, burning, burning ever closer to the packed powder in the barrel. It did not help that I did not know exactly how fast it would burn.

'Hold on,' he said. 'Who are you? I've never seen you before.'

'Fernandes,' I told him. 'Only come over a few days ago from the other ship.'

'From the *Vera*?' he asked. 'Do you know João?'

'Yes,' I said. 'Look, can we talk in a minute? I'm desperate for a piss.'

He shrugged and turned away. I walked a little aft to where I knew one of the mooring ropes was, and hitched up my shift. I heard his footsteps receding, and I reached over the side and took the mooring rope in both hands. Then I swung over and lowered myself hand over hand into the water so that he did not hear any splash. I cast off shift and hose as having no further use to me, and swam several strokes under the water. I hoped he would simply assume that I was too tired to go back and speak to him again.

A few minutes later I waded ashore onto the familiar rocks, never more happy to do so, and walked swiftly to the tree line where I had left my mantle and boots. Once inside those I was soon warm again, and I sat down to see what happened.

It took longer than I thought. I sat and waited, but there was no activity on the ship that I could hear. The sentinel had not been alarmed by me, it seemed. I waited another hour or so.

Then, quite suddenly, a bright orange flower blossomed inside the ship, a shaft of light that lit up the sky and sea, and that was followed by the loudest sound I have ever heard, a blast that reverberated around the bay, and then there was a second blossom and a series of blasts, three or four in rapid succession. The vague outline of the ship turned into a blazing inferno, and things began to rain out of the sky into the sea and onto the land. I stepped further back into the shelter of the trees, but there were no more explosions. The ship continued to burn, and then, slowly at first, but with increasing rapidity, it began to settle lower in the water. The stern was first to dip below the surface, and then the rest of the ship followed it, slipping down and extinguishing the flames as it went. Within a few moments, the water and the sky were dark again, and it was as if Gaspar Corte-Real and his fleet had never been in our bay.

I never found any sign of what had happened, except for a few barrel staves and some singed pieces of furled sail that were washed up on the shore, and which Oubee's people took. The Portuguese did not come again to the new found land while I was there.

I took the remnants of Qantoc's tribe to Oubee's village and told him what I had done, and then went with him when he moved his people inland, away from the fish and the fishers of men. For seven more years I lived as a Beothuk, learning to hunt, visiting the coast only when necessary and becoming a complete woodsman. Then, in the late spring of the eighth year, Oubee brought his people back towards the coast, and there in the bay was a ship.

On the shore a group of men were gutting fish and salting them from a line of barrels. Two of them had detached themselves from this group and were trundling a water barrel across the rocks on rollers. I waited until they had started to fill the butt and made sure that they were unarmed. Then I stepped out from the cover of the trees and stood so that they both could see me.

One nudged the other and they turned to look at me, both of them alert and cautious, tensed for action. I could see their eyes running along the edge of the tree line, looking for any companions I might have with me.

I waited, and then held up both my hands, palms outwards so that they could see that I was unarmed too. When they had digested this I stepped down the slope, keeping my hands in view, and stopped about ten paces away from them.

'Portugueses?' I said.

They looked at each other.

'Euskara? Français? Vlaamsch? Españoles? Italiani?'

They stared at me, and then one of them spoke to the other in a language which, although I did not understand it, I was able to recognize from my brother's struggles with it as a boy. I laughed aloud in recognition. '*Bore da*,' I said. 'You are Welsh, then, is it?'

They were clearly astonished to be spoken to in their own language, and stood as if struck dumb.

'*Saesneg?*' I said, and then added to their confusion. 'Do you speak English? I speak English.'

'How?' asked one of them, regaining his composure.

'I meet Englishmen here, many years in the past, when I am a boy. They are fishermen, like you.'

'From Bristol?'

'Yes. Some say their home is Bristol and some say their home is Swansea.'

The taller of the two let out a shout of surprise, and then they both advanced on me and clapped me on the back and shoulders. 'We know those men,' the taller said. 'We sailed from Bristol, too, and we are both from Swansea.'

They took me over to the fish stages and shared their food with me, and when their companions who had been fishing turned up, they too sat with me and I had to answer questions.

'Who is your king?' one man asked me.

'My king is Oubee,' I said. 'This is his land. Who is your king?'

'Our king is the King of England,' he said.

'I know England is far across the sea,' I said. 'How is England? How goes it there?'

He shrugged. 'England is England,' one said. 'It stands where it did.'

'When I spoke to the English men many years ago,' I said, beginning a little fishing expedition of my own, 'they told me that their king was called Henry.'

'Why, so he is,' another man said. 'Well remembered.'

'He must be a very old man, to reign so long,' I said.

'No, he is both a very young man, and a great man,' the first man said.

'How can he be young?' I asked. 'He is king when I speak to the men of Bristol, and that is more than a score of years ago, when I am a boy.'

They looked at one another, and then one said, 'Oh, he's thinking of the old king. No, old King Henry died, what, two or three years since.'

'So does not his son, King Arthur, now rule?'

'King Arthur? Nay, he is but legend.'

'No, Jem,' said the other man. 'Don't you recall that old

King Henry had another son that died as a boy, an older one, and his name was Arthur.'

'He did,' his companion said. 'It was so. Arthur, who died while still a boy. This red man is better informed than I am. How do you know so much?'

I ignored the question. 'So who now reigns in England?' I asked.

'King Henry – the Eighth, isn't it?' one of the men said.

'That's the very one,' said the other. 'He took his elder brother's place and was brought up to the crown.'

I stared out over the ocean as the realization slowly dawned on me. I was free to go home.

Peace

After 1512

I made myself as useful as I could to the Welshmen and their English companions. I supplied khalibu meat and furs in exchange for bits of metal, and from time to time brought baskets of berries to vary their diet. I listened carefully, and there was no sign that they intended to capture or enslave any of us. From time to time I slept and ate on board, and I helped with the fish gutting and salting as I had all those years before.

In late summer it was time to go. I begged the captain, a Bristol man called Jay, to take me with him to see all those places I had heard so much about from his men. He warned me that I would be shown as a curiosity in England, but I said that I had no objection to that, and in the end he agreed to allow me to work my passage as an ordinary seaman.

I had already approached Oubee and told him that I was leaving. He had tried to dissuade me, but the homesickness was on me, and I would not be turned away from my purpose. I took a goodly supply of red clay with me, to maintain my pretence, and my mantle and boots, for the warmth in them, but nothing else of that lovely new found land and its gentle people.

We sailed in what I discovered was early September, and after a passage of twenty-nine days sailed into Bristol Channel and past Brandon Hill. The local men were all excited and went off to see their families, leaving just a few of us on board to guard the ship and its cargo, so there was nothing easier for me than to disappear. I slipped away from the ship on the second night in port, carrying a bundle of old clothes. When I was missed the hue and cry went out for a red man wearing a deerskin cloak. An itinerant English sailor, newly washed, was able to stand on the corner in his patched clothes and say truthfully that he had seen no such man, after which he melted away into the darkness and stepped out of the ken of the nobility.

Of my life thereafter there is but little to tell. My days of adventure were over, and I settled to a quiet and peaceful life, with but perhaps one moment of drama, which I shall relate ere long.

I was nearing forty years of age, but my life in the forests had made me fit and strong. I was sinewy, and took pleasure in doing things well. Bristol was thriving, and there was a call for new houses for the newly affluent. With no other skills but my strength, I took work as a labourer for a builder, and learned some of the skills of that trade. I moved in time from the mere shifting of rubble to the manufacture of bricks, recalling the skills I had first learned on the Çanaga so many years before, and that led later to redeveloping my knowledge of their laying. It was pleasant work. Having no ambition to move on and find my fortune, I became seen as reliable, and having no family to care for I was a man freely able to go where I was needed and where work was available, and for a period of twenty years or more I became an itinerant builder, taking my skills from place to place. I wandered much of southern England, rarely venturing into the north, and many a house built in those years has its fair share of bricks made or laid by my hand.

I was still Richard, but I took the name of Grey. It was one that I felt I could answer to, being my mother's name after her first marriage and the name of Thomas, my childhood chamberlain and half-brother, but not one unusual enough to draw undue attention to me, as Woodville or Plantagenet would surely do.

At the end of these years I found myself at Eastwell in the county of Kent, and, hearing that a local knight named Sir Thomas Moyle was looking for skilled bricklayers for a new house he was building, I called to see his overseer and was taken on. The overseer had originally looked askance at me because of my age, but I was able to convince him of my fitness, and was able to supply him with the names of others I had worked for who had found my work satisfactory.

His other layers were in the main young and boisterous, and because he had to be away from the site so often he appointed me chargehand, with the task of keeping them applied to their work. This spared me much of the physical work, and the building grew apace.

Then the village was visited with a disease that laid low all who it came in contact with. It began with one of the itinerant brickmakers, who suddenly began to shiver violently one day, and then fell to the ground, unable to stand upright. At first we thought naught of it, thinking that he had caught a chill, but by the end of the working day three more men had been struck down. A hospital of sorts was set up in Sir Thomas's barn.

The next morning half the men did not report for work. I went along to their lodging, only to find that half had fled. 'It is the English Sweat,' one of those still there told me. 'He who catches it will die for sure. Do you not recognize the signs?'

I did not. The disease had been introduced to England at the time of Bosworth (some said even that it had entered the country in Henry Tudor's army) and killed many then and in numerous outbreaks since, but at the time I had no idea of what he meant.

Nonetheless, on the way back to the site I was overcome very suddenly with a sense of apprehension, followed within a half hour by cold shivers, great exhaustion and severe pains in my neck and limbs.

I fell to the ground, and after some time felt myself lifted and carried, and before I reached the barn I was hot, and sweat began to pour from me. I felt only heat and a blinding headache, and then I must have become delirious, for I found myself beset on all sides by people of the past – my father came and spoke to me, and so did Jehan, and my brother Edward rose before me in graveclothes and smelling of ashes. My uncle Richard appeared before me, hanging naked across the back of a horse, and there too were Bemoy and Alacho, the African bleeding from a dozen stab wounds, and the boy who had held my horse's bridle at Exeter, and behind him a host, two hundred Cornishmen and a crew of drowned Portagees, and to each and all of them I called, and screamed, and begged mercy, and cried aloud for water for my dreadful thirst.

And then a week later the fever broke, and I was myself again. Seven of our workmen had died and been buried in a mass grave in the village churchyard, but we that survived, although desperately weak, were otherwise unscathed, and were soon recovering and able to stand up and move around.

As soon as I was able I went out into the fresh air and sat beneath a tree on the village green. The sun was strong and my spirits had been lifted, and I took out a book to while away the time. Such days of leisure were rare, and I intended to enjoy this one.

I had not been long at my reading when I saw two figures coming towards me. One of the girls who had been looking after us was pointing at me, and I recognized the man with her as Sir Thomas, whose house we were building.

I struggled to rise as he approached, but he flapped a hand at me and told me to sit down again, which I was glad to do.

'What is't you do, sir?' he asked, and held out a hand for my book.

'Read, Sir Thomas,' I told him, and held out the tome. 'Ovid.'

He took it, looked at it with interest, and returned it to me. 'You enjoy reading?' he asked.

'Yes, sir.'

'A rare accomplishment for a layer of bricks,' he said, 'and it is an even rarer accomplishment to do so in Latin. How did you come by this language?'

I had my story ready – it had been long practised and polished, and flowed from my mouth like pure truth. 'I was not always a workman,' I told him. 'In my youth I was a churchman, destined for the priesthood, but my sense of vocation left me, and I returned to the world, bringing with me only my knowledge of the language of the church.'

'I hope that you may say truth,' he answered, 'but the story you tell now is not that which you told Meg here.'

I looked at the girl. 'I have not spoken to Meg,' I said, 'except to ask for water or some food.'

'That was in your normal state,' he told me. 'It is what you said to Meg in your fevered state that troubles me.'

'I have no recollection of saying anything,' I said. 'I am sorry if, while my mind was wandering, I said anything to offend either your worship or this good lady. It was no doubt the ramblings of a troubled soul.'

'I hope so, Richard Grey,' he said, 'for if it were aught else then what you spake was treason.'

'What?' I sat up straight. 'What treason could I speak?'

'Meg, tell him what you heard him say, as you told it to me.'

Meg swallowed hard, and then began her story. 'While lying in the torment of fever, Master Grey did say to me that he was not what he seemed, and that in truth he was Richard Plantagenet, true King of England, and that our King Henry was a liar and a thief that had stole the kingdom from him.'

Thus does the unconscious mind betray the conscious. I had no doubt that I had burbled such things to the girl, for whence else could she have heard them?

I smiled. 'I think you must have misheard me, Meg,' I said. 'It is impossible that I could have said such things.'

'That you did, sir,' she said, 'and not only I heard them, but Ann Banks too – but not as much as I, in truth.'

'Thank you, Meg,' Sir Thomas told her. 'You may return to your duties now and must speak of this to no one unless I give you leave.' He waited until she had curtsied and turned away, and then he said to me, 'I know you are weak and tired now after your illness, and in this state you can be of no danger to any man, and I would not tire you further with questions, but when you have back your strength I want a long talk with you, and I want the truth. When you feel strong enough, come to the house.'

He rose to his feet and looked down on me, and I nodded my acquiescence.

I went up to the house some two days later. Sir Thomas's kindness in giving me time to recover was a godsend, for it enabled me to concoct a story that might hold water. I could not go against my promise to Henry Tudor, but I had to tell this good knight something.

'I do not remember my mother,' I told him, 'and do not know who she was, but as a boy I was boarded out with a Latin schoolmaster, who acted as father to me, and was paid for my bed and board by a man that came every quarter day. When I was about twelve years of age, one August, the man came again with a horse and took me with him across the country. I was taken to a field where a battle was to take place, and was taken to the tent of the king, Richard. He acknowledged me as his natural son, and said that he had wanted to see me before the battle, as it was a battle for England, and should he lose he would not be allowed to live. Then he gave me a purse of gold and bade me haste to London, there to await news. If he won the battle, then I was to attend him on his return; if he lost, then I must shift for myself. He lost, Sir Thomas, as you know, and I went for a sailor and remained at sea for some years before returning and becoming a builder, as you see me now.'

'You were at Bosworth?' Sir Thomas said.

'I was,' I said, aware of the sin I was committing in lying to this good man.

'Did you see Richard fall?'

'No, sir; by then I was from that place.'

'He died unshriven, you know,' Sir Thomas said.

'That was not his choice, sir; when it was reported to him that there were no chaplains in the camp to say mass, he replied that if their quarrel were God's, then they needed no supplications; if not, such prayers were idle blasphemy.'

Sir Thomas grunted; he had been taken in, for I could ever tell a credible tale. 'I know not what to say,' he said. 'What will you do now, if your secret is out?'

'I am too old to worry about such things,' I said. 'I have a little money saved; I will live out my days in the village here if you give me permission.'

Sir Thomas gave me a little plot of land in the field nearest the river, and I builded a small house for myself, and have lived there since, and my secret is still safe.

Except from one person.

It was a few months after the conversation with Sir Thomas Moyle, long after I had forgotten I had even had it, when a shadow fell over my book as I was sitting beneath the willow tree.

I looked up, but the sun was shining directly into my eyes and I was dazzled, and it was a moment or two before I realized that there was a man standing there, a large, bulky man. I rose to my feet. 'I beg your pardon, sir,' I said. 'I did not see you there.'

He must have seen that I was squinting, for he moved two paces to his right. I could see a party of people, some on horses, afar off, and Sir Thomas with them. I looked again at the man beside me, saw him more clearly, and fell to my knee.

'Forgive me . . .' I began again, but he reached out a hand and drew me to my feet.

'Richard is your name, I believe,' he said.

'It is, Your Majesty.'

'And a bricklayer who reads Latin, I believe.'

'Sir.'

'How old are you, Richard?'

'I believe, about three score and five, Your Majesty.'

'Your left eye . . .' he said.

'An accident in youth, sir. It was a disfigurement, but the vision was not much impaired.'

'The bastard son of Richard the usurper, I hear.'

I looked at the ground. Let him think that if he wished.

'I think that to be a fairy story, Richard.'

Now I looked up again at him.

'A Richard you may be, Richard,' he said softly, 'but not the Richard that Richard says he is. I know my history, Richard, and some of its secrets, too. You have broken your solemn word, then, Richard.'

I looked at him. 'Sire?'

'If you are the man I think you are, I believe you promised my father never to enter this realm again while either he or his successor was alive.'

'Not so, sire,' I said.

'Which is not so?' he asked. 'Is it not so that you have broken your word, or not so that you are the man I think you are? Or both? Or neither? If you are the man I think you are, then your life stands forfeit to me. If you are not he, then you have never given any such word, and you have no idea what I am talking about.' He paused and looked round at the nearby party, and then turned again to me. 'But you do know what I am talking about, don't you, Richard?'

I had had enough of hiding and deceit. 'I do, sire.'

'So your word is broken, and your parole worthless.'

'No, sire,' I said again. 'It is true that in another life, when I was another man, I gave my word to your father, but I am not forsworn, for I kept my promise to the letter.'

'Do we speak of the promise never to reveal your true identity? That you have kept indeed, and kept well for more than two score years. But that is not the promise I mean, is it, Richard. Did you not promise never to return to these lands while he lived?'

'Indeed, sir.'

'Or while his successor lived; went it not so?'

'No, sire, it did not; the king bade me remain in exile while he lived, and in the lifetime of the crown prince, his son, Arthur, whom he thought should succeed him.'

There was a moment of silence, and then, 'Ha!' The king let out a whoop, and slapped his thigh. 'Is that the lie of it?' he said. 'He told you Arthur, did he, and thought not of me? Well, that was the very way of the man, that is sure. Second sons are ever ignored.'

He walked in a small circle, looking the while at me, and then came to a halt again, facing me.

'So, Richard – or Uncle Richard, I suppose that should be – do you yet have designs on my throne?'

Now it was my turn to laugh. 'Indeed, sire, I do not, nor have had these forty years. I was young then, and knew not the value of peace and quiet, a warm hearth and a good night's sleep.'

'Did you keep your other promise?' he asked.

I knew the one he meant.

'I did, sir. There are no sprigs of the bush to come and annoy you. I have not lain with a woman since Katherine was taken from me in your father's time.'

He shook his head. 'Chastity and celibacy together; now those are two virtues neither of which I shall ever be able to lay claim to – nor indeed hope to. I have been studying the papers

344

of the time. The secret ones, too. You'd be surprised how many secrets there are.' He paused again. 'Or then again, perhaps you wouldn't. Morton ordered you killed, you know, but by the time my father found out about it Morton had died himself, and no doubt sweats for it in hell even now. You know about Katherine? She married again, you know, three times.'

'I did not know, sir.'

'Well, she thought you were dead,' he said. 'Even so, she waited fifteen years. Dead now, of course.'

He must have seen my reaction to this. 'You did not know?'

I shook my head.

'I'm sorry. I thought you would know; but there is no way you could, is there? As you say, you kept your promise and did not go near her.'

'She thought I was dead,' I said.

He nodded and looked out at the river. The silence hung in the air. 'Well,' he said eventually, 'what must I do now? Do I bring you to court to live in brilliance and splendour?'

Again, he was quick to see my reaction. 'Fear not,' he said. 'If you do not want it then be sure that I do not either. What will you do – live out your days here on this riverbank?'

'If Your Majesty permits.'

He smiled. 'Contrary to rumour, Richard, I do not execute every man I meet. If you present me no problems then I shall not bother you again. You can live peacefully in your cottage and read the works of our distinguished uncle.'

He was observant, then – he had spotted that my book was not a Latin one, but Anthony Rivers's 'Dictes and Sayings of the Philosophers'; I read it frequently, not just for the wisdom it contained, but because it reminded me of Katherine, who had been reading it on the day she trothed herself to me.

I caught the smile on the king's face and returned it. When he smiled he much resembled his grandfather, who was also my father. I thought to tell him so, but decided 'twas inadvisable;

my father had died much younger than Henry was now, and it was not only in the face but in the corpulence that they were alike.

The sun was setting now, and we stood and watched as it sank towards the river. 'Do you remember finding me in the cupboard and teaching me to sing?' he asked suddenly.

'I do, sire,' I said, 'but I must confess I am surprised that Your Majesty can remember such a moment.'

'If you knew how rare were the moments of proffered kindness in my childhood, you would not say that,' he said. 'You did not know me, and wanted nothing from me, but offered me help and a smile and a kind word. Oh yes, Uncle Richard, I remember.'

The group of courtiers had begun to move hesitantly towards him, and he turned and waved them away with a cry of, 'All right, all right! I'm coming.'

He smiled again at me. 'I must be from hence. The cares of state . . .'

I made to kneel, and he stopped me. 'Princes do not kneel to princes, Richard, nor age to youth. Relative youth, anyway. Live in peace.'

'Thank you, Your Majesty,' I said, and watched as he turned away and strode across the meadow towards the group of anxious men.

He had gone no more than twenty paces when suddenly he turned on his heel and hastened back towards me. I stood, unsure of what to do, and he came close and stood no more than a pace away.

'Moments of kindness,' he said. 'They are rare and precious. I just gave you a moment of sadness, I think, in telling you that your lady was dead, even though you must have feared that was the case.'

I looked at the ground, and nodded.

'Let me recompense you,' he said. 'I know you can keep a

promise, so I ask you to promise me that you will do nothing – no actions, no enquiries, no attempts at contact – over what I will now tell you. It is for your ears only, and for the peace of your soul which I have disturbed this day. Do I have your word?'

Puzzled, I gave it him.

'Know then,' he said, his voice dropping to a conspiratorial whisper, 'the fate of your child.'

I felt a hand of ice grip at my heart, and for a moment forgot how to breathe.

The king waited until I was myself again, and then went on, 'He lives, a prosperous gentleman. He was taken from your wife when he was ill as a small child, not long before you were "executed", and then she was told that he had died of an illness. He was placed with a family, as you were in Tournai, but his family was English and knew nothing of his past. He was provided for, and studied in Italy, he became a physician, and he married into the family of a good man, albeit a stubborn one. He is eminent in his profession, and is a son that any man could be proud of. He will never be King of England, but he is loved and safe in a good family and valued among men.' He looked at me. After a few seconds, he asked, 'Is it a moment of kindness?'

I felt the tears prick my eyes. 'It is, my lord,' I told him. 'Thank you.'

'I am content, then,' he said. 'You know, yours is a strange story, Richard, but a good one. In fact, it is a most preposterous story. You must write it down.'

'Yes. Perhaps I should.'

'You misunderstand me,' he said, and looked at me pointedly from under those heavy brows. 'I mean, you *must* write it down.'

'Oh, I see.'

'And it will be for me to read,' he said, 'but of course no one else must see it.'

'No.'

'You understand, of course?'

'Of course.'

'Remember your promise, then,' he said again. 'Not a word, now.' He turned away again, and then suddenly was once again beside me. 'One more thing,' he said. 'If you wish to do so, resume your own name; I shall make no comment. Better to die a Plantagenet than a Grey or a Woodville, eh?'

'Or even a Warbeck,' I said.

He laughed aloud, and threw his final sentence over his shoulder as he walked away. 'Or a Warbeck,' he called. 'Oh yes, especially a Warbeck.'

Author's Note

Any historical novel is a combination of various Rumsfeldian factors, and in particular the combination of known knowns with unknown unknowns. When I set out to write this book I thought I knew most of the known knowns about Perkin Warbeck; it turned out that what I knew would set klaxons sounding on *QI*, in that what had been taught to me at school about Perkin was mostly nonsense, and that there was much more to him than meets the eye. The unknown unknowns, of course, were less of a problem, as I simply made them up. Thus the book became, as is I suppose inevitable, part history and part conjecture, a conjunction of what is known or probable with what is possible, albeit sometimes unlikely.

If Richard of York survived the reign of Richard III (which is the basic premise I have adopted) and emerged as Perkin, then there are six years to fill before we meet any firm historical facts. What I have written is not at all a likely explanation of Perkin's life, but it is a possible one. This, of course, is where the fun lies, and it has been a lot of fun finding out where he might have gone and what he might have done. I emphasize the 'might'.

For this note, I thought it best to take the narrative chapter by chapter and explain where the ideas were gleaned from.

Prey: The river trip with the assassins is invented.

Prince: The early life of Richard of York is well documented, and was as outlined in the early pages. This narrative continues from my novel *The Master of Bruges* (Macmillan, 2010). The arrival of Hans Memling, the Flemish painter, and his involvement with Richard was first conjectured in that book, as was their friendship with William Caxton.

Private Citizen: Perkin's boyhood is not documented in any detail, but given Richard's known musicality a place in the Tournai cathedral choir would not seem unlikely.

Pressed Man: Perkin's 'confession' says that he worked for a Jan Strewe in Middelburg and went to Portugal with Edward Brampton as a family servant, but left his employ not long after arriving in Lisbon.

Privateer: Vaz da Cunha is a historical figure, as is Bemoy, and the voyage to Jaloof really took place. There is no evidence that Columbus was aboard, however. The geographical details of the Senegal river (i.e. the Çanaga) are from Barbot (op. cit.).

Pêcheur: Pierre Jean (Pregent) Meno was a historical person, although his involvement in cod fishing is fictional. I owe the details of this and some subsequent chapters to two serendipitous finds: in January 2010 I was in Cambridge and short of something to read, so I popped into a charity shop and bought (for 55p) a book called *Cod* by Mark Kurlansky, which detailed the fifteenth-century fishing trips to the other side of the Atlantic by Basque and Breton fishermen. Later, back home, I went to the parish jumble sale, where I bought Ian Wilson's *The Columbus Myth* for 10p. Never was 65p better spent.

Primitive: The Beothuk were a genuine tribe, and did cover themselves with red ochre, giving rise to the name 'Red Indian'.

The tribe, never numerous, died out in 1829. The ceremony which Perkin describes is markedly similar to that undergone by Captain John Smith in Virginia almost a century later, when he was 'saved' by Pocahontas. It is likely that Smith merely mistook an adoption ceremony for a genuine threat to his life.

Pretender: Perkin/Richard's arrival in Cork marks the beginning of what is known historically about him. Most of the details about Charles VIII are taken from contemporary descriptions. A fuller (fictional) account of Richard's interview with Maximilian is in *The Master of Bruges*.

Princeling: Richard's friendship with Maximilian is historical, as is his summary of Anglo-Burgundian relations at this period. Richard's adventures in Kent and Waterford are historical, but his involvement in the fighting in the north of Ireland is fictional.

Peregrinator: The main facts are almost entirely historical; only the details are fictionalized. Richard landed in Scotland in November; he was married by January.

Patriot: Richard's squeamishness and naivety have been remarked on by a number of commentators. He advanced only four miles into England before returning, unhappy with the way things were going.

Pragmatist: Two armies did melt before Richard without a blow being struck; in the narrative, how this was achieved is conjectural, but by no means implausible. It is not known why Perkin fled east, towards the advancing Henry, instead of west; my solution is, again, conjectural. Henry VII never seemed to be able to get Pierrechon's name right; 'Perkin Warbeck' was an anglicization of the sounds, while 'Piers

Osbeck' may simply be a misreading – 'Wer' coming out as 'Os' from the manuscript.

Probationer: The errors and discrepancies in Perkin/Richard's 'confession' have never been satisfactorily explained. Many of them (such as 'Antwerp' for 'Ouldenarde') may well have been no more than careless copying. There are copies of the confession, Perkin's letter to his mother and Henry's exultant announcement that he had caught Perkin in the municipal archives in Courtrai (Kortrijk) in Belgium.

Provocateur: Richard's meeting with Bess is fictional. The court poet, John Skelton, took against Perkin, and wrote the mocking poem about him that Richard mentions. It is quite long, and very scathing. My using the subsequent mockery as Richard's reason for escape is, however, conjectural.

Prisoner: For whatever reason, Perkin/Richard's face was disfigured after he was placed in the Tower, presumably to remove any remaining resemblance to Edward IV; de Puebla remarked on this in his report to the King and Queen of Spain. Such an action would be both cruel and pointless unless those responsible had another motive, which I have duly supplied. The sentence which Perkin repeats to the bishop is verbatim.

Personator: From this point on, all is pure fiction, although Thirkell did fit out an expedition to the new found land from which he returned safely, being back in London by 1502. Gaspar Corte-Real sent fifty-seven 'Red Indians' back to Portugal to be sold as slaves, but his own ship disappeared without trace after the rest of his flotilla had left. There was a long-lasting legend that early English explorers in North America had been greeted by a native speaking Welsh; as late as 1806 Lewis and Clark were told to look out for the Welsh-speaking

Indian tribe as they moved west on their ground-breaking expedition.

Peace: The story of a Richard Plantagenet working as a bricklayer in Eastwell in Kent is well known (see David Baldwin's *The Lost Prince*). The king's visit, of course, is fictional. The story of the doctor who '. . . studied in Italy . . . became a physician, and . . . married into the family of a good man, albeit a stubborn one' can be found in *Richard of England*, by Diana M. Kleyn, although she and I have given him different identities.

Select Bibliography

Baldwin, David, *The Lost Prince: the Survival of Richard of York*, Sutton Publishing, 2007

Barber, Richard (ed.), *The Pastons: A Family in the Wars of the Roses*, The Folio Society, 1981

Barbot, Jean: *see* Hair, Paul

Costain, Thomas B., *The Last Plantagenets*, Doubleday, New York, 1962

Fields, Bertram, *Royal Blood*, Regan Books, HarperCollins, 1998

Gies, Joseph & Frances, *Life in a Mediaeval City*, The Thomas Y. Crowell Company, USA, 1969

Hair, Paul (ed.), *Barbot on Guinea*, Hakluyt Society, 1992

Jones, Evan, *Alwyn Ruddock: John Cabot and the Discovery of America* in *Historical Research*, Vol. 81, issue 212

Kendall, Paul Murray, *Richard the Third*, Allen and Unwin, 1955

Kleyn, Diana M., *Richard of England*, Kensal Books, 1991

Kurlansky, Mark, *Cod*, Vintage Books, 1999

Marshall, Ingeborg, *A History and Ethnography of the Beothuk*, McGill-Queen's University Press, 1996

Norwich, John Julius, *Shakespeare's Kings*, Viking, 1999

Oman, Sir Charles, *A History of the Art of War in the Middle Ages*, Vol. II, 1278–1485 A.D., Greenhill Books, 1991

Peacock, Annabel, 'The Men of Bristol and the Atlantic Discovery Voyages of the Fifteenth and Early Sixteenth

The Shadow Prince

Centuries', unpublished MA dissertation, University of Bristol, September 2007

Quinn, David Beers, *England and the Discovery of America*, 1481–1620, George Allen and Unwin, 1974

Weir, Alison, *The Princes in the Tower*, Pimlico, London, 1992

Wilson, Ian, *The Columbus Myth*, Simon and Schuster, 1991

And, for the entertainment of it:

Ford, John, *Perkin Warbeck*, London, 1634

Lindsay, Philip, *They Have Their Dreams*, Portway, London, 1957

Morgan, Terence, *The Master of Bruges*, Macmillan New Writing, 2010

Penman, Sharon, *The Sunne in Splendour*, Penguin Books, 1982

Shelley, Mary, *The Fortunes of Perkin Warbeck*, Routledge, London, 1857

Finally, I must salute above all others my bible, my constant companion throughout the writing of this book, without which it could never have been completed – simply the best book ever written on the case of Perkin Warbeck:

Wroe, Ann, *The Perfect Prince*, Random House, 2003